PHANTOM HEART

Kelly Creagh

PHANTOM HEART

VIKING

VIKING
An imprint of Penguin Random House LLC, New York

First published in the United States of America by Viking,
an imprint of Penguin Random House LLC, 2021

Visit us online at penguinrandomhouse.com.

Library of Congress Cataloging-in-Publication Data is available.

Printed in the United States of America

ISBN 9780593116043

10 9 8 7 6 5 4 3 2 1

Design by Kate Renner
Text set in LTC Cloister Pro

For Katie McGarry, who hates dead things but loved this book.

*And for Gina Possanza, who appeared at my window
just when I needed an angel.*

PART
I

ONE

Stephanie

"He has lights for eyes."

Brushing a few errant curls from my face, I glanced up from my homework and leveled my little sister, Charlie, with the full blast of skepticism she deserved. Ignoring her wasn't working.

This whole week, she'd been talking about *him*. The masked man who lived in our new house. Our newest oldest house.

"There's nothing in your closet, Chuck," I said for the tenth time in four days.

A glower of indignation replaced the saucer-eyed stare of fright she'd been projecting my way ever since the sun had set, taking with it the cozy yellow glow that had surrounded our house—an older-than-Christmas Victorian.

"Don't call me Chuck."

I pushed off from where I'd been lying belly-down across my metal-framed bed, calculus book open.

"All right, Chess," I grunted, opting for the more acceptable nickname Dad had given her. I didn't feel like trading Charlie's six-year-old fear for her six-year-old fury: stomping and top-of-the-lungs screeching.

I took Charlie's small hand, and she gave my fingers a squeeze.

"He talked to me last night," she whispered, creeping me out. "He asked me questions."

"Well." I drew her toward the hallway. "Did you tell him to mind his own beeswax?"

Her feet stalled on the creaky, bare-wood floor. "He has bees?"

"No." I bent down, bringing us eye level. "It's a way of telling someone to leave you alone."

"So . . . you believe me now," she said, like stating that out loud would make it true. "That he's *in* there. Zedok."

She pointed down the long hallway to her doorway at the far end.

With the upstairs hall and bathroom lights off, I had to admit the trek to her bedroom *did* look ominous.

"There's no one in your room, Chesser." I hit the switch that sent light bursting from the huge, original-to-the-house crystal chandelier that hung over the grand staircase. "This is a big old house, and old houses make noises sometimes." Realizing I'd just repeated something I'd probably heard responsible adult figures say a billion times, I made an amendment. "Just think of it like house farts."

Usually, fart talk got laughs from Charlie. This time, I didn't get so much as a smile. Gently, I tugged her forward. It was like trying to drag an anvil.

"Houses shouldn't have other houses inside them," she said.

"That's right, they shouldn't," I agreed.

"This one does." Again with the whispers. Like she was afraid someone was listening in.

I knelt in front of her. "What's really going on, Chess? You never asked to sleep in my room when we were at the last house."

"Because there wasn't a man in the closet at the last house."

Fair enough.

"Look. Do you want me to *show* you that there isn't anyone in your closet?"

Charlie nodded, her eyes unblinking and silver-dollar-sized.

Her seriousness, coupled with her apparent confidence in my being a formidable opponent to her imaginary not-friend, made me smile.

I stood and meandered into her darkened room, where I flipped the light switch. I pivoted to face the closet in question. The door was open already, the small space inside empty.

Having inhabited the house for only a week, none of us had finished unpacking yet. Tired of having to box things up shortly after unboxing them, we'd all become accustomed to living in the land of limbo regarding our stuff. And Dad, perpetually "just about to" finish a place, never encouraged us to use anything as practical as a closet to store our clothes.

For us, "home" had never really been a location.

At least not since Charlie had come along.

"See?" I said, turning my gaze on my little sister, who stood toes-to-the-threshold in the doorway. "There's no one there."

To this, she said nothing. Just stared at the cracked plaster wall inside the otherwise vacant closet.

"There *was* a house in there," she said. "Like ours but nicer."

My shoulders slumped. This was dumb, and my calculus was getting cold.

"How about this," I offered, plucking her stuffed octopus,

Checkers, from her bed. "How about we swap rooms tonight? I'll sleep in here, and Chess and Checkers can sleep in my bed."

"He can get to your closet, too," Charlie replied without missing a beat.

"Great," I said, officially fresh out of patience. "So, either way, you can send him to me, this Zeebo guy—"

"Zedok."

"Right, okay." I'd probably regret humoring her later. "You can send him to my closet, and I'll tell him to get lost."

"He told me to tell you he can see you in your dreams." Her thumb crept toward her lips—a nervous habit that usually meant she was afraid she was about to get in trouble. "And that you wouldn't believe me when I told you about him. So he told me to tell you that he knows you like that boy with the blond hair."

"Chris Hemsworth?" I asked, unimpressed.

"Kyle," she replied.

I scowled at her, though the only one I had to be angry with was myself. Most likely, Dad had asked her to get the scoop on Kyle, a cute guy in my chemistry class, who I might have brought up once or twice, just so Dad wouldn't be so *Dad* later when and if I actually made a blip on Kyle's radar. As a result, Charlie had just factored Kyle into the sensory overload that came with yet another full-scale change.

Probably, the shadowing me through the house and "monster in my closet" talk also meant something more important was at play.

Charlie was feeling the move. And maybe the same sense of isolation that had begun to nibble at me in this decrepit once-upon-a-time palace was eating at my little sister, too.

This house *wasn't* like the others my father had flipped. This Addams family mansion meets Poe's House of Usher was, by far, my father's most ambitious.

Not to mention his most risky.

The other houses, shotguns and suburban bi-levels, had taken three to four months to turn around with the help of a contractor. This one would require more than the projected six months. Which was good news for me, because that meant I might actually get to finish my last year of high school at Langdon. And even though there were only the three of us—me, Charlie, and Dad—I liked the idea of a bigger house that had room to stretch out in. I also liked the idea of a graduation ceremony at which I would not be seated next to total strangers.

Maybe I'd have friends who lived close enough to come to the party I'd already planned out in my head. One that would strategically place my tank-top- and booty-shorts-clad body next to Kyle's muscled and tanned one.

Of course, it *had* also crossed my mind that Dad had picked this project to give Charlie and me a chance to actually get used to the taste of the tap water somewhere. Then again, he could just as easily have bought this thing purely on the grounds that it included an ancient, inoperative piano.

Because though Dad happened to be the most functional and pragmatic dad in the history of dad-dom, I happened to be the only one who understood that, deep down, he also sometimes wasn't.

"Stephanie," whispered Charlie. "I'm scared in here."

Did she mean her room? Or the house.

I knew better than to ask.

Instead, I smoothed my brow and approached her with a smile. Charlie was right. There *was* something in this house. The same something we'd dragged with us to every house since leaving Syracuse. A ghost, I guess you could say.

The kind that lived in the heart, though.

"C'mon, you." I handed over Checkers and hoisted my little sister into my arms. "Slumber party time. Just for tonight, though, okay?"

"'Kay," she said, soft in my ear, though the tenseness in her tiny frame told me that she hadn't been paying attention to my words. That, instead, as her focus remained trained on the doorway to her closet, her little girl's mind fixated on the creature it had cooked up.

The imaginary, lights-for-eyes, dream-spying creeper she'd dubbed "Zedok."

An entity whose appearance in our lives had, I was sure, little to do with the move and more to do with the fact that Charlie had reached an age where she was starting to notice what was missing.

Who was missing.

TWO
Zedok

Crayons littered the worn parquet floor in front of the parlor's drop-cloth-covered piano.

My piano.

Charlie sat in their midst, coloring the sheet music she had discovered within the piano's bench.

My music.

I approached with slow steps, my shadow enveloping her small form.

Charlie did not turn to peer back at me. She merely slowed her progress in obscuring my work with her own.

Somewhere above, on the second floor, a door slammed and a girl's voice shouted about coffee, the smell of which filled the mansion to its brim.

The girls' father, the estate's new on-paper owner, a Mr. Richard Armand, barked a reply from his place in the nearby kitchen. Another upstairs door slammed. The sound of rushing water and the clanking of dishes followed.

For days, similar racket had floated through the walls of *this* house—the decayed living version—to mine. The preserved dead one.

Gritting my teeth, I told myself I was lucky to have a child as young as Charlie within my reach—a girl whose psyche, unlike her elder sister's, had not yet been sealed by the rust of logic and reason.

In theory, Charlie should help expedite everything. Exactly *what* end she would expedite if she continued to decimate my work, however . . . Well, that remained to be seen.

"What have you done?" I demanded.

Charlie did not reply. Instead, she climbed to her feet, clutching one of her crayons as though it could serve as a weapon. Her gaze flicked from me to the open doorway and back again.

She looked up, staring straight into my eyes. Through the holes of my mask, I returned her gaze. Until the illustration at her feet caught and stole my attention.

A hooded black figure marred the sheet music. His gray-colored mask, with its somber expression and muted features, had been rendered with some accuracy. The child had even drawn dark lines to indicate the mask's grate-like mouth, consisting of skeleton keyholes.

From there down, the cloaked form dissolved into one long smear of darkness. Which I supposed was accurate enough as well.

"Is it not bad enough that you and your family have invaded my home?" I asked. "You would also render useless the only blessed thing that keeps the worst at bay?"

"S-Stephanie says you need to get your own beeswax!" the trembling girl replied with more tenacity than she'd yet been able to muster in my presence.

"Stephanie," I scoffed, not even bothering to decipher the meaning behind her wax comment. Because the subject of Charlie's sister was precisely what I needed to speak with her about. "It would seem that, despite your efforts to convince her, Stephanie still does not believe in me. And she will neither see nor hear me until she does. Do you know what that means?"

The crayon between Charlie's hands finally snapped under the pressure of her grip, making me pause and, for the first time since entering the room, examine my conduct.

Seeing my music in ruins—unsalvageable—had brought me closer to that edge I so feared. More even than before because there were people in the house. And that was something that put *me* in a tight grip. Only *I* could not afford to snap.

The Armands certainly could not afford for me to.

"It means," I said, attempting to soften my tone, "that you and your family will not be leaving as soon as you need to. Which, if it happened today, would still not be soon enough."

Thus far, Stephanie had proved to be my biggest obstacle.

In contrast to her younger sister, Stephanie seemed to understand too much about the world. Far more than any young lady of my day would have dared to boast.

In the end, though, neither Stephanie nor her father could prove any *real* match for me. No one—no one aside from the medium, that was—ever had. And was that not precisely why I needed this family to depart?

"Why do we have to leave?" challenged Charlie. "Why don't *you* leave?"

"Because I am cursed," I snapped. "My soul has been shattered, its shards shackled to this estate. Its pieces lie strewn about me in much the same way your crayons now lie strewn about you. Do you understand?"

She shook her head.

My frustration renewed, I took another step, more of her crayons cracking under the heel of my black riding boot. Stopping short, I bent to retrieve my mangled work.

"Your drawings. Shall I assume they are all of me?" I asked, and, this time, she nodded.

In response, I tore the papers into shreds and flung the scraps toward the room.

"*There*," I growled as I swung to face her again. "*Now* do you understand?"

Charlie scurried to put the piano bench between us.

"You're a bad man!" She gripped the bench, the fury in her voice scarcely contained.

"*Yes*," I hissed back at her. "I am."

Her body shaking, she actually chucked the two halves of her broken crayon my way.

The pieces bounced off me and tapped against the floor. I threw my cloak back, causing her to yelp and, like a frightened mouse, take refuge beneath the piano's drop cloth.

The toe of one shoe still poked out from beneath, though, its smallness inciting me to once again check myself. For her terror did not serve my purpose. Not so much as her *influence* did. And, at this juncture, I needed more of the latter than I did the former.

"I suppose you *do* understand," I muttered, more to myself. "In your own way."

"I'm not scared of you."

I curled one hand tight enough to cause the leather of my glove to creak. Then I released the clench, tucked my hands behind my back, and resolved to begin again. Why terrify Charlie outright when she herself could not bring about my goal of an empty house?

Things were not going as planned, though. Nearly a week had passed and no matter what proof her younger sister supplied, Stephanie refused to buy into even the possibility of my existence.

"I don't need *you* to be frightened of me," I told her.

"Good!" Again, this came from behind the cloth. "'Cause I'm not."

"Then you won't be averse to helping me."

"Stephanie's going to make you get lost."

"That I am lost already is the issue at hand," I said, pacing while I addressed the piano.

"Are you going to hurt us?"

I frowned, the question burning through the lingering scraps of my anger.

"It is not my wish to," I admitted. "And that is why you, your father, and your sister must go."

Charlie lifted the fabric, one eye peering out at me. "How did you get torn up?"

How to answer her? How to make a child understand when I still, even after all this time, did not fully grasp the particulars myself?

"Is your face torn up, too?" she pressed. "Is that why you wear a mask?"

The lights flickered, the bulb of a nearby work lamp dying with a soft *pop*. I sneered behind the mask that obscured the whole of my countenance, papery lips peeling back.

"Yesterday," I said in an effort to steer both of us back on course, "you accompanied your father into the basement. You are not to go down there again. By yourself or otherwise. Do I make myself clear?"

"Why? Will you hurt Daddy? Or Stephanie? If they go down there?"

"I don't know," I said. Because, truly, I did not.

"W-what are you?"

I crossed to the piano and flipped up a portion of the sheet to reveal both the huddled girl and one corner of the instrument's keyboard, aged and broken.

Once, my hands, like a pair of lovely spiders, had climbed over these very keys, coaxing such sounds from their hidden strings. And the music I had played—how it had filled the house that, on this side, lay in ruins around me. How it had filled the *soul* that lay in ruins on the other.

And this version of the piano. The real and true version. Did I gravitate to and guard it the way I did because we two were so alike? Too damaged to issue forth anything but the discordancy with which our hollow bodies had become wracked?

"I'm no longer certain of what I am," I murmured.

"Charlie!" called Stephanie, her feet pounding down the stairs. "Charlie?"

Her courage bolstered by the approach of her sister, Charlie darted from her hiding place, shoes pattering over the scattered and torn music I could not have played anyway.

"Charlie!" cried Stephanie when her sister stopped just short of colliding with her. Simultaneously, she took in the scene. "Oh my gosh. What happened in here?"

Charlie peered from Stephanie to me and back again, still holding on to the hope that her sister might, at any moment, perceive my presence.

It was a hope we shared, if for different reasons.

"I—I was coloring," answered Charlie.

"I see that. But why did you rip your papers up and throw them everywhere? That's not nice."

"*I* didn't do that."

"Let me guess," came Stephanie's dry reply. "Zedok came in here and ripped up your drawings."

"And then threw them," Charlie said.

"Oh yeah?" sighed Stephanie, bending to gather the bits of paper into a stack. "Why would he do that?"

"I got in trouble," Charlie whispered. "For coloring."

"What?" Stephanie crossed to the crayons. "You're not in trouble. Just c'mon. Help me pick these up."

As the two set to work tidying up—Charlie keeping a watchful glare on me all the while—my gaze slid from the girls to the piano's keyboard, where I laid two fingers.

"Listen," Stephanie prattled while she returned the crayons to their designated tin. "I've got to get to school early to finish my homework, so Dad's going to drop you off. But I'll pick you up later, okay?"

When I pressed the chord, Charlie jumped, startled by the dissonant sound.

Stephanie, however, displayed no reaction whatsoever. Rising then, she approached the piano. She hesitated, though, after taking hold of the dustcover, her free hand falling to the naked keys. She did not press them. Instead, she trailed her fingers over the keys that remained—and over the sockets of those that did not.

I checked the girl's features to find upon them an expression I could not help but recognize.

She was listening. To . . . music.

The fact that she could hear it and I could not provoked within me a soundless echo of envy. The emotion fled as quickly as it had come, though, replaced by a more horrible sense of curiosity. Horrible because, unlike envy, curiosity was something I knew better than to entertain.

And yet, from this near a distance, a dullard could not have missed the pain that briefly knitted Stephanie's brow.

I glanced back to Charlie, as if she might provide me with some clue to its source.

But then Stephanie severed the moment by tossing the piano's dustcover back into place.

"Let's get you some breakfast," she said to Charlie, turning away from the instrument, and from me. "You're looking a little pale."

With that, Stephanie took her sister's hand and led her from the parlor with Charlie watching me until they both vanished.

And then abruptly, I was no longer the only hidden thing present in this parlor. This house.

Just now. What music had resounded through Stephanie's memory?

Whose music?

Dangerous questions I had no business pondering. Especially when a certain vow made to a certain nuisance obliged me to remain *out* of the affairs of any living person I encountered.

Regardless of what Stephanie had heard, my only concern should be that she had not heard *me*.

Perhaps, though, after this latest interaction, Charlie would say something that would begin to change that.

For today, I would have to use my invisibility and my silence to my advantage and plan a subtle yet less deniable strike to augment my efforts.

For how much larger did shadows loom when you were not watching them lengthen? When you'd convinced yourself they were not even there?

Large enough to swallow you whole before you were ever aware night had fallen.

A truth I wagered no one in the world understood better than I.

THREE

Stephanie

This guy. This. *Guy.*

I glanced up from the calculus that, thanks to Charlie, I hadn't finished last night.

It should have been easy enough to knock out, if only I hadn't, somewhere along the way, managed to pick up a super-distracting shadow.

He sat two tables away in the otherwise empty school library, his face half hidden behind a thick novel. He hadn't turned a single page.

Occasionally, I *would* catch his eyes flicking my way, the lenses of his black, thick-rimmed glasses reflecting the fluorescents overhead, making it impossible to read his expression.

Hipster Glasses, I'd taken to calling him, had made his first appearance yesterday—same bat time, same bat channel. For that reason, I might not have been so paranoid. Thing was, he had also made his second and third appearance yesterday, too.

At lunch, he'd twice passed my table, gripping his tray and slow-walking by, like he couldn't figure out how to get to wherever he usually sat. Then, after last bell, I'd found him leaning against a row of lockers near mine, pretending to read that same book.

This morning marked the end of this peripheral hovering being coincidental. And I wanted to tell him I knew where he could find a friend as creepy as him, but that it would require him to come over to my house and, apparently, stay the night in Charlie's closet.

Standing, I shoved my book and notepad into my messenger bag. If I confronted him now, that would leave him the weekend to think about what an unsubtle weirdo he was. It would also guarantee that, except for today, I wouldn't have to awkwardly run into him again.

Hipster Glasses stiffened as I approached, his suspender-clad shoulders going rigid.

I guess he was hoping I would stroll on by. When I stopped to stand to one side of his table, his eyes flicked to mine, visible for the first time through those lenses.

Wow, they were blue.

"Hey," I said.

"Uh..." He blinked at me, his dark, floppy-in-the-front, vintage, college-contour haircut trying (not unsuccessfully) to be retro-cool. "*Hhhhey.*"

The way he drew out the "h" annoyed me, because it suggested that *I* was the one behaving oddly here.

"I don't date," I said. "I don't do homework for hire. I don't do or sell drugs, either. And I don't like being monitored."

His face went crimson, which was exactly the reaction I'd been going for. It forced him out of hiding and dismantled any potential excuses or explanations he might have gone for.

"I'm not monitoring you." He snapped his book shut, eyes

darting, perhaps searching for the librarian or anyone else who might overhear our conversation.

"Really," I said, my tone as deadpan as my stare. "You *haven't* been following me?"

"Following you, *yes*," he said, smart enough, apparently, to recognize the corner he'd been backed into. "'Monitoring' suggests I've conducted surveillance on you. Recorded and reviewed data. There's a difference."

He was schooling *me* on vocab?

"You *do* know how stratospherically creepy you're being, don't you?"

"Yes!" he shouted at the book. I could tell he was genuinely angry at himself and not me. Not only had a deeper and more scarlet crawl begun to work its way up from the collar of his white button-down shirt but, from this close, I could actually feel the heat of mortification radiating off his inflamed skin.

Well done, Stephanie. You have appropriately cowed Clark Kent's lurker second cousin.

"You know—" I began, but he cut me off.

"I've been *trying* to figure out how to talk to you without weirding you out," he said, shooting straight out of his seat to stand up. *Up, up, and away.*

I swallowed hard, tilting my head back to take in his height, half expecting his nose to start bleeding.

"Mission unaccomplished," I said, resisting the fierce urge to step back from him. Which would be giving him a win. And since when did standing up make someone kind of maybe hot?

Broad shouldered with limbs almost too long for his body and this chic geek thing happening with his clothes, he looked as if, after tripping out of a 1940s newsroom, he'd tumbled into a taffy puller.

"I'm not a stalker." With this declaration, he shifted his weight to one Converse-clad foot, his big hands going to his tapered waist. My gaze lingered on his muscular, hair-dusted forearms, bare of the sleeves that he'd rolled to the elbows. Mm. Nice build, but . . . *so, so* no.

"Okay," I said. "So let's start there. If you're not a stalker, then why have you been following me?"

"It's not *you*," he hurried to say. Probably because the librarian, Ms. Geary, had returned to her post behind the checkout counter, signaling that we were minutes from first bell. "I'm not interested in *you*. It's . . . it's your . . ."

"My what?" I prompted.

"It's your house."

I squinted at him, unconvinced. "My *house*? Is that some weird euphemism for—"

"*No!*"

We both glanced to Ms. Geary, who glared bullet holes into Hipster Glasses. Turning back to me, he lowered his voice again. "You live in Moldavia."

"*Romania?*"

"No." He held up a hand, like *I* was trying *his* patience. "That's what the house is called. *Was* called. Before . . . just—it's haunted. Like . . . *really* haunted."

My glare dropped into a glower. One that dripped disdain. And skepticism.

"You're following me around because you think my house is haunted."

"I'm following you around because I *know* it is," he said, those blues igniting with a strange hunger. "Surely I'm not the first one to tell you that."

Technically speaking, I had to grant him that. Sure, Charlie had said she'd seen some creeper in the closet. But once I'd had her tucked in with me, the witching hour had come and gone with no more mention of monsters or ghouls in the walls. We'd both slept. Soundly.

And then there was the fact that I didn't believe in ghosts. Or anything else that couldn't be measured, documented, or, you know, *proven*.

"You *are* the first one to mention it, actually," I semi-lied. "Because I haven't *told* anybody yet which house I moved into."

He went pale, the crimson hue draining from his face in an instant.

"I . . . I keep up with the house," he stammered. "It's been empty for years. And no one ever stays there for more than a few months."

"Probably because it's barely habitable," I said.

"It came cheap, didn't it?"

"We bought it 'as is.' Because it's falling apart. That's why we're flipping it."

I frowned. Why I was telling him this?

"Did you even check into the history before you bought the thing?" he asked, folding his arms.

"What is it that you want?" I folded my own arms, mimicking his pose. This must have made him uncomfortable—*more* uncomfortable—because he dropped his arms.

"I was just . . . curious," he began. "I've never spoken to anyone who lived in that house before. I wanted to ask, I dunno, if you'd seen or experienced anything . . . abnormal."

"*You're* abnormal. Does that count?"

He looked toward the counter, where Ms. Geary busied herself with checking in items and pretending not to be listening in.

Glancing down, he nodded at his shoes.

I stifled a victory smirk, *almost* feeling sorry for him.

"Actually," I said, softening my tone, "there *was* something weird that happened the night we moved in."

Slowly, he lifted his eyes to mine, trying, I could tell, to gauge my level of sincerity.

"I heard this voice coming through the wall. It was this . . . guy."

Though Hipster Glasses didn't ask what the voice had said, that exact question swirled in his widening and too-serious scowl-stare.

So I went in for the kill.

"He said his name was Buddy Holly, and to tell you he wants his glasses back."

With that, I marched past him, shooting one last glance to Ms. Geary, who I swear smiled, though she never looked up.

"Hey," Glasses called to me. I stopped but didn't turn around.

"You know who Buddy Holly is?" he asked.

Overhead, the bell rang.

I glanced back at him from over one shoulder. "There's no such thing as ghosts."

"Well, you should give me your phone number," he called,

apparently no longer caring about what Ms. Geary had to think of any of this. "Just in case it turns out there is."

"Don't you already know it?"

I spun quickly so he wouldn't see me grin and, with that, hurried into the crowded hall.

FOUR
Zedok

The saw's cry had ripped through the halls of my side of the house—a harpy feasting upon its still-living prey, gleeful in its viciousness.

The man responsible for creating the infernal racket, Mr. Armand, stood in the center of the parlor, this version of which, with its cracked-plaster walls and pockmarked ceiling, scarcely resembled my own.

A pair of safety glasses shielded the man's eyes as he worked. Eyes that did not see me, though I stood just beneath the archway leading into the parlor, between the open pocket doors.

I had watched Mr. Armand this way for over an hour. With such a horrid noise filling both versions of the house, what else was there to do but stew at him?

If he felt my presence, he never let on.

Not that I had expected him to. I had been in Mr. Armand's dreams as well as Stephanie's, and he had seen me no better than she had. Though since his work centered on uplifting the travesty this side of the house had become, I had indulged in the temptation to direct his mind's eye toward images of the mansion as it had once been.

He would not be staying long enough to achieve even halfway similar results. Still, I'd taken small pleasure in informing him just how to get it right.

Large and powerfully built with dark brown hair, beard, and mustache, Mr. Armand reminded me of the shipyard workers I had glimpsed when I first arrived in America. And in that moment, with his eyes on his work but his mind so clearly elsewhere, I had to wonder which of us more closely resembled a ghost.

Neither of us, I'd say, quite so much as *Mrs.* Armand, who, through the very act of failing to exist, had begun to make her presence known.

Family photographs had appeared in the home, but none depicting her. Talk of her had been even scarcer. And Mr. Armand chose not to wear the ring I had twice now witnessed him pull from a lockbox to examine before replacing it.

Stephanie's interlude with the piano that morning had stayed with me despite all my efforts to dismiss it. Now Mr. Armand's intermittent glances at the piano had confirmed the thing I had come to assume.

That Mrs. Armand was not absent. Not so much as she was gone.

Also, that the pain here was still fresh.

Though I did not celebrate its existence, I could admit that there were fewer poisons more potent than loss.

My curiosity quenched, I left Mr. Armand to his pains and swept toward the grand staircase, which, like this side of the house itself, could now be called "grand" only in its ruin.

Had Charlie been present, she might have heard me approach the second floor. As it was, both girls were at school.

Clearing the remainder of the steps, I moved down the hall—and passed through the open doorway of Stephanie's room.

Until now, my sense of propriety—ingrained into me by my own mother from nearly the moment of birth—had prevented me from trespassing into Stephanie's quarters. Now, though, reason and purpose, not to mention the increasing deficit of time, demanded I ignore my breeding in favor of doing all I could to investigate this small chink I may have located in Stephanie's impenetrable armor.

Avoiding my cloaked and masked reflection in the mirror of Stephanie's dresser, I searched for my in.

"Spartan" was the word that came to mind when I took in the extent of her possessions, most of which remained sealed in columns of stacked brown boxes.

There was one item, however, that caught my attention.

A simple porcelain angel, her wings tucked, knelt on Stephanie's nightstand, her faceless countenance downcast as she harkened to the music of her silent lyre. The size of a swallow, the angel sat close to the pillow where Stephanie laid her head at night.

Its presence there intrigued me.

Stephanie had neither seen me nor sensed me in any capacity since her arrival. Even when I had dipped inside her dream, she had not perceived me.

And so, forced into the role of voyeur, I had observed her in her sleeping fantasy bestow her affections on the yellow-haired boy. The one who I had ascertained, through the eavesdropping of her conversations with her father, went by the name of Kyle Benedict.

My being invisible to Stephanie, though, did not disturb me quite so much as the presence of this angelic statue.

Because its placement in her otherwise unadorned room suggested that she reserved for the artifact some measure of reverence.

Also that she *did* believe.

The stoic and levelheaded Stephanie. The sensible and seasoned scholar.

Could she truly believe in something as otherworldly as angels? Or was this figure, like Mr. Armand's coveted ring, yet another idle and hollow token of loss and remembrance?

I plucked the angel from her place, taking her prisoner within my palm. Then I frowned into the face she did not possess, my ears tuned to the epiphany she whispered voicelessly to me.

Did I not also have a face I no longer possessed?

I glanced away from the angel, doing something I took pains never to do, and offered to Stephanie's standing mirror my masked and cloaked visage.

Two pinpricks of light regarded me through the holes of the mask. I looked away, my thoughts unfurling faster until suddenly, a breakthrough.

Indeed. Why had it not occurred to me before how thoroughly I had been going about this the wrong way?

Stephanie, more pragmatic than arithmetic itself.

Given her disposition, would it not take *months* of my wheedling at Charlie for her to even notice the smallest hint of my presence?

Him, though . . .

Truly, who would Kyle Benedict be next to *him*?

Had Stephanie not proven with each of my efforts how there existed in her world no room for monsters in masks?

Might she entertain, however—should one make an appearance within her next dream—an angel?

When it came to angels, I of course knew none. Thanks to the curse, I never would.

I had once, though, been well acquainted with a devil.

One who'd never had even the slightest trouble passing for just the opposite.

My plan decided, a check of accomplishment registering in my hollow chest, I turned to make my exit, along the way depositing Stephanie's figurine atop her dresser.

Charlie could rest easy tonight. Perhaps every night after as well should I, through this new avenue, succeed in obtaining the audience I *truly* sought.

That of her elder sister.

FIVE

Stephanie

"Well, Dad, you did it," I said, joining him where he stood on the cobblestone walkway. We gazed up at the monstrosity that loomed like a grizzled beast before us. Our new house. "You've successfully turned us into the Munsters."

Red ivy clung to the turret that rose three stories high, capped by a spire. The home had a second, shorter turret at the rear, but its roof blended with the jutting, tent-shaped sections crowning the rest of the house. While the home's gray stone structure gave the exterior a Wayne Manor feel, the actual architecture and facade made me think of a creepy old-fashioned dollhouse left in the attic to rot.

"At this stage," Dad said, speaking up at last, "I think it looks more Addams Family myself. They always struck me as having a bit more class, y'know?"

"They *did* have a butler," I admitted.

With a fast slapping of shoes, Charlie barreled past us in her purple puffer jacket, toward the crooked-limbed maple on the leaf-covered front lawn. I only saw what had lured her there when the creature she'd spotted sprang into flight.

A huge moth.

The bug fluttered off the tree's trunk just before Charlie could grab it, ruining its camouflage. How had Charlie even seen it?

While Charlie jumped after the ugly thing, I handed my father one of the heavy brown paper grocery bags weighing down my arms.

He took the bag and asked the obligatory, "How was school?"

"Okay," I said, supplying the obligatory answer. "Except I found out that, apparently, our house is haunted."

"Humph." Dad retrieved the other bag from me.

"So," I said, pulling the rest of the groceries from the Civic, "when were you going to tell me we had specters?"

He smirked. Dad didn't believe in ghosts any more than I did.

"Why bother when I knew the neighborhood kids would do it for me?" he replied. "You know, I'm surprised it took this long. I thought for sure you'd come back on Monday with some cock-and-bull story."

Charlie whooped past us, back to the car, where she'd left her My Little Pony lunchbox.

"First off, Dad, you have to live in a *neighborhood* to have 'neighborhood kids' and, secondly, unlike you, I do not broadcast the fact that I live in an ancient Victorian deathtrap."

"Oh, c'mon. It's not *that* bad." His mouth quirked, dark beard wrinkling. "As long as you stay out of the basement."

"Why? Did you go down there today?"

"No. I'm actually kinda scared to go back down there."

"Because of the ghosts?" Now it was my turn to smile.

"Because I'm pretty sure we're going to need a new furnace, and

I don't even want to know what it's going to cost to heat a place like this. And because I still need to get an estimate on installing a washer-dryer setup down there. You know. The *really* scary stuff."

"Yeah, well." I glanced behind me to where Charlie pulled open the Civic's rear door. "I wish you would have told me up front whatever the realtor said about this place."

"Why's that? See something strange?"

"Not me."

"Chess?"

Our eyes met for the first time, Dad's hazel stare shadowed by his heavy brow and, I was glad to see, by concern, too.

"Last night, Charlie complained about a man in her closet. I'm worried the kids at her school may have said something to her. Apparently, this place is some kind of paranormal hotspot. Or am I telling you something you already know?"

"Humph," Dad said again.

"*Dad.*" I glowered at him. "What did the realtor say?"

"Nothing." He shrugged. "When I asked if this place was haunted, I'd meant it mostly as a joke. You know, to make him sweat since they're supposed to disclose stuff like that if you ask."

"And he just said, 'Yes, here be ghosts'?"

"He checked his papers and stated the place was 'rumored to be.' But no stories. Why? You hear some good ones today?"

"Nothing specific."

"Well." Dad laughed, a soft sandpaper-on-stone sound that I loved. "Might be a fun research project. And, after what I discovered today, I know where you can start."

"Where?"

"Let's just say that if I ever see that realtor again, I will live up to my former reputation and jack him in his clean-cut jaw."

Dad had a bit of a record. After he got out of the service and before he met Mom, he'd gotten into a few bar scuffles. One turned out to be the chair-smashing, bottle-over-the-head sort. I never knew about the brawl until after Mom passed. When I'd turned sixteen, though, Dad had sat me down and confessed everything. Not in a get-it-off-his-chest kind of way, but more like I was some kind of lawyer who needed to know the whole truth. He'd said he wanted me to be informed in case it ever came up again. He'd also told me he did time for assault.

Not a *long* time, he'd said, making it clear that the man he'd pummeled *had* walked out of the hospital without permanent physical damage. But he'd also wanted me to know why, even though he'd spent several years in anger management and therapy, normal jobs weren't going to be an option for him. Not the good kind that would allow a single father to properly care for two daughters.

The only part of the story I side-eyed was that last part. Because his Richard Smash days were so far in the past that I felt sure he could have settled in any town he really wanted to.

But Dad needed his projects. And to not be in any environment that encouraged looking back. And I needed him to be Dad.

So, house flipping we a-went.

"What did he leave out?" I asked. The realtor must have omitted some truly odious piece of information for Dad to even joke about breaking his longstanding no-violence track record.

"You know all that tall grass in the back? Close to the woods?"

"Yeah?"

"Turns out there's a family graveyard hiding in one patch."

I sucked a hissing breath in through my teeth.

Selling a house rumored to have ghosts was something we'd dealt with before. Successfully, too, since—as far as amenities went—ghosts weren't real. Sometimes buyers even *wanted* a "haunted" house.

But bodies in the ground? Not a good selling point.

I tilted my head at him. "Can't you sue him for that?"

"Not on an 'as is' buy, turns out," he said, making it clear his brain had already traveled these neural pathways and that he'd probably even made some phone calls.

"Well." I sighed, giving him a pat on the back. "We've got six months to figure it out."

"And six months to keep it hidden from Charlie."

Like so much else, I added in my head.

"Easy enough," I said with a shrug. "The grass will hide the graves for at least another month. After that, we can get some tarps to hide them for the winter. It's too dangerous for Charlie to go that close to the woods anyway."

"You be careful if you go back there, too," Dad said. "There's a lake beyond the trees that belongs to the next lot, and probably snakes and varmints and everything else in those woods."

"For the moment," I said, "I'm good just navigating the obstacle course that is our house."

"Three weeks from now, you won't recognize the place." His chest puffed as he shifted his weight from one steel-toed work boot to the other.

Charlie popped between us, then, with a loud "Boo!" before

erupting into giggles, even though neither of us had jumped.

"You want me to make this chili or what?" I asked them.

"With spaghetti!" chimed Charlie.

"The stove works now," Dad offered.

"That's lucky."

Surprising me, Dad set the groceries down on the walkway. He looped an arm around my shoulders and jostled me into him so that the scent of his Old Spice deodorant wafted over me.

He planted a kiss on my hair.

Affection from my father usually came awkwardly and out of the blue like that.

For me anyway.

But the one-armed hug was his way of telling me thanks.

Thanks for being me. And for helping him play understudy to the person we both missed. The person Charlie had never known.

Dad gathered the groceries again with calloused hands.

I knew better than to try to help him, so I went back to my car to get the rest.

I stopped, though, jumping at the sight of the gigantic moth from the tree, which had perched itself, wings outspread, on the edge of my open trunk, its dark body contrasting starkly with the Civic's bright blue finish.

The thing, mammoth in size, as big as my palm, flickered its yellow-accented wings, its segmented, cigar-thick abdomen giving a shudder. Then it took off, flittering up and away.

But not before I had glimpsed the strange emblem on its back.

The symbol, a brownish-yellow skull, must occur naturally in the species.

Still, it disconcerted me nonetheless.

♪ ♩ ♪

SEQUESTERED IN THE attic, I sat on the antique periwinkle chaise lounge I'd found there and smirked at my phone screen.

"Lucas Cheney," I said, eyeing the profile I'd finally managed to bring up in a search. Officially, Hipster Glasses had a name.

Too bad my recon-slash-procrastination session would soon be over since, due to his locked profile, I couldn't glean much more from social media than that. Aside from some basic info and a few photos of him decked out in his Archie duds, it was tumbleweeds.

"Figures," I muttered, dropping my cell into the cushions.

Then, cringing at the attic I still did *not* want to get started on, I picked it up again.

This Lucas guy was, after all, way more fun to look at than the disaster spread out before me. He was interesting, too, because why, in every one of his photos, did he look like he was headed to a sock hop?

I *could* ask him about that. I could also ask him more about the house.

Maybe I should have given him my number when he asked for it. Then again, maybe I *would* have if he hadn't point-blank said he wasn't interested in *me*.

Rolling my eyes at Lucas, I abandoned my phone again and stood, eager to let in some fresh air. This attic smelled like a tomb.

After putting Charlie to bed, I'd tromped up here with every intention of clocking in for my first day on the part-time job that came with every new house. Dad always paid me an allowance to tackle a few of the more menial tasks while he took on the grunt work.

At first glance, though, this attic, full of cobwebs and several decades' worth of junk, had only inspired me to take a load off. Because, wow. This one was going to take a while.

Still, I had to start sometime.

Carefully, I picked my way over a pile of rolled-up carpets, heading toward the window. I had to yank the rusted crank several times, though, before the casement pivoted open with a teeth-jarring screech.

Spiced autumn air surged into the room, cooling my cheeks while the wind whipped at the short stretch of woods flanking either side of our winding driveway. The trees tossed their fiery arms this way and that with a low and traveling *shhhhhhhh*.

I leaned through the window overlooking the old iron fire escape that zigzagged up the rear of our house, and took a deep swig of the air that was fresher and cleaner here than it had been at our last house. Though the musty plant smell that rushed my nostrils promised rain, I hoped for Charlie's sake it wouldn't storm. She'd actually let me put her in her own bed that night, and though she kept glancing to her closet, she never mentioned her monster.

I turned and scanned the dancing-dust-mote- and junk-filled room for a good place to start.

Too bad I didn't have a strong, awkward, and ghost-obsessed boy here to help me.

Grinning in spite of myself, I headed to the corner that held the most promising artifacts: a stack of old steamer trunks.

Grunting, I hauled one onto the floor, then I flipped the latches and opened the lid. Apparently, though, someone had already beaten me to this punch. The trunk, empty except for a child's yellow-ribbon-wrapped straw hat and a smattering of papers and photos, had been looted long ago.

So much for treasure hunting.

I gave the papers a cursory once-over, and just as I was about to close the lid, one of the papers lining the bottom of the trunk—a photograph—caught my eye.

I dipped my hand into the trunk and withdrew the sepia-toned image of a wealthy-looking Victorian family. Posed against a non-descript backdrop, they seemed to watch me through the crackled window of time and space.

Well, *three* of the four figures did.

A pretty woman in an elegant lace gown with Gibson Girl hair held center place in the photo. A cute little girl who might have been eleven or twelve stood in front of her dressed all in white, her own hair done in braids. To the woman's left stood a glowering man with dark hair and a matching handlebar mustache. To her right, there stood another male figure. A *young* man by the looks of his one visible hand. I couldn't tell for sure because a black blotch that seemed to be part of the photo itself obscured the whole of his head.

Maybe the heat or cold of the attic had damaged the photo? Or maybe just time.

I rooted through the papers and, in addition to a faded ocean liner ticket from London, I found another small full-body photo—this one almost halfway blacked out.

A single figure—the same young man from the family photo, I guessed—posed as the portrait's subject. He wore a long black dress coat open over a waistcoat. One hand held a violin. The other gripped its bow. Above that, the photo dissolved into the same blackness that had ruined the previous photo. Again, the blotching obscured the man's face and head. All except for the very edge of his sleek and longish black hair.

My immediate guess was that he had to be the son of the couple. Which would make the little girl his sister. Could the family be the original owners of the house?

I looked up as a breeze rushed in through the window, sending a flutter of loose papers over the attic. In the distance, a rumble of thunder sounded.

"*Great.*" Dropping the photos, I hurried to the window and cranked it shut, eyeing the storm-darkened clouds above.

If Charlie woke and the power went out, she was going to lose her mind.

I made a beeline for my phone, but paused when my foot encountered one of the papers the sudden gale had sent scattering off a nearby desk.

Sheet music?

Bending, I plucked the yellowed paper from the floor. Then turned to find another pair of papers filled with more music, the notes of which had been etched onto the lines by hand.

No name or signature headed or footed any of the papers. Still, the romantic in me wanted to believe the long-gone mystery violin guy had been the composer. The paper felt and looked old enough, but the notes themselves gleamed crisp and fresh. I ran my thumb over a quarter note, causing a faint smudge that, if nothing else, proved the intricate piece to be unquestionably modern.

Forgetting my phone for a moment, I took to the task of gathering the other sheets. Though I told myself it was because the ballad was handwritten and therefore original and possibly one of a kind . . . I knew that wasn't the real reason.

Mom. *She* was the true reason.

For the second time that day, a wave of crushing sadness washed over me. And there I went again, careening backward through the years until I was once more seated on a piano bench next to my mother, my small, Charlie-sized legs kicking in time with the metronome while Mama sang . . . and played.

That bench. It was a spot she and I shared well into the years my feet no longer dangled. And those were the years when *I* had done the singing.

That morning, it had been the memory of her music—something that I recalled now better even than her face—that had killed me.

Now? In this moment? It was the fact that Charlie would never have her turn on that seat.

And this music, like that old piano, was what screamed these brutal truths at me in a way that refused to be ignored.

At the same time, the collection of carefully placed notes beckoned to me in their hidden language, a vernacular that my mom had taught me to decipher and translate through the sweet mixture of sound and soul.

I'd stopped singing after she died.

Well. I'd stopped taking lessons.

Sometimes I still sang. Usually when I was in the house by myself. Or to Charlie at night before bed. I never told Charlie the songs were Mom's. I just sang them so that she would have some pieces of Mom, even if she couldn't know those pieces for what they were.

Dad and I. We did what we could to keep Mom out of Charlie's daily life. Far enough out to keep her from asking too many questions, the answers to which were bound to cause pain.

One day soon, though, Charlie would find out the truth.

It was a day I wanted to hide from, and one that Dad wanted to run from.

I sighed, scanning the notes, refusing to blink so that my tears would dry before they could fall.

"So. You had some reasons to be sad, too, huh?" I asked the music, the melody of which could have scored a tragic romance.

Flipping through the pages, I hummed a few bars of the haunting ballad, quietly, just in case Dad happened to be near.

Though my love of music had survived my mother's death, Dad's had not, and that's why I did my best to leave him out of it.

He never said anything, but I could tell that music—certain types that included my singing—bothered him. And yet, he hadn't so much as lifted a finger to evict the old, broken, and tuneless grand piano sleeping under that dustcover in our ancient new parlor.

I might have taken that as a sign he was finally starting to heal. If I wasn't so afraid it happened to be a sign of just the opposite.

"Steph?" came my father's voice from the base of the staircase, startling me into silence. "Mind coming down and giving me a hand with something?"

"Coming," I called, grabbing my phone.

Then, unable to help myself, I rolled the sheet music into a tube, taking it with me.

Because, for the same reasons Dad needed silence . . . I found myself needing a song.

SIX

Zedok

This time, when Stephanie dreamed, against all odds, she *did* see me.

My plan to appear to her not as I was, but as I once had been . . . worked.

Though the curse had disallowed the survival of even a single untainted likeness of my former self, I had never forgotten the face that could have once been found in any mirror.

The face was not one easily forgotten. Nor, for that matter, easily ignored.

This dream of Stephanie's had begun similarly to the last one I'd attempted to infiltrate, the school setting unfurling from the darkness of her unconsciousness. She entered through the dissipating void, her attention fixed on something ahead of her—someone. Yet a fleeting scan of the crowd showed no trace of the yellow-haired star of her previous fantasy.

As Stephanie approached, I let the scene unfold as it would, resisting the temptation to take hold of the dream and spin it my way. Instead, I took my place amid the other phantom players, ironically the least phantom among them.

Eyes locked on me where I stood close to one metal-compartment-lined wall, Stephanie gaped at me as she passed. Her steps slowed, retreated, and then abruptly halted in front of me.

We stood but a few feet from one another, and I watched her as she watched me—as the hallway cleared of students and noise far faster than it would have in reality.

At last, her complete concentration had become mine.

I waited, leaving first words to her, for allowing her to initiate our conversation would help to embed me more firmly in her dream. And in her mind.

Her first utterance, though, left much to be desired.

"Uum," she said. And then nothing more.

Ah. *Erik.* He had always had this effect on people. On debutants in particular—those elite young ladies of my day. The girls who, each fancying herself the ingénue in a play full of villains, had volleyed against one another to win a more favorable union than her rivals. Which one of them would not have poisoned the other's punch for but a single dance with *Erik*?

"Where did *you* come from?" Stephanie asked, before sending a glance around the vacated hall, as if she'd only just noticed we were alone. Then she gestured to the rapier I wore. "Are you with the drama club or something?"

Her casual demeanor suggested she had yet to realize this was a dream. I had hoped that my dated wardrobe would help hurry that part along.

"Forgive my intrusion," I said with a small nod. "Though we are not yet formally acquainted, you should know our paths have crossed before. That is why I am here."

She frowned, her hands clasping tight the strap of her shoulder-slung bag.

"I don't think so," she said. "Last I checked, I was the only new student here. Besides, I think I would remember someone . . . British."

An involuntary smile touched my lips—*Erik's* perfect lips. Because, while I was sure I would never know, I assumed my nationality had not been the first word to spring to her mind.

Had I really forgotten how much power lies in beauty? It was a power I missed. And one that apparently held even more sway with Stephanie than I had initially wagered.

My smile faltered, which suggested that some part of me had been secretly hoping Stephanie would prove herself different from the girls I had once known. That she would surprise me.

All the better, perhaps, that she did not.

"I am not a student of this school, Miss Armand," I clarified. "My formal education, in fact, was acquired over a century ago."

She took a sudden step back from me. "How do you know my name? Who are you?"

"I am," I answered quickly, "the rightful heir and lord of the estate your father has just purchased."

She squinted at me before again inspecting the hall that held none but the two of us.

"The truth is," I admitted, "I have endeavored to garner your attention for some time. And now that I have it, it is imperative that you absorb every word of what I am about to tell—"

"This has to be a dream," she mumbled suddenly, providing the answer to the riddle as it occurred to her. Her eyes returned to mine. "You can't be real."

"Though this may be a dream," I hurried to say, "I'm afraid I cannot agree with your second assessment."

Now that Stephanie had become cognizant in her dream, the likelihood of her waking and severing our connection increased. Contrary to my assertion, she still believed me to be a figment. If I said just the right things, though, I could now, perhaps, begin to change that.

"Every word your sister has uttered about the presence on the estate is true," I said.

"Presence?" Stephanie took another retreating step. "What are you talking about?"

"There is an unfathomable darkness in this home," I said, reclaiming the distance between us. "The product of a curse. An infection that extends through the manor's walls as well as its grounds. As a result, you and your family are in grave danger. I do not wish for any of you to be hurt or worse. And that is why you must all leave. Immediately."

"Leave," she repeated in a deadpan tone that insinuated I had not heard the lunacy imbued in my own words.

"The monster your sister speaks of is *real*," I told her. Which, just as everything else I'd relayed to her, was true enough.

Stephanie drew a breath. Then she started to say my name. "Zedo—?"

I raised a finger to stop her—boldly pressing it to her lips. Keeping my stare fixed on hers, I waited to be certain I had her silence. Only then did I withdraw my finger, which I pressed for one moment to my own lips.

Awed, and perhaps a bit shaken by my gall, she merely blinked.

When I spoke again, I chose my words with the utmost care. "Take caution with that name," I said. "He will hear you whenever you or anyone dares speak it."

"Riiight," she said, unconvinced as ever. "You still haven't told me your name."

"I am Erik," I said, lying to her for the first time. And I did consider it a lie. For though I had once been Erik, I was no longer. And had not been for over a hundred years.

"*Erik*," she said, repeating the name in a way that made me flinch. For, though there was one other person who insisted on referring to me as such, to hear that name uttered aloud was to be reminded of everything I had lost. Everything I no longer was, and could never be again.

"I must go," I told her, my central aim now achieved. "But you should heed my warning. Get out. *Leave* Moldavia. Or, one way or another, *he* will make you."

I ended the dream there by opening my eyes—casting their glow upon the hearth I had seated myself in front of prior to my meditation.

And now I was back. On my side of the house. Once more locked within the shell of the thing I had just warned her against.

SEVEN

Stephanie

I woke up at four fifteen that morning—right after the dream ended.

I didn't even try to go back to sleep, either. I wouldn't have been able to. Not with that face—that voice—still echoing in my mind.

With the hope of grounding myself in reality, I got up. Clad in T-shirt, pajamas pants, and robe, I padded downstairs to make myself a cup of coffee. Four sips in, though, and I was still asking myself the same ludicrous questions. Why, for the first time since I'd entered it, did the house feel so . . . off? And why had that dream felt more real than this moment that *was* real?

I pressed the tips of my fingers to my lips, where the sensation of his touch lingered. Though no one had touched me at all.

The mind was a funny thing. Scientists wanted to say that outer space was the final frontier, but I would argue that it was the human brain. And mine? Between yesterday and today, well, it had somehow fallen into a black hole.

Two cups of coffee and almost a half hour of total silence later, though, and I managed to sort the dream out in its entirety. Well, nearly.

The tall, dark, and molten-hot stranger standing at the lockers? Nothing more than a fancy chimera Frankensteined together by my subconscious, which had excavated the parts both from yesterday's interaction with Lucas and those freaky faceless photos I'd found in the attic. How could I be so sure? Because Sir Steamy McDreamy had referred to the house as "Moldavia." And Lucas had been the first person to utter that name to me.

Boom. Mystery explained.

The dream had also revealed another layer of my inner world that I couldn't help but examine now, too.

This Erik guy. I might not have even stopped to pay him any attention in the dream if he hadn't been sooooo . . . Well, for lack of a better term, *beautiful*.

Even now that face reverberated through my memory as sharply as it had in the dream.

Gripping the handle of my coffee mug, I frowned into the cooled light-brown liquid.

My attraction to the dream figure . . . Did his appearance mean I legit had the hots for this Lucas character? Like, without even realizing it with total waking-mind coherence?

I could totally admit Lucas was cute. But was the dream telling me I wasn't letting myself admit just *how* attractive I thought he was? Or was the entire interaction with Erik just supposed to highlight how conflicted I felt about kind of being into someone who had also kind of been creeping on me?

Tired of Sigmund Freud–ing myself, I finally shoved the coffee away and stood.

It would be six soon, and Dad would be up and I wanted to make him and Charlie breakfast before we all dug into the day's projects. Which meant I had an hour left to satisfy one curiosity, at least.

♪ ♩ ♪

PRE-MORNING DARKNESS STILL swathed the estate by the time I got dressed and made it out the back door.

Flashlight in hand, I stepped down from the dry-rotted, wraparound porch and into the milky mist that enshrouded the grounds. Just down a short path, the metal frame of a gazebo-shaped conservatory poked through a tangle of bramble and brush.

While the intact panes of the glass house shone opaque in the starlight, the missing ones gaped black, making the thing look like some giant bug with too many open mouths and even more sightless, cataract-clouded eyes.

Though I had forgone exploring the property until now, I'd already inspected the conservatory, which had been just as overrun by plants on the inside as on the outside.

Of course, there'd also been evidence that the glass house had once been truly beautiful. An oasis of plants and peace.

Had the lady of the house hosted tea parties there? What sorts of plants had she grown?

Almost certainly, there had been roses. Victorians loved their roses, right?

Dad would raze the glass house for sure, but I couldn't help wishing he would restore it. A functional conservatory wasn't something that could drive up the home value enough to cover the cost of its restoration, though. Or counteract the fact that there were dead people buried thirty yards away.

My eyes slid to the shadowy line of the woods.

I wanted to believe simple curiosity led me to investigate the graves. But there was no denying my sudden interest in them had more to do with my dream.

I couldn't bring myself to say that I was "scared." Things were definitely *odd* here, though.

But accumulating weirdness aside, you couldn't get much more concrete than graves. Graves had dates and names. Graves had *facts*.

Steeling myself, I trudged toward the thickest section of tall grass, the soles of my rubber Wellingtons tromping over leaves and twigs. So far, the heavy Maglite I'd brought hadn't been a huge help, what with the mist deflecting the strong white beam, dispersing the light.

As I got closer, I veered in the direction of a set of oddly spaced trees. That was, they weren't part of the forest. Thorn bushes huddled around their bases, while downed limbs and twigs tangled in the weeds.

And there. Straight ahead, I spotted them.

The graves. Three total.

I actually held my breath as I approached the two that stood right next to one another, one half sunken in the waist-high weeds.

WILLIAM THEOPHILUS DRAPER read the first stone, right below the epitaph of BELOVED FATHER AND HUSBAND and above the dates listed as February 18, 1859–December 21, 1903.

CHERISHED WIFE AND MOTHER was the predictable epitaph for the second, half-sunken gravestone—Lillian Angelique Draper's.

I frowned at her grave. At the worn dates. They couldn't say what I thought they did.

Approaching the stone, I crouched and brushed away the layer of clinging dirt. Then I traced the mossy numbers with a finger.

Born March 25, 1865. Died December 21, 1903.

Almost against my will, I glanced to the right. To the third grave.

This one was for PRECIOUS DAUGHTER, Myriam Elaine Draper.

Again, though, the listed dates had me pausing. Or *date*.

She had also died on December 21, 1903.

Since she'd been born August 29, 1891, she would have only been twelve. Same approximate age as the girl from the photo. Her parents. Their ages would match the photo I'd found, too.

Though there was no way to be sure—not without further research—I could only presume that whatever had killed one of them had killed them all.

In that instant, the force of the tragedy bowled into me.

Could the home's reputation owe to the fact that the family somehow died inside the house or on the grounds? Perhaps there'd been a gas leak or carriage accident.

Of course, they must have been together. To have all died on the same day . . .

Except. What about the other figure from the photos? The blotted-out young man?

A shudder of soundless movement near one of the trees caused me to start and stand.

I walked toward the movement and spotted the source.

Another moth.

The creature, as large as the one I'd found yesterday, trundled over the trunk of the tree.

Crunching over twigs, leaves, and uneven ground, I made my way to the maple. Peering into the tree's branches, I searched for more of the beasts.

I found a second moth only when I looked down again.

This one, a little smaller than the one Charlie had chased in the front yard, sat perched on the edge of another stone.

Another *gravestone*.

I dropped once more into a crouch.

The moth flitted aside as I cleared the leaves, grass, and muck that had camouflaged the stone.

"*No*," I whispered at the name that had been carved there more than one hundred years ago. A name that could not really be there. "There's no way."

And there shouldn't have been.

Because that name. Its presence there suggested the impossible.

That other things, things that weren't supposed to exist at all, had really been there, too.

EIGHT
Zedok

Tick, tock, tick, tock went the mantel clock. My father's clock. Doing its normal job of wearing through my sanity.

Pacing in the parlor on my side of Moldavia—a frozen-in-time version full of finery, decorated in my mother's good taste, and furnished by my father's bottomless wealth—I tried to ignore its ticking, the only sound that disrupted the midnight silence of the house.

Always, its doleful, monotone song served as the only music I knew. The sole accompaniment to the soundless nocturne my existence had become.

I could compose, yes. Requiems, concertos, waltzes, and anything in between. I could inscribe entire cantatas—an *opera*, should I so wish. And composing occupied me so thoroughly that, for the time I could remain absorbed in the task, it held the power to lift my mind out of my wretchedness. Which was why I coveted the hours that, until the Armands' arrival, I could spend in unencumbered labor on the other side of the house.

Yet, no matter where I composed it, I could render to my music no real life. Not without a heart.

My latest effort, a simple ballad, sat abandoned and unfinished in the attic of the Armands' side of the house. Too distracted by the memory of my encounter with Stephanie that morning she had entered the parlor to collect Charlie, pausing at my piano to harken to her secret music, I'd stopped mid-note and left the pages where they lay atop my father's old desk—a place well out of Charlie's reach.

I could have returned to the work. The quiet was such that I might have been able to stay enveloped in my labors until just before dawn, when Moldavia's new tenants again awoke to traipse through my family's manor with more racket than a traveling carnival.

Though how could I have hoped to focus on music after last night's tête-à-tête with Stephanie?

Since our interlude, I'd had difficulty placing my thoughts on anything else.

Most disturbingly, I found myself inexplicably desirous of another conversation with her.

For that reason more than any other, I had resolved to stay well out of her dreams this night. I had, after all, accomplished what I'd sought to. I'd planted the seed that would soon grant me greater influence in her waking life. Why engage with her a second time?

No doubt my interest in speaking with her stemmed from the fact that inaction had never been a comfortable choice for me. Especially in situations where time insisted on working against me. But then, I assured myself, no move at all on my part was still, in this instance, a move. Because Erik's absence from her dreams tonight—was there any better way to encourage her to seek the answers out for herself? And she would go digging. As smart as she was? As determined as she could be?

Would she hate Erik after she learned what he had done?

Of course, how could she not.

Abruptly, I halted my pacing. Scowling beneath my mask, I glanced to the piano, yearning, as always, to play.

My inability to produce so much as two complementary notes was one of the crueler twists of the curse.

Not only was I to be haunted by the fragments of my own splintered soul along with all the memories of this house, but I was also to be mocked by this pristine instrument that, though it shone with lacquered blackness, would produce for me no more music than its ruined twin. Miraculously, the piano, my piano—the version I considered to be the true version—still occupied the same space on the Armands' side of the home.

Despite whatever meaning it held for the Armands, though, the instrument would most certainly not be suffered to remain much longer. Another cause for concern, since the last man who had entered this house with the intention of removing my piano had left the premises . . . rather worse for wear.

A similar fate awaited the Armands. How well I knew it was only a matter of time.

If only Stephanie were not so . . .

"Headstrong," I mumbled, my voice muffled by my mask as I swung into a turn, retracing the steps I would momentarily turn to retrace again. "Contrary."

What else could I say of her?

"That she is coarser than bramble," came my dry reply—and almost through a laugh. "Forthright," I added. "Yet obstinate and hard-nosed. Intelligence and beauty to spare, yes, but absolutely no refinement. What would my parents have said of her? I cannot even imagine. Myriam, on the other hand, would have been nothing short of entranced, I have no doubt."

What was I doing speaking out loud this way to no one? Though I sometimes conversed with my masks, those loosened shards of myself that paraded about me, through the house and over the grounds—ghosts of my own soul—I seldom uttered aloud my thoughts. Why do so when, too often, I had my masks to do that for me?

Was I merely pronouncing for my own benefit my opinions of Stephanie as I settled upon them?

"Not quite," came a caustic voice to my left—a voice I knew well. One that could hardly be counted as a voice at all.

I froze at once. My gaze trained on the piano, I dared not look.

Though it was not uncommon for me to be joined at any moment by one of my masks, it was quite unusual for *him* to appear so suddenly and without *some* heralding.

And what was it that had lured him from his normal dwelling place of the cellar?

Had Mr. Armand's recent excursion there agitated him as I had feared it would?

"You truly cannot guess what has beckoned me from below?" asked the mask, answering my thoughts, which were as much his as they were mine.

My masks. These personified slivers of my soul. One or indeed *twenty* of them could be found—at any given time—milling about the magnificent mansion or its snow-covered grounds. Unlike me, however, the masks remained confined to this parallel, suspended-in-time version of the house. Thankfully for the Armands, my masks could not pass between both versions as I could. Also unlike me, the masks possessed no corporeal form under their masquerade garb.

This mask, though—the one who called himself Wrath—was, with his crimson uniform, trailing cloak, and shining silver death's head mask, perhaps the most arresting of them all.

And the shard of my soul *he* represented—arguably the most heinous—fit too well with the image he presented.

"Do you hazard a guess?" he asked, dark amusement backing his distorted baritone.

I did not bother to answer. Because I *did* know—at least in part—what had caused his emergence from the cellar.

In the past, my masks had each had their turn at me. Over the decades, I have worn their various guises and, in so doing, have become the aspect of myself they represented entirely.

Control was what Wrath was after now. The control that, fortunately for the Armands, the mask I wore now—that of Languor—currently enjoyed.

Alternately, however, that meant that I, on some level, must want Wrath to win control also. For, in the same way my thoughts were the masks', so, too, were the actions and words of the masks my own.

Wrath's appearance portended all the disaster I hoped to circumvent. For it meant that he *already* had reason to want to take hold of me and, therefore, the fate of Moldavia's occupants.

"Leave me," I snarled at the mask. "Take whatever it is you think you know and go sink back into your hole. Whatever plan you have to ensnare me, it won't work."

"Fool. You are ensnared already."

"I told you to *go*," I warned, a dangerous tremble starting in my form.

"My eyes," Wrath said, that awful voice slicing deeper the gash of my growing anxiety. "To look through them would show you the truth. Should you wish to see it."

"My *wish*, monster, is for you to return to your hell and thus leave me to mine." I swung to face him. He sat upon the pale blue chaise near the parlor's bay windows. A stag's antlers crowned his hooded head. Dual pits of nothing watched me through the silver skull.

"That is not your wish," Wrath whispered, his words soft and supercilious, the collection of syllables akin to the guttering of flame.

I squared my jaw. And regarded him in stubborn silence.

For his presence alone told me he *must* be right.

"Very well. What is it, then?" I dared to challenge him, my dread of his answer echoing through my chest, that empty space that had once housed both an intact soul and its beating vessel. "Speak, and say what it is we *do* wish."

Wrath did not answer. Instead, his nightmarish visage rose to a height that matched my own. Next, he placed a gloved hand over his mask and took it away to reveal a face of nothingness. With the slow and measured steps of a pallbearer, he approached me. I stood my ground in spite of my wariness.

Stopping mere feet from me, he extended one crimson-clad arm and offered with his gloved and ring-lined hand his silver mask of irreverence, malice, and destruction.

Did he think for one moment that I, knowing what he was, would willingly *take* it from him?

Horror warred with my incomprehension, until my eyes fell to the shining metal of the proffered mask.

Like a mirage, another face appeared in the skull's mirrored surface. Quickly, the vision swam toward focus. And the face . . . it belonged to a girl.

Stephanie.

Tick, tock, tick, tock went the mantel clock, counting the seconds in which my fingers crept, of their own accord, toward the mask. Toward her.

As they did, a low rattle entered my awareness.

The house. It had begun to hum around us, causing the knick-knacks to clatter on their surfaces, the legs of the furniture to tremble against the floor, and the strings of the dormant piano to unanimously elicit an ominous wail of warning.

Terror for what I was doing, for what I'd nearly done, prompted me to rip the mask from Wrath's grip and toss it to the hearth, where it dissolved to vapor before impact.

At once, the tremoring of my world ceased. The piano's voice died.

At my side, Wrath's looming figure undid itself, his crimson cloak and officer's uniform unfurling to nothing, even while his low and unsettling laughter—always the last part of him to leave—echoed as fading thunder through the parlor.

NINE

Stephanie

With a loud scrape of chair legs on linoleum, I dropped into the seat across from his, prompting all four people at the lunch table to look up in surprise.

The petite, blonde, braid-wearing girl seated next to me fixed me with a scowl.

Dead ahead, Hipster Glasses gaped with the highest degree of shock of anyone.

I leaned forward over the table. "We need to talk."

"Uuhh." He shot a glance to his cohorts, who consisted of Braid Girl; a Black guy with short dreadlocks, a yellow peanut M&M T-shirt, and a septum piercing; and a pale goth kid with silken shoulder-length black hair and an enormous silver cross looped around his neck. "I thought we already . . . talked."

Hipster Glasses shot Braids a more panicky glance.

I sensed there might be a thing there. At the very least, he didn't want her to know the details of our last conversation.

"We need to talk *again*," I clarified. Right when I'd been about to expound on why, though, Braids cut in.

"Yeah—*hi*." Pivoting toward me, she offered her hand. "I'm Charlotte."

"Stephanie." I gave her hand a quick shake before turning my attention back to Hipster Glasses. Or rather, Lucas.

"Oh, um, sorry," said Lucas, sounding dazed. "I should introduce you. This is Patrick." He pointed to the kid with the piercing. Patrick gave me a what's-up chin lift, which I returned. "And that's Wes. Alternately known as the Priest."

"A pleasure to make your abrupt and unexplained acquaintance," Wes said, winking at me in a distinctly come-hither manner.

"Uh . . . you too," I murmured, and returned my attention to Lucas.

"Listen," I said, lowering my voice, "I need to know what you know about my house."

"You know," came Charlotte's voice from my left, "if you have an issue, you should really go through the website."

I frowned at her. She bit into her apple at me.

I quirked a brow at Lucas. His eyes, widening, darted between me and Charlotte.

"Website?"

"Yeah, *website*." Charlotte said, "As in a dot com address on the World Wide Web? There's a form you're supposed to fill out on our contact page if you want help. That way we can schedule accordingly. And keep our cases straight."

"Helps us weed out *basket* cases, too," said Wes, making Patrick snicker.

Okay. So I hadn't exactly endeared myself to this group. I wasn't trying to be invasive. But it had been Lucas I'd wanted to speak to. Apparently, a lunchtime conversation with him was a package deal.

Lucas hadn't been in the library that morning, and after our last interaction, I somehow doubted I'd find him milling around my locker again after final bell. I needed to talk to *someone*, though. Because Erik's name showing up on that grave *after* the dream-visit? It couldn't just be happenstance. Not only did all the moving parts defy coincidence and leap officially into the realm of the outright bizarre, they involved Charlie.

"Cases?" I asked Lucas. "What kind of cases?"

"We're paranormal investigators," explained Wes, his tone suggesting that this information was public knowledge.

"You mean like *ghost hunters*?" I asked Lucas, whose face went as crimson as it had on Friday. Either he was embarrassed by this revelation or felt he would be as soon as his friends discovered how he and I had already met.

"You are currently sitting with the entire SPOoKy team," said Patrick.

No kidding, I wanted to say, but managed to keep the comment in check.

"Which is an acronym for the Scientific Paranormal Organization of Kentucky," Wes clarified, plucking a pudding cup from the table. He gestured to me with it as if lifting a brandy snifter. "Though I feel you should know that I offered the single declining vote for adopting *that* particular moniker."

"Oh," I said. Because "wow" seemed too snarky, and I was already in the red with these guys.

"Yes," Wes replied, "I much preferred Southern Masters

of Otherworldly and Troubling Hauntings or, if you like, SMoOTH."

I nodded at that. Because what else could I do?

At least now Lucas's comment in the library about collecting "data" made more sense. And this news about his being a paranormal investigator supported his claim that his interest in me had, in fact, been about Moldavia.

While all this made *me* feel better—about Lucas and my sort of having a crush on him—*he* seemed squirmier now than ever.

"Yeah." Lucas cleared his throat. "I should have told you that when we, uh, discussed things on Friday. Like I said, I just didn't want to . . . weird you out."

"Wait," said Charlotte, cutting in. "Lucas, what's going on?"

"I just moved here from St. Louis," I told her.

"Yeah," replied Charlotte. But it might as well have been a "duh."

"And so ensue-eth the brandishing of claws," recited Wes in an eerie monotone. "The gnashing of teeth. The desperate attempts to undermine one another in the pursuit of my ardors." He held up a halting, silver-ring-lined hand. "Ladies, take heart, I am not as celibate as my nickname might imply."

"Shut up, man," Patrick said, shoving Wes's hand down. "Nobody wants your creepy ass."

"She lives in Moldavia," said Lucas.

Wes's near-smile fell. Patrick's expression sobered.

Charlotte's glare went from glacial to apprehensive.

"You live in Moldavia." Wes repeated the statement, his pale gray, kohl-rimmed eyes boring into me.

I chose that moment to speak to the table at large. "Okay. Will someone—I don't care who—please tell me what the story is on my house?"

"What'd you see?" Patrick asked, causing Charlotte's stare to bounce between everyone.

"Buddy Holly come back?" With this question, Lucas tipped back in his chair, folding those finely sculpted forearms over the dark pinstriped vest he'd buttoned over a white dress shirt. Which, I had to admit, looked snappy on him.

"Try Zedok," I said.

The front legs of Lucas's chair came crashing to the floor, his glasses knocking askew.

Wes's spoon made a crash landing on the floor.

"Nope," said Patrick. "We're all booked up with nope. Indefinitely. Sorry for your luck."

"*Trick*," chided Lucas, and it took me a second to realize that was another nickname.

"Oh, *please*," said Charlotte. "She's *messing* with us, you guys."

Lucas frowned at this. At me, too. Like he thought Charlotte had to be right.

But I didn't care what any of them thought of me or my motives for joining their lunch table. Not after a reaction like *that*. Not as long as someone started telling me what was wrong with my house.

"What about the name Zed—"

Wes hissed—actually *hissed*. Wincing, he held up a finger.

"*What?*" I splayed my hands.

"Names hold power," answered Wes. "To speak a demon's name is to summon it."

"*Demon?*" Internally, I officially started to freak. Because Erik said something similar in the dream. He hadn't called Zedok a demon, but he'd told me not to say the name.

"Wes is our resident demonologist," explained Lucas in a dismissive tone. "He thinks every haunting is demonic."

"And Lucas," Wes retorted, "is our resident fearless leader and professional debunker. His superpowers include dismissing full-bodied apparitions as fart clouds."

"Excuse me if I didn't want to scare her, *Wes*," Lucas said through gritted teeth.

"Sounds to me like she's got good reason to be scared, *Lucas*."

"Guys." Charlotte again. "*Hello.* She's lying. You know as well as I do where she got that name."

"Excuse me," I said to Charlotte, because if there was one thing I could not stand, it was people talking about me like I wasn't there. "My six-year-old *sister* is where I got that name."

"You sure your six-year-old sister wasn't in the next room when you were watching the documentary?"

"I don't know anything about a documentary," I said, officially starting to hate her. "She's been talking about this Zedok guy since the night we moved in."

"Okay, yeah," Wes said through an uneasy grin. "Can we not . . . say that name? I think we'll all have a far more pleasant afternoon if we refrain from invoking the infernal."

"What are you all *talking* about?" My blood started to race again, both with fear and mounting agitation.

That's when Charlotte veered on me. "Oh, come *on*. You got the name off of that TV special *Paranormal Spectator* did on the house six years ago. It doesn't take rocket science to figure out that you watched the 'Phantom Fury' episode over the weekend. And now you're messing with us. Or Lucas. I'm just not sure *why*."

That last bit she aimed at Lucas while I gawped at her, still too stunned by the invoking-demons remark to formulate a coherent thought.

"Charlotte." Lucas leaned forward to prop his folded arms on the table. "Chill for a second, okay? Let's just hear what she has to say."

"I didn't watch any stupid documentary," I snapped. At all of them. "This . . ." I hesitated before saying the name again, strictly for Wes's sake. "My sister started talking about this . . . ghost thing or whatever right after we moved in. I thought she was making it up. But now . . ."

I trailed off, suddenly unable to articulate anything more. Because how could I tell them about the dream with Erik without sounding crazier than I already did?

"But now you don't think she's making it up," Lucas finished for me.

Okay. So at least *he* believed me. That I wasn't fabricating this as a way to get back at him.

Right now, though, I still didn't know *what* I believed.

Before yesterday, I'd believed that dead people were dead and that if there were such things as spirits, they didn't stick around on earth to haunt the living.

Maybe, I had wanted to believe, souls transformed into angels.

Because Mom had believed in angels.

"I don't know," I said finally. "I just thought that, since you seemed to know so much about the house, you might be able to tell me something useful."

"Well," said Wes, "*something* must have happened. Or else you really are pulling our chain. On a side note, chain-pulling is a pastime I, too, enjoy."

"Quit being a creep, Wes," snapped Charlotte.

"Just creepin' it real," replied Wes.

"Please forgive my asinine *ass*-ociate," said Patrick, holding up a hand to block Wes's face from view. "His mom forgot to staple his tact to his shirt today. Not to worry. He and I are going to have a talk about it later. But, in the meantime, give it to us straight. Did you see him?"

No one moved or spoke for several seconds. Not even Charlotte. Their waiting on tenterhooks made me want to give them *something*. But all I had was the truth.

"I haven't *seen* anything," I admitted, keeping my gaze on Lucas. "Not . . . exactly."

"How do you not exactly see something?" Another question from the enchanting Charlotte.

"What about your sister?" prodded Lucas, like he didn't want Charlotte's question to derail my answer. "Has she seen him?" The intensity of his stare told me his heart had to be pounding as fast and hard as mine. From fear or excitement, though . . . Well, I guess I didn't know him well enough to say.

"She blames a lot of stuff on him," I said. "She says he talks to her. I thought he was some kind of imaginary friend but—"

"What does she say he looks like?" This question from Patrick, who, along with Wes, had also begun to take me more seriously.

I shrugged. "She says he wears a mask."

Several things happened all at once.

Patrick threw up his hands, saying, "I'm out."

"Holy shit," Wes muttered before making the sign of the cross at me.

And though Lucas did his personal best to keep his poker face, the quiet way he sat back in his chair told me that I had obliterated the doubt in him, too.

"Oh, for Pete's sake, you guys," spat Charlotte. She stood fast enough to cause the legs of her chair to screech. "I'm not sticking around for this." She took up her tray. "We're serious investigators. Not gullible idiots willing to risk our hard-earned reputation on something that was proven to be a hoax anyway."

"They never proved or disproved anything," argued Lucas.

"Rastin came out and *said* he faked it," Charlotte snipped back.

"Who's Rastin?" I asked. "And faked *what*?"

"Controversial clairvoyant," Wes answered in an aside. "He had an episode during that, uh . . . episode."

I scowled, the already tight knot of worry in my chest constricting. "What kind of episode?"

"Like you don't know," scoffed Charlotte.

Lucas cut in. "Boq later claimed Rastin only said he faked it because he was *afraid* of what the entity might do if people went snooping around the house."

"The episode was . . . bad," Wes said, answering my question.

"*Rastin's* episode," clarified Patrick. "'Phantom Fury' itself was actually pretty awesome."

"Though you have to agree that the show itself isn't as good as *Ghost Adventures*," said Wes.

"Ghost *Yellers*, I think you mean," snorted Patrick.

Charlotte brandished a finger at Lucas, ignoring the others. "That's because it was Boq's show on the line!"

"Boq *died* shortly after that investigation, Charlotte."

I blinked at the dual rapid-fire discussions happening around me until the gravity of what Lucas had just said finally hit me. Someone *else* had died in the house?

"Later. Of *natural* causes."

"A heart attack at age thirty-eight is *not* a natural cause!"

"She watched the documentary, Lucas."

"She said she didn't!"

I folded my arms. Because here I was again—just part of the scenery. And what the hell was I even still *doing* here? Why hadn't I, at the barest mention of there being a documentary, gotten up and walked away from these Winchester-boy wannabes?

Since I didn't have an answer to that, I stood, officially done.

"Wait. Stephanie. Where are you going?" Lucas asked.

"To the library to see if they have this stupid documentary. Something tells me I'm better off watching *it* instead of trying to get something coherent out of any of *you*."

"*Don't*," said Lucas, and I jumped when his hand, warm, caught me by the wrist.

I swung with a glower to face him, and he released me, retracting his hand as though my skin had burned him.

"Don't watch the documentary, I mean," he said, probably as aware as I had become of the three sets of eyes now trained silently and unblinkingly on the two of us. "Let me come over first."

"*What?*" Charlotte and I both blurted in unison.

"Let me take a look around the house," Lucas said. "Inside, I mean. Make a preliminary sweep. Document your experiences before you get any more outside information."

"Dude." Patrick's brows lifted. "You sure that's a good idea?"

"Information is why I'm *here*," I said. "And did you say some guy died of a heart attack inside the house?"

"Not *in* the house," corrected Wes. "Three months after filming."

"In his sleep," amended Patrick.

"But there was also the piano guy who died," said Wes.

"The *piano* guy?" I asked Lucas.

"I'll tell you everything you want to know." Lucas held a staying hand up to Wes and Patrick, who went obediently silent. "I promise. I'll even let you borrow my DVD of the *P.S.* documentary. But first, let me come over."

"Um," I said, still caught off guard by the notion. Because if he was asking to come over to my house right in front of a bristling Charlotte, and she wasn't chiming in to forbid it, wasn't that pretty solid evidence for them *not* being a thing? "Well. My dad's doing a lot of work in there. We'd . . . have to stay out of his way."

"You've *got* to be kidding me," said Charlotte.

"I'm coming, too," said Wes, his words tumbling out fast, as if he'd only been waiting for the invite to drop.

Patrick saluted us. "Y'all have fun. Send me a postcard from the fourth dimension."

"Just Lucas," I said. "My dad would have a coronary if I brought home a paranormal investigative team." As if having Lucas over wasn't going to be tricky enough. "You can come tonight. Six o'clock."

"Lucas, we have practice tonight," Charlotte said, her voice quieter now.

"We can practice tomorrow," replied Lucas.

Huffing, Charlotte spun and marched away.

"Listen," I said to Lucas, staring after her. "If you have to practice for something—"

Lucas shook his head. "It can wait. And don't mind Charlotte. She's this way with everyone when she first meets them."

I glanced to Wes and Patrick to see if they would back that statement up, but both avoided meeting my stare.

"I'll be there tonight," he said, rising to his towering height and collecting his tray. "Six."

With that, he hurried to catch up with Charlotte, leaving me with Patrick and Wes, both of whom eyed me as though I were a witch marked for burning.

"Is it really *that* bad?" I asked. "The house?"

"Since this seems like it's heading toward being an official SPOoKy investigation," said Patrick, "I get why Lucas doesn't want you to be influenced by any outside information or history yet. So, for now, I apologize, but mum's the word."

"But, for the record," Wes interjected, those storm-gray eyes alight with quiet foreboding. "Yeah . . . it's that bad."

TEN
Zedok

The camera bag that the boy carried told me exactly what he was, if not who.

From my second-story perch, through the window of the turret, I marked the young man's approach as he made his way to the porch.

He was as tall as I was, though broader, of course, in the shoulders.

Beneath his attire, I imagined he must possess a muscular form, for he stood quite straight. The lightness of his step betrayed his engagement in some regular physical activity, too.

I sneered, despising him straightaway, as I did any and all who dared to carry the hated title of "paranormal investigator."

Normally, it took loud announcements and flashy appearances before inhabitants called in reinforcements. Researchers, shamans, members of the clergy, and certain meddlesome mediums had all encroached upon these grounds before, each harboring the futile hope of eradicating the blight that plagued Moldavia. That was to say, *me*.

The trespassers nearly always bore the same array of useless equipment. And always wreaked more destruction than good. On themselves as well as on me . . .

So far, the only thing setting this creature apart from the others was his age.

My guess was that he could not yet be eighteen. And so no more than a year younger than *I* had been at the time the curse had decimated my world.

Reason dictated he must be a schoolmate of Stephanie's. An acquaintance. She had not resided in the area long enough to acquire any more meaningful relationships. At least I did not think so. Regardless, he was here, and thus represented a complication I cared not for.

What did he know of Moldavia? What had he told her? Or what had *she* told *him*?

Had Stephanie spoken of Erik?

Perhaps I should have warned her not to.

The boy knocked, the noise rankling me to the bones.

If Stephanie *had* told this boy about her encounter with Erik, did not his presence on these grounds suggest that he believed her?

His status as an investigator aside, was that not on its own enough to make him officially my enemy?

ELEVEN

Stephanie

"**H**ey, come on in."

Standing beneath the porch's stone portico, Lucas gripped tightly with both hands the shoulder-slung strap of a camera bag. While I stepped back to make room for him to enter, he gave me a tight and apprehensive smile.

What had him so on edge? Was it the house? Or possibly . . . me?

"Thanks," he said, and did this weird ducking walk into the foyer. Like he was stupid excited and trying (and failing) to contain it.

I tried not to smile as he trailed right past me to stand in the center of the foyer.

"Oh, wooow," he said, turning in a slow circle so he could get the panoramic view. "This place is *unbelievable*."

"I'm just glad there's running water."

He marveled at the dusty but lit chandelier that dripped crystals. "No, it's beautiful," he said, his voice breathy and lost and actually kind of sexy.

He floated farther into the foyer, as though drawn inward by an invisible force, gaping at the walls as he passed them like they were coated in gold instead of cobwebs. I waited while his wandering took him all the way to the grand staircase. Propping one foot on the bottommost step, his hand going to the newel post, Lucas peered up to the second floor.

"Geez-O-Pete," he whispered, his fingers twining the newel post's decorative cap—which then promptly came off in his grip.

"*Hey!*"

Lucas and I jumped in unison when my dad came tromping in from the back hall, his brow knit with annoyance. "What the deuce did you just do?"

"Oh," Lucas uttered, his entire face becoming one big O of shock.

"*Dad,*" I warned, while Lucas took two retreating steps from the stairs. After drifting too close in my direction, it dawned on him that he still held the amputated cap, which he slowly extended toward Dad. Dad marched over to him, scowling hard until, suddenly, a smile broke through the Incredible Hulk facade.

"I knew it was like that," he said, accepting the piece from Lucas. "Haven't glued it back on yet."

Pressing a hand to my chest, I rolled my eyes at my father and his guerrilla warfare tactics while Lucas's whole body sagged with relief.

"Dad," I said again. "This is Lucas Cheney. The friend from school I'm doing that report with?"

I nodded at Lucas, whose panic returned in an instant, his eyes snapping to mine.

Relax, I tried to convey, *be cool and just play along.*

"Richard Armand," Dad said, offering his hand to Lucas, who accepted my father's stiff military shake. I cringed inwardly, hoping Dad's grip wasn't as crushing as it looked. "Stephanie says you two are working on a local-history project for school?"

"Y-yes, sir," said Lucas, though I could tell it caused him deep unease to lie.

"What's with the camera bag?" Dad said, his seriousness returning, genuine this time. "Are you two taking photos in here for this thing?"

"Oh. Uh . . ." Lucas fidgeted with the bag strap, like he was fighting the urge to deny the thing was even his.

"*Chill*, Dad." I looped my arm through one of my father's giant ones and gave it a squeeze. "We're just documenting a few things. Like the differences between the main stairway and the servants' stairway and other Victorian-era things like the butler's pantry and the dumbwaiter."

"Son, you just going to stand there and let her call you names?" Dad asked.

"Uh, yes, sir?" replied Lucas.

"Good answer," said Dad. "But, seriously, these photos aren't going to end up on Facebook or YouTube or some kooky ghost-hunting site, right?"

"N-no, sir," said Lucas, who then seemed to stop himself from what he was about to utter next, probably some memorized, knee-jerk spiel about case confidentiality.

"Dad's not ready to show anything off yet." I gave Lucas a pointed glare, hoping he now understood how my father felt about the spirit realm and those who wanted to tap into it.

"Nothing worth showing off." Dad backtracked in the direction he'd come. "You can probably tell, Luke, that I've only just started patching up the place."

"It's Lucas, Dad," I corrected.

"Lucas," replied Dad. "As in George. Got it. Maybe I should make it easy on myself and just call you Skywalker."

"Well, sir," said Lucas. "I've been told I *am* strong with the Force."

"Ugh." I palm-slapped my forehead. "*Don't* encourage him."

"Hey." Dad pointed at Lucas with the newel cap. "Who shot first?"

"Uh, that would be Han, sir."

Dad grinned. "I like this kid," he said, continuing to aim the newel cap at Lucas, not like he was a person but, rather, an interesting specimen of fauna I'd retrieved from the woods. One he was even considering letting me keep. "I left Chess in the yard, so . . ."

I waved him on.

"Dinner in an hour, Steph," he said over his shoulder as he turned. "Skywalker, I hope you're hungry."

With that, Dad was out of sight again, giving me the chance to breathe a sigh of relief.

"I guess I should have asked permission first about the camera," mumbled Lucas.

"Permission granted," I said. "And don't mind my dad."

"Easy for *you* to say. You forgot to mention your dad was the Brawny Towel guy."

"He's really just a big teddy bear." I smiled, nudging him with one elbow.

Lucas didn't look convinced.

I grinned. "We'd better get started with this investigation before he and my sister come back in. So, where to first?"

"Well, that depends," he said. "Where would you say your concerns first began?"

Mine? The answer to that would be the graveyard. But that would be the wrong place to take Lucas with my dad prowling around outside.

"I guess, technically, that would be Charlie's room," I said. "So, this way."

"*Charlie* is your little sister?"

"Yep," I called back as I reached the stairs. Gripping the now headless newel, I turned with a smirk and waited for him to join me. "And I just *dare* you to call her Chuck."

TWELVE
Zedok

"It's speculated in some circles that closets, as a general rule, can be problematic."

The boy's voice drifted to me through the halfway open door of Charlie's bedroom, which once, long ago, had been my bedroom. Erik's.

I stood just without, hoping to ascertain how much information had been passed between them, and whether there were plans to involve any likeminded *friends* of this zounderkite. Similar to cockroaches, there was never just *one*. Out of pure curiosity, I also wished to gauge the nature of their relationship.

"Closets?" Stephanie asked him. "Really?"

"A famous investigator and researcher once stated that you were asking for trouble if you left your closets open at night," the boy droned on, the irksome know-it-all cadence in his voice making me wish upon him a slow and agonizing death. Did I hear he would be supping with the family this evening? Pity the grounds did not produce any belladonna. "There's some conjecture that closets can hold or trap energy and, possibly, act as vortexes between dimensions."

"Vortexes," Stephanie repeated without inflection.

In reality, he was not so far off from the truth, though "portal" would have been a better word. I had passed from one side of the house to the other many a time through that closet. Closets, though, were not my only means of transport. In Moldavia, all doorways and thresholds held, for me alone, the power to open to one version of the house or the other.

"I'm not asking you to believe it," replied the boy with a shrug that suggested he meant what he said. "I'm not sure *I* believe it. But, all the same, it can't hurt for your sister to sleep with the closet closed from now on."

"Point taken," Stephanie mumbled.

She said something else then, but I missed it on account of the fast thudding of small steps. Charlie came barreling up the stairs, and just before she could round the banister, I managed to retreat into the door's shadow.

THIRTEEN
Stephanie

"**W**hy are you in my room?" Charlie asked.

Lucas and I hadn't been in her room for more than five minutes before she'd come running up the stairs. No doubt Dad had sent her to spy on us.

Thankfully, I'd already gotten a chance to tell Lucas about her initial conversations with Zedok, her claims of there being another house, and the business surrounding her closet.

"Charlie, this is my friend Lucas." I gestured toward Lucas, who'd been waving some colored-light-studded remote-control-looking device over the closet's back wall.

He'd already snapped plenty of pictures, checking the view screen after each batch of shots, his expression giving nothing away. But I could tell by the way he'd taken his time soaking it all in that, for him, just being here was a big deal.

"Hey there," Lucas said, smiling at my sister, causing a pair of dimples I hadn't noticed before to appear. "Nice to meet you, Charlie."

Charlie just stared at him, her head tilting back as Lucas drew nearer, like it was a skyscraper that approached her and not a person.

He lowered himself onto his haunches and offered Charlie his hand. Instead of shaking, though, she gave him five.

"What's that?" she asked, pointing to the device in his other hand.

"This is an EMF detector." Lucas held up the device with the colored lights. "That stands for 'electromagnetic fields.' I was just seeing if there were any readings in here."

Charlie pointed to the stack of boxes in the corner near the window. "All my books are in there."

Lucas laughed and obligingly looked. But his smile fell when he spotted something on one of the window's panes—a large leaf plastered to the glass.

Er. A large leaf with legs.

The moth, one of the giant skull-decorated variety we kept running into, inched up the pane, moving toward the jamb.

"We've seen those everywhere," I said. "I'm guessing they're a local breed?"

Lucas didn't answer, but went to the window, dropping his EMF detector onto Charlie's bed. Charlie wasted no time in going for the device, which she scoured for buttons. Lucas, in the meantime, raised the window with strong arms, taking care not to scare off the insect.

To my horror, he looped an arm outside—and grabbed the thing.

Adding to my unease, he brought the creature inside, cupping his other hand around it to create a makeshift cage.

"Oh my God," I whispered the instant the insect began to emit a high-pitched squeak-screech. "Is it really making that sound?"

Lucas didn't answer. Instead, he peered into the gap between his two hands.

Curious, Charlie dropped the EMF detector back onto the bed and went to Lucas's side. She teetered on her toes, trying to see.

Lucas, in a daze, crouched again to let her look, though his focus on the creature remained unwavering.

"You said you've seen more of these?" he asked, his face graying before my eyes.

"Yeah." I shrugged. "Why? They're not dangerous, are they?"

"They're not *indigenous*," replied Lucas.

"You mean to this area."

"I mean to the United States." He stood quickly when Charlie's curious fingers got too close, and promptly chucked the thing out the window.

While it flittered away, vanishing into the deepening dusk, Lucas shut the sash and flicked the latch.

"Charlie," said Lucas, his attention returning to my sister. "Stephanie says that you don't like to sleep in your room and that your closet bothers you. Can you tell me why?"

At once, Charlie's demeanor changed, her carefree smile failing, those small brows coming together. I hated to see the peace drained out of her like that. But I couldn't be mad at Lucas. He hadn't said anything scary—hadn't mentioned anything at all about Zedok. He'd only asked her a question. Seemed *I* was the one to blame here. Because, until now, I'd been all too quick to dismiss Charlie's claims about her monster. All because it wasn't something that fit into my paradigm. In that moment, though, I found myself fighting off the awful thought that Mom would have listened to her.

"Charlie," Lucas prompted again as Charlie glanced back in the direction of the door. "Is there something the matter?"

Instead of answering him, Charlie zoned out, going still and quiet, something she hadn't done since the other morning in the parlor when I'd found her standing in the middle of her crayons and all those scattered papers.

"She never used to do this before," I said in a half whisper.

"She does it often now?" Lucas asked, his own voice tight and low.

"Sometimes," I offered. "Whenever she talks about *him*."

"Charlie, what is it?" Lucas asked, suddenly raising his voice to just above normal volume. "Is there something there?"

Charlie's thumb went to her lips and hovered there as her gaze remained locked on the door, which hung half open. Before, this kind of behavior hadn't done much more than annoy me. Now it sent arctic chills up my spine.

Slowly, after receiving no answer, Lucas went to retrieve his camera from where he'd set it on a nearby chair. Then he drifted to where Charlie stood, the floorboards creaking under his feet.

As though in answer, an echoing creak sounded from out in the hall.

Startling me as he sprang into action, Lucas leapt for the door, which he threw open.

FOURTEEN
Zedok

Quicker than I would have thought possible, the young man burst into the hallway where I stood, his two staggering steps bringing us abruptly face-to-face.

Face-to-mask.

I remained frozen in the place where I'd moved to gain a better vantage point from which to observe this intruder. And now my efforts had rewarded me with as good a view of him as I could have hoped for.

"Charlie, did you see something?" the boy asked, even as he gazed right through me.

It came as no surprise. Unless they were as young and unconditioned as Charlie, even those who believed my existence was possible rarely perceive me before I offered undeniable proof. The boy *had* heard the creak of my footfall, though. An important thing to note.

Charlie latched herself to Stephanie's legs, watching me from behind them, one eye hidden, which told me her silence was something I could bargain for.

While the boy squinted and searched the gloom, I wrapped a hand about the hilt of my sword and began a slow retreat in reverse down the hallway, careful this time to keep my steps deliberate and silent.

Lifting his camera, the boy snapped a photo, the spark of its blinding flash igniting the hallway like a bolt of lightning. He shot the camera again and again. I would not show up in his photographs, though. Not until I was something he was willing to see.

As I went, I pressed a finger to the keyhole mouth of my mask, cautioning Charlie against revealing my presence. She blinked at me, frowning, but nevertheless, the child did as I bade and kept my secret.

FIFTEEN

Stephanie

Dinner turned out to be awkward times five centillion plus pi.

At least during the first half, with Dad asking Lucas leading and uncomfortable questions like "Were you two paired for this project at random, or did you choose to work together?" and "Where are you planning on going to college, Lucas?" and, my favorite, "Do you have a job, Lucas?"

To my amazement, Lucas dealt with each inquiry with graciousness and an odd finesse I hadn't expected. He'd been fumbling and awkward during our first meeting in the library. Tonight, though, his air had become that of a congenial scholar. Sherlock Holmes meets Peter Parker. All business but with a bit of warmth and wry wit thrown in.

Also, I couldn't help but notice that, whenever possible, Lucas took pains *not* to lie to my dad.

He'd thankfully also taken the lead on my "school project" angle. But each time the subject came up, Lucas had—after supplying some polite though evasive answer—steered the conversation back to my father's plans for the house. A smart move on Lucas's part because Dad loved to talk about his work to anyone who'd listen. And as Lucas asked question after question, my father's stern demeanor finally started to crack.

"And this is going to sound weird," Dad said at one point in the conversation, "but at least once a week, I have a dream about how this place used to look. Y'know. Back in the day."

Wait. *Dad* was having dreams, too?

Lifting one plaid-flannel-sleeved arm from the table, Dad pointed in the direction of the parlor. "The fireplace in the front room, for example. In my dream, it had decorative glazed tiles surrounding it. Painted with sparrows and flowers that matched the wallpaper. There was the carved figurehead of a deer, too. Antlers and everything. That's all gone now. But I can see in the framework on the iron facade where there had once been tiles. I must have glimpsed that detail before and my brain just . . . filled in the rest during REM. The subconscious is one heck of an organizer, isn't it?"

"Y-yeah," Lucas stammered, his smile uneasy.

"You didn't mention the dreams to *me*," I said.

Charlie, who had rushed through her dinner so she could get in her tablet time before bed, sat in the hall outside the kitchen, the device propped on her knees.

"Because you're always wrapped up in some textbook," Dad scoffed.

"Since you've been here," prompted Lucas, "have you seen . . . y'know, anything out of the ordinary?"

I froze. *Oh geez.* He went there.

Dad grinned at him and wagged his eyebrows once. "You mean like a ghost?"

"Dad doesn't believe in ghosts," I interjected quickly, in case

Lucas needed *another* reminder that this was territory that need not be tread upon.

"I *am* aware, though," Dad countered, "that this place has a history of ghosts. I'm assuming, Lucas, that since you're from around here, you know something about that?"

Dad chewed his next bite of roast in expectant silence. This time, I held back from swooping in to offer Lucas an out. Because *he'd* been the one to bring it up. And because the proverbial can had *so* already been opened. Also, there *was* the little fact that Dad hadn't asked anything I didn't want to know myself.

"Well," Lucas began, shooting me a meaningful look, "I know that this house was built for a well-to-do family of four in the late 1800s."

"The Drapers," Dad mumbled with a note of contempt that had nothing to do with the Drapers themselves and everything to do with their bodies being six feet under our property.

"Oh, you know about them," Lucas said.

"Well," Dad began, "the realtor told me they were the original owners. He also mentioned that this place had a reputation. What he didn't tell me was that the Drapers had all died here on the same night and that foul play was suspected."

"What?" I said. Though I knew about the dates, this was the first mention I'd heard about anything nefarious.

"Found out *that* little nugget at the local hardware store today." With this, Dad balled up his napkin and tossed it onto the table. "Apparently, the Drapers' eldest, a kid named Erik, got himself mixed up with some kind of cult."

I slowed my chewing to a halt, my eyes bugging at the plate of food I now couldn't hope to finish. Dread spread over me like a frost, and I laid my fork down.

"The Order of the Mothmen," muttered Lucas, and immediately I lifted my widened stare to him.

"You know something about it?" asked Dad, who perked with sudden interest.

"The Order of the Mothmen," Lucas repeated, speaking softly while sparing a glance toward Charlie, who stayed absorbed in *Frozen*. "They were a bunch of teen boys who were, much like the rest of the aristocratic world at that time, interested in Ancient Egypt and the occult. During the Victorian era, exploration of Egypt, along with the emerging practice of Spiritualism, was all the rage. People had Egyptomania. And anything having to do with the mystery surrounding death intrigued them."

"Sounds about right," huffed Dad with a laugh. "Victorians were a morbid bunch."

"That's putting it mildly," agreed Lucas.

"So," I began, not finding the humor anywhere in this, "what was this Order supposed to be about?"

"Well." Lucas's gaze bounced from me to Dad, as if he hoped my father would butt in and end the conversation before it could start. But Dad was too intrigued. Not because he believed in the paranormal but because here, finally, was someone willing to tell him just what he'd gotten himself into in terms of investments. "Supposedly, Erik, whose parents emigrated here from England when he was twelve, was the founder of the Order. Erik, it was said, had always harbored an interest in the occult, pseudoscience, locks, puzzles, and illusion. Stuff like cryptographs, magic, conjuring, and ciphers."

I pursed my lips in thought, intrigued on more levels than one. Lucas, it seemed, had told this story before. Maybe it was a campfire favorite. Or perhaps he kept a running case file on this place.

"About this Erik," I said, officially glad I had not yet told Lucas about the dream. "What did he look like?"

"No one knows," said Lucas. "There aren't any surviving photos of him. Which, weirdly enough, fits with the curse. It was supposed to have obliterated all images of him. Because, as the story goes, he was unusually handsome."

"Oh yeah?" I muttered more to myself than to either of them.

"Curse?" Dad asked. "No one's said anything yet about a curse."

No one but Erik himself.

"When Erik turned sixteen," Lucas continued, his stare lingering on me in confusion before returning to my father, "he started meeting in secret with schoolmates. Sons of other wealthy socialites. It was said that they called themselves the Order of the Mothmen because Erik, who had an obsession with bugs, thought that moths were the ultimate masters of disguise. It's rumored he resented both his looks and his station, since they contributed to so much of his life and future being written out and orchestrated for him. So as the Order began to grow, the members took to wearing masks during their meetings. In a way, I think wearing a mask allowed Erik to become something else, you know? *Someone* else. Someone more in control of his own fate."

"So you're saying Erik is supposedly one of the ghosts haunting this place?" I asked.

"Um," Lucas said, "not exactly. The legend says that, when Erik was seventeen, he enrolled in university. His parents wanted him to study medicine. Erik agreed so long as he could continue his music studies as well. Apparently, he played the piano, the violin, and also sang really well. Like, at prodigy level. Anyway, during the following winter, after Erik turned eighteen, Erik's family made a return visit to England without him. Erik held a secret masked ball here at his parents' estate. A mummy-unwrapping party."

"A mummy *what*?" I asked.

"At the time," Lucas said, "there were a lot of amateur archeologists traveling to Egypt. Brits and Americans who were excavating near the pyramids and in the Valley of the Kings in Thebes."

"Oh yeah," I said. "They gutted a lot of the tombs. Egypt is *still* trying to get their artifacts back."

Lucas nodded. "And mummies, of course, were everywhere. Abundant and considered to be worthless by the foreign excavators. That was, until high-society people started buying them and having them shipped to England and the States. From there, the mummies became the center of lavish parties."

"Don't say it," I muttered, my stomach giving a flip. "They unwrapped the mummies for fun."

"Pretty horrible, huh?"

"Not to mention totally irreverent," I added.

"And this Erik kid held one of these parties here?" Dad asked.

"Legend states," replied Lucas, apparently throwing caution to the wind on the whole "the less you know" approach, "that the mummy the Mothmen had procured for their unwrapping party had been an ancient priest of Anubis, the Egyptian god of the afterlife. Supposedly, this priest had also been a mystic and magician.

Basically, all those traits that the members of the Order of the Mothmen, and Erik specifically, sought to emulate."

"So they got that mummy on purpose?" I asked.

Lucas shrugged. "It's assumed so. Some also speculate that the party was less of a party and, well, more of a . . . ritual. And that Erik was attempting to siphon the mummy's former powers into himself."

"So what happened at this twisted little soiree?" Dad said, eyes flicking in Charlie's direction.

"Nothing." said Lucas. "That's to say, the party itself went off without much evidence that the ritual—if there *had* been a ritual— had worked. Everyone went home. Leaving Erik here alone. That night, though, the story goes that the mummy, which had been laid out and unwrapped in the dining room, well . . . supposedly, he rose from the dead."

"Oh, *nice*," I hissed, my throat suddenly tight, the food in my stomach churning.

"As retribution, the mummy was said to have placed a curse on Erik," said Lucas. "One that killed his entire family the very night they returned home from their trip to England. Right before Christmas. No one knows how it happened or even *what* happened. The servants just awoke that day to find Erik and his mother and father and younger sister, Myriam, all dead. All sitting around the same dining room table that the mummy had been unwrapped on."

"Quaint," said Dad. "The realtor conveniently left out all of that. But I'm assuming now, since you know so much, that what you've been telling me is common knowledge?"

"The stories vary," Lucas said, like he was offering some small consolation. I was glad, though, that Lucas had picked up enough on Dad's personality to know that his irritation rested with the people who'd sold him the house and not the messenger. "Most people have heard about the mummy-unwrapping party. As far as the Order of the Mothmen, though . . . Well, I wouldn't say those details are *widely* known."

"Oh, well," Dad muttered to himself. "The mummy is the *least* damaging part, isn't it?"

Lucas cringed.

"What . . . happened after that?" I heard myself ask, picturing the gravestone in the backyard. The stone that listed Erik's name.

"The day before the bodies were to be buried," Lucas said, "one of them went missing."

"Two guesses whose, right?" Dad laughed, his chair groaning as he sat back and folded his arms.

"They never found him?" I asked.

"There's some thought that maybe there were body snatchers involved. It wasn't uncommon back then. There were people known as Resurrection Men who dug up the bodies or stole them from morgues to sell to doctors and scientists. For someone as prominent as Erik to have been stolen, though, well, that would have been unusual."

"There are other versions of the story, you said?" This from Dad.

"Well, yeah. Some speculate that it was the Order of the Mothmen who took Erik's body and, in the practice of the ancient Egyptians, mummified him and entombed him in some unknown location. The thought is that they did so as a means of appeasing the spirit of the Egyptian priest they'd offended. Others say it was the mummy himself who took Erik's body."

"To do what with?"

I don't know why I asked. I wasn't sure I wanted to know the answer. Maybe it had been my scientific instincts that had insisted I overturn each rock that presented itself, regardless of what horrors I might find beneath.

Lucas's warm voice again washed through the quiet that had settled among us.

"Going back to Egyptian myth, it's important to know that Anubis was not only the god of the Egyptian afterlife and of embalming, but he was also the deity responsible for admitting souls *to* the afterlife."

"Kind of like an Egyptian grim reaper," I said.

"Yeah," Lucas replied. "In a sense. Only Anubis was responsible for performing the ceremony known as the Weighing of the Heart. To the ancient Egyptians, the heart was considered the seat of the soul, and Anubis was said to personally weigh each heart on a set of scales to determine whether to admit you to the afterlife. Some versions of the story state that, because Erik had removed *his* heart during the mummy-unwrapping party, the reanimated priest mummified Erik and removed his heart in turn, an action that then doomed Erik to walk the earth as a living corpse."

"I thought you said Erik wasn't the one haunting the grounds," I said.

"I said it supposedly wasn't Erik's *ghost*," Lucas clarified. "Since he doesn't have a heart, he's said to be stuck here. Along with the Egyptian priest. Both of them in . . . uh . . . tangible form."

"So we have zombies," Dad grunt-laughed. "This keeps getting better and better. Buildings, I can fix. Reputations?" He shook his head. "Not so easy. And you know what's *really* going to be fun? Trying to get contractors on site in the spring."

"Maybe I shouldn't have said anything," mumbled Lucas.

"Ah." Dad waved a dismissive hand. "No. I'm glad you did. Better to know, right? In reality, I've got plenty of time to think of ways to debunk all the bull. All the same, though, you seem to know quite a bit about the woo-woo junk surrounding this house. You don't believe in any of it, do you?"

"N-no, sir," Lucas said. Another lie? Hard to tell this time.

"So what do *you* think happened?" By asking the question, I was kind of being a jerk. Because I'd perhaps already heard what Lucas believed. But this was the most sensible way to ask for the skeptic's version of the tale.

"Well, there are a lot of people in town who think Erik killed his family, faked his death, and ran off."

At this, my jaw dropped.

"Hmm," mused Dad. "Any reason for that belief beyond the thought that the kid was just a psychopath?"

"A significant portion of the family fortune was never found."

"Ah," Dad said, like Lucas had just told him the painfully obvious answer to a riddle.

After that, conversation turned on a dime, speeding into the realm of *Star Wars*, rock and roll, and sports Hall of Famers.

I tuned them out, my brain beta-waving through all that Lucas had revealed.

If Zedok was real, and what Lucas had just explained him to

be—a rightfully teed-off walking, talking dead guy—then wouldn't I have seen him, too, and not just Charlie? It was doubtful as well that an Ancient Egyptian priest would be speaking English to my little sister. And Erik. If he truly had been evil—a psychopath, my father had called him—would he have warned me in a dream to leave?

Stephen Hawking's theories surrounding a multidimensional universe *could* allow for something like spirits—in some capacity—to exist.

But reanimated mummies? Walking corpses?

Not. Possible.

♪ ♩ ♪

I WALKED LUCAS out to his car after dinner, wishing the whole trek that I'd grabbed my jacket instead of just a cardigan. While the late September days here could get up to seventy, the evenings had no interest in pretending like summer was still a thing.

"Here," Lucas said once we reached his car, a red Dodge Dart, and he opened the passenger's side door for me. "Get in and I'll turn on the heat."

I climbed in, huddling into the seat as he shut the door after me. Taking advantage of the time it took for him to round to the driver's side, I scanned the immaculate dash and floorboards. Because you could tell a lot about a guy by the way he kept his car. He drove a stick shift instead of an automatic, too, which was hot in a James Bond–ish kind of way.

Once inside, Lucas started the car, and music began pouring

through the speakers—old, slow-swaying, big-bass music with some dude singing about asking a girl to dance with him, and a chorus of guys in the background with harmonized "doo-bee-doo"s and "wa-wa-wa-wa"s.

I tilted my head at his radio, which, instead of switching off, Lucas turned down to a low, mood-setting buzz. Like this was 1952 and we'd just "parked" on Lover's Lane.

A moment later, he flicked a switch that sent lukewarm air rushing from the vents.

"Your sister," he said, killing the mood I guess he *hadn't* been setting. "You know, I think she saw something in there today. Normally, I don't like to jump to conclusions regarding the status of a site. But, given the history of the property and Charlie's involvement, I think there's enough here to warrant concern. This thing. You said she's been talking to it?"

Thing. It. His choice of words was not lost on me.

Was this the moment to tell Lucas about my dream encounter with Erik? Or . . . was it better to wait?

"Stephanie?"

"Mm?"

"Can I ask . . . where your mom is?"

I flinched, blindsided by the question. Then again, we *were* dealing with ghosts here. How could I hold it against him when I'd also thought that Charlie's invention of Zedok somehow tied back to the person Dad and I made it a point never to talk about?

"She died," I said. "And . . . Charlie never knew her."

I left it at that, confident that his powers of deduction would lead him to connect the dots.

"I see," he said. "I'm . . . really sorry."

God. We needed to change the subject. Because no matter how much time passed, the pain never eased. And I didn't know Lucas well enough to cry in front of him.

"What the heck are we listening to?" I asked him suddenly, waving a hand over the car's stereo as the song switched to another just like it.

"Oh, this?" he asked, graciously allowing the abrupt shift in topics. He offered a smirk and turned the volume up a few ticks. "Let's see. This one is 'Be-Bop-A-Lula' by Gene Vincent and His Blue Caps."

"It sure is," I muttered.

"First recorded in 1956," he went on. "And not to be confused with the 1945 hit 'Be-Baba-Leba' by Helen Humes, which is killer-diller. I've got it if you want to hear it."

Killer . . . diller?

"Soooo," I said while he dug for his phone. "I'm just going to ask outright. What is your deal with this stuff?"

"Stuff?"

"Yeah. You know. The . . ." I gestured to his radio. "And the . . ." I nodded to his pinstriped vest. Then tapped the side of my eye, indicating his glasses.

"The music?" he asked, a bemused smile making those dimples reappear.

"The music," I said. Because, okay, we could start there.

"You don't like it?"

"I never said that."

"*Exactly.*" He held up a finger. "Because everyone likes music. And *this* music? Man, it just *cooks.*"

A grin I couldn't help broke onto my face. "That so."

Lucas nodded along, his knee bouncing, his eyes connected with mine, like he was waiting for me to hear the same thing he was hearing.

"It's . . . nice," I allowed. Because this was all making me like him way faster than what I felt prepared for.

"The swing-eighths just make it *so* danceable."

I blinked at him, curious. "By swing-eighths, do you mean, like . . . a quarter and eighth note triplet?"

He paused in his jamming, brows lifting in happy surprise. "You read music?"

My smile faltered, but I quickly recovered. It was too late, though. He'd noticed.

"Used to," I said. "You do, too?"

"Actually no," he replied, again accepting the spotlight as I swiveled it back his way. "I study the rhythms and the instruments. Because if you don't get the music, you don't really get anything, you know?"

I didn't know. And yet . . . I did.

"You're a dancer?"

"Isn't everybody?"

"*No,*" I said, again through a smile that snuck up on me. Something that happened often in his presence.

"You'd be surprised."

"I never said I wasn't."

He grinned at me, and my world seemed to shift and grow a little warmer, like the sun had finally come peeking through the dark clouds.

"SPOoKy is doing lunch in the gym tomorrow," he said. "To make up for tonight's missed rehearsal. Sooo. You should stop by and I could show you a step or two . . . if you want."

Whoa. Talk about mixed signals. He was inviting me to hang out with him and his friends again, but during a time when he and Charlotte would presumably be dancing?

"Maybe," I offered. Because I didn't want to spoil the moment by asking about her. I was enjoying his company too much. Along with the growing hunch that he might be into me as much as I was into him.

A long patch of silence passed between us then while his stereo serenaded us.

"Thanks, by the way," I told him finally. "For coming out and assessing our zombie infestation."

He gave a soft laugh. "I'm really not sure how much I helped. Actually, I think I might have tripled your dad's normal stress level."

"You helped," I assured him. "At least I know to keep a closer eye on Charlie for the time being. I also know where I can report anything strange."

"Speaking of," he said, reaching past me to the glove box, "I know we have to tiptoe around your dad about it, but if something else weird does happen, or you need anything . . ."

He offered me a small white slip of paper.

"What's this?"

"It's . . . my card," he explained. "Or *our* card. As in SPOoKy's."

"Your *card*?" I asked. Because who in high school had a card? "Whose number is this?"

"Er. Well. That . . . would be mine."

"You're giving me your number?" I asked, because I couldn't seem to help myself. But maybe to get a little more flirting, I first had to give some.

"N-no," he said. "I mean, yeah. But . . . not because I want you to call me."

"So, you *don't* want me to call you."

"I didn't say that."

"Okay," I said, flashing him a smile, one that made the worry creasing his brow lessen. "Then . . . maybe I will."

With that, I let myself out of the car and jogged back up to the porch, where I offered one final wave before returning to the house that, whether it was truly haunted or not, was, for the first time, a house I was glad we'd moved into.

SIXTEEN
Zedok

Irate, I paced in the hallway between the girls' rooms, pausing long
enough with every pass to peer toward the banister overlooking
the foyer, anticipating Stephanie's return.

Already, ten minutes had elapsed since she'd exited *alone* with
him. And that was four times longer than propriety would have ever
permitted any young woman of my time to be left in the sole care of
such a man.

And Mr. Armand. Where was he while his eldest daughter frat-
ernized with some pompous and self-serving . . . *mucksnipe*.

With that interloping idiot. That meddlesome *cur*.

What gave him the right to spew such a slanderous mangling of
facts?

At last, with a familiar whine, the front door swung open,
prompting me to take two sharp steps to the banister, which I seized
with both hands.

Alone once more, Stephanie entered the foyer, her ebony curls
shining like coal in the glow of the chandelier as she shut the door
softly behind her. She then drifted to stand just below the enormous
light fixture . . . and me.

She held in her hands some bit of white paper, which she studied with barely subdued delight.

My grip tightened on the banister, and as she passed out of sight beneath, I resolved to speak with her again.

Tonight.

SEVENTEEN

Stephanie

"What were you thinking inviting him here?" asked a voice, *his* voice. "All things considered, that was quite possibly the *worst* thing you could have done."

Encased on all sides by pure nothingness, I spun in place, searching the void for the source of the admonishment.

"Where are you?" I asked the darkness.

"Here," came the same accented voice from behind me, and, whirling, I suddenly found myself facing him. He stood just a few feet away from me, even more beautiful than I remembered, one hand perched on the hilt of his rapier. He had on the same dark slacks, gray waistcoat, and black riding boots as last time. Now, though, he wore an ebony cloak. His black chin-length hair stirred in a breeze I didn't feel.

"Where . . . where are we?" I asked next. This had to be another dream.

"If you'll permit me," he said as, with an absent wave of his hand, the blackness encircling us began to morph, filling in with the details of a stately room.

A lavish parlor, complete with pocket doors and a shining parquet floor, unfurled into being, the details devouring the nothing the way flame consumes paper. I gaped at him and then the parlor, which I recognized as ours. Except not the current version with its cracks, missing plaster, and dust. Instead, a far grander version of the room surrounded us, complete with a working fireplace accented by the same bird-painted tiles my father had mentioned at dinner.

I crossed to examine both the tiles and, positioned just above the crackling flames, the antlered figurehead of the stag my father had also described. Above the deer, on the mantel, ticked a small clock. One that marked the time as just after midnight. Which, if it was accurate, meant I must have only just fallen asleep.

"Please," Erik said, "if you would take a seat. There's tea if you like."

I spun from the fireplace to note the sudden existence of a coffee table set with a beautiful silver tray. A filigreed teapot and matching cups kept company with a spread of pastel pastries and delicate finger sandwiches.

It all looked so real. And lacing the air? The faint scents of candlewax and lamp oil, burning firewood, lemon, lavender, and roses.

A moment more passed in which I had to convince myself I really was dreaming.

"Erik?" I asked him.

"Ah, you remembered my name," he replied, his tone wry, sardonic.

"You," I said then, almost in a whisper. "You're . . . dead."

The words prompted him to scowl at me, though he didn't look any less gorgeous for it.

"And you, Miss Armand, are still standing. Tell me, shall I invite you to sit again, or is this a conversation for which you will insist upon being as unconventional as ever?"

He spoke like he knew me. Or . . . like he'd been observing me for a while. Something he'd alluded to in the last dream.

"I don't even know what conversation it is we're supposed to be having," I said, taking my turn to be snappish while still reeling from the abruptness of his appearance.

"The young man," he said with impatience. "We are discussing the young man."

"Lucas?" I gestured toward the bay windows, which showed only the blackness of night.

"He must not be allowed to return," Erik said. But I only half heard him, because there was still too much that needed to be cleared up.

"You're *not* just a dream . . . are you?" I asked him, not certain yet if I wanted him to be real. Maybe not if the second version of the story Lucas had told us, the one in which Erik had killed his parents and sister, was true.

"I told you previously that I was not," he said. His surliness. It couldn't really be all because of Lucas . . .

"You also previously told me I should get out of my own house." I folded my arms.

"Advice I still stand by," came yet another acerbic reply. "And even more adamantly now. Because, by inviting that *fool* over here, you have hastened us *all* toward what I am certain shall be an unbearable outcome."

Questions piled behind my lips. First thing first, though.

"So you were listening in?" I asked. "You heard what Lucas told us at dinner . . ."

"I did not murder my family, if that's what you're asking," he said, the vehemence in his voice almost covering the barest of trembles. His eyes, filled with indignation—and pain—fastened on to me, until he severed our locked gazes by turning away. "Though I was . . . responsible for their deaths."

Well. That was vague.

But maybe, with a little push for specifics . . .

"What about the rest of it?" I asked him, because obviously he *had* been listening in. "The curse."

"I already informed you there was a curse," he replied.

"Yeah," I said, turning slowly in place, fascinated by the grandeur of the room. "But you didn't tell me what the curse was. *He* did."

"He knows *nothing* of the curse," snapped Erik, though his words scarcely registered because, by then, I'd spotted the piano.

Black and shining, sleek and majestic, the instrument occupied the same corner as it did in our parlor. Far more beautiful than anything we'd ever owned, it struck me as something Mom would have gasped at the sight of, too.

I went to it, my shape silhouetted in its gleaming, polished surface.

The keys, not a one yellowed or chipped, shone white as snow.

White as the lilies that had covered my mother's casket.

Unable to help myself, I slid onto the bench. And now here I was again, inside the shell of a memory. Though, this time, within the confines of a dream.

I put my fingers on the keyboard, hands taking up the familiar positions my mother's always had, as if doing so could somehow summon her.

I pressed the white E key and then the black D-sharp, alternating between the two until moving to B, D, C, and onward, the notes falling together, becoming a melody. The pattern repeated itself again, and then again, varying slightly as I coaxed it along. It flowed through me and from the piano, building all the way to the place where it . . . stopped. Well, where *I* stopped.

A shadow fell over me, and I turned to find him standing at my left, his form backlit by the glow of the fireplace. His eyes, more penetrating even than before, bored into me.

"What are you doing?" he demanded, his voice even more intense than his gaze.

I retracted my fingers from the keys, curling them inward.

"Don't," he commanded.

"Don't what?"

"'Für Elise,'" he said, gesturing to the keyboard. "You cannot just cease in the middle . . . You must play the rest."

"I don't know the rest of it."

His attention went from me to the piano, his expression crestfallen.

"I'm sorry," I stammered, quick to slide out from the seat I should never have taken. "I never learned. We—"

I stopped myself there, the silence sweeping in to surround us once more, though uglier than before since it was now filled with everything I didn't want to talk about.

"We?" he ventured. "You're speaking of yourself . . . and your mother?"

My eyes narrowed at him. "How do you know about my mother?"

"It was merely a well-aimed guess."

"A *very* well-aimed guess."

He pressed his lips together in thought. Then he peered toward the fireplace, the light illuminating his too-handsome profile.

"Her absence," he said finally, his focus returning to me after a beat. "It looms."

I didn't know how to respond to that. Especially not when his words provided uncomfortable evidence that he really was able to listen in on us and possibly see us, too.

"We shan't talk about her if you do not wish to," he said. "Trust me when I say . . . I understand."

I'd been ready to rail at him. To lash out. Suddenly, though, I couldn't. Not when his words carried far more weight and sadness than needed to convince me what he'd said was true.

"Your family," I said. "They've been gone a long time."

"It feels that way," he admitted. "But . . . only when it doesn't."

Those words resonated with me in a way no one else's had.

Mom had been gone for six years now. Most of the time I remained acutely aware of the years that had passed. Sometimes, though, like lately, things got raw. Other times, in brief nanosecond moments of extreme excitement or disappointment, those instances when your first gut instinct was to run to the most important person in your life, I even still forgot she was gone.

"It's like he said, then?" I asked. "The curse killed them and . . . you as well?"

"The curse is mine alone to bear," he said with conviction. "And duly so. Though . . . it is true their deaths were a consequence."

I tilted my head at him, reading him true for maybe the first time.

"But then . . . that would mean you've been here for over a century. You *can't* have spent that whole time blaming yourself."

He flinched, his expression pinching. Almost as if, just as he had done with me, I'd glimpsed—or rather, prodded—some hidden and too-tender facet of his pain.

"Yes," he said after several long beats of silence, his words strained, his collected demeanor threatening to crack, "well . . . it *was* my fault."

At this response, my heart issued for him an almost debilitating ache. Immediately, I fought the urge to apologize—right along with the impulse to keep prying.

Because now more than ever, I wanted to know what had happened to him—what had *really* happened.

Instead, I gave him the same moment to recover that he had granted me. Then, taking my cue from Lucas, I jumped to a new topic—or, at least, a previous one.

"Could . . . couldn't *you* play it?"

"I beg your pardon?" he asked, taken aback.

"'Für Elise,'" I said. "Why don't you play it for me?"

"I can't," he said, even more devastation underscoring his tone than before.

"Oh," I muttered. "I guess he got that part wrong, too . . ."

"Which part?" Erik asked, distracted, a scowl touching his brow as he divided his attention between me and the piano, as if trying to figure out which of us was to blame for his confusion.

"Lucas. He said you could play."

"I *can* play." His hand curled into a fist. "I just cannot . . . play."

"That's not contradictory."

He turned away from me to face the piano. "I could have played it. Once."

"So, you *were* a musician?"

"I *am* a musician. I just . . ."

"Just what?"

"I just . . . Could you try again?" he said to the instrument. But, of course, he had been talking to me. "'Für Elise.'"

"I told you, I don't know—"

"Play what you know."

"But I—"

"*Please.*"

He turned those eyes on me again. But, once more, it was his voice that pierced me.

That word. He'd uttered it as a genuine plea. And in that lone syllable, I again detected an all-too-familiar note of pain. The kind that, when it rings out, causes all similar surrounding chords to vibrate right along with it.

Not sure what I was doing, I reclaimed the seat on the bench.

"Stop," he said before I'd played so much as the first two notes. "Andante. Slowly, but not too slowly."

"I know what 'andante' means." I shifted and started over.

"Softer," he corrected.

Again, I stopped, and I might have gotten angry with him if he hadn't swept his cloak back in order to take the seat next to me, the motion sending a waft of lavender my way.

"See here," he said. "The opening notes. They are one entity, linked as they walk out of the dark together, born from the nothing, surprising and yet undeniable, like the first stirrings of love. Your fingers. They need only caress the keys. Let them fall as feathers. Like so."

His right hand went to mine, his third and fourth fingers, cool and a little rough, overlaying my own. His words, combined with his touch, caused a thrill to rush through me and heat to rise in my cheeks. I held my breath as he pressed each of my fingers just the way he'd said, one after the other in the same pattern. He halted at once though when the music came out discordant, distorted, and wrong. The notes that themselves had, a moment ago, resonated with such beauty now clanged eerily, off-key and garbled.

Erik's hand lifted instantly from mine. I kept my own where they were, unable to move, my skin still buzzing from our connection, my body humming from his nearness, my ears and mind shocked by the unnerving sound his influence had elicited from the instrument.

He drew his hand away from the keys, though his eyes remained fastened there, the momentary flash of brightness in him dimming.

"You see now what I mean," he muttered.

And I did.

"It's . . . part of the curse," I guessed. "You can't play anymore because you're a ghost."

"I am not a ghost," he corrected darkly. "And neither, I must tell you, is he."

"He," I repeated. "You mean Zedok."

He didn't admonish me for saying the name this time. But he didn't answer me, either.

"Who is he?" I pressed. "What *is* he?"

"Not what you think," murmured Erik, "I can promise you that."

Another unenlightening answer. But did that mean Lucas's story was wrong? Erik had said it was. Perhaps Zedok *was* a demon.

"He's what's keeping you here," I said, lifting my hands from the keys and slowly placing them in my lap. "He—*it*," I corrected, adopting Lucas's label for the monster. "It's keeping you prisoner."

To this, Erik said nothing, just observed the piano with a stricken expression that echoed the one from before. But maybe he *couldn't* tell me. Could the same thing preventing him from playing music also somehow prevent him from revealing the truth about the curse?

"Lucas said you were—"

"That boy," he said, Lucas's name apparently jolting him back into the moment. "It is imperative that you forbid him or any more of his ilk from entering the premises again."

"Lucas came here to help. And if he knows something about what's going on here, then I don't see why—"

"Because!" he said, rising from the bench. "Bringing him here is akin to striking a match in a cellar full of powder kegs!"

I twisted to peer after him as he strode away, back toward the fireplace. He stopped there, a pillar of darkness in the gloom. But . . . there was light inside him, too. I'd *felt* it just now. When he'd talked about the music . . .

Pushing off from the bench, I started in his direction, stopping just short of him.

"Erik," I said when he failed to say anything else, "I . . . I want to help you."

And I did. Because if there was one thing I understood about him, it was the pain.

He glanced over his shoulder at me, his expression grave. "There is perhaps nothing you could have said to frighten me more."

We stood apart like that for a long time. Like both of us had too much left that we wanted to say but no way of articulating it.

"The reason he is not to return," Erik said at last as he again approached me, "is because I cannot guarantee it will not be the last thing he does." He lifted his hand, his knuckles drifting close to my cheek. "Not when things are as they are. Not when I can scarcely protect *you*."

Just when he would have touched me, the dream ended, and I started awake. And as I found myself back in my bed, my thick coverlet fortifying me against the creeping cold, I stole a groggy glance at my bedside clock.

Its face read 12:45. Which meant I'd been asleep for less than an hour.

My eyes then trailed past the clock to where I'd placed my mom's angel figure. Where I'd *re*placed it.

Two days ago, before my first dream with Erik, I'd come into my room to find it had been moved.

At the time, I'd blamed it on my dad. Charlie wasn't tall enough to reach my dresser. Now, though, I could only question that assumption. Because Dad never came into my room. And even if he did, he never moved my stuff.

These occurrences. The dreams. The graves. The stories. They could only really wind me up if I let them.

I rolled onto my back again, and as I gazed at the twin fissures crisscrossing the plaster of the ceiling, my mind returned to Erik and the vision I'd just left. One I couldn't seem to shake the feeling had ended . . . because he'd made it.

EIGHTEEN
Zedok

I rose from my chair as I opened my eyes, simultaneously casting their glow upon the hearth.

Atop the mantel, my father's clock ticked as it had in the dream, its chiding rhythm beating into the brain I no longer had.

As it counted the never-ending seconds, I stood in awe of what I had just done. Or rather, all that I had *not*.

My sole purpose in speaking to Stephanie at all had derived from my need to incite her and her family to *leave*.

And I had again delivered my foreboding message, yes, but far less effectively than I could have if I'd only stopped to think for one moment about my approach. But I hadn't. Instead, I'd become possessed of the desire to gain a modicum of absolution from her.

I'd wanted to absolve *Erik*.

But . . . I *wasn't* Erik.

That Cheney boy. That *stupid* boy. His jumbled version of the story had riled and incensed me. More than what he had gotten wrong, though, it had been the details he had gotten *right* that had angered me.

Yet, I should have counted his meddling as a favor.

If I'd had the presence of mind to appear to Stephanie in tonight's dream not as the glorious Erik but as the horrendous masked figure she had finally begun to believe in—would not the boy's precursory tales have only aided my efforts?

But no. I had elected to sit down with her. *At the piano!* As if the two of us were contemporaries. Or more ludicrously—as if she had been my friend.

And then there had been the *music*. Hesitant and clumsy, it had fallen unexpectedly out of her fingers to land incomplete at my feet—the fractured bones of a long-dead memory. But those notes. Though lifeless, they had still possessed enough of the soul of the masterpiece to send a shock through the scattered shrapnel of my own.

Though I should have liked to blame my derailment upon the music, the truth was . . . I knew better. There was something else at work here. For I had been diverted from my purpose before her fingers had touched those keys. From the very moment I had entered the dream. Or perhaps . . . even before.

Wrath's prior visit swam to the surface of my memory along with the image that had manifested within the specter's grim mask.

Stephanie.

As far as reasons went, I could only think of one that might explain why I had seen her, and it had everything to do with the fact that I had dared to become Erik.

In resurrecting him, even if only in image, I had done both myself and the Armands—Stephanie in particular—a critical misdoing. I had tasted forbidden fruit. I had been made to remember what life had once been like. What *humanness* had been like. And perhaps *that* was what Wrath had attempted, in his own way, to forewarn me of.

But a herald, no matter how ominous, was still only a herald.

So long as I took charge and changed courses swiftly, I yet had time to rectify my missteps. Thankfully, my blunders had done me the one favor of providing the means to their undoing. Through Erik, Stephanie *had* come to believe in Zedok. Enough at least that, to get to her, I no longer needed her sister to serve as emissary.

Tomorrow. It *must* be tomorrow that I—

I paused, sensing the presence of another mask in the room. Whirling, I drew my sword and, in the same motion, extended the blade toward the open pocket doors where I had expected to find Wrath.

But it was not Wrath who stood within the doorframe. Instead, a *female* figure watched me through the almond-shaped eyes of an all-white mask.

Not all of my masks were male. A few were and, in the instance of Hope, *had been* female in outward appearance. Unlike their male counterparts, my female masks had—until now—always taken on the guises of people Erik had known while alive.

This mask, though, I could not now recall having ever encountered either in life *or* death.

Her dress, a deep burgundy, complemented her raven hair, loosely wound into an elegant chignon.

"Who are you?" I demanded of her, forbidding myself to ascribe to her the likeness of another young woman. Not when there wasn't any. Not when there couldn't be.

The mask did not answer. Only lifted one lace-gloved finger, which she pressed to her lips before her figure began to unfurl to mist.

I could not fathom which part of me *she* represented, and I should have been glad to see her go. But her unraveling, just like her appearance, instead triggered within me a terror I was sure I had not entertained since that horrible night when the Egyptian priest had left me with all I had stolen from him and could not give back, passing once more into the hereafter to leave me . . . with me.

Powerful as my fear surrounding this new mask was, it still could not trump the deeper feelings of shame held over the harm I had caused the priest, whom I had ripped from eternal rest by dabbling witlessly in matters I did not understand.

His resulting fear and pain upon reawakening had since become all too understandable to me.

And in removing his heart, had I left him with any other choice but to extract mine?

Though my remorse surrounding my egregious actions had always remained one of my keenest emotions throughout the decades, the knowledge that my heart had granted my victim passage home *had* always counted for me as a small measure of balm.

But . . . the appearance of this newest mask obliterated even that modicum of sustaining solace. For what else could she be but evidence that it was all happening again? That, due to the same enduring distortion in my soul, I was rushing headlong into even deeper spiritual debt—if that was possible.

Whatever the mask was, she served as an ominous reminder of how the greater and more terrifying mystery had always revolved around the question of which part of me had been debased enough to desecrate the priest's consecrated form and disrupt his sacred slumber in pursuit of my own gain.

It spoke volumes that I still did not know myself well enough to say—not even after all this time. Yet the answer I suspected was the one I feared and loathed the most: that this particular corruption—the smear of hubris and the stain of entitled arrogance—lurked in *every* mask.

My soul had shattered so easily, and its enduring frailty suggested that there had not been much holding it together in the first place. Something that hinted at a more horrible truth still.

And that was this: that the true reason the curse was irreparable . . . was because I was.

NINETEEN

Stephanie

Unable to pay attention in any of my morning classes, I spent the first half of the next day replaying my latest dream encounter with Erik in my head. Over and over again, I heard his cryptic answers and, over and over again, I tried—and failed—to decipher them. Then the bell for lunch rang, and even though Lucas had invited me to the gym, I made myself go to the cafeteria. I even got in line, telling myself it would be a bad idea to seek Lucas out. Because what would Charlotte do if I interrupted the rehearsal that had been rescheduled because of me? But then, when I got to the tray station, it occurred to me that it would be far worse for Lucas to think I wasn't grateful to him for coming over last night. Or that I wasn't interested . . .

With that thought, I bailed on lunch and rerouted to the gym. On the way, though, I continued to vacillate, my steps alternating between quick and slow. I wanted to see Lucas, but I didn't want to be a nuisance. Then again, Charlotte really hadn't minded being one yesterday...

Arriving at the gym with little more than half of lunch period left, I stalled in front of the open double doors. My heart gave a flutter when Lucas glided into view, moving backward to one of his old-school doo-wop songs. An echoing flitter of jealousy flapped through my gut when Charlotte slid into view, extending a hand to Lucas, which he took.

I held my breath, my insides twisting as he pulled her close in a dance pose, his free arm wrapping her waist.

"*Shoo-doop shoo-bee-doo,*" chanted a quartet, the accompanying piano and pace-setting drums issuing soft and sultry from a nearby portable speaker.

Augh. Coming here had been a mistake. I started to back away before either of them could spot me, but then someone called my name.

Seated several rows up on the bleachers, next to Patrick, Wes waved a sandwich at me.

"What's shakin'?" called Patrick through the otherwise empty gym. "Hopefully not your house." He popped a Dorito into his mouth.

Dropping Lucas's hand, Charlotte spun to glare at the doorway. At me.

Oh boy.

Lucas, his expression brightening, broke away from her and jogged to meet me. And he might have looked utterly ridiculous in his newsie-style cap, bow tie, cropped pants with suspenders, and tawny argyle socks if he hadn't looked so smoking hot.

"Hey, you came," he said, actually pulling his hat off. Like somebody from the jazz era might do before opening a conversation with a lady.

"Um," I began. I shifted uncomfortably under his gaze. "Yeah. I—"

"Worry not, fair maiden!" Wes called to Charlotte. "*I shall dance with thee!*"

With that, Wes descended the bleachers. He closed the distance between himself and Charlotte before hauling her off her feet and tossing her over his shoulder. Charlotte yelped and then, unable to help it, she laughed as Wes began to fake waltz. He grinned at me while he turned with Charlotte.

"I told y'all we need to get a spray bottle for him," said Patrick, kicking back with his soda. "Don't tell me it's not in the budget."

I would have laughed myself if Lucas hadn't chosen that moment to take me by the hand and lead me out of the room. He drew me up a nearby set of steps to an empty landing. Sunlight streamed in through the stairwell's big windows, highlighting the faint sheen of sweat on his brow.

"Everything all right?" he asked me.

Why was he so warm? Probably, he was this way with everyone.

I pointed back the way we'd come. "Sorry I interrupted." Again.

"You didn't interrupt," he said. "We were just cooling down. We're actually in really good shape."

Yeah. I would say you are, too.

"Uh." *Focus, Stephanie.* "What exactly are you guys rehearsing for?"

"Oh." He stuffed his hat under one arm. "Charlotte and I compete together. There's a big shindig happening this Saturday. It's an annual deal. We took home third last year."

"Wow." I grabbed one of my elbows, trying not to come off like I cared too much one way or another that Lucas and Charlotte had been dancing together for years. "You guys must be really good."

He shrugged. "We're better than we were last year. Which is good since the prize money really helps with supplies for SPOoKy. Last year, the winnings helped us get our thermal-imaging camera."

"You guys are really serious about this ghost-hunting stuff, huh?"

"We're as serious as you can be about anything when you're in high school," he said, doing his underplaying, dismissive thing. "But enough of my blabbering. What's something you like to do? What are you passionate about?"

Even in the face of these questions, I managed to keep my smile intact this time. The words to answer him with, though, proved more difficult to conjure. What was I "passionate" about? It *used* to be music. It used to be singing. It used to be chasing notes and some-times still, when I got the itch, writing down words to songs that didn't exist. Then Charlie had appeared.

"I guess I don't have a lot of free time these days."

"You've got to help your dad a lot," Lucas guessed, stuffing his hat into a back pocket.

"We help each other," I said. "Charlie helps, too."

"You and your sister are pretty close," he observed.

"She drives me crazy sometimes," I laughed. "But she's . . . well, she and Dad are . . . everything."

Lucas nodded, listening—*actually* listening.

"Speaking of Charlie," he said. "Sheeee . . . have an okay night?"

I gave a nod. "More or less."

He frowned at that, tilting his head at me. "Did she mention another encounter?"

"Um, no." I folded my arms and leaned a hip against the wall, trying to gain a little distance from him so some of my brain cells could regenerate. Because that smell of aftershave mixing with his sweat? It kept bringing me . . . *images*.

"Well, it seems like there's something," he said.

That morning—all day, in fact—I'd spent as much time waffling on how much to tell Lucas as I had on whether to seek him out in the first place. And now here I was, face-to-face, *wanting* to tell him about my dreams with Erik. But after Erik's adamant warning that I needed to keep Lucas off our property, I'd convinced myself not to. Though Lucas could probably offer insight into my theory that Erik, if in fact he was real, was being held prisoner in the house by Zedok, I could think of no better way to have Lucas tromping straight back into Moldavia than to open my mouth about it.

Then again, what if Lucas didn't believe me? Would telling him about my conversations with Erik just convince him I was as attention-seeking as Charlotte had accused me of being?

For the time being, until I could get *proof* that Erik *was* real, it was probably best to keep Lucas out of my house.

"Things are . . . okay at the moment," I said, which wasn't a lie. Of course, it also left me high and dry regarding the reason for my being there.

"Soooo . . ." He gripped the window ledge, leaning into it and maybe even a little into me. "Since you're not here to tell me there's blood dripping down the walls—"

"That doesn't really happen," I chided him, but only because I wasn't sure.

"What I was saying," he went on, "was that if you're not here about your house, then, well, you must have come for your dance lesson."

My mouth popped open, but a smile fought its way through my shock. "Oh, I *don't* think so."

He pulled his phone from a back pocket.

"Let's ssssee here," he muttered, his thumb tapping the screen until, suddenly, music started pouring from its speakers.

Stiffening, I glanced up the stairwell and down. No one was there. But it wouldn't be too much longer before the bell rang and the halls flooded with people and—

"Wait a second," I said, glancing toward his phone. "Is this a Buddy Holly song?"

"Who?" he asked, taking hold of my hand after setting his phone on the windowsill.

I didn't get to say anything else, because that's when his other hand went to my waist. My free hand went to perch on his bicep, which might as well have been forged from iron. I mean . . . holy Winter Soldier, Batman.

For one heart-stopping moment, I felt sure he would draw me against him like he had Charlotte, but he stopped short, keeping a middle-school-dance distance from me instead.

"The basics go like this," he said. "Take your right foot and step back, then rock back onto your left again."

My head swimming from his nearness, from this delicious trap I'd somehow fallen into, I did as I was told.

"Good," he said, the scent of his good-boy Dial soap and whatever styling gel he used to get his hair to do its all-American thing washing over me. That, along with his heated touch, made my blood simmer under my skin.

"Now," he continued, "take three steps to the right. Then repeat to the left."

Smiling in spite of how ridiculous I felt, I again followed his lead.

"One, two—one, two, three, one, two, three," he said, marking our time until we had a rhythm going. And then, suddenly, we were dancing. To a Buddy Holly song. With Lucas now giving me the subtlest and sexiest of practiced pushes whenever we returned to the rock step.

"See?" he said. "I told you everybody dances."

"You're giving me way too much credit," I managed. "We're pretty much just doing the same thing over and over."

"That's how it starts with everything you learn," he said.

He raised his arm, gave another one of his expert pushes, and spun me. The world blurred for a second, the sun and the stairs and Lucas all whirring by until he stopped me, bringing us together, his arm now wrapped most of the way around me.

Never before had I been given the opportunity to examine a bow tie so closely.

"Ope," he said, releasing me. "S-sorry about that. Force of habit."

He stepped back, straightening his glasses with the hand that had all but burned its imprint into my back.

The silence pulsed between us, filling the space that, a moment before, hadn't existed. A space I wished had stayed nonexistent, if only a moment longer.

"Uh, listen," said Lucas at last, his hands delving into his pockets again, his gaze falling to the floor. "The bell's going to ring, but while I have you here, I want to ask you something."

Holy crap. Was he legit about to ask me out? I should let him. I totally needed to. I really *wanted* to. So then why was I ready to head him off at the pass to be sure I understood fully his relationship with Charlotte?

"Armand!" came Wes's familiar voice to my left, causing me to jump and Lucas's jaw to jut with sudden annoyance. "Come to this barn dance competition thing on Saturday."

"What?" I eyed him where he now stood in the middle of the vestibule leading to the gym.

"Yeah," said Lucas, surprising me when he cut in. "You should come. There'll be food. And, of course, dancing."

"But . . . I'm not really a dancer." And Charlotte hated me.

"You don't have to dance if you don't want to," Lucas said. "You can just chill and watch the competition. We can hang out between sets."

"And *I* can hang out during," Wes said, pointing at me. Then he winked before backing away. "Just think about it."

"Yeah, no pressure," said Lucas.

"But if you *do* come," added Wes, "we can be gorgeously uncoordinated and sedentary together."

I smiled—a little nervously. Was Wes flirting with me? Or just messing with me?

"Dude. You serious right now?" Lucas asked Wes, making me do a double take between the two. Because that seemed the sort of thing one guy friend might ask another if he felt his buddy was encroaching on his territory.

"I dunno," said Wes as he pantomimed lifting a Dracula-style cape over his nose and mouth before arching one sculpted brow. "*Am* I?"

With that, Wes skulked back into the gym as, overhead, the bell sounded.

"Ignore him," said Lucas. "He wears the same socks, like, every day. I'm pretty sure he sleeps upside down in his closet, too—but, yeah, totally think about coming out on Saturday. If you're not busy, that is. There'll be a live band. I could even show you a couple more moves. I mean . . . if you wanted."

"I see you're not writing me off as a lost cause."

"Well, you know," he said. "Thought the least I could do was return the favor."

I grinned and shook my head at him, blushing as the dividing doors on the floor above opened, releasing a group of chattering underclassmen.

"Wait, though," I prompted, hoping the moment hadn't flown. "What were you going to ask me?"

"Oh," Lucas said as students filed past us, a few of them offering curious glances our way. "I wanted to see if you'd . . . let me walk you to class."

An obvious lie. I'd already learned Lucas touched his glasses when he fibbed. But just because his bravery had fled didn't mean he wouldn't find it again later.

"Won't you be late?"

"Just let me grab my stuff."

Without waiting for an official answer, Lucas popped his hat on and bolted back down the stairs and into the gym, where he'd left Charlotte. Who, if I wanted to save myself from falling for a guy I couldn't have, I was going to have to find a way to ask about. *Stat.*

TWENTY
Zedok

Before the week was out, I told myself, the family would be gone.

Wrath would return to his basement, the mysterious new mask would dissolve into the ether, and *I* would return to my work. I would think no more about the Armands. In a year or so, Stephanie would have become as distant to my thoughts as the summer was to my world.

I glanced around the vacant, time-eaten parlor as though it might hold assurance for me.

On this side—the Armands' side—no oriental carpet softened my step. Paper peeled like dead skin from the walls. A filmy layer of grime, fuzzy with fragrant sawdust, coated all.

Skirting the two wooden sawhorses supporting the interrupted work of Mr. Armand, I strode again to the mantel atop which I had, over an hour ago, deposited Stephanie's angel. Its placement there, upon the exact spot where my father's clock had once sat—still sat on my side—was all part of my plan.

I had not expected to be left waiting quite so long, however.

Stephanie. Where was she?

I turned to the piano. And sighed inwardly at the sight of it.

"My oldest friend," I told the sheeted instrument. "What a mirror image the two of us have become."

I went to hover over it and placed my hand upon the covered keyboard.

Normally, whenever I attempted to play, my mind could not connect anything into a melody. Last night, however, marked the first time since being put under the curse that I had been able to achieve something other than a one-note dirge. Granted, I had been playing *through* someone else and in a dream at that. Not to mention the result had been as startling as it had been disquieting. For instead of either sound *or* music, my fingers over Stephanie's had produced a sort of . . . wail. Though the sound itself had been horrible, it still counted as the nearest thing to actual music I had ever been able to produce.

Well. Without a heart.

Once or twice, as an experiment, I had dared to implant a substitute for the heart that had been quite literally torn from me.

The experiments had always worked. And they had always failed.

I had already resolved that there would be no more substitute hearts. Not after my father's already broken pocket watch had ruptured in my last attempt.

I lifted my hand from the piano to trail fingers over my empty sternum. My hand stopped to gather the fabric of my dress shirt into a tight fist, and for an instant, I imagined I could still feel the pain from the watch's fracturing.

"She is late," I told the piano.

On Tuesdays, Stephanie ran the errand of laundry after school.

Last Tuesday, she had come home late in the afternoon—around teatime. It was nearly half past five now, though, which meant she had likely become involved in an additional activity.

Straightaway, my thoughts went to the boy. She would no doubt have seen him today. Perhaps she was with him now.

With irritation, I tore free the piano's cloth cover. The heavy fabric fell away, puddling at my feet to reveal the travesty beneath.

Hideous, broken, *wasted*, the monstrosity bellowed its silent misery at me.

I turned my back on it, doing my best to stifle the fury that my carefully orchestrated plans might have been undermined by *him* of all people. So much, after all, had gone into the devising of this latest strategy, including the evacuation of the house. Soon, though, Mr. Armand would return from the errand I'd sent him on with Charlie. If Stephanie arrived after that, all of the day's efforts would have been for naught. And if the increasingly erratic behavior of my masks was any indication, the time I was so used to having in excess was already well on its way to running out.

Time.

Habit prompted me to glance toward the mantel, where I'd set Stephanie's angel.

And that was when the most insane of impulses overcame me.

At that moment, I wanted nothing more than to take the angel from her new perch and return her to the place from which I had taken her. This I wanted to do so that Stephanie might yet pass one more peaceful day doubting the monster existed so that I, as Erik, might spend one more congenial night in her company.

So strong was this urge that, after only one moment more of

deliberation, I might have snatched the angel from her place and hurried to undo my trap. And I would have, if the jingling of keys followed by the creaking of the front door had not heralded the arrival of one of the home's occupants.

Frozen and listening, I waited for Charlie's voice to signal that it was she and her father who had returned.

Instead, the voice was *hers*.

"Dad?" Stephanie called, prompting me to turn. "Charlie?"

TWENTY-ONE

Stephanie

The house roared quiet back at me. Instead of entering, I stared up the empty staircase, my hands tightening on the basket of freshly folded bed linens I held.

Still bewitched by the memory of my last dream with Erik and needing also to bring a touch of *life* into this place, I'd picked up a dozen red-on-the-inside-and-white-on-the-outside "Snowfire" roses from the florist I'd found next to the laundromat.

Just because we couldn't restore the conservatory didn't mean we couldn't have roses.

The plastic-wrapped flowers lay atop the clean sheets, their scent mingling first with the detergent and then, as I crossed the threshold, with the aroma of fresh sawdust and million-year-old wallpaper glue.

Last night, Dad had torn down as much of the old wallpaper as he could in the parlor, leaving the more stubborn patches for today. I should have heard him in there now, scraping away. For some reason, though, he didn't seem to be home.

"Hello?"

With my back to the still-open front door, I waited another few seconds, not sure why I was holding out for a response when I had already seen that Dad's red F150 wasn't in the drive.

I guessed the good news was that I wouldn't have to explain to him why I was late. Not that I'd get in trouble for joining SPOoKy for after-school ice cream anyway, which Lucas had invited me to while walking me to class.

On a side note, how adorable had it been to watch Lucas power run down the hall after seeing me to American lit? Answer: *very*.

Still, I didn't want Dad jumping to conclusions about me and Lucas. At least, not until I came to my own conclusions about us.

The bad news about Dad being out? This officially marked the first time I'd been in the house alone.

Normally, such an event would have been cause for celebration. A reason to crank my music, take a long soak in the clawfoot bathtub, or catch up on my huge to-be-read pile.

Thanks to the dreams with Erik, though, the house didn't feel as empty as it should have.

I shook my head at myself. Because this—loitering in the foyer of my own house, harkening to my nonexistent ESP—was stupid.

Kicking the door shut behind me, I tucked the basket of linens under one arm and started for the kitchen. But at the entryway to the parlor, a tug in my gut caused me to look inside.

Though my gaze first zigged to the uncovered piano, it immediately zagged to the mantel.

To my angel.

I dropped the basket onto a nearby antique corner chair. Unlooping my purse strap from over my head, I let the bag fall to the floor. Next, I strode up to the mantel and stared right at my angel.

This marked the second time it had moved. Seemingly on its own.

Yet there were only two people who could have moved it in either instance. Dad, knowing how much the figurine meant to me, wouldn't have touched it. Unless he'd found it lying around somewhere. And hadn't it been on my nightstand last night? A place well within Charlie's reach. She could have taken it and left it somewhere. In that case, Dad *would* have moved it someplace where it wouldn't get broken or smashed.

Like the mantel.

And there you have it, my dear Watson. Mystery sol—

Boooooooooooonmmnnggggg.

Yelping, I retracted my hand from the figurine and spun to face the room.

The low and out-of-tune note, issued from the enormous grand piano, resounded around me—*through* me—as my eyes took in its un-sheeted form.

I held my breath and scanned the vacant room, my blood pumping hard and fast through my veins, propelled by the eerie sensation that, though there wasn't anyone in sight . . . there *was* someone there.

The same someone—the same some*thing*—I'd felt before.

No. No, there *wasn't*.

I tried to take my mind down the first rational route I saw—that I must have *imagined* the note being played. But my logic refused to follow. Not when I could still *hear* the fading reverberations of the note as it slowly died out.

I grabbed my angel from the mantel, then forced myself to trudge past the piano that Dad must have uncovered because he was planning on dismantling it soon. I returned to the basket of clean laundry and, willing myself to stop shaking, laid my angel atop the bedsheets, next to the roses.

Basket in hand, I left the parlor quickly, and with a determination I was still waiting to feel, I marched into the kitchen, where I found a note from Dad on the counter.

All four smoke alarms were beeping when I got back from picking up Charlie.

Couldn't find any 9Vs, so we went to Wally World.
Shouldn't be gone long. Tacos for dinner.

—Señor Dad

All four smoke detectors? At the same time?

Still no reason to get psyched out. Whoever had last replaced the alarm batteries would have done so all at once. It made sense they'd all go out together, too.

After putting the roses in water, I started up the creaking stairs with the laundry. Normally at first, then my steps quickened. As if speed could help me escape the sensation that someone followed close on my heels.

Reaching the second-floor landing, I swung around the newel and made a beeline for my room. There, I set my angel back on my dresser, where Charlie couldn't get it. Then I scooted it all the way back.

There.

Lingering for a beat, I frowned at the angel's featureless face, wishing in that moment that I could have the person who it represented instead.

Mom. The angel had been hers.

Unlike Dad, Mom had harbored a baseline belief in supernatural forces. Though, as a scientist, she could always explain away the weird stuff, too.

I guess I was like her in that way.

I left my room at a brisk walk and headed toward Charlie's.

Until today, I'd encountered no evidence beyond dreams and stories. Now, though, by working off the suggestions that had been fed to it—that this house was haunted—my ego was doing its *job* by trying to protect me from a perceived threat.

But it was my rational mind that could protect me from the ego's predisposition to freak out.

The house was old, the floorboards creaked, causing one of the strings in the piano to vibrate, and Dad moved my angel to keep it safe.

Erik was a dream—an archetype representing both my grief and my growing feelings for Lucas. And while some kids chose to have an imaginary friend, Charlie had decided to conjure an enemy. Which, given that the stories surrounding our house were public knowledge, had probably come from something she'd heard at school.

Zedok was just her way of filling the vacant spot in her life she'd begun to take note of, her mind working off suggestion as well to transform the invisible elephant in the room into an invisible masked man.

I pulled a twin fitted sheet out of the basket in Charlie's room, wishing all the while that I'd thought to turn on Spotify or something. *Anything* to drown out my thoughts and other hard-to-explain noises.

Singing to myself, I pushed the piano incident to the back of my mind and got to work making Charlie's bed.

The music I'd discovered in the attic had contained no lyrics, but I'd still found the melody as haunting as it was unforgettable. I'd pulled the sheet music from my schoolbag while waiting for the laundry to dry, deciphering the notes like runes, humming the refrain to myself and cementing it in my mind. Though sadness threaded the notes that both dipped and climbed, above all, strange beauty underscored the song, which had died uncompleted and mysteriously mid-note on the final page.

Though the music had never been finished, the ballad's chorus existed in its entirety, and I clung to the memory of it now, repeating it with differing syllables while I hoisted the sheet high over the bed so I could float it down over the mattress. The moment after it settled atop Charlie's bed, though, the spine-prickling sensation I'd first experienced when I'd opened the front door returned.

Turning my head, I settled my gaze on a chair that had been pulled out from the corner. Closer to the foot of Charlie's bed. As though someone had drawn it out so that they'd have a better view of my sister while she slept.

Dad again.

He didn't have trouble sleeping so much anymore, but when he did go prowling, it was always to check on us.

Though I kept singing, my focus remained fully on my fingers clutching tightly to the selvedge of the white sheet. I eyed the chair. Then, unsatisfied with the way the sheet had settled, I fluffed it up once more.

Then I did something I hadn't planned. On my next cycle of the refrain, I pitched my arms toward the chair, sending the sheet at and over it.

Over the invisible person who had been sitting there.

The figure shot to their feet, sending the sheet to the floor before the thin layer of white fabric had had time to fully betray their outline.

But there was no denying I had seen the impression of a mask.

A scream erupted in my ears. Propelled into flight by the most primal fear I'd ever experienced, I didn't know it was mine until I reached the stairway banister.

My body moved on its own, legs carrying me from the danger while my mind tried to work out how I hadn't been grabbed or stabbed. Or worse.

Ripping open the front door, I fell out of the house, tripping down the front porch steps and landing hard on the walkway, my palms the only things stopping my nose from crashing into stone.

I flipped myself and crab-crawled back from the open mouth of the front door, screaming again in the face of nothing, because I had fully expected to see someone there, ready to descend upon me.

There was no one. Not in the foyer or on the stairs.

Flipping myself again, I pushed up from the grass I'd retreated into and fumbled to my feet. From there, I ran pell-mell for my car, which I'd left parked in the drive.

Latching on to the handle, I yanked at it with an anguished cry.

My keys. I'd left them in the house.

Right along with my phone.

TWENTY-TWO
Zedok

My God. That voice. That *voice*.

The curse. Was it not *enough*?

Shall I forevermore now have that *voice* ringing in my hollow head as well?

I did not know where she had gone after seeing me—only that she had fled the house. For the moment, as I tore up the servants' stairs and into her version of the attic, I told myself I did not care to where.

A black lie. But at least I *could* still lie to myself.

With fast footsteps, I tore across the room to the desk, where I already knew what I would find.

My music. It was gone. *Of course* she had taken it.

Hadn't I known from the first notes that it had been mine? Even having never heard it with my ears, I'd have recognized it anywhere.

I fixed my hands on the desk, and before I could grasp that I had already begun to lose control, I threw it over. It landed with a deafening crash that shook the room—perhaps the whole house, though there would have been no one here to hear it.

No one but the masks.

The masks. What would they do to me now?

Wrath had seen this coming. Had there been some hint of her unearthly gift that I had ignored? Was *this* what Wrath had been alluding to? The reason I'd seen her face reflected in his mask and what had summoned the new masked figure who had looked so much like her?

While Stephanie might have been someone who would have caught my eye during my life before the curse, the thing that I was now could have, before today, sent her away with nary a wit. Even if she *had* intrigued me.

At least that was what I had been prepared to *make* myself believe at any cost.

But now . . . ?

The ringing of Stephanie's voice. It had done what *I* had been unable to. In essence, it had ripped the mask from the truth. And now here I was, left to gaze in horror at what lay just beyond.

Stephanie. *Stephanie.*

How had this happened?

I replayed the events of our encounter again in my head, buying my mind another moment before having to put my realization into something so inescapable as words.

Her porcelain angel. She had discovered it in the parlor as I had intended her to. And my pressing of the piano note. That, too, had been another purposeful test, issued to see if I had yet infiltrated her mind enough to be perceived.

From there, I had followed her to the second floor and into Charlie's bedroom with the goal of gauging what effects my tactics had thus far rendered. From there, I *had* meant to frighten her. But then. Then she had begun to sing. And the force, the *power* of her instrument had washed over me, weakening me into the unquestionable need of a chair.

The music she had woven for me on the piano, luring and lulling as it had been, was but noise next to that voice.

My very *bones*. They'd reverberated with her refrain. And how my hollow chest had ached from the beauty that had devastated my senses.

Rendered defenseless in her presence, incapable of departing or even moving, I had listened, transfixed. I'd not had sagacity enough even to discern that she had detected my presence. Neither had I possessed the power to shield myself in any way from the onslaught of her song. Or, for that matter, that damnable sheet!

What was I to do when she returned? After such an encounter, could I even hope she *would* come back?

Of course she will come back, you idiot.

And when she does, all you will want—all you might ever long for now until forever—will be to hear, to feel, those liquescent notes filling the void you have become. That angel's voice that allowed you to taste for the first time the heaven you shall never know.

I spun to face the room that, like all of the house—*both* versions—served as just another chamber of my sprawling tomb.

But the accumulated clutter from all the lives the home had known could not barricade me—or insulate her, for that matter—from what would now hurry to consume us both.

Now that I knew what she was to me . . . Now that I understood what I had allowed to happen . . .

Wrath.

Was he waiting for me on the other side even now?

If he were to conquer me, would he not—would *we* not—then take the girl?

There would be no reasoning with myself. For, with the donning of that mask, all reason would dissolve—vanish as the day does into night.

Oh, Stephanie. Before this hour, before this day, your name had been but a collection of syllables attached to a face I had believed— perhaps in folly—that I could still have eventually forgotten. Now . . . now it was a song. One I wanted to whisper if for no other reason than its pronunciation counted as a music I *could* make.

I cringed beneath the mask and, with the steps of a man condemned, carried myself to the tarnished version of the chaise that sat in the parlor. Collapsing onto the seat, the one Wrath had occupied nights ago on my side of the house, I scoured my mind for a solution to this cruel twist.

But, with the first sliver of bliss I had tasted in nearly one hundred years fading, *hatred*, deep and dark as a mire, began to well up within my emptiness to blot out all equanimity.

The roses she had brought with her. Had the boy given them to her?

But then, who else?

I did not despise him for coming here. Nor for telling Stephanie the things he had about me. *No.* I hated him because he had dared to occupy a space I could never hope to. The one next to Stephanie.

I hated him almost equally for being all the things I had once been.

Handsome. Strapping. Charming. *Alive.*

These emotions, Envy and Spite, would both converge upon me if I could not wrest them from my consciousness.

Perhaps Madness and *not* Wrath would have me then.

And there would be no telling how that would end.

Stephanie. What would happen when she returned to her house?

What would happen to either of us, both of us—*all* of us—when I made the inevitable return to mine?

TWENTY-THREE

Stephanie

I'd texted Lucas late last night. Which was probably why he'd never texted back.

Charlie had slept beside me, tucked under the covers of my bed, this time at *my* behest.

After the incident in her room, I hadn't gone back inside the house until she and Dad had returned from their battery run.

I hadn't bothered telling Dad what had happened. He wouldn't have believed a word of it anyway. Would the Stephanie I had been when we'd first moved into this place have believed me? Knowing Dad, he'd have put me in counseling or taken me for a head scan. Because fixing things was what Dad did. But this wasn't something Dad would be able to fix.

Lucas, possibly, *if* I was lucky, might be another story. And the truth was, I'd wanted so badly to call him. I hadn't dared, though. Because Erik had pretty much proven he could hear any conversation in the house. And if Erik could, that probably meant *he* could, too. That must have been why Erik wouldn't confirm my guess that he was a prisoner, just like, I was starting to realize, my family and I were becoming.

And Erik. I'd wanted to talk to him, too. Because now there could be no denying that he *was* real. Still, a conversation with him would have required me to fall asleep. Something that I wasn't sure I'd be able to do in Moldavia ever again.

Now that I was back at school, though, I was free.

Locker doors slammed and students passed me in the hall, a few giving me curious glances, probably wondering what I was doing anxiously loitering next to my own locker. If I cared, I could've pretended to look for something important or peruse my phone. But I couldn't afford to miss Lucas if he decided to meet me here as I'd texted him to.

But as the hall began to clear, and Lucas's face wasn't among those on their way to class, my heart began to sink.

How could someone I'd known for such a small amount of time have done so much to earn a place there? Probably because he cared. And because I, to a certain extent, had let him.

I turned my head in the direction of the thinning stairwell traffic, waiting for him to just appear, the way Erik did in my dreams. Maybe Lucas hadn't gotten my text. Maybe he was ignoring me. Maybe he'd left his phone at home or—

"Hey, what are we looking at?" came a breathless voice from behind me. I jumped, then spun to regard Lucas, who had come from the other direction.

"Oh," he said, straightening his short, vintage-style tie. "Sorry about that." He smiled an involuntary smile at having accidentally startled me. That was, until he realized that I wasn't smiling with him. His expression immediately sobered. He *almost* got the chance to ask me what was wrong.

Dropping my books, I collided against Lucas, wrapping my arms around him tight.

Being frightened like that. It had taken me right back to that moment in my sister's room, when that sheet had settled over . . . over something that wasn't supposed to be there, its whiteness conforming to the contours of a figure.

A masked figure . . .

A flush rushed to my cheeks the moment I realized I was publicly embracing Lucas Cheney. Who, so far, had yet to hug me back.

As I hurried to draw away, though, his arms settled around me, pressing me to him. For one blissful moment, I sagged against him, letting my tired eyes fall shut. His warmth engulfed me, along with the scents of sandalwood, peppermint, and soap. All of it transported me from the terror of yesterday, and this reality where I lived in a horror-filled house, to a better world. One where there was only me and Lucas.

"Something happened," he said after a pause that I got the sense he'd wanted to prolong, his voice a rumble that I felt more than heard with one of my ears pressed to the stiff fabric of his white button-down shirt.

I nodded. Then, gripping those iron biceps, I pushed back, forcing us apart. Lucas relented, his arms hesitant but obliging. I took a breath, staring straight into the buckle of the skinny belt he wore high around his waist along with a pair of wide-legged Dagwood-style trousers.

"Sorry I missed your text," he said. "I crashed early last night and woke up late. I didn't see it till this morning. But, you know . . . you can always call me."

I took in a slow, stilted breath. "I wanted to. But . . ." I trailed off, clueless on how to begin. Because the incident with the sheet sounded crazy inside my own head. Putting it into words would no doubt make it doubly so.

"It wasn't Charlie this time, was it?" he guessed.

I shook my head, my eyes following the trail of his tie to his collar and, finally, to the unearthly blues behind those glasses.

"What was it?" he said, his gaze searching mine. "Tell me."

Here was the moment I'd been anxious for ever since yesterday. Why should I be, though? This was Lucas, after all. The boy who waved electromagnetic-field-measuring gizmos at closets. The boy who believed in a hereafter. The boy who had been *right*.

"I saw him," I said. And, because I wanted to leave no room for doubt, I uttered the name I wasn't supposed to. *"Zedok."*

TWENTY-FOUR
Zedok

In Moldavia, doorways and thresholds held, for me alone, the power to open to one version of the house or the other.

Before yesterday, I had never been selective about how I made my comings and goings between the two houses. Until yesterday, whenever I had needed to return to my Moldavia, it had been the nearest door or archway that had served best.

But after hearing Stephanie sing, the metaphorical trapdoors that surrounded me had all presented themselves as more trap than door. Because with the revelation of Stephanie's seraphic voice, there would be no telling which of my masks would be there to greet—or ambush—me behind any one of them. Knowing what I and thus they now knew, which one of them would not rend through the other in order to lay command of me?

And so I had spent that entire night in the attic pacing—and contemplating—which doorway to step beyond.

It was true I could have bided my time indefinitely. But then, there really *was* no way to hide in perpetuity from oneself. And the longer I waited, the rasher, the harsher, the more restless the masks would grow. Never mind the fact that now *both* the girls would surely see me if I remained on their side. Perhaps I had even disturbed their sleep with my restless footsteps. What I did *not* need at this juncture was to give Stephanie cause—any more than I already had—to throw Erik's cautioning to the wind and seek further assistance from that camera-toting half-wit. Doubtless, his bungling would trip the final wire upon which we all now balanced.

There was also the little matter of my current mask. Already, Languor had failed me in more ways than I wished to tally. He would need to go. There was only one mask I could think of, though, whose influence would not guarantee more bedlam. Whose strength, too, might be enough to defend us from the others—from Wrath.

If I was lucky, if Stephanie was, he still dwelled where last I had left him.

Finally obtaining a grasp on myself, I descended from the attic and exited the house by way of the back door. From there, I strode with purpose down the dawn-lit pathway of Stephanie's world to the devastated conservatory. There, I passed through the ramshackle door of the broken glass house into the pristine but night-darkened interior of my own.

Once, long ago, the conservatory had overflowed with life. Ferns, hostas, and lilies, along with any number of other flora, had spilled from the glass doors and pivot windows.

Thanks to Myriam, during the spring and summer, roses had bloomed here in excess, their resplendence outshining lesser blooms.

This spot had been a favorite for teatime with my mother's acquaintances. And how often had she herself sought the companionship of the blooms in order to conduct her sketching and knitting?

Only shriveled and dried blossoms remained on the vines now, their papery, freeze-dried heads held hostage by the yellowed and thorny cages of their own petrified vines.

If there was one feature I missed in my wintry Moldavia, it was the roses. But nothing here lived. Nothing save for the moths. And, perhaps, the memories tied to this glass house.

Happiness had dwelled in the conservatory once.

Now the ghost of that happiness was all that remained within its boundaries.

Of all my masks, I knew of only one who could withstand the painful recollections that haunted this place.

Against all expectation, I found him here. He stood with his back to me, a silhouette facing the windows, his gloved hands clasped behind him.

"So," I said in a whisper. "After all this time, you *are* still here."

Unlike Wrath, I had neither seen nor heard from him in decades. It must have been at least that long since I had entered this conservatory.

Knowing what part of my soul this mask represented, I had never questioned his absence when he'd first vanished. Contrariwise, I had never had the need to confirm nor seek out his presence.

Until now.

He turned to face me, revealing his mask.

Time-crackled gold affixed his nose and lips in calm, straight lines. Matching gilt-leave filigree accented this lower diamond-shaped portion of the mask by chasing the borders between it and the upper midnight-blue segment that surrounded the almond-shaped eyeholes. At his forehead, on a patch of parchment-colored paint, a few black notes dotted the lines of a music staff.

Valor.

If there was a Horatio to my Hamlet, was it not him?

As if in answer to this second and internal question, Valor removed his mask.

Perfect darkness waited within his hood.

Observing me through that void, the figure extended to me his mask in the same fashion Wrath had.

This time, though, as I made my way to him, I laid a hand with eagerness over my own gray mask—a mask I had stolen from Languor at some point in time that I could not now recall.

Valor watched unflinchingly on as I removed Languor's mask, which I laid upon a plant stand beside a pair of Myriam's discarded gardening gloves.

Accepting Valor's from him, I placed it—both his countenance and identity—over my own.

Instantly, his figure unraveled, his cloak unfurling—vanishing— before reappearing to settle upon my own shoulders. Turning, I found my prior mask, Languor, reformed. He stood now beside the plant stand, Myriam's gloves clenched tightly in his fist. Lost to his reverie, he paid me no mind as my free hand fell to wrap the hilt of Valor's sheathed saber, different in ornamentation from Languor's rapier, though no less lethal.

And so I found myself looking *out* through those almond-shaped eyeholes that I had, the instant before, gazed into.

Regarding the outer world, I saw and heard everything in the same manner I had in the moments before. Nothing external had changed.

Within, though—fully present now in Valor's awareness—I *was* able to sense and conceive of a new course of action. One that hitherto had not occurred to me. One that would *never* have without Valor's influence.

Valor and I. We would speak to Stephanie again.

And, of course, what *else* would Valor have me do . . . besides tell her the truth?

All of it.

TWENTY-FIVE

Stephanie

I'd never cut a class before in my life. Before today, I'd never had a reason to.

After I'd finished telling Lucas what had happened in the house yesterday, starting from the smoke detectors and ending with the sheet, the final morning bell had rung shrill through the hall, causing us *both* to start that time. Neither of us had laughed then.

Classroom doors had shut all around us, one teacher poking her head out into the hall to narrow her eyes on us, which prompted Lucas to gather my fallen books from the floor. He'd then taken my hand and led me wordlessly in a direction opposite my first class. I hadn't even protested. Because, in that moment, the only thing that had mattered was that Lucas believed me.

He'd taken us straight to the library. And though Ms. Geary had eyed us with as much (if not more) suspicion as the hallway teacher, she didn't try to stop us on our way past the circulation desk. Maybe that had something to do with the fact that Lucas and I were holding hands—a stark contrast to what she'd observed the last time we'd both been here together.

Lucas took us all the way to the last row of computers. He claimed a seat in front of one of the desktops, drawing me into the seat next to him. As far as places where we could talk went, there had to have been better. But, when Lucas drew his backpack into his lap, I got the impression he hadn't brought me here for conversation. His real reason became clear when he produced from his bag a DVD case, which he handed to me.

So. Here it was. The documentary.

Paranormal Spectator, the title read.

A bald man in his thirties glowered at me from the cover, his meaty arms crossed over his bulging chest, black T-shirt straining against his biceps, his too-serious and war-ready eyes chiseling through me. Behind him, my house lurked like a monster, ready to pounce and devour.

So. *This* was the guy who had died three months after filming. He looked too fit and, as Lucas had cited, too young to be the victim of a heart attack.

I flipped the DVD over and found a kinder face waiting on the back.

"That's Rastin," said Lucas as I studied the man. "He lives in LA and travels all over the world helping with cases."

Rastin had thick, black, and short-cropped hair; a neatly trimmed goatee; and glasses. His dark eyes had a warm, soulful essence to them. He struck me as more genuine somehow than the Hulked-out guy on the front.

I trailed a finger down the episode descriptions until I found the one for Moldavia.

Episode 6: "Phantom Fury"

*Joe Boq investigates one of Kentucky's most notorious
Victorian mansions. Joined by special guest, renowned
medium and clairvoyant Rastin Shirazi, Joe attempts
communication with the spirits haunting the allegedly cursed
estate of Moldavia. But things take a shocking turn when a
malevolent entity attacks, resulting in the only instance thus
far in Paranormal Spectator history of a lockdown being
aborted.*

"What?" I blurted, ice water flooding my veins as my gaze
snapped up to find Lucas freeing a pair of earbuds from his bag. He
said nothing, but tapped a finger against his lips, shooting a furtive
glance toward Ms. Geary.

Lucas took the case from me and loaded the disc into the CD-
ROM tray. He plugged in the earbuds, handing me the right bud
while he inserted the left in his ear, an action that forced us to lean
in toward one another.

After a goofy and overdramatic intro with spliced, static-slashed
images and ominous voiceover narration, Joe Boq appeared on
my front lawn. He started talking at the camera WWE-wrestler
style, restating some of what Lucas had said about the mummy-
unwrapping party. All the while, Rastin stood quietly to the side,
his eyes fixed on the camera until, at one point, he slowly turned his
head toward the house.

The scene cut away then and showed the team inside, asking dumb questions to the air while holding digital recorders like

interview microphones. Lucas paused the video. He turned toward me, an action that nearly brought our foreheads together.

"Whenever *Paranormal Spectator* visited a place," he whispered, "they tried to gather evidence like EVPs or anomalies on camera. Sometimes, they even tried to take action against a spirit, with the hopes of clearing a property. Shortly after the team entered the basement of your house, Rastin attempted to perform an exorcism . . ."

He fast-forwarded, stopping when the clairvoyant, Rastin, emerged in the doorway of our cellar. Limp and addled, Rastin leaned against Joe Boq, one arm looped around the other's shoulder for support.

My unease ratcheted even tighter as, cast in the eerie, greenish-gray tint of night-vision, the segment played out like a scene from one of those low-budget, shaky-camera horror films.

Blood started to stream from Rastin's wide eyes, which had rolled into the back of his skull so that only the whites showed between fluttering lids. The blood gleamed black in the night-vision and leaked from Rastin's nose, too, smearing his upper lip.

"Tell us your name, *demon*," commanded Boq.

The rivulets of blood ran into Rastin's mouth, staining the teeth around which writhed lips that then formed words.

"I am Zedok," Rastin growled at the camera, a hundred voices seeming to issue through his throat while his blood-smeared fingers reached for the lens. "I am he who enters through darkness and takes leave by the same route. To come for me is to find me. To strike against me is to fuel me. To invoke my name is to invoke my *wrath*."

The camera tilted, the lens dropping from Rastin's face.

"No!" shouted Boq. "Keep rolling."

"He's bleeding, man," said the camera guy even as the screen righted itself on Rastin once again. White foam now began to issue from one corner of Rastin's mouth, mixing with the blood.

Boq stumbled out of the basement doorway, tripping on the top step. Rastin went down then, to the floor. The camera followed him there, where he began to convulse, a seizure wracking his body. He arched with a silent scream.

"There's something in his mouth," the cameraman said, and I shuddered as I focused in on Rastin's parted lips.

"Shut off the camera," Boq said. "Call 911."

"There. Look! There's something *in* there, man. It's coming out!"

The thing—obviously alive—emerged from the back of Rastin's throat, a pair of probing antennae coming into view first within the dark cave of his mouth. Two twitchy front legs followed, popping out over Rastin's bottom lip. A glossy black head and a pair of shining milk-white eyes glowed in the glare of the camera light.

"I said turn the damn thing *off*!" shouted Boq, his hand closing over the lens—blocking out the sight of the bloodied moth just as it freed itself from Rastin's gurgling, foaming mouth.

By then, I'd had enough. Jerking the earbud from my ear, I scooted back from the table, bending forward at the waist, and tried to breathe.

Nausea churned my stomach, threatening to have me upchucking all over Lucas's oh-my-god-are-you-for-real black-and-white saddle shoes.

"What did I just watch?" I asked at last, hoping against all hope that Lucas would confirm what Charlotte had said about the episode being fake. Because, more than anything, I wanted to believe that was true. But the moth. It had been the same kind I'd been seeing all over our estate. And that name. At least now I knew why Charlotte had assumed I'd gotten it from this DVD. Unless another kid at school *had* told Charlie about this documentary, and I was seeing things, then all of this *was* real.

Our house had a demon. And it had Erik, too.

Erik. He'd told me from the start that I needed to leave. He'd been trying to protect me—my family, too. What had he endured because of that?

And how the hell was I going to tell Dad we needed to move?

If he refused, it would be impossible to convince him we could never go down to the basement.

"That's why the moth worried me so much," Lucas said. "Charlotte thinks that *Paranormal Spectator* planted them on the estate when filming the episode. But some people say that Rastin inadvertently bridged to an alternate dimension—where the moths come from."

When I didn't say anything, Lucas laid a warm palm on my spine.

"Why did you show me this?" I asked.

"So . . . so that you would know what I know," he replied.

"That can't be the only reason."

"Stephanie," he said, like the answer was beyond obvious. And it was. But I still wanted him to say it. "We need to get in there. We need to start documenting solid evidence."

We? He was talking about SPOoKy. But Erik had told me explicitly *not* to let Lucas or anyone else like him onto the property. That had to mean paranormal investigators. I didn't want to consider the repercussions if I *did* have Lucas back. But then, hadn't I just seen what could happen if I didn't?

"I don't need evidence," I said. "I need help."

"Stephanie. In this field, evidence is the only way to *get* help."

I could read between the lines. He was trying to tell me, as gently as he could, that what was going on in my house required more help than he, or SPOoKy, could offer. He was telling me we needed professional help.

"You . . . you said Joe Boq died," I said. "But what about Rastin? What happened to him?"

"They wouldn't have aired the episode if he hadn't lived," said Lucas. "Actually, Charlotte's main reason for believing it was a hoax is because they did air it. That, and Rastin came out and said it was a hoax. But, clearly, that was just to keep people away."

"So . . . he's okay?" I sat up, though my eyes remained in my lap, as if that could protect me from the answers I didn't want.

"W-well," Lucas replied. "He's purported to have a heart murmur because of the incident, but . . . that's all hearsay. He's never confirmed that."

"What about the piano guy?" I asked him. "Wes mentioned a piano guy."

Lucas sighed. "I guess you and your dad didn't wonder too much over why there was still so much stuff in the house."

I shrugged. Dad made a habit of swooping in to buy places that had gone into foreclosure, or from sellers who were eager to liquidate properties. That was one of the reasons why, so often, the homes came with extras—junk the previous owners couldn't be bothered to clean out. Moldavia, in that respect, had been no different. Except, of course, that a lot of the antiques seemed as though they could have been original to the house. Including the piano.

"Someone tried to remove it," I guessed. "And then what?"

"Heart attack," Lucas replied. "Died on the spot. Left the property in a bag."

I balled my hands into fists, shutting my eyes again—eyes that had gotten no sleep last night and might not again tonight. Because, in going to Lucas, the only thing I'd accomplished was making this all worse, just like Erik had said. And not just for myself.

"Then you know why you guys can't come," I said.

"If I can't come," he replied, his tone soft and, remarkably, unafraid, "then you can't stay there."

I looked up to him, a sad smile tugging at my lips. "So then are *you* going to tell my dad why we have to abandon his newest investment?"

"N-no," he said, as he glanced away from me. "I'd like to still be allowed to see you."

For a moment, the storm inside me calmed by a degree. The words "see you." The way he'd said them. It suggested that he was pursuing me. But, again, the urge to ask about Charlotte rose within me. More than anything, I wanted to fast-forward to the moment when she wasn't constantly hovering between us—just another ghost in a world that had, for me, become populated with far too many. But, in this moment, I had a bigger problem on my hands.

Frowning, I bit my lip, wanting to tell him about Erik now, too. But I was still hesitant to hand him that part of the puzzle. Because if Lucas learned any more about what was happening in my house, he'd insist on coming over with SPOoKy.

"What am I going to do?" I whispered, almost more to myself than Lucas.

"There is one thing . . ." he said.

I eyed him, reluctant. Because surely whatever his suggestion was, it would involve something that I'd already forbidden.

"I think I know someone who can help," he replied. "Someone we can talk to who won't need evidence. If . . . if it's okay with you, I'll try to contact him."

I couldn't bear the thought of anyone being hurt because of the thing in my house. But if Lucas knew someone who might be able to do something . . . Well, that was better than any other alternative.

"Okay," I said.

"That still doesn't solve the problem of what happens in the meantime," Lucas replied.

"In the meantime?"

"Yeah," he said. "I don't . . . I'm really not sure how soon this guy will get back to me. I've only met him once. It could be right away. But. If it isn't . . ."

His unspoken question hovered in the air between us. What would we, or at least I, do until then?

"In the meantime, I'll do what I've been doing until now," I said simply.

"You mean . . . just sit tight?" He folded his arms like it was the last option he himself would have proposed.

But to that, I could only shrug. Because I still wasn't quite ready to tell him that I also had someone I could, so long as he showed up again, ask for help.

"I don't like the idea of your going back in there," he said.

"I don't think I have any other choice," came my reply.

"You'll call me this time," he said. "If anything else happens. Whenever. Even if it's the middle of the night?"

"I'll call you," I said.

And though I meant the promise, I also hoped I wasn't going to be given any reason to keep it.

TWENTY-SIX
Zedok

Remaining on my side of Moldavia, I reemerged from the conservatory, making my reverse trek to the rear door of the house, this time with steps that sank into deep snow.

As I approached, I scanned the darkened yet still somehow eye-like windows of the house that once, so long ago, *had* been a home. An unquiet mausoleum now.

As I crossed the threshold, my hand itched to draw my weapon.

But as I made my way through kitchen and hallway, foyer, and, finally, parlor, I found no single other version of myself lurking in the gloom. After all that had happened, should I not have been beset by them? One at least?

Anyone who knew less about their own deeper nature might have found comfort in such seclusion after so much fear of waylay.

What this ominous solitude brought to me, however, amounted to just the opposite.

Because if no mask appeared to stop me in my plan or even to advise me against it, did that not suggest the plan itself—the only one Valor and thus I had concocted—was somehow . . . faulty?

TWENTY-SEVEN

Stephanie

*R*oses. *Everywhere.*

Their aroma, so distinct, pervaded the space, potent enough to make my head spin.

I drew a breath, sharp and short, recognizing my impossible surroundings for what they were. The *conservatory*. Not the old and ruined one behind our house. Instead, I'd been transported to a replica of its past, one resplendent with greenery and studded with innumerable buds, all different colors, each in various states of unfurling. And my presence here. It could only mean . . .

I turned to find him standing at the opposite end of the room. A dark figure against a flower-dotted backdrop, he regarded me with an unreadable expression. For a long time, I just stared back, awed all over again by that face, which never stopped being arresting.

That night, after I'd gotten home from school, I'd taken care to try to keep my family together in the house. I'd done homework with Charlie in the parlor while Dad continued chipping at the wallpaper. When bedtime had rolled around, I'd sent Lucas a requested all's-well text before curling up in my bed again with my little sister.

This time, I hadn't wanted to fight off the sleep that I likely wouldn't have been able to anyway.

And this—*he*—was the reason why.

Still, I hadn't been sure he would come. I'd started to worry that my encounter with Zedok meant something terrible had happened to Erik.

"You . . . you're okay," I said, breaking the silence. "After yesterday, I wasn't sure what to think." He didn't say anything, which made me nervous. Because he hadn't been this quiet in any of our previous meetings. And that expression he wore, like *I* was the ghost here, suddenly made me anxious that I'd misread him. "*Are* you okay?"

"In truth," he replied at last, without a trace of any of the coldness he'd shown before, "I am not."

I frowned and took a halting step toward him. I wasn't 100 percent certain what to do, either. Especially now that there was so little room left to doubt that Erik wasn't just a dream.

"Something's wrong," I guessed, my heart speeding up. "Besides the curse, I mean. Something happened."

"Something has . . . happened," he conceded.

I started toward him. His brows lifted slightly in surprise as I approached, but he didn't continue. Not even when I stopped right in front of him. Instead, his eyes searched mine.

"*Erik*," I prompted when his answer never came.

He started. Then his expression darkened. Immediately, though, he banished the scowl behind a mask of indifference, and with a half-hearted gesture to the walls surrounding us, he strode away, moving toward the pillow-piled wicker furniture that occupied the center of the spacious room.

"Do you like it?" he asked.

"Like what?"

"The conservatory," he said. "I thought you might take pleasure in seeing it."

"It's . . . beautiful," I admitted, though cautiously, still baffled by his words, not to mention this sudden and near-total shift in him.

"I could not help but notice how rarely in this house—large though it is—you manage to enjoy moments that are wholly your own," he went on to say. "Though I possess time in abundance, as commodities go, it's rather ill-suited for lending, wouldn't you agree? It is true as well that I cannot bring you roses, but . . . as you can see, it is well within my means to transport you to them."

I wanted to smile at this gesture—at his words, too. My concern wouldn't let me, though. And now there arose a new concern. One that asked where all this was coming from.

"To see you standing among them, though," he went on without seeming to noitce my confusion, "it now leads me to wonder if the beauty is, in truth, all mine to behold."

I blinked, uncertain for an instant that I could have heard him right.

"Erik, what are you talking about?" I asked him. Because I wanted to know if the blush that rushed to my cheeks truly had any business being there. Or if this was all just part of his . . . Victorian-ness?

"You returned home yesterday with roses," he said, still way over in the left field of Wait, What Is Happening? Stadium. "They . . . were a gift, no doubt."

"I got them from the florist."

"*You* bought them?"

What was he getting at? "You're stalling."

"I am," he admitted, keeping his back to me, the response giving me *zero* comfort.

"Why?"

"Because now that you're here, with me, I find the words that I had resolved to say to you suddenly more difficult to summon than anticipated."

Talk about non-answers. "Just spit it out."

He glanced over his shoulder at me, his scowl returning. "Spit . . . it out?"

"Yeah," I said. "It means—"

"I can deduce what it means," he said, cutting me off.

"Then why can't you just say it?"

"Because I fear what you might think," he raced to say. A blunter answer for sure, but still useless.

"Are we in trouble now?" I asked, cutting to the chase because one of us needed to. "Me and Dad. Charlie. Is it too late?"

He spun to face me, his cloak whirling with the motion. "No. Of course not. I don't think I would be here now if it was."

"I don't understand." I opened my arms, then let them flop to my sides. "If you're stuck here because of the curse, then where else would you be? Why won't you tell me why, *specifically*, we have to leave? More importantly, why won't you let me help you?"

"I'll thank you not to berate me when the very reason I have come is to tell you everything," he said, that familiar chill in his tone returning, his words silencing me. He paused and, seeming to check himself, he began again. "You'll forgive me for prolonging the moment. How can I help it when I know that, as soon as I finish telling you all I've come to say, you *will* go?"

His voice, one of the surest things about him, all but died on that last word. As if, after trying so hard to convince me to scram, he'd suddenly changed his mind.

"You're . . . different," I said, scanning his attire that had changed along with his demeanor. Still garbed in mostly black, he now wore a royal blue embroidered waistcoat. A silken black cravat replaced the white one he'd worn before. A spotless ebony dress coat accompanied matching slacks, while his shoes shone in the moonlight that streamed through whatever scant patches of window the roses failed to blot out.

If it was possible for him to look more handsome than he had before, well, he managed it.

"I am different," he agreed. "But then, how could anyone not be after hearing you sing?"

I shut my mouth, stunned by the question. "You heard me?"

The tiniest of smiles touched his lips, accompanied by a short, ironic laugh. His gaze broke from mine to focus on one green-vine-covered wall. "With a voice like that, what angel above your head or demon beneath your heel could *not* have heard you?"

Again, heat rushed to my cheeks. I folded my arms, a gesture that I'd probably hoped would bring comfort, or a sense of protection from his sudden but not altogether unwelcome barrage of flattery. It did neither.

"Stephanie," he went on, still without returning his eyes to mine. "I cannot hope to put into words the exceptionality of your gift. And I would be a liar—*more* of a liar," he corrected, "if I did not confess to you how fervently I wish, for your sake as well as for mine, that I had never heard you sing my music."

"*Your* music?" My blush intensified, to the point where I couldn't have hoped for even one second that he wouldn't notice. Apparently, being in a dream didn't change physical responses. Surely I was now as scarlet as half the blooms surrounding us.

"I daresay only Odysseus, in his circling of the Sirens' island, could have understood the depths of my ecstasy in hearing the perfection of your song," he continued, his use of the word "ecstasy" causing me to lift my hand to my brow so that I could physically shield my face from his now unrelenting gaze. Probably, in his time, that word hadn't carried any of the more salacious connotations it did now. Or . . . had it?

"Conversely," he went on, "only a drowning man could fathom the ineffable agony that came in the moments, in the hours, after you fled my presence."

Immediately, my head jerked up. "*Your* presence?"

"I did not mean to frighten you," he said.

I shook my head, once again lost in the labyrinth of Erik's words. "Are you saying that was *you*?"

His eyes shot away, searching the air for the answers he was having trouble giving me. When they returned to me again, they did so only in a sidelong glance, one full of darkness and secrets.

"Stephanie," he said. "What I have come to tell you is . . . that I have kept from you the whole truth of this place. Of myself, as well. As a result, I am more afraid for you than ever."

If it was *him* I'd seen under that sheet and not Zedok, then . . . wasn't there *less* reason for me to be afraid now?

"The figure under the sheet," I said. "It had on a mask."

"Yes," he replied, uttering the word like he despised it.

"Zedok wears a mask," I continued.

"Yes," Erik said again, the repeated one-word response fanning the flames of my frustration. But then my mind derailed, flying off in the direction of something else he'd said.

"That music couldn't have been yours," I insisted. "The paper was old, but the notes were fresh."

"That is because I had just written them."

"No," I argued. "That's not possible."

"I've come here to tell you that it *is*."

"Then what are you saying? That the details of the curse, the things that Lucas told me, are *true*?"

Sudden anguish swept over his expression. "I confess I don't quite know where to begin. So much of what the boy told you . . . I admit I didn't want you to know. It never occurred to me why. Not until yesterday, when it all became terrifyingly clear. I know I can't expect you to understand why it has come to this. Not when our moments together have been so few and brief. Yet, after decades of solitude, after so much *silence*, how could our interludes not have become as music to me?"

I blinked several times, my blush flaring anew.

Sometimes the way he phrased things, like poetry was an actual language, made me want to second-guess his meaning. Often, the things he said *did* seem to have two meanings. But had he just admitted to . . . caring about me?

That still didn't explain why he was having so much trouble saying what he came here to say. But if he wasn't going to tell me outright, maybe I could guess.

"He plans to target me specifically in order to get at you," I said. Though that didn't strike me as something he should have difficulty saying. "Because we're becoming . . . friends."

"Is that what we are?" he uttered through a dry laugh, like he didn't believe it. "How ever did I manage to earn something so precious? And yet . . . I cannot accept. For it is too reckless a thing for me to allow."

I frowned at him and, suddenly, not giving a rip about any demon, made my way to him, past the smattering of furniture to stand just in front of him, as close as we had been the night before last when we'd stood together in front of the fireplace. When he'd almost touched my cheek. Now his scent, one of lavender and honey—and something more caustic that I couldn't name—fought with that of the roses.

"We're friends if I say we're friends," I told him.

"And so you speak music as well as you sing it" was all he said, a rueful almost-smile tugging at his lips.

Peering up into his face and into those sad eyes, so beautiful, I couldn't stop myself from reaching up to him. My fingers hovered close to his jaw, closer than his own had come to mine that night. But then, before I could make the connection, he caught my wrist. Not roughly, but with an abruptness that suggested my touching him was something he legitimately feared.

He squeezed my wrist, scowling. Just when I thought he might admonish me or sweep off again, he stepped *into* me, leaning down far enough almost to allow his forehead to touch mine, the silken strands of his dark hair falling to mingle with my curls.

And now I had an answer as to what he, in his own Erik way, had been trying to tell me.

Our moments together *had* been brief. But each more intense than the last, as if building toward this moment. One that had maybe become *too* intense. And yet . . . I couldn't pull away.

"Tell me what to do," I said in a whisper. "The curse. Tell me how to break it. Tell me how to set you free and I will."

"There is no cure," he answered, a tremor in his tone, like he was trying to convince himself to let me go even as I was trying to convince myself to pull free. "The curse is absolute, and there is no hope of undoing it."

"Then I'll *change* it," I said. Because, curse or not, the world still answered to certain rules. My world might have been irrevocably altered since we'd moved into Moldavia, but the earth was still spinning and he and I were still here. Separated by time and death but, simultaneously, by nothing at all. If that was possible, then so was his freedom.

My freight train thoughts halted then, stalled the instant he moved in by another inch, his lips hovering that much closer to mine.

Would he really . . . ?

More importantly . . . did I want him to?

Seriously. What was I doing? I should have been stepping back from this stranger who I already knew was *dead*. And what about Lucas? Did a kiss in a dream count as a real kiss—something that could potentially destroy what awaited me in reality? That question alone should have been enough for me to draw away. But then . . . what I wanted in that moment was clear enough since I *wasn't* stepping back.

"*Stephanie.*"

Before I could stop them, my lids fluttered to half-mast, my own lips parting in anticipation. Because no one had ever said my name that way. Soft as a prayer, each syllable laced with longing.

Erik guided my hand down, his grip on my wrist loosening so that his fingers, as rough and cool as I remembered them, could trail to find and twine mine. He came closer, until we were pressed together, just a breath apart, his hand clutching mine tightly, as though we weren't hovering on the verge of a kiss, but at the edge of some great divide. I gripped his hand in return, squeezing, a response that I'd meant as encouragement.

Instead, the action seemed to jar him from a spell. He pulled back, his fingers releasing my unyielding ones, his expression nothing short of horrified.

"Forgive me," he said, his words made more of breath than voice. "I . . . should not have dared come to you again."

"Erik—" I tried to tug him back to me, but he continued his retreat, dispelling as he did the greenery-covered windows, the walls of vines, the cobblestone floor, the roses, and, with them, their scent.

"Wait," I said, squeezing even harder the hand that dissipated from mine, suddenly as intangible as smoke. "Erik, please—"

But it was too late. He'd gone. Leaving me to the blackness that fast rushed up to consume everything and, along with it, me.

TWENTY-EIGHT
Zedok

*P*ain, unmistakable and wrenching, echoed through my empty chest, resonating inexplicably from the hollowed place where there was nothing—no heart from which such agony could derive.

The sensation, like an all-consuming rift had opened within me, came mere seconds after I had ended the dream with Stephanie.

I had only just risen from the armchair, and weakened by the onslaught, I staggered to the piano, which I leaned against for support. The keys, in response, uttered a discordant clangor.

God. What . . . *was* this? Lifting one trembling hand, the same one Stephanie had clenched with her own in the dream, I gripped at my waistcoat, wadding the material into my fist, as if the action might help to alleviate the feeling that, any moment, I would collapse into myself and implode as a dying star.

If only I could be so lucky. If only *she* could.

Gritting my teeth, I forced myself upright.

This anguish. Was it meant to serve as some form of punishment?

Doubtless Lucifer himself would not have dared what I almost had. To touch lips with the purest of angels.

One moment longer with her, and I'd have done the unthinkable.

How could I have let this happen?

Fury overtook me, driving me to shove the lone standing lamp from the piano's closed lid. It crashed with a horrible racket. The knowledge that my surroundings would not permanently sustain any damage only served to fuel my ire.

I stumbled to the mantel next, which I cleared with a sweep from both arms, sending the decimated artifacts toppling to shatter against the floor. Chief among them was my father's clock. How many times, in a bid to win refuge from its incessant ticking, had I broken it?

Stephanie. How could I save her now that I had allowed her to become entangled in the strings of the heart I did not have?

I stilled. The remnants of the ache abating once again, ushered away this time by the realization that I was not alone.

I had a visitor. Not another mask, though.

Instead, I had company in a much truer sense.

And *his* presence. Should I not have sensed it the very moment he had encroached upon my domain? No doubt I would have had I not been with *her.*

"How long have you been there?" I asked him.

"Long enough," answered the man.

"I thought I told you never to come back."

"You did," he said. "But I thought we also agreed that you would not give me reason to."

"And yet, having no reason has never stopped you before."

So. He knew of the Armands. It had been my intention that, by the time he became privy to such information, the Armands would be gone. Though I wanted to ask him how he had come by the truth so soon, I refrained. For did the answer, whatever it was, matter at this juncture?

In command of myself once more, albeit with some tremulousness, I eyed him from over one shoulder.

He sat on the chaise, having invited himself in per his usual annoying habit. Though I hated that he had borne witness to my brief lapse, it did please me to see that he, too, was attempting to hide the slight tremor in his own hands and frame. His fear, more than anything, told me that he could not be counted responsible for the attack I'd experienced.

The man, a *living* man, was none other than the famed psychic medium Rastin Shirazi. Six years had passed since we'd first been introduced. And does any manner of meeting acquaint two souls quite so well as a duel to the death?

"You should leave," I said. "Things never bode well for either of us when you are here."

"And yet you know as well as I do," said Rastin, "that I am not *really* here."

"Indeed," I grunted, hating him. For his stubbornness. For his horrible habit of dropping in on me whenever he pleased. Perhaps what I hated most about Rastin, though, was the conflicting *gladness* the sight of his meddlesome face brought to me in this moment. "I suppose it could be said that *I* am the only one who is truly here."

This last part I uttered as a test. To determine exactly how much he knew.

"Except I know that is not currently true."

"Is it not?"

"Erik—"

"*Don't*," I said, cautioning him against the use of my Christian name. I had shed it for a reason, adopting in its stead—as a reminder—the alias I had operated under while carrying out all the dark dealings that had led to my perdition. And the resurrection of my given name. Wasn't that how we had all gotten here—to this dire predicament?

"I know that there are people living here," Rastin said, for once arriving at his point with relative swiftness. "After I discovered as much to be true, tell me, what other choice did I have but to confront you?"

"Oh, I don't know," I said. "There is always the option of minding one's own business."

"Given the circumstances," replied Rastin in that grave, scolding, and almost parental tone he sometimes liked to take with me, "I'm afraid that you *are* my business."

"Well. As you can see." I paused to gesture to the broken clock and the rest of the mantel debris. "I have everything well in hand."

"Clearly," he replied as he regarded me over the narrow frames of his wire-rimmed glasses.

As before, he sported the same neatly trimmed goatee and mustache. A gray scarf, worn over a black blazer, looped his neck. He appeared thinner and more worn than in times past, though, his face prematurely lined.

My fault, I was certain.

"I would offer you tea," I said, as if it was possible to divert subjects with him. "If you were actually here to drink it."

"Just now," he said, ignoring me, "you were in pain?"

Once confident I could do so without wavering, I pivoted to face him, and for the briefest of instants, terror caused his face to pinch, his fear springing from the memory of that night in the cellar. With Wrath.

For good reason, Rastin had not stepped physically onto this property since that initial meeting of ours. The fact that he was here in spirit form, his body elsewhere in the world, afforded him the luxury to depart in the same manner in which he'd entered—within the blink of an eye. Even in his current astral state, though, he was still quite vulnerable. I could do him a great deal of harm if I chose to. Lucky for him, Valor harbored no temptation to do so.

"I was in pain, yes," I admitted after several beats.

"You have implanted another false heart," he guessed.

"My dear Rastin," I said through a short and humorless laugh. "You might fancy another trip to the brink of hell, but I personally have quite had my fill. Tell me, though, so long as we're on the subject of one another's health, how fares your own heart? No doubt it still troubles you."

Whenever the opportunity presented itself, I never shied from offering him a reminder of what his attempt to dislodge me from this estate had cost him. I did this because I didn't like feeling responsible for him. But Rastin's little stopovers. Did they not suggest that he felt responsibility for me, too?

"I'm here to *talk* and, for now, that is all," Rastin snapped, taking my reminder as a threat. How characteristically melodramatic of him.

"Well," I said. "You are a funny sort of diplomat to request peace but, in the same breath, hint at war."

"The *people*, Erik," Rastin replied, his initial fear of me waning, his bravery coaxed forward perhaps by the observation that I was not currently under the influence of a mask dispossessed of reason. "I'm here because of the *people*."

"Oh, I have no doubt they are why you are here," I spat with a bitterness I could not fully bring myself to feel. Because the sudden appearance of the only person who had ever attempted to break my curse so shortly after Stephanie's proclamation that *she* would be the next to attempt the task . . . Well, it suggested the influence of the miraculous.

"Erik, there is a *child* here," he pressed. "A little girl."

"There are *two* girls," I corrected. "One six. One seventeen. And Mr. Armand, their father, is in his forties. Do you think these are details I might have missed? How quick you are to assume I have not already taken pains to see to their eviction. I'll have you know that I have tried and have thus far failed. Armed with that knowledge, tell me, medium, what is your plan?"

"This." He gestured to me with one hand. "*Speaking* to you— one man to another. My plan, in other words, is to ascertain what *your* plan is."

It did not escape me that he'd referred to me as a "man." Or that we were having this exchange in civil tones. A far cry from how we had conducted our business the last time he'd visited me in this manner. Though I did not recall which mask had held me in its thrall then, the knowledge that it had not been Valor's was enough to tell me I could not have been half so sane.

"Your appearance," I muttered. "I must say, I *do* find it rather opportune."

"O-opportune?" he stuttered, fully on edge once more.

"Indeed. One day sooner and you would not have found me so hospitable. Who knows *what* you might have discovered had you come a week from now? But providence, it would seem, *can* be bothered with my plight after all. Though not, it appears, until the moment it becomes someone else's." I laughed, and a backward glance toward Rastin showed he was far more disconcerted even than before.

"Tell me, Rastin," I said, barreling on. "Your powers. Is it fair to assume they have grown since the last time you attempted to exorcise me?"

"I was mistaken to—"

"Answer the question," I snapped. "Granted a second chance, do you think you could succeed?"

At this, he stood, openly galled now. I, too, could not help but be flabbergasted by my newest and perhaps even more insane plan, which I found myself uttering aloud in real time as it occurred to me.

"You are toying with me," he accused. "You hope to lure me into a trap."

"I am not."

"You must be."

"The exorcism," I said in an effort to refocus him. "If I agreed to submit to it, would you try again? That is why you return here, is it not? Because you hope to find me in a state that would allow you to try again someday. And your heart. Surely it cannot be so damaged that—"

"It would be a *cleansing* this time," he corrected, his concern over the fact that I might be tricking him lessening by a fraction. "And my strength in this matter is not half so important as the fact that I now know what it is I am dealing with."

"And what, precisely, is *that*, Rastin? Please, if you would, enlighten me. For that's a puzzle I myself have never gained a satisfactory answer to."

"A cursed human spirit," Rastin said.

"An unbreakable curse, allow me to remind you. And *am* I still human? Under what authority do you make such a bold assumption?"

"Just because a curse is irreversible does not make it unbreakable," he argued, ignoring my question. "Every curse can at least be undone. Even one as terrible as yours."

"Do you really think so?" I asked, not bothering to hide my skepticism.

Rastin spread his hands. "You said it yourself. Would I return to this house time and again if I did not? Would I be here now?"

"So then. Do I have my answer?" I asked him. "You truly feel you could succeed? You are *certain*?"

"Certain?" He shook his head. "No. Confident? Yes. But, Erik, what has led you to this change?"

"*There has been no change*," I growled, clenching one hand into a fist. "That is why your confidence must become your certainty. For should you fail, I *will* kill you this time, Shirazi. You and I are both aware that is not a threat so much as it is a warning. To us *both*."

At this, he scowled. "If there *is* any hope for my success, then I need to know why you wish to try again. It could be that very reason that sees us through this time."

"I . . ." I began, then stopped myself. Because, while I wanted to put him off, I could see his point. Also, in keeping my horrible secret, was I not leaving a terrible gap through which Stephanie might still fall? And lastly, if I was to sell myself out, should I not do it as thoroughly as possible while I still had the chance? "The girl, Rastin," I blurted. "It's the girl."

"The little one. She reminds you of your sister. Is that it?"

"*No*," I snapped, hating him for prying at me like this. And yet, here was my opportunity to admit my deepest fear to the one person who could do anything about it. "The . . . other girl."

"What about her?" Rastin pressed, the sudden reluctance in his tone suggesting he suspected the truth even if he remained unprepared to believe it.

"You said she is seventeen," he said, making the connection on his own when I did not immediately answer. "A year younger than you were when . . . Oh. Oh dear. You like her."

"I don't *like* her," I said, speaking through gritted teeth. Because of how garish he made it sound. As if she were some sort of pastry— something to merely like or dislike.

"Love, then," he said, the very word causing an echo of that grim pain to return.

Was it that? I would not have thought it possible.

"How?" Rastin pressed.

To that, what could he expect me to say? How could I explain to him the way she had about her? Her manner and intelligence. Her fire. How could I make him understand that her presence in this house had *done* something to me? *Awoken* something—galvanizing me without my even being aware.

But Wrath. *He* had known it all along.

"I don't know how, Shirazi," I said, a new tremor starting in my limbs, as though it was God himself I was confessing to and not a mere man.

But it was out now, and I had said as much as I could bring myself to say.

"This mask you're wearing," he demanded. "Tell me what its name is."

Did he still think this was a trick?

"Valor," I said. "For now . . . I am Valor."

Though the tension in his frame did not leave him, it did seem to subside slightly with this answer.

"I have never encountered you in this mask before," he said.

"As well you might not again," I warned. "Which is why, if we are in agreement, we must act quickly."

"You would submit yourself willingly to the procedure?" prompted Rastin, at last beginning to believe. To hope. "You would . . . participate?"

"No more questions, Rastin. You will come to finish what you began, or you will not."

Would he be so cruel as to reduce me to begging?

Rastin, perhaps sensing that I was close, did something he had never before. He took several steps toward me, enough to leave a short space between us. Then he did something even more remarkable than that. He placed a hand, heavy and warm, on my shoulder. Though Rastin was not truly here with me in physical form, his powers were such that he could make it *feel* as though he was. He squeezed the jutting bones there, an action that stunned me far more than anything he had said or could ever say to me.

"Of course I will come."

Silence pulsed between us.

Responsibility.

Perhaps that had been the wrong word to describe the nature of our understanding of one another. What was that old saying about the enemy of my enemy?

Though Rastin was not my friend, he was perhaps the closest thing I had ever had to one.

At least before Stephanie . . .

"How soon can you be here?" I asked, new fear creeping over me. For had we not already conspired on too much aloud in the presence of something that could just as easily unravel it all?

That was to say . . . me.

"I am currently far from here," said Rastin. "Half a world away. But I will leave at first opportunity."

Gratitude and a small measure of relief coursed through me. And yet I could not thank him. I dared not for fear that, in doing so, I might curse the plan we had made. The one that, in obliterating me, would save her.

"Erik," Rastin said, channeling my attention to him again with his release of my shoulder.

"*What?*" I snapped. For maybe now I *was* Erik again. Maybe *she* had made me so.

"For this to work, you know you will need—"

"A heart," I finished for him.

This I did know. And yet I had hoped he would not advise me to implant one.

"Not yet," I said. "Not until you arrive. I can't risk its rupturing. Not with the family here."

"You risk more without one."

He was right. But wrong as well.

If I put a heart in, it would draw my spirit together and focus it. With the pieces of my soul banished back into my body, my masks would not be free to have at me. Wrath would be relieved of his power to overtake me. Unless of course something caused the heart to break. In which case I would lose control no matter what.

In short, it was a gamble either way.

"Do it now and buy us time," Rastin urged. "Buy *me* time. There is something I will need for the cleansing. It will take some doing to get. And you said yourself you might not be as you are for much longer. The next mask. Are you willing to wager you will be as cooperative as you are with this one?"

"I..." I said, because his argument was sound. And yet pure lunacy. "I make no promise."

"I don't need one," Rastin said as he took two retreating steps from me, his form fading out even as he did so. "If you truly care for her, then I know you will do it."

With that, he flickered away. Leaving me, for the time being, on my own.

If not alone.

TWENTY-NINE

Stephanie

I opened my eyes to the whispery shuffling of paper.

A cursory glance to my digital clock told me I'd slept beyond the dream with Erik and through most of the night. Apparently, though, Charlie hadn't.

She sat on the floor with her back to me, her tin of crayons open beside her.

In the glow of the nightlight that I'd moved from her room to mine, she colored furiously something I couldn't see.

"*Mmph.*" I pinched my eyes shut for an instant, as if I could squeeze an hour more of sleep into the span of a second. Then, slowly, I leaned forward to peer over Charlie's shoulder and froze at the monstrous scarlet image marring the sheet of white copier paper.

"Charlie. What is that?"

She paused in her scribbling to glance back at me, then lifted her finger to point at my closet door. Which stood open. *Wide* open.

It had been closed when we'd gone to bed. I'd made sure.

"You . . . you saw that?" I asked her. "That thing came out of the closet?"

"No," said Charlie. "He said he can't come to our side yet."

Our side? Yet?

I froze, my insides icing over. "Is that Zedok?"

"He said he was," replied Charlie with a shrug. And her nonchalance was the most disconcerting part of all of this.

I tilted my head at her, my bleary mind trying to distill her words into something that made sense. Like Erik's though, none of them did.

"I thought you said you'd seen him before," I pressed.

"I did," replied Charlie. "But he didn't have a skeleton face then."

Tossing the covers off, I swung my legs over the side of the bed and hurried to shut the closet. Then, leaning my back against the door, I frowned down at the drawing.

"How long did you talk to him?" I asked Charlie. "What else did he say?"

"He watched you sleep for a long time," she said, peering up at me, her eyes shadowed beneath by small dark circles. "I asked him if he was Zedok, and he said yes. Then I told him he didn't *look* like Zedok."

I shook my head, almost afraid to ask. "And . . . what did he say?"

"He just said, 'Yes, I do.'"

THIRTY
Zedok

"**D**id you see what he did?" whispered the first of the two sibilant feminine voices. "What he brought with him from over *there*?"

A second voice then. "You don't think he's seriously considering—"

"*Hush.* Do not even say it. He knows better. Which is why he never agreed to it."

Seated at the piano on my side of Moldavia, the lamp I had demolished the prior evening now intact atop its lid, I lifted my right hand.

"What does he think he's doing?" hissed the first.

"You mean besides imprudently courting disaster?" scoffed the other.

Ignoring the whispers, I laid my gloved fingers onto the keys.

I could not play "Für Elise." But . . . I could remember the feel of her hand beneath mine. The discordant, corrupted music we had made together in the dream.

And here I was, for the hundredth time in as many minutes,

hopelessly lost in the thought of her, left grasping in vain for the ghost of one of our few moments together.

"He won't do it, if he knows what is good for him," hissed the lower of the two voices, her words meant more for me than her companion.

"But why else sit down at the piano with it? He means to play. He wishes to escape."

"It is my conviction that he knows better than to think he can."

Again, my mind swept through the memory of last night.

She and I. We had been so close. Drunk on her nearness, lured by her words, her beauty—that voice—I had craved more. So much more.

Had I ever longed to touch someone so?

In closing my eyes, I was able to block out the keyboard's black-and-white lines, but not the whispers or the ticking mantel clock, which, like the other things I had destroyed last night, had repaired and reset itself.

"Well. Are *you* going to stop him?"

"*We* are. Of course we are."

This was why so much of my written music existed on the Armands' side of the house.

All of my composing transpired there. Where these two particularly obnoxious monstrosities could not follow me.

"Dearest Spite," hissed the softer of the two voices. "Did you *hear* what he just called you?"

"Oh, Envy, *dear heart*," answered the second voice, hoarser and deeper in register. "We are both well aware that, of the two of us, he only ever thought of *you* as obnoxious."

Slowly, I turned my head to glare at them through a single eye-hole of Valor's mask.

Adorned in emerald and burnt coppery orange respectively, the two women occupied the ever-popular chaise by the parlor's bay window. They watched me from behind fluttering lace fans while, at their backs, the sheets of snow that never ceased to fall in this realm filled the window's view.

Spite and Envy—or, as I had once referred to their living equivalents, the Scorpion and the Grasshopper—represented a pair of debutants who had once dueled for the opportunity to win my betrothal. Though their representatives were now long dead, their doubles had taken it upon themselves to carry their predecessors' venomous yet saccharine war into my damnation.

Appropriately, Envy wore the mouthless mask of a bug-eyed grasshopper while Spite's mask reflected the likeness of an armored scorpion, her long braid, fashioned to resemble the creature's lethal tail, draping one shoulder.

Moving in tandem, they plucked their saucers from the coffee table's colorful biscuit-laden surface, pinching the handles of their respective teacups.

Ludicrously, they raised the tea-filled cups to the spots on their masks behind which their lips ought to have dwelled, pretending—as their counterparts had in life with so much other business—to sip.

Both phantasms exhibited enough of their once-living twins' less-than-civilized characteristics that I was loath to think of them as *ladies*.

"Come now," chirped Envy, "there was a time once when you thought of me as a lady."

"There was a time also," Spite replied, the purr in her tone suggesting she'd been waiting for just such an opportunity to strike, "when he thought of you as an abhorrent mollisher."

"Well." Envy gave an absent wave of her gloved hand. "*You* would know, seeing as you made it your business to know everyone else's. And I daresay he never cared much for either you or me. Though I am certain that, between the two of us, he *did* prefer *me*."

I turned my attention away from them, focusing on the subject of their previous debate.

The rose, which now lay atop the piano's gleaming music shelf.

I had stolen it—extracted it from the dozen that had, in fact, *not* been a gift from Stephanie's young man.

All this because Rastin had prescribed a heart.

The rose was an obvious choice. One that, because of what it represented to me, might find the strength to hold. Stephanie, after all, had brought the flowers here. And last night, at my devising, we two had been surrounded by roses, their heady scent assailing us, filling the moments I had stolen with her.

"Yes," snickered Envy, "but he very nearly stole more than mere moments."

"She very nearly let him, too," replied Spite, scandalized. "Imagine what she will say—what she will *do*—when she learns the truth?"

"You mean that she was nearly kissed by the only true monstrosity among us?"

The two of them dissolved into titters. But, too preoccupied with the weight of my decision, I had little care available to give their words.

The rose. Miraculously, it had not died as I'd feared it might when I'd touched it. More importantly, it had not withered upon my bringing it into my world.

Nothing on my side of Moldavia lived. Nothing but the moths that had been summoned to coexist with me as yet another constant torment. Nothing until now.

If only *she* could live here.

"He is having a dangerous thought," whispered Spite to Envy.

And she was, of course, correct.

Even as Valor, it appeared I was not immune to these feelings. Even now I missed her. Yearned for her presence. To hear her say my name.

Undone by her so thoroughly, I had failed even to tell her one thing of true consequence. Yet there was some solace in the fact that I had, as Valor, possessed enough courage to beseech Rastin's intercession.

Which was why I needed to implant the heart. The rose.

For him to make another attempt at what he liked to assume would be my deliverance, his plan required my soul to be all in one place. Yet my soul was in shambles for a reason. Why risk attempting to focus it now? What if Rastin was wrong? What if I was better off as I was while I waited for his arrival? Empty? Splintered. Scattered.

The hearts—objects not meant to harness a soul—*always* gave. As a result, the masks, having been silenced for that time, all came bursting out of dormancy to rain down on me, all of them all at once seeking their revenge. And to take hold . . .

This rose. Would its implantation put Wrath to bed for long

enough? Rastin had promised he would come soon but . . . when? What if he was delayed?

But then . . . what if he was right?

What if Wrath, or any other mask, overpowered me?

After all, they all wanted what I did. Unfettered by reason, though, which one of them would not find a way to *take* it? Take *her*.

She would hate me then.

Decided, I grasped the rose.

"*Don't*," warned Envy.

"Remember what it cost you last time?" hissed Spite.

Ignoring them both, determined not to buy into their warnings— my own nagging doubts—I allowed my fingers to find the buttons of my waistcoat.

"He's going to do it!" cried Envy, her voice shrill with a panic that was more my own than hers. "I told you! Didn't I tell you?"

"The pain," said Spite. "It will be so much worse . . ."

Resolute, I took the rose and snapped from its stem the half-unfurled bloom.

"It *will* break," said Envy.

My waistcoat open, I paused at the task of unbuttoning Valor's white dress shirt.

And here was where I wavered.

Because Envy was right.

My heart. It would break. Just as all the others had. Perhaps this time, though, it would rupture even as soon as I inserted it.

Because Stephanie was *not* here with me. And could *never* be.

Deep down, didn't I understand that was the true reason for the pain?

Valor, though. *Without* a heart, was he strong enough to protect her? Was Erik strong enough? He had been strong enough last night. Both to stop me from sealing our fate with a kiss that could only have driven me mad and to conspire toward my own destruction.

Closing my hand around the rose, I crushed it, deciding anew that Valor *was* strong enough. And that I was, too.

That, for the time being, we would have to be.

THIRTY-ONE

Stephanie

I hadn't planned on going to the dance. I wouldn't have, either, if Dad hadn't point-blank made me. But I wasn't sorry I was here now, parked just two cars down from Lucas's Dart.

The good news was that, in exchange for agreeing to "get out of the damn house already," I'd been able to make Dad promise to take Charlie to dinner at Chuck E. Cheese. Which would get them out of the house for a while, too.

Also, there *was* the really shiny silver lining that I was going to get to see Lucas. I'd seen him at school yesterday and the day before, but only fleetingly since he and Charlotte had spent lunch rehearsing again. I'd stayed away this time, granting them space due to the competition being so close. I'd been thinking about him all day today, though, resisting the urge to text him since I knew he had to be prepping for tonight. Was he nervous about competing? If he wasn't scared to go charging into haunted mansions that had played host to several fatalities, then maybe not.

Again, I'd flip-flopped during the drive here on whether or not to tell him about Erik. Really, though, how could I? Now that

Erik had almost kissed me. Like *that* wasn't going to be an awkward conversation.

Yeah, hey, Lucas, I realize that you and I might be a thing, buuuut remember that Erik guy you told me about? He's approximately twenty times more smolder-y than described and, just FYI, I think he has a thing for me. Also, I almost let him lay one on me in a dream. Anyway, I'm not sure if I should feel guilty about it, because it's still not clear if you and Charlotte do more than just slow dance together.

I sighed. Loud and long, grabbing Charlie's drawing from where I'd laid it in the passenger seat. Marring the white page like an angry wound, an antlered skull-faced figure in red glowered up at me.

Though my sister's recounting of her latest conversation with the thing had repeated itself umpteen times in my head, the meaning still evaded me. I could have pressed her. But I didn't want to make whatever was happening more real for her than it already was. Instead, what I *wanted* to do was take this drawing in with me to show Lucas.

I shouldn't bother him with it tonight, though. Certainly not during his competition, which was looking like a way bigger deal than what had been sold to me.

Vehicles packed the gravel-and-grass lot, and the lit-up barn glowed like the jack-o'-lanterns set up on the surrounding bales of hay.

Inside the barn's mouthlike door, girls and guys my own age mingled with women and men in their twenties and thirties. While the men sported slacks and vests, bow ties and suspenders, the women wore floral-print dresses that matched kerchiefs tied around their heads, or flowers tucked into short, vintage dos.

For a moment, I panicked. Lucas hadn't mentioned a dress code. Not that I owned a single silk flower barrette anyway. I'd waited to leave the house until Charlie and Dad were secured in his truck, and though I wasn't late because of it, I certainly didn't have time now to go home and change out of my tight-fitting dark-wash jeans, short leather jacket, boots, and black boatneck blouse. Wes had said the party would be in a *barn*, after all.

Start time had been stated as eight p.m., and my dashboard clock had just flipped to read eight forty-five.

Okay, so I *was* late.

Making the executive decision *not* to show Lucas the drawing tonight, I tucked it into the glove box. Then, hoping I hadn't missed his and Charlotte's number, I let myself out of the car and trekked up to the barn doors, over which hung strands of orange and purple Christmas lights.

Within, big bourbon barrels served as drink tables while rows of hay bales provided bench seating. Farther away, against one wall, wheelbarrows filled with ice and old-fashioned glass-bottle colas flanked a long table packed with autumn goodies.

More lights wound around the support beams and rafters, and at the far end of the barn, to the right of the dance floor, the live swing band played at a breakneck pace.

The band had a singer, too—a woman in bright red patent leather pumps, matching lipstick, and a black cherry-dotted dress. She jived in place as she sang, her smoky voice all "daddy" this and "baby" that.

Nearly everyone in the barn had gathered to watch the competition from the perimeter of the dance floor, whooping and whistling their encouragement and, whenever a girl went popping into my view from over their heads in an aerial, shouting with awe.

Woooow. O-kay. Were there different levels to this thing? These had to be the pros.

I scanned the barn's interior but didn't see anyone from SPOoKy. So I sidled up to the edge of the crowd, where different perfumes and colognes mixed with the scent of straw, cinnamon, and cider.

And suddenly, among the competitors, I spotted them. Lucas and Charlotte.

Seeing them standing together at the edge of the wood floor, the next in a queue of couples waiting their turn to dance, I couldn't help a grin. Lucas looked *good*, clad in a smart vest and lemon-colored tie, black straight-legged trousers, and his saddle shoes, the number ten fastened to the cuff of one leg. He clapped along with the beat, his eyes alight with excitement, locked on the couple currently strutting their stuff. That was, until the pair started to shuffle out of the way.

And then Lucas tugged a beaming Charlotte onto the open floor.

My grin faltered as the skirt of Charlotte's dress, as short as it was yellow, whirled out as Lucas twirled her, her equally yellow Keds carrying her away from him and then close again. *Really* close.

They latched hands, rotating as a unit, Lucas's free arm going to Charlotte's waist as though to keep the centrifugal force of their whirling from sending her careening into the band.

As I drifted closer to the scene, wading through the crowd of onlookers, the tension in my chest wound even tighter.

"Wow" did not begin cover the acrobatic spectacle playing out before me. And damn did they look *amazing* together. Like a couple who had just jitterbugged out of a time machine—Lucas with his hair a total mess from all the action, Charlotte with her poison-berry lipstick and Marilyn Monroe smile.

They were in the zone.

Until Charlotte's eyes drifted to where I stood.

The moment our eyes met, her smile became less exuberant.

But then I couldn't see her face anymore, because Lucas had hauled her toward him again, ducking low as she braced her hands on his shoulders. Then his hands disappeared up her skirt. He lifted and Charlotte went airborne, her legs opening to allow her to clear Lucas's head leapfrog style as he pitched her up and over—like someone tossing away a paper cup.

With more poise than a cat, Charlotte landed on her feet. Grinning once again, she ended their dance with victory fist pump to the air. Lucas laughed and smoothed his tousled hair as they jogged off the floor hand in hand.

The tightness in my chest puddled away, twisting into a cold knot in my stomach. I shut my eyes, trying to block out the memory of something that was only, I *knew*, a dance maneuver.

Physics. It was just . . . physics.

"You okay?" came a low voice to my left. "You look a little nauseous."

I opened my eyes and, forcing myself to smile, turned to regard Wes, who peered down at me through a cautious side-eye. Though I wasn't sure what Wes's visit would bring, I was sort of glad I was no longer the only one here who didn't look like she'd popped out of a Humphrey Bogart film.

"I'm fine," I said. "Just a bit of a . . . headache."

Augh. Why was I lying to Wes?

"How come you don't do this, too?" I gestured to the dance floor, trying to deflect. The music had slowed now, allowing the competitors a break and the novices a chance on the floor.

"Why, Miss Armand, are you asking me to dance?"

"What?" I needed to backtrack. "*No.*"

"I accept." Taking my hand, Wes began to weave his way through the crowd to the dance floor.

"Wes," I protested, yanking. "I told you, I don't know how to dance."

He paused to glance back at me, his silken black hair catching a violet glow from the party lights. "You don't have to dance. Just drape your fine self languidly over my fine self and let me sway you."

Had the circumstances been different, I probably would have told Wes to back off and take a hike. But I had no idea where Lucas had gone. So what else was I going to do? Stand around and look pitiful?

Surprising myself, I allowed my free hand to float up and perch on Wes's shoulder. As I did, I looked toward where the row of competing dancers had stood.

"C'mon, work with me here, Armand," Wes leaned down to whisper. "You want to speed this all up, then don't let him see you looking for him."

I tensed, ready to pull away, but he held on, keeping me close.

"*Relax,*" he urged. "I'm not trying to steal you. Just like I know you're not really into dancing with me."

"You don't have to say it like *that*. Dancing with you is fine. And wait, speed *what* up?"

"I saw you when you came in," he said, giving another shrug. "And let's just say . . . I get it."

He paused to twirl me. With some annoyance, I went along with the spin. Then Wes drew me into him again, bringing our bodies flush. "Here's hoping he saw that one, huh?" Biting his bottom lip, Wes waggled his dark brows at me.

I rolled my eyes, unable to stifle a laugh.

"Thaaaat's the ticket, Armand," he said. "Go on. Say yes to the Wes."

"*Hey.*"

I jumped as Lucas appeared at our side from nowhere.

"Greetings, my liege," said Wes, though he never broke his stare from mine. "Stephanie and I were just . . . catching up."

"Yeah. Mind if I cut in?"

For the span of several seconds, Wes kept his eyes trained on me. He winked. "Who gives this woman to be joined in slow, sultry dancing? Reluctantly, I do."

Scowling at Wes, Lucas slid into his spot.

"One more thing." Wes inserted an arm between us, issuing each of us a hard glare. "Don't forget to leave room for the Holy Spirit."

With that, Wes departed, heading toward the snack table, where I caught sight of Patrick chatting up a cute girl wearing a rival school sweatshirt. Next to him stood a perturbed-looking Charlotte.

A warm, almost burning hand came to rest at the base of my spine while the trumpets wailed low, cymbals ticked a soft beat, and someone plucked an upright bass.

Lucas took my hand and swayed me from one foot to the other.

All around us, other couples executed saucier and more daring moves, the men sending the women into perilously low dips, the women sliding up close to the men, hooking a leg around one of theirs, tango style.

Lucas's cologne—subtle, sharp, and masculine—blended with the underlying scent of his skin and sweat, the mixture taunting me. We turned together, and somewhere in the midst of the rotation, he drew me snug against him—closer than during our impromptu stairwell dance lesson. The sensation of our hips pressed together made me dizzy.

"When did you come in?" Lucas asked. "I kept looking for you."

So. Charlotte hadn't told him I was here.

"Just now," I said. "Well. A few minutes ago. I mean . . . I saw you guys."

"Oh, you saw us?" Lucas brightened.

"Yeah. You guys are . . . kind of amazing." Could he detect the jealousy in my voice? "How long have you two been, uh, doing this?"

"Since grade school," he said. "My mom owns a dance studio."

"Whoa." He and Charlotte had been practicing and performing together almost their whole lives. And it showed.

I don't know why, but in my head, this dancing hobby of theirs had been one thing. A somewhat corny, old-school, kitschy, niche thing. Like square dance or polka. Something seniors did on the weekends. Not a pop-up, in-your-face, socially accepted metaphor for sex.

"I was starting to think you weren't going to come tonight," he said.

"How could I miss it?" I asked, because with Charlotte watching from wherever she was while Lucas swayed me, I could now assume they weren't together. Though it remained a mystery why she still seemed to despise me.

"Because you've got a lot going on," he said. "Helping your dad with the house. Keeping watch over Charlie. The house itself."

A small smile curled my lips, and new warmth spread through me, because it suddenly occurred to me that Lucas must have been watching the door for me since the start of this thing, scanning the crowd for my face, and holding on to the hope that I *would* make it here tonight. Not just the barn and the party but *here*, meaning his arms.

"I can't stop thinking about you," he said. "Truth be told, I can't stop *worrying* about you, either."

Turning my head, I let my eyes fall shut as I pressed my cheek to his chest.

"Your friend," I said, relishing in the feel of his silk tie against my skin, the underlying heat of him, and the steady thump of his heart. "Please tell me you heard from him."

"It's getting worse," he guessed, his tone dropping, anxiety squeezing his voice.

Scowling to have my bliss obliterated just before it could fully be born, I opened my eyes again. I frowned and blinked, though, distracted by a glimpse of Charlotte in the crowd.

Hold up. Was she dancing with . . . *Wes*?

"Rastin hasn't gotten back to me yet, but I'm still hoping he will soon."

Lucas's words caused my head to snap forward. My eyes burrowed holes into his tie, which I now had the urge to yank so I could bring him down to my level.

"*What* did you just say?"

"It's possible he hasn't gotten my message," Lucas said. "There wasn't an email listed, so I sent it through the contact form on his website. He probably gets tons of messages. But I'm hoping he'll respond to mine ASAP since I put Moldavia in all caps in the subject line."

"Wait. You're telling me you messaged *Rastin*? As in the moth-regurgitating wonder Rastin?"

"Y-yeah. Sorry. I-I probably should have told you that's who I meant."

Probably?

"You never said you knew him!"

"No," Lucas said, "I—I don't. I mean, I *did* meet him once at the Mid-South Paranormal Convention a couple of years ago. He signed my EMF detector . . ."

I dropped my arms from Lucas's and took a step back. "You messaged a famous medium about my house."

"Is that . . . not okay?"

Not if it meant the media or some paranormal TV show crew was going to come parading over our lawn or knocking on our door. Dad would go *nuclear*.

"You really think he's going to respond?" I asked, because what else could I say? The trigger had already been pulled.

"If . . . if Moldavia wasn't a hoax," said Lucas, his hand held out for mine like he was hoping I'd step back into the spot I'd left, "then . . . how could he not?"

Maybe because he'd almost *died*? Seriously. Was Lucas legitimately from Mayberry?

"Lucas," I began, but stopped when a certain yellow-bedecked someone sidled up next to him.

"Hey," Charlotte said, glowering at me as she spoke to Lucas. "Stephanie needs a drink. Don't you, Stephanie?"

Lucas's hands went to his hips. "Char—"

"You're being really rude," said Charlotte, giving him a shove. "Look at her, she's parched. Don't worry. I'll keep her company till you're back."

Lucas dropped his arms, his shoulders knitting. Again, he opened his mouth to argue with her, but she shot him a glare and he pivoted toward the drink station. Charlotte, in turn, spun to regard me, her eyes full of something that scared me.

"Do you know why I'm here?" she asked.

"Be . . . cause you hate me?"

"Close," she said. "I'm here because I hate that look on my best friend's face. The one he was wearing just now? Yeah. FYI. That's not going to fly."

I folded my arms, irritated, beyond confused, and maybe a little embarrassed.

"Like he's all smiles whenever he's tiptoeing around you," I said. Because why not add defensive to the list?

She rolled her eyes at me, and just when I'd thought I'd gone too far—poked the ponytailed bear past the point of fury—Charlotte laughed.

"Please. You think we don't talk?" she challenged. "You think I don't know your hair smells like the 'ocean at midnight' or whatever? Even though I told him that's probably just coconut curl cream."

Hold up. Lucas talked about me? That way? To *Charlotte*?

I opened my mouth to ask the question I hadn't even finished formulating in my head yet, but Charlotte held up a hand, stopping me.

"Here's the rundown on me and him," she said, like she'd read my mind. "We dated over the summer. That was awkward sauce, and it didn't work out. Now he's smitten with you, and you're all I ever get to hear about."

"But you—"

"I didn't like you because I thought you were judgy, and fake," she prattled on. "But Lucas says you're cool and that your house might actually be a portal to hell after all, and I realize that's gotta suck. So I'm over it, and if we end up getting along—no promises— you're going to lend me that jacket."

I shook my head, trying to keep up. And to believe my ears.

"Also," she said, hand going to her hip as she cocked it to one side. "I don't know what's going on with you two, but he's coming back now, so here it is, simple as I can put it. Move in or move on, but don't mess with him, and don't break his heart."

Lucas reappeared then, the warning glare in Charlotte's shimmer-shadowed eyes intensifying on me before shifting to him. "Is that cider?"

"Y-yes?" he said.

Snagging the drink, Charlotte then took a sip. "As you were," she said. Then she stalked off, taking the cider with her.

"God." Lucas ran a hand through his hair again.

"She . . . um. Just that she likes my jacket."

"Listen," he said. "I have to go after this song. They're going to start semifinal rounds. But before anyone else can interrupt, I wanted to ask you if . . . next weekend. I mean, I know you're really busy, but . . . well, I was wondering if we could, er—we as in you and me. Like . . . *just* you and me. If we could—"

"Yes," I said.

"Uh. Wh—I haven't even—"

"The answer's yes," I repeated. "Whatever it is. I . . . I'd love to."

A smile, huge, broke onto Lucas's face. "Wow. Really?"

"Yeah," I said, his smile spawning one of my own. How could it not when, thanks to Charlotte, I now knew exactly where I stood with him? In a place that, despite Charlotte's pending approval, just so happened to be right where I wanted.

"That's . . ." He laughed. "That's great."

Taking my hand, he drew me into him again, as close as before, his warmth—in every sense of the word—enveloping me.

A modicum of peace settling over me for the first time in days, I again laid my cheek against his chest, within which his heart beat with a more frantic rhythm. I grinned once more. Had he been that nervous? Or was he just that glad? Maybe he was both.

Lucas turned us with the music, and as he did, I spotted Charlotte, stationed once again at her post near the snack table.

Our eyes met and she lifted her cider to me in a "that's more like it" gesture before draining the drink . . . and marching away.

♪ ♩ ♪

THAT NIGHT WHEN I got home, I of course had to give Dad the rundown.

Yes, I had fun. Yes, there were a lot of people there. *Yes,* Lucas and I danced. Yes, I would be seeing him again—on Friday, if that was okay—and yes, actually, it *would* be a date.

After making a show of deliberating, Dad—who seemed secretly glad about the whole thing—gave his blessing. More questions had predictably followed after that, though. Like where we would be going, if Lucas would be picking me up, if I'd made Lucas aware of my midnight curfew. Oh, and if Lucas had tried to kiss me yet.

"No offense," I told him, helping to gather some of the day's debris into a trash bin, "but that's kind of none of your business."

"Yeah," echoed Charlie from behind her tablet. "That's kind of none of your business."

"Skywalker better watch himself," Dad said.

"In case you forgot, you like Lucas," I reminded him.

"That was before he tried to kiss you."

"Oh my gosh," I said, giving in. "He did not try to kiss me, okay? There was no kissing." Which was the truth. Because after Lucas and Charlotte had placed first in the competition, the five of us had all walked out to the gravel parking lot together, everyone laughing and celebrating. While Patrick and Wes debated over which piece of equipment SPOoKy should use the prize money to invest in, Charlotte and Lucas had gushed together about the other dancers, and how they'd only narrowly won against the couple from Radcliffe.

I had meandered behind everyone, trailing along like a party

balloon, content that even though I wasn't part of the group officially, I officially wasn't *apart* from it, either. How would that change
after this coming week? After tonight, I felt it was bound to.

"No kissing?" Dad had asked next. "Really?"

"Really," I promised.

"Huh," came Dad's reply. Followed by the infuriating response
of "Well, what the heck's the matter with him?"

Shortly after that, I gathered up a sleepy Charlie, glad Dad
had let her stay up to wait for me instead of putting her into her
bed. After brushing our teeth, we both retreated to my room, and
Charlie, who for better or worse was now becoming accustomed
to the new sleeping arrangement, nestled into her usual spot with
Checkers.

As I lay next to her, staring at the same old two crisscrossing
cracks in my ceiling, I let my mind wander back to my dad's question.

If Lucas had been given the chance tonight, *would* he have kissed
me? Maybe a better question was if kissing was part of his plans for
Friday.

The thought of him leaning down to press his lips softly to mine
made my skin tingle. Until, suddenly, my thoughts circled back on
themselves, flying in reverse through time to another boy who *had*
tried to kiss me.

Erik.

Would I finally see him tonight? What would I say to him if I
did?

I'd have to tell him about me and Lucas. Which probably meant
I'd have to tell Lucas about Erik now.

The quiet of the house settled around me, the silence broken only by my sister's rhythmic breathing. Rolling my head to one side, I eyed the closet door, which I'd made sure to shut before climbing into bed. I willed it to stay that way, simultaneously trying not to think about the figure from my sister's drawing.

Erik. Two nights ago, he'd tried to tell me something and hadn't gotten to.

Though he'd also said he shouldn't have "dared" to come to me again, I had to believe he would still eventually return. He'd already admitted to caring about me. In a weird way that I didn't fully understand, I guessed I'd come to care about him, too. Enough so that I had meant what I'd said about wanting to help him.

He'd said the music that I'd found was his, alluding also to the fact that he'd physically written it.

I am not a ghost.

Erik's words rang through my head, suggesting things I didn't like to think about. Still, he couldn't have meant that the stories, the ones Lucas had told us, were true. Could he?

"Erik," I said under my breath. Could he hear me? "We need to talk."

I watched the closet door, waiting for something to happen. It never did, though. Still, I kept watching, all the way up until my eyelids grew heavy and at last . . . fell.

THIRTY-TWO
Zedok

"She's been home for some time now."

Seated on the wicker settee, surrounded by the gnarled vines of my sister's long-dead roses, I peered toward the doorway, within which stood the mask who had spoken.

He wore a black-and-white ensemble of medieval nobility complete with an ostentatiously plumed hat. His mask, which resembled the painted black-and-white face of a court jester, bore the most malicious of grins. Between his hands, he shuffled a deck of cards, white as the snow that blustered in behind him.

"Care to know where she was?" asked the mask.

"No," I said, regretting that I had chosen the conservatory this evening for a hideaway. My masks tended to stay away from here, but there also happened to be only one door. A door that this mask now blocked.

"Yes, you do," the mask said, sending the cards rushing from one black-gloved hand to the other in a rapid, streaming shuffle. "Or else I wouldn't be here."

"I've no interest in games," I said to the mask. "Go away, Guile."

"Perhaps I will," he said as he spread his arms with the softest jangle of hidden bells. "After a while."

Irritation rankled me. Because though I had come out here to be away from the house and, more importantly, Stephanie, the mask spoke true. I *did* want to know where Stephanie had been that evening. But then . . . wasn't that because I already suspected?

"I heard her and her father talking through the walls a short while ago," said Guile. "Turns out she has been to a dance." He formed the cards into a fan and gave himself a fluttering waft. "Bet you can't guess with who."

He plucked one card from the lot and held it out to me, back-first.

"I don't care," I said.

"Yes, you do," repeated Guile, who flipped the card to reveal the knave of hearts. "We *all* care. You're just the only one who doesn't *want* to."

"I'm the only one who knows I *shouldn't*," I snapped, even though the conversation could only prove circular from here, as they all inevitably did.

"That you shouldn't doesn't mean you don't," mused Guile. "But then, why shouldn't you care?" he challenged. "Because you're dead? Because you're a walking nightmare? Because your face is—"

"Enough," I said, standing. "Leave, or I shall make you."

"Make me, and I shall return."

What was the purpose of this torment? Guile had to know he could not win in a match against Valor. He could not possibly be here with the hopes of besting me and transposing masks.

"What is it that you want?" I asked him.

"You know what I want," said Guile, his voice dropping low.

Again, he shuffled the cards and plucked another from the deck. He held it out to me, back-first once more. "And this time, you don't even need to guess, do you?"

Without waiting for a response, he flipped the card, revealing a dark-haired queen of hearts. I dropped my gaze from the card, willing myself not to acknowledge the identity of who it represented.

"She will see him again," I said. A question masquerading as an observation.

"Soon," answered Guile as he stepped my way, the queen of hearts extended to me. "Quite soon, in fact."

"It doesn't matter," I reminded myself, for I *did* have a plan.

"Mm, yes, the plan," Guile replied to my thought, halting his approach, causing the extended card to vanish with a flick of his wrist. "Listen. *About* that . . ."

THIRTY-THREE

Stephanie

I hadn't been asleep for long before my eyes opened.

I wasn't sure what made them pop wide, the sleep in them gone in an instant.

Most likely, it had been the cold that had settled over me, emanating from the place where Charlie had been sleeping next to me. *Had* been. But no longer was.

My metal-framed bed creaked as I pushed myself into a sitting position.

Immediately, my gaze went the floor, where I had found Charlie coloring early yesterday morning. Though her crayons lay scattered about, *she* wasn't anywhere to be seen.

"Charlie?" I murmured, half stumbling out of bed to face the closet door, which stood closed, just like I'd left it. I tore it open. Nothing. Cracked plaster and emptiness.

I hurried out of my room, my feet carrying me fast in the direction of my sister's pitch-black doorway. Grasping the banister overlooking the chandelier and the foyer, I halted with a gasp. Clad in her pajamas, Charlie stood below, her small form bathed in the night's blue-tinted gloom.

"Charlie," I said as I rounded the top newel. From there, I hurried down the steps to my sister's side. Kneeling next to her, I grabbed her by the shoulders and spun her to face me.

Though I'd expected to find her in some sleepwalking state since it wasn't like her to wander at night, I instead found her fully awake, Checkers dangling by a tentacle from one hand. She blinked at me, brows arching to vanish beneath her bangs.

"What are you doing down here?" I asked, smoothing her hair, my panic subsiding.

Instead of answering, she pointed to the pocket doors leading into the parlor.

"What?" I said, "What is it?" I stood slowly, taking my sister's hand as I did. "Did he come back? Did you see him in there this time?"

"Don't you hear it?" whispered Charlie, her fingers giving mine a squeeze. "Listen."

I stilled and, staring through the open pocket doors and into the silent, darkened parlor, I did as she said . . . and listened.

For a long moment, nothing happened. Then, just when I'd been about to pick up Charlie so that I'd have her in my arms, a single faraway piano note reverberated from within the parlor.

A small gasp escaped my lips. A week ago, I might have been more shocked by the sound. But the note was too similar to the one I'd heard the other day when I'd come home to find my angel on the mantel. Though I hadn't gotten the chance to ask Erik in the last dream if he'd been the one to move the figurine, I now had to assume it was him. He'd confirmed his had been the form I'd glimpsed under that sheet, so wasn't it safe to assume he'd been the one to play the piano note?

As though in answer, the note sounded again. Low, long, and resonant, it reverberated through the room. Still, its ringing didn't fill the space like the out-of-tune note that day had. Instead, beautiful and mellow, it seemed to come from . . . somewhere else.

"You hear it, don't you?" Charlie asked, giving my arm a tug.

I glanced down to her, into those big eyes that begged for reassurance and for some sign that she wasn't alone in her experiences anymore.

"I hear it," I told her, my voice shaking.

"It keeps going," she said, her own voice calm and wondering.

Erik. Could it be he'd heard me whisper his name? What was he trying to tell me? Something, apparently, that couldn't be said in a dream.

"Charlie," I whispered. "I want you to stay right here, do you understand?"

She nodded, her hand relaxing in my grip, as if the repeating note held some kind of hypnotizing power over her.

Stepping away from my little sister, our hands parting, I drifted into the parlor, my steps slow and measured. I kept my gaze locked on the covered piano. Muffled, the repeated note seemed to come through the walls while also resonating from the area in which the piano sat. Except that, broken and ruined, the piano under the sheet could not have produced such a sound.

I stopped in front of the instrument, my eyes scanning the seat and the covered keyboard, searching for any sign of movement. There wasn't any, though.

"Erik?"

All at once, as if in speaking the spirit's name I had dispelled him, the sound stopped. I waited for the note to begin again. When it didn't, I let my hand, trembling, drift toward the cloth covering the piano. One tug was all it took for the drop cloth to fall, revealing the skeletal and wrecked thing that, like the rest of our house, had once, long ago, been something majestic.

"Erik," I said, softer now because I didn't want Charlie to hear me talking to no one. "If that was you . . . can you give me a sign?"

Nothing. Except . . . a new sound. That of gentle ticking.

I turned my head slowly toward the fireplace, the perceived source of this new almost-noise. Our mantel didn't hold a clock.

But then . . . didn't Erik's?

THIRTY-FOUR
Zedok

"**W**e heard you talking," said Guile. "You and the medium. Did you think we wouldn't?"

Of course, I *did* know the masks would have heard. Even in the midst of colluding with Rastin, I'd understood that few other parts of myself would want the plan to transpire.

"It is the only way," I said.

"It is not," argued Guile, who approached by another step. "By the by, I feel obliged to inform you that we all find it incredibly rude that you chose not to consult a single one of us regarding your plot."

"Oh?" I remarked, almost wanting to laugh.

"Yes. Wrath in particular was quite put out."

Wrath. Why had I not seen him since that night he had appeared before me in the parlor? I kept waiting for his strike—anticipating that it might come at any moment. But, if what Guile was saying was true, why was he here in Wrath's stead? Out of all my masks, Guile presented the *least* threat.

"Ah," said Guile, once again latching on to my unspoken thought. "That may be true. But isn't it always the least threatening part of ourselves that offers the most ominous the opportunity to operate? A mask for our masks. A wild card, if you would." With another flourish, he produced a joker card. "And don't you suppose it would then be true to say that I, by proxy, would be *the* most dangerous? To Valor, at least."

I frowned at both him and his most recent selection from his deck, not liking the suddenly dizzying turn of this conversation. Done with Guile, I moved to pass him. He skittered to block my path, arms outheld, the absurd feather on his hat dancing.

"Stand aside, Guile."

"You cannot go yet. Because, well . . . you see, we are going to take her."

"What are you on about?"

"That is why the others sent me. To tell you it will happen tonight."

Was there truly some part of me as idiotic as this?

"You see," Guile hurried to explain, "with the medium on his way, and you dithering over a heart, and the boy so close to stealing hers . . . Well, when might we ever again get another chance?"

Thoroughly done with his antics, I drew my sword and brandished it at the mask.

"I'll not tell you to stand aside a second time," I said. "Go scurry back to the others. Tell them what you already know. That it is useless to try to convince me."

"Why, Valor," said Guile through a short laugh, "whoever said we needed *you*?"

THIRTY-FIVE

Stephanie

Scowling, I left the piano, and as I approached the mantel, the ticking grew louder. I went all the way up to the place where I'd found my angel. And there, I stared at the patch of paper-peeled wall from behind which issued the ticking.

Tick, tock, tick, tock.

Tilting one ear toward the sound, I leaned in, certain of what I was hearing but equally sure it couldn't be real.

"Charlie," I whispered to my sister. "Do you hear the—?"

Wham!

I yelped, spinning away from the mantel to face the pocket doors that had slammed themselves closed, shutting me in.

On the other side of them, Charlie screamed.

THIRTY-SIX
Zedok

The child's shriek—it ripped clear and sharp through the night, coming from the house.

"*Charlie?*"

"Your turn now, Valor!" chortled Guile as he unleashed his deck at me.

Panicked, I charged through the flurry of cards—all faces—shoving aside Guile as I did. He laughed and staggered out of my way, putting up no fight whatsoever—something that terrified me almost as much as Charlie's cry.

THIRTY-SEVEN

Stephanie

"Charlie!" I hurried to the doors but halted in my tracks when, just as swiftly as they'd come crashing together, they flung themselves apart.

My breath caught at the sight of the foyer that lay before me. Even in the midnight dark, I could tell it wasn't ours. Not with its beautiful wood paneling that gleamed in the cold glow of soft silver moonlight. What was happening?

I switched from foot to foot, fighting with the impulse to rush through those doors again, because that's where I'd left Charlie. But Charlie wasn't there anymore.

"Charlie?" I called into the foreign foyer, my voice ringing through the house-within-a-house that Charlie had already tried to tell me about. She had seen it, too. Through the doorway of her closet.

"Steph-nie?" rang Charlie's petrified voice from right in front of me, but as muffled and distant as the repeated piano note and the ticking clock had been. Instinct taking over, I surged forward, straight across the threshold and into the house that was not ours.

Unthinking, I dashed across the foyer and into an opulent dining room with walls swathed in smooth and seamless scarlet and gilt-leaf paper. Four high-backed chairs surrounded a cleared and polished table. One long enough to hold a body. A mummy.

Dazed, I retreated from the room with a whimper. Panic then nipped at my sanity, threatening to devour my whole mind the moment I found myself once again facing the closed pocket doors. I went to them, throwing them apart myself this time.

But our parlor was gone—changed to mirror, in every detail, the lavish one from my dream with Erik. All except for the bay window, which, instead of showing a world of nothing, now displayed one of whiteness. *Snow* blanketed the grounds, huge tufts of it falling at a breakneck pace to fill the sill.

Tick, tock, tick went the black clock now situated centermost on the mantel.

The parlor. If . . . if I went back inside. If I shut the doors and opened them again, would that take me back? Desperation rising to shunt my fear aside, I moved to cross the threshold.

I froze, though, paralyzed by sudden movement in the darkened hallway, and I turned my head to find something lurking there, watching me from within the shadows.

A silhouetted figure.

With lights for eyes.

THIRTY-EIGHT
Zedok

Had I possessed the capacity to breathe, I would have stopped forever at that instant.

Lips parted and eyes wide, Stephanie Armand herself stood in the flesh before me, inexplicably transported to my side of Moldavia. Terrified, she watched me in silence, the glow from the winter moon streaming in through the stained glass encompassing her in the most befitting of halos. Even locked within the grips of alarm, she was beautiful.

She saw me now, though. At last she believed. But what she saw—no doubt it was the source of her terror.

"Stephanie," I said, forcing myself to formulate words. "How did you get here?"

At the sound of my voice, she stiffened. Her frame, now ramrod straight, became still as death, her face white as talcum.

"*Erik?*" she whispered with barely any voice at all.

"Yes," I told her, uncertain of what else to say, though petrified of what this interlude would lead to next. Somehow, working outside of my cognizance, the masks had conspired to lure her onto this side. And now where were they? In entering the house, had I, too, fallen prey to their trap? No matter the answer, this crisis demanded of me one thing and one thing only. I had to get Stephanie back to her side *at once*.

"I don't understand," she half gasped. "This . . . this doesn't feel like another dream. Is it?"

God. What to do? What to say? If only this *was* a dream. I could go to her. I could—

"Your eyes," she said. "Charlie said—"

Knowing better than to sheath my sword, I tightened my grip on its hilt. Then, left with no alternative, I took slow steps toward her, allowing the gloom to peel back from my form. At the sight of my mask, Stephanie pressed her back into the front door, her chest rising and falling with greater frequency.

"I am not the monster," I told her. A lie. But I would have said anything to keep from triggering the utter panic that was reaching its boiling point within her. In order to return Stephanie to her side, I would need her to trust me. Allow me near enough to take her hand. "Please. You must believe me."

"Stop," she commanded, holding up a palm to me.

I complied. "Stephanie, there isn't—"

"Take off the mask," she demanded. "If it's really you, then . . . show me your face."

I stilled, an unbearable silence elapsing within the boundary of several seconds.

"That's . . . not possible," I said at last.

Her jaw setting, she pushed off from the door. Then she came at me, reaching toward me as she had in last night's dream, this time with the hopes of winning my mask. A victory I could not allow. I would have stopped her had she not halted herself, her attention stolen by something at my back.

The renewal of her terror told me who—what—it must be. Raising Valor's saber, I whirled on my enemy, but only just in time to allow his gloved hand to close over Valor's mask.

THIRTY-NINE

Stephanie

"Erik!" I shrieked, darting forward to latch on to the attacking arm of the crimson-clad figure from my sister's drawing. In the same motion in which he ripped Erik's mask free, though, he, Zedok, flung me off.

The force of the throw sent me reeling. I met the floor hands-first, my hair falling forward to obscure my view.

Even in the darkness, though, I had seen a portion of his face. Erik's.

Just the sliver of a glimpse was all I'd caught. A blur of grayish-yellow. Parchment-colored skin stretched over a jutting cheekbone.

It *was* true, then. The story. The legend of Erik's walking corpse.

A shadow fell over me, its edges encompassing the place where I half lay, half knelt on the beautiful carpet. The merest glance upward showed me that the shadow possessed antlers.

Fumbling to my feet, I lunged for the front door but cried out when a hand stopped me, taking hold of my upper arm. It spun me easily, and that silver skull mask floated nearer, visible through the screen of my tousled curls, its grinning face coming within an inch of mine.

"Did you see?" he demanded, his distorted voice a scarcely contained rattle of rage. "Did you see us?"

Us?

"Let *go* of me!" I twisted in his grip, hating how small and weak I sounded.

"No? But you *wanted* to see, did you not?" Zedok asked, cocking his head at me.

I shrieked in protest as he hauled me in front of him. Hooking an arm around my upper body, he forced me to face the hallway and the cloaked figure now kneeling within it.

Erik, his back to us, hood still up, held one hand to his face. The other searched in vain for the mask that did not lie anywhere in the path of his searching fingers.

Because it lay on the floor behind him—between us.

The skull-masked figure moved us forward. I dug my heels into the carpet and skidded, being edged against my will toward the hunched figure.

"*Look*," rumbled the voice at my back.

As we drew closer, my gaze fell to the blue-and-gold mask, which stared sightlessly—soullessly—upward.

Though I wasn't sure how, I was certain that when he got close enough, Zedok would destroy the mask. Crush it underfoot.

"Take a good look at your *Erik*!" Zedok growled again, his deep and shredded voice curdling my blood.

"Close your eyes, Stephanie," warned Erik, who kept his back turned to us. "You mustn't do as he says, or he will have us both."

I ignored them, keeping my focus on the mask.

"Turn around, Erik," I called to him.

Erik stiffened at my command, and Zedok laughed, buying me the time I needed.

I slid my foot forward, hooked the mask under my toes—and kicked it toward the huddled figure.

I didn't have time to see if the mask got to him, because, with a growl of rage, Zedok hauled me back, walking me in reverse until my spine met with the front door. His masked face hovered close to mine—so close that I could see my own frightened expression multiplied within two rows of grinning silver teeth.

"You have bought yourself but moments," he hissed. "Rest assured, though, we *will* have him. And then we will have you."

"No, you won't!" I took hold of his silver mask, and without knowing what I was doing, I tore it away.

His laughter filled the room again as the mask came free to reveal a face that was not there. Then his cloak and unraveling form dissipated into nothingness, his mask evaporating from my hand.

After that, silence—the deafening, screaming sort—resettled in the foyer, where I once again found myself alone with Erik.

He stood against the wall now, one hand gripping his chest as though in pain. The other held his mask over his face, like he feared I might try to take it again. Or that someone else—some*thing* else—would.

So. Here was his secret.

Why, though, had he told me not to look? Because he hadn't wanted me to see? Or because seeing would have cursed me, too?

I gasped for my breaths, shaking where I stood.

"You're hurt," I said, pushing aside my need to piece things together when clearly the danger wasn't over.

"My dear," he managed, "you have no idea."

The response—so distinctly Erik—made me go to him.

"Charlie," I pleaded, terror squeezing my throat, making my words tight and pinched. "I . . . she was there and then . . . when I got here . . . Please. I need to get back—"

"He cannot reach her," he answered, straightening from the wall and lowering his hand from his mask. "At least not . . . at the moment."

"He got to me," I protested. "And you."

"Stephanie," he said, his voice tense and breathy. "Do you trust me?"

The question, along with its quietness, sent a peal of warning bells ringing through me.

Instead of answering, I glanced over my shoulder, toward the dining room, where yet another dark figure now stood, this one wearing a long-beaked crow's mask, his black garb that of a highwayman. My horror grew tenfold then at the sight of several more figures lining the stairway. A jester with a harlequin mask. A woman with a grasshopper's mouthless face. Next to her, another beautifully gowned lady in a scorpion's mask. All along the banister overlooking the chandelier—and us—gathered more figures, all of them materializing out of the shadows.

"Quickly," muttered Erik. "My sword is behind you."

And that was all he needed to say. Twisting, I lunged for it. No sooner did I lay hold of its hilt, though, than the figure in the bird mask bolted toward me. I had enough time, but only enough, to toss Erik his weapon before one gloved hand took hold of me.

The bird-masked figure ripped me away, tossing me back, into

235

another figure whose mask I could not see. Those who had occupied the stairs and the second-floor landing came pouring down toward me. The whispering menagerie of masks then blurred into a kaleidoscope of crackled ivory, tarnished silver, and antique gold. Countless empty eyeholes whirred by, the repetition of my name creating a low but deafening hiss.

"Erik!" I shrieked, twisting amid the collage of false faces, searching in vain for his mask among the others. He'd vanished, though, and I couldn't get to him. Yanking myself from the grasp of one figure only resulted in my being snatched by the next.

That mask passed me to another, and then that one to another as they maneuvered me down the back hall.

As I went, an ominous tinkling drew my attention upward, to the chandelier that swayed above me. How had I been carried this far so quickly? And who were these figures? Where were they taking me?

Only when the chandelier passed out of sight did it dawn on me where we must be headed. When we entered the kitchen, I knew for sure.

Wrenching my body, I managed to swing myself around in the whispering mob, which fell suddenly silent as the cellar door opened itself wide to a vat of blackness.

"No!" I yelled, but then my instinct to fight dissolved into dumbfounded wonder as a stark white mask, that of another woman, bled through the darkness.

The girl, adorned in an elegant drop-shoulder gown of burgundy, her raven hair piled atop her head and studded with tiny roses, extended one white-gloved hand to me, as if expecting me to take it. As if she thought I'd *want* to descend with her into whatever horror waited below.

Captivated by her undeniable resemblance to me, I stopped struggling against the other masked figures so intent on bringing the two of us together.

And though I didn't dare take this figure's waiting hand, I did not try to pull away, either, when she reached to take mine.

FORTY
Zedok

I fought my way through the figures, sword-to-sword and blade-to-dagger. In each instance, I won the fray by ripping my assailant's mask free.

Despite many of them reassembling to block me a second time, I progressed in the direction Stephanie had been taken. Though I anticipated the moment Wrath himself would reappear, he never did. Why bother when he had so many masks willing to bring her *to* him?

If that were to happen, I was sure he would present me with a choice. Give in to him willingly, or have my mask again stripped away in front of her. Either scenario would doom me to become Wrath, and Stephanie's liberty would be forfeit.

Always, Wrath played to win, and now it all became clear. My resolve as Valor to see Stephanie free of this place, free of me, did outweigh his—*my*—desire to possess her forcibly. And so Wrath's aim had not been to challenge Valor outright, as I had feared. Not so much as it had been to undermine that resolve by decimating me.

He knew what I knew. That I could not have withstood the sight of Stephanie's face had she seen mine.

Valor would have cracked, and Wrath would have won me. But . . . was there truly not *one* other shard of my soul that wished for her freedom? Was there no other glimmer of light amid the shrapnel of my ravaged spirit?

It would seem not.

Delayed and parried, attacked and detained, I won my way to the kitchen at the great cost of time, certain I would find her already transported to the bowels of the house. Miraculously, though, I arrived at Stephanie's side in time, if only just.

A gentle tug on my part was all it took to dislodge the porcelain facade of the mask whose likeness and name I now could no longer deny. With the dispatching of Desire, I turned to the real Stephanie.

My plan from this point had been to flee with her, to put as much space as possible between her and the greedy hands of the distorted soul that wanted her at all costs. From there, I would fling open the first door I encountered and see her through to her side. But the execution of that plan was not to be. And this time, it was none other than Stephanie herself who thwarted my efforts. Or the efforts I would have made, if she had not, in that moment, devastated me utterly by canceling the distance between us with a swiftness I could not have stopped, her arms lifting to wind around my shoulders and draw me into the first embrace I had experienced in over a century.

Time fell away, the world as well, while within me, bliss warred with agony.

Had I ever known either of them until that instant when her fiercely beating heart crashed against my nonexistent one?

Warmth. I had forgotten what it felt like.

"Human," Rastin had called me. This moment suggested that, perhaps, against all odds, the medium was right. For human was how she made me feel.

Distantly, I became aware of the masks unfurling around us, each of them dispersing as if suddenly relieved of their power to be. Why? I could not know.

Stephanie. This girl who embraced me in spite of now knowing what I was.

She had to be the reason why.

Masks or no, though, she needed to leave.

My hands. They trailed up her arms, gloved fingers unable to help stealing a forbidden caress on their way to wrapping her wrists. With gentleness, I undid the link of her arms. That I was able to do so gave me hope. For her.

I turned from her then, staying connected to her by one hand only. With it, I drew her from the kitchen and into the darkness of the hall.

"You must go," I told her without stopping or looking back. Because I could not risk vacillating for even one more instant. Not when it was her freedom, her sanity, on the line. "You must leave here tonight. Take Charlie and your father and never return."

Hurried steps, far more certain in their purpose than I, brought us to the front door. Though she yielded and followed, I registered resistance, too. Either she did not trust me or she somehow sensed my plan to eject her from my world and was now hesitant to leave. For what reason, I could not fathom.

The masks had gone. But I was not fool enough to believe they would not return. Now was our only chance.

I gripped the front door handle and pulled open the entrance to Moldavia, hauling Stephanie through and releasing her with momentum into the glow of her own porch light.

Stephanie freewheeled into the autumn night, her beautiful dark curls flying forward to frame her stricken face. She reached for me until the moment she stumbled down from the stairs and over her front walkway.

I kept my arm extended toward her, shocked by my own action. That, after having been so close to holding her, I'd actually let her go.

"Erik!" she shrieked. "Look out!"

But I'd already felt them. The return of the masks. The innumerable hands that gripped me and drew me backward, into the house that would forever hold me prisoner.

She charged up the porch steps, concern and terror twisting her no less lovely features.

Terror for the masks. And concern . . . for *me*.

Mercy. Could I believe what I was seeing? That she would again cross the threshold of this hated place, risk life and freedom to reenter its boundaries for *my* sake?

I kicked the door shut, blocking out the sight of that expression, so wrought with distress.

The realization that she *cared* what became of me, no matter in what capacity, coupled with the knowledge that I—some version of me—had done her harm, brought with it the return of the pain.

Awful and searing, it bloomed once again from the center of my chest. I cringed beneath my mask, grasping at the spot, as though that could do anything to lessen the ache while the masks dragged me backward.

My conversation with Rastin. My resolution to try to go so that she could stay . . .

My masks had borne witness to all of this. In the same way they had overhead Stephanie's voice. The same way they had been present for all my interactions with her.

No doubt they had also relished her embrace.

They would set another trap. And keep setting them. Until they had what they wanted.

What *I* wanted.

But what I wanted was *madness*.

Madness . . .

Out of all my masks, *he* was the only one that floated. Like roiling clouds of smoke, his coal-colored silk robes swirled and wafted every which way, winding and unwinding about him.

He hovered above me now, twining the chandelier while Guile, Spite, Envy, Guilt, and Shame forced me down, struggling, to the floor, their collective laughter echoing in the cavernous space.

His whole visage, apart from the white and gold-filigreed three-faced mask itself, gave the impression of a blot of black ink that had been dropped into water. Through his nebulous form raged a lightning storm, jagged white illuminating the insides that, as was true in my instance, too, he did not possess.

The chandelier swayed as Madness circled it, trailing a gloved hand over its dripping crystals.

Until this moment, I had tried to fight against them if only to buy the Armands time. Enough to allow them to vacate the premises before I became something worse than what I was.

Delaying the inevitable seemed to be a knack I'd never lost.

Valor was doomed. And if he was, then so, too, was Rastin. So were we all if Stephanie did not do as I had instructed and seize her chance for freedom.

I wanted her to go. I wanted her to stay.

A moment ago, one wish had been stronger. Now, in her absence, the other grew to consume me.

Closing my eyes against the hisses and whispers of the masks, I did something I had not done since I was a small boy.

I prayed. To the God of the Bible, no less. My father's God.

Let her leave, I pleaded even as I opened my eyes to see the bird-masked Malice do the honor of pulling my mask free, like a magpie ripping flesh from a carcass.

The masks screamed and recoiled.

Wails of horror filled the house—mine among them.

Because of what would come next.

Please, I beseeched. *Let her leave unharmed.*

This I repeated in the mind that would soon be taken from me as well.

Because even as I willed her to take flight and never look back,

I could not bear the thought of never seeing her again.

Above, Madness's head rotated, his three-in-one face aiming itself directly toward me.

"I don't know who you think you are begging," he growled, his three distinct voices speaking at once. "No one can hear you in there. No one but us."

Madness laughed. And then he dove for me.

FORTY-ONE

Stephanie

"**N**o!" I shouted the moment the door slammed shut in my face.

Immediately, I latched on to the knob, only to find that it wouldn't twist in my grip.

Somewhere inside, Charlie wailed.

"Charlie!" I pounded the door. "Dad!"

I'd seen and felt so much that could not be explained. And now here I was. Back in the world I knew, locked out of the house I didn't.

Just when I'd decided to abandon the front door and try the back entrance, its stained-glass sidelights and transom lit up—signaling that someone had come into the foyer.

The sound of Charlie's crying grew louder. A large shadow painted the panes. The lock clicked. Then the door opened, and I found myself staring up into my father's stunned and sleep-drawn face, my little sister bawling in his arms.

Behind him lurked the stripped walls and creaky worn floors of our house.

"Where in God's name have you been?" Dad bellowed at me, furious and frightened.

"We have to go!" I said, collecting Charlie from him, her face red and streaming with tears. She clung to me, small arms wrapping me tight. "We have to get out of the house. Now!"

"Why?" he demanded. "Stephanie, what the *hell* is going on?"

Leave, Erik had said. But where were we supposed to go? More importantly, how could I convince my father to take us away?

"Dad, *please!*" I pleaded as, inside, the blazing light from the chandelier flickered a warning. "I-I'll explain everything on the way, I promise. But right now, we need to *go*."

He studied me, eyes searching.

"Fine," he said as he strode back into the house. "Stay here while I get my keys."

"Wait—" I called, cut off by the exact thing I had feared might happen if we became separated by entryways.

All on its own, the front door swung shut with sudden violence, slamming in my face.

"*Dad!*"

Charlie screamed. Shuffling her to one arm, I took hold of the doorknob. The nightmare wasn't over yet.

Inside, through the stained glass, the lights flickered a second time.

"Dad!" I shouted again, rattling the locked door in its frame. "Go out the back! Get out of the house!"

I didn't wait for his reply. Instead, clinging fast to my little sister, I tore around one side of Moldavia. Reaching the rear door, I found it wide open, like someone was playing a game with me.

"Dad?" I screamed into the house—and felt my heart immediately loosen when he came into view, his expression even more confounded as he took in the sight of the lights going haywire.

Sensing another trap, I waved him toward us.

"This way, Dad! Hurry!"

Scowling more out of confusion and irritation than fear, he started in my direction, closing the distance with a fast walk.

"Run!" I yelled too late, bits of plaster raining down on him. Then came the tinkling of crystals followed by the snick of metal snapping.

It careened into view then—plummeting straight for his head.

The ancient and dust-caked chandelier.

I took care in crossing to Stephanie's side.
Not to be seen.
To steal there. Before she could **leave**
me.

*How did we come to
the landing so fast?*

How else?
Through Charlie's closet do—   **Or**, rather, us.

*Stop. Leave your
knife
sheathed.*

I

Don't!

want to do this.

But.
How else to make her **stay**?

No. Not the chandelier.
You mustn't.

Ha ha! Yes, the chandelier!
Smashing idea!

You'll kill him.

Only if he's lucky!

Tell me.
If she is to **go**, what other choice have we?

None!
Your knife blazes.
You must

not

aim for the chain!

I
I
I

I

I
HER
There's no more time.
No matter what we now be**come**.
chhhccckkk
The chain cried only once at its severing.
Mr. Armand dove, of course. Perhaps in time. Perhaps not.

Yes. What a crescendo!
What a display!
The cacophony of crystal kissing—rending—the floor.
The light snapping of bone.
Bravo!

See what you've done.
The girls. Now they
are crying, too.

It

doesn't matter.

Not when time wasn't impo rtant to be gin w ith.
No t whe n i t was n't import a nt to m e.
N o t whe n **we**'d b e e n s o un **will** ing t o se e re as o n.
T i m e . . . B es i d es i t, w e **have** so l i t t l e l e f t.
A n d t h e h **o u r** s.
d i d s h e n o t m a k e t h e m s o m u c h m o r e b e a r a b l e ?

True. Time didn't matter. Not to me.
Not without her.
But.
It was about time, I would say.
For we'd never liked that chandelier any**way**.

FORTY-THREE

Stephanie

Charlie and I rode to the hospital in the ambulance with Dad. After the chandelier's chain had snapped, the fixture had plowed into the wood floor, landing with enough force to crash partway through.

The noise had been like an explosion. So had the impact.

Splinters and shards had flown, pelting the walls.

Running on pure adrenaline—pure panic—I'd barreled through the back entrance to where Dad lay unconscious, one leg pinned beneath the chandelier's heavy metal frame.

I hadn't really been thinking about what I was doing. I didn't even remember putting Charlie down. I'd only wanted to get to the only parent either of us had left.

I'd called 911 after that. And as soon as Dad was admitted to a triage room, because I hadn't known what else to do, I had called Lucas.

He came. Of course he came.

"Are you okay?" was the first question out of his mouth when he'd arrived in the waiting area. I'd told him over the phone that Dad had suffered a broken femur and a concussion.

If I was going to be truthful, I would need to tell him no. And that I wasn't sure I ever would be "okay" again.

There'd been only one other time in my life when I'd been less okay. And that had been the night Charlie had been born. The same night Mom had left us—all three of us—forever.

But I couldn't think of *that*. Not right now. Not if I wanted to keep the sanity that I felt fairly certain I still had.

I had Charlie in my lap, too, her little head resting against my shoulder, thumb shoved into her mouth. So I couldn't fall apart into little pieces like I had back then.

"Dad's going to be okay," I muttered at last to Lucas, who'd waited more patiently for an answer than I would have. "So . . . I'm okay."

I said this purely for Charlie's benefit. But I gave Lucas a look that I hoped conveyed all I *couldn't* say. That I was terrified. That there were things I needed to tell him with words. At the same time, I relished the sensation of his shoulder pressing into mine as well as the embrace of his jacket, which he'd insisted I wear when he saw me shivering. Could he guess that I hadn't been shivering from the cold?

Either way, the jacket calmed me. It was safe. The same way Lucas felt.

Guilt lobbed itself on top of my dog-piled emotions, telling me I should have told Lucas everything sooner. About Charlie's drawing and Erik, too. Would any of us be here now if I had?

Surprising me, Lucas took my hand. Perhaps his way of conveying that he got the gist of what I was trying to telepathically communicate.

The contact, warm and gentle, soothed the rawness inside me.

Throughout my life, people had always commented on how mature I was for my age. And maybe I was that way naturally. But after Mom passed, I hadn't really had any other choice but to grow up fast. Not when Dad stayed lost longer than me. Not when Charlie couldn't know how broken her arrival had left us.

So I'd been the one to keep us knitted together after the shattering earthquake of loss. As much as any eleven-year-old girl could. I'd learned how to change diapers. I'd done some trial-and-error laundry. I'd insisted on things like puzzle nights, and taco dates, and other things that removed us from our suddenly too-empty home. And I'd babied the baby when Dad hadn't been whole enough to attempt it.

I'd done all right. Up until tonight. When I'd finally reached the moment I'd always known would come sooner or later—though I never would have dreamed it would arrive this way. The moment when I wasn't sure I could handle being the glue. When my years of life experience and my book knowledge didn't add up to *enough*.

On the bright side, it certainly felt better not to have to face this moment alone.

I shut my eyes to stave off the tears that I'd managed to hold at bay this long. Instead of more sadness and fear, though, a gratitude so intense that I began to shake washed through me. And now, in order to keep from having a total breakdown, I had to squeeze the big warm hand that felt nothing like the last one I had clasped.

Exhausted and numb, I tried to fit some of the puzzle pieces of the nightmare together.

Zedok. He had to have been responsible for the chandelier. While that part seemed obvious, nothing else did.

All those masked figures. Who or what were they? Prisoners just like Erik?

According to Lucas and the *Paranormal Spectator* documentary, only four people counting Erik had died as a direct result of the curse. But Lucas said that the mummy-unwrapping party had taken place during a masquerade . . . Could *everyone* who had attended the party have become trapped in the house? Victims of the curse?

If that was the answer, it still didn't explain the masked girl in the cellar doorway. The one who had looked just like . . .

I glanced toward Lucas again, suddenly wanting to let everything come spilling out. Clearly, he suspected the cause of the chandelier crash. What must he be thinking?

He wasn't asking me for the same reason I wasn't telling him. And that was because of Charlie.

"Rastin," I said, my voice sounding like a stranger's to my own ears. "Tell me you heard back from him."

"Ah," Lucas said, his grasp on my hand tightening, the squeeze telling me that yes, he had been reading between the lines. "N-no."

I shut my tired eyes, allowing the force of that one word to detonate through me in a bomb of silent devastation.

Over the intercom, someone paged a doctor. Various beeps floated this way and that.

Soon, it would be morning. Dad would wake up. He would ask

me again what had happened. After that, only one thing was certain. He would insist that we, all three of us, go back to the house that Erik had told me never to enter again.

And Erik. *Poor Erik.*

I couldn't get the sight of that cheekbone out of my mind. Or forget the way his skeletal hand had clasped mine. The too-angular feel of his form when I'd flung my arms around him, pressing my body against his rail-thin one.

Dead. He was dead. But somehow . . . alive.

The horror of it caused me to convulse once, which caused Charlie to whimper and cling to me harder, and Lucas to squeeze my hand again.

Erik was still in that house. And had been since he'd died. A prisoner. Forever.

Even if I *could* somehow convince my dad to leave, how could I go knowing that Erik was still there?

"There's . . . something I forgot in the house," I said to Lucas, who slowly turned his head my way. "I have to go back for it."

"You can't," he said. "Not alone."

I fell silent at the implications.

"Your dad," Lucas said. "He'll probably be here all day. And they'll come . . . if I call them."

I gathered his meaning with the same reluctance as before.

"It's almost morning," Lucas said, his way of pressing the issue when I didn't answer. "Does Charlie have somewhere she can stay?"

Since I was still a minor, Charlie and I had to stay with a

friend's family until Dad got discharged. But I could just tell the hospital I was riding with Lucas to pick up my stuff from the house first.

Deciding to spare Lucas the details, I nodded in answer to his question.

In response, he released my hand, then walked out into the hallway to make his call.

FORTY-FOUR
Zedok

Luckily, Mr. Armand had survived the attack.

Still, though, there was no cause for relief.

Standing beneath the pristine twin of the chandelier on my side of Moldavia, in the exact place where it lay decimated on the Armands' side, I glanced to where the discarded mask of Madness lay on the floor, shuddering from the aftershocks of its defeat.

Once more, I wore the countenance of Valor. Paradoxically, our reunion was owed only to Madness, whose violent actions had brought about the one thing that could have returned me to my senses.

In inflicting injury upon Mr. Armand, I had left him and thus his family with no other choice but to come back and to stay. For where was one such as Mr. Armand to go with a broken leg? Aside from that, were not the man's savings as well as his livelihood instilled within this house?

This war against myself. As always, I stood only to lose it. The only difference now was that I had something to lose.

Rastin. Where are you?

At last, Madness's mask dissolved. Released from my fear that he would rise as soon as my back was turned and usurp me a second time, I turned on my heel and strode down the dark hallway. From there, I once again passed the threshold between worlds to enter the Armands' sunlit kitchen. Morning light glinted on the surface of the cluttered table.

In the center of the bric-a-brac and scattered papers there still dwelled the vase of roses.

Keeping my gaze on the flowers, my hand went to the cravat lacing my throat, pulling it free. Next, I undid the buttons of Valor's waistcoat.

Distress sneaking over me, calling me to stop as I had last time, I seized one of the blooms before I could convince myself to delay this dark surgery further. I snapped its head from its stem, prepared to do what I should have done. What the medium had instructed me to do. But then the ominous click of the basement door followed by the slow creak of its opening halted me.

"Shall we ever forget it?" asked a horrible voice.

I spun to find him framed in the cellar doorway, a blood-red figure backed by the blackness of our basement.

"Her voice, you mean?" I asked. Because, with the invisible barrier between houses separating us, it was safe to converse with him.

"Her arms," Wrath corrected. "Locked around us that way. Like we were more to her than what we are."

"Than what we ever could be," I said, taking my turn to correct him.

"Yes," he agreed, the calmness in his answer startling me.

"You want her that badly," I whispered. "Enough to take her by force? To keep her with you against her will?"

"I tried to tell you."

"You tried to *trick* me."

For once, his skeleton's face seemed to echo as much sorrow as it did rage. "So make me go away," he said. "Make us all go away. If you can."

"And here I'd thought you'd come to dissuade me," I remarked bitterly.

"I think we agree she must return," replied Wrath. "Bereft of Hope, you now hold in your hand your final defense. Hers. So I know what you will do. Unlike you, I do not expect Valor to behave any other way than how he must. As is true of the rest of us, you cannot help yourself."

Could it be he was being genuine? Or was he merely trying to enmesh me in some new plot? Either way, it didn't matter. Wrath was right. There were no other options left to me.

Without another word, I seated myself in one of the Armands' chairs. Keeping the rose clasped loosely in one gloved hand so as not to damage it, I then pried open with the other the final barrier of Valor's white dress shirt.

The slit made by the Egyptian priest in my lower left side still existed and so would serve as my avenue. And with no muscle or sinew, no organs or collagen to contend with, I found the contortion needed to properly place the rose within the center left of my rib cage easy enough to execute.

The moment I released my hold on the rose was the moment that flower became heart.

With a crackle of straining bone, I withdrew my arm and hand.

Though I did not have to look to know Wrath had vanished, I turned my head to peer at his doorway anyway.

It of course stood empty, the piece of my soul he represented once more quarantined within my bosom, lashed together with all the others by an object as tenuous as my certainty that in doing the only thing I *could* do . . . I had done the right thing.

FORTY-FIVE

Stephanie

After seeing Charlie off with our friend's mom, who I fed an excuse about needing to stay with Dad, I left the hospital with Lucas. And finally, during our ride to the rendezvous point with the rest of SPOoKy, I confessed to him about the interactions with Erik.

I started with the pictures I'd found in the attic. From there, I told him about meeting Erik in that first dream and how he had warned me of Zedok. I explained about finding the graves behind our house, and how Erik's name on the last one had led me to seek Lucas out. I even told him about how adamant Erik had been that I not have investigators over to the house. That Erik had admitted to being the figure under the sheet, and about the promise I'd made to Erik to free him. I left out the detail of the almost-kiss, though. And also all those things Erik had said to me leading up to it.

Things were already so complicated. And, after all that had happened between me and Lucas at the dance, sharing that particular brush with Erik seemed like something that could only tangle things further. So, instead, I launched into a play-by-play of last night's events, starting with Charlie waking up in the middle of the night and ending with the chandelier.

As far as answers went, I had no solid suggestions to offer him. Just the pieces to a scattered puzzle. A mangled, nonsensical mess that Lucas let me dump at his feet.

To his credit, he drove with an impassive expression while I laid out everything, including Erik's battle with the other masked figures, and how he'd fought to free me from them. I explained about the two sides of the house, too, and how Erik had ejected me from his own shortly before the chandelier had come down.

"Why didn't you tell me any of this before?" he asked, predictably. "The dreams, for instance. Erik. Did he tell you not to?"

"No," I said, fidgeting. "I just spent so much time wondering if they really were dreams or not. And besides that . . . I didn't want you to think Charlotte was right about me."

He got quiet after that, driving a while longer, then taking another turn toward our destination. Finally, just when I thought Lucas wouldn't say anything else, he spoke again.

"You care about him."

I glanced his way, but he kept his eyes on the road. Oddly, there'd been no jealousy in his voice. There had been something else, though. Something like worry mixed with mistrust.

"Dad is why I have to go back in," I admitted after a pause. "But Erik is why I *want* to."

I only really worried about what Lucas thought of me after that. Because he immediately went silent again. Not only that, but, having reached the café where we'd be meeting the team, he parallel parked with way too much ease, never having to redo or hold up traffic like I would have.

That was what made me sure he'd written me off.

Killing the ignition, Lucas turned to look at me. He was about to say something, until he stopped himself, his jaw flexing.

This was it. Any second now, he'd accuse me of lying or suggest I seek professional help. He'd tell me to get out of his car and never—

"I believe you," he said.

Several beats passed in which I didn't breathe.

"You . . . do?" I asked, in case he might have changed his mind in the seconds it took me to find my voice.

"What I meant to say," he corrected, "is that I believe that's what you experienced."

I frowned, nausea churning in my empty stomach. Because that was basically a polite way of saying he *didn't* believe me.

"I know what I saw," I said.

"I'm not saying you didn't see it," replied Lucas. "And I'm not saying what happened to you, Charlie, and your dad wasn't paranormal. Obviously, Zedok is as real as we've all been afraid he was. But the legend of Moldavia is just that. Ghosts, even demons. Stephanie. They . . . they're not physical beings."

"I already told you," I started again. "Erik *isn't* a ghost. He said so himself. I didn't believe him either. Not until I saw him. Not until I—" I stopped. I could feel myself dancing around a few key details. The almost-kiss. How I'd flung my arms around Erik in that moment when I'd been so relieved to have him at my side again—a familiar presence in a sea of strangeness. Did I think Lucas would judge me? Was I afraid he'd feel betrayed? Or was I more afraid he would refuse to help me help Erik?

"I know you saw him," Lucas said, taking my hand in a gesture that, though sweet, told me he most definitely did *not* know. Which made me worry that whatever he was planning to do with SPOoKy might be a bad idea. Perhaps I should have gone back into the house for Erik alone. But then, that felt like a bad idea, too.

"Lucas—"

"The incident with the sheet," he said, interrupting me. "Erik confirmed that was him, right? But, in that moment, he wasn't really there. Physically speaking, I mean."

"Not in the same way as last night," I agreed. "But . . . he *was* there."

"But do you see what I'm saying?" he asked. "If he was *real* then you'd have seen him then, too."

I went silent. Lucas had a point, which was too logical to deny. Either Erik was a ghost . . . or he wasn't. But then, on the flip side, sheets couldn't settle over mist.

"I know none of it makes sense," I whispered at last. "I can't explain it. And I don't expect you to—"

"We know how to perform a cleansing ritual," he blurted. "To clear a property of spirts. As investigators . . . it's pretty much all we've got."

Turning my head to stare forward, I went silent. Because what he was telling me was that SPOoKy was equipped to handle *ghosts* . . . and ghosts only. Still . . . the cleansing ritual was *something*. And Zedok at least had been a ghost. Or something like one. He'd dissolved into nothing when I'd pulled his mask free. Perhaps a cleansing ritual could get rid of *him*.

Then again, hadn't an exorcism ritual almost killed Rastin Shirazi in front of a camera?

"Spirits," said Lucas, "certain kinds of darker entities can make you see things. They can cause hallucinations."

"You think Zedok made me see those things?"

"I think something did."

"What about Erik?"

"I . . . I'm not ready to tell you what I think about Erik," he said, a comment that caused my stomach to unwind so that it could twist itself the other way.

"Why?" I demanded.

"I'll tell you," he promised. "But . . . only after we do this. For now, just know that I have my reasons."

What did he think? That Erik wasn't who he said he was? That he could somehow be in league with this thing? Or even that he didn't exist at all? Whatever Lucas thought, I had no other choice but to wait and find out.

"What happens to us if it doesn't work?" I asked instead of pressing the issue.

"Then, whatever this thing is, it's out of our league anyway," he replied, like he'd already thought that part through. "And we'll have to try something else. But right now, I think you have to agree, as far as options go, this is the only one we have."

I frowned, still discomfited by his refusal to see things from my perspective—to even bend just a little. "But just in case it's *not* a ghost we're trying to get rid of—"

"Stephanie."

"*What?*"

"Do you trust me?" he asked, turning his head to me with those beautiful, oceanic eyes.

In response, I could only gape at him. Because why did he have to ask me *that* question?

"I'm afraid to," I said. "Especially when you don't know what we're up against."

"That's just it," he said. "I think I do."

"I see," I said, reading the subtext loud and clear. *My* opinion couldn't be trusted.

He went silent. Which at first made me even angrier. But then I asked myself what it would mean if Lucas was right about my having hallucinated. I'd done my job by telling him what had happened to me. Now it was up to him to tell me what that meant. I didn't like it. But he'd asked me for my trust—something I *wanted* to give him. And he'd never given me a reason not to grant it.

"Okay," I allowed after several beats. "I trust you. But then . . . what now?"

He let out a sigh, as if he'd been afraid he wouldn't have gotten past this barrier with me. In truth, he still hadn't. But I needed help and so did Erik.

"As the story stands," Lucas plowed forward, "I can tell you right now, the others won't believe it. But if I give them my version, I think they'll believe me."

"So . . ." I paused, not understanding. "What are you saying?"

He frowned. "I'm saying that you should let *me* do the talking."

And so it went that the rest of the SPOoKy team got an abridged and much more academic version of the previous night's events from Lucas, who had translated everything I'd told him into far more technical (and far vaguer) terms.

Phrases like "multiple aggressive dark apparitions," "open portals," "vortex hotspots," "psychic attacks," and, the most ambiguous of all, "confirmed nonhuman entity" got dealt around the coffee shop table like cards at a blackjack game.

I eventually tuned out the jargon talk, my mind taking me back to the previous night. To my impromptu embrace with Erik.

I'd been so terrified and so relieved to see him that I had just rushed him, winding him in my arms.

His frame had felt like that of a scarecrow. Light and hollow and . . .

I flushed at the memory of it—of his scent, which, like his voice, had been so familiar. And the way his gloved hands had lingered as they'd traveled along my arms, tenderness lacing the action.

Then there had been his *eyes*. Those lights-for-eyes that, according to my sister, were supposed to belong to Zedok. Zedok's eyes, though, had been blacker than black—two empty and night-filled pits of nothing. Had Charlie seen both figures and somehow confused the two? Or was this solid evidence that Lucas could be right? That Erik *wasn't* real. That he was, essentially, a trick.

The prospect caused my heart to contract and pound almost painfully hard.

I didn't want that to be so.

If not for that embrace with Erik, Lucas might have convinced me I'd hallucinated the whole ordeal. But that encounter, I couldn't have imagined.

And neither could I believe now that Erik, in all his turmoil and sadness, was not a prisoner of the monster.

I scowled at the tabletop. Confliction and confusion, and a hint of longing, warred with my fear of going back inside that house.

It didn't help that the legend Lucas had told us fit with all I had experienced firsthand. Everything but his assertion that the entity in the house was "nonhuman." Because if Zedok was the Egyptian priest, then he *would* be human. But then, *he* had been incorporeal, and garbed like another masquerader, so that didn't fit. And what about Erik? Lucas never mentioned him once to the others. Would the cleansing set him free? If it worked, would I even get to say good-bye . . . ?

"So who's in?" Lucas asked when he finished his debriefing.

I glanced up at this to find Charlotte staring straight at me.

I returned her gaze unblinkingly, and she frowned.

"I'm in," said Wes.

Eyeing Wes, Patrick gave a long sigh of mock resignation. "I guess that means I'm in, too, because who else is going to watch you?"

I smirked at Patrick, and he snuck me a wink, which told me a smile was all he'd been after.

Charlotte opened her mouth next, and I braced myself, waiting for her to start rattling off reasons why we shouldn't be messing with stuff this dangerous. She didn't, though. Instead, she seemed to rethink whatever she'd been about to say and, averting her gaze from mine, gave Lucas a stiff nod.

♪ ♩ ♪

LOW-HANGING CLOUDS, DENSE and dark, threatened rain the whole drive to my house. They didn't make good on the promise, though, until all five of us were standing under the portico of Moldavia. Now here we all were, at the threshold, with everyone in SPOoKy aware that, in being present for this cleansing thing, they were risking more than they had at any prior investigation.

The plan was to split up in pairs while one person waited at the door. I had been the one to insist on that last part to ensure we had a way to escape. Patrick had volunteered for the job, and no one had fought him on it. After Charlotte called dibs on going through the main floor with Lucas, Wes had jumped to say he would take the upper floors with me. I could tell Lucas had wanted to protest on both counts. I agreed to the arrangement, but only with the stipulation that no one went into the basement. According to Lucas, though, the basement had to be cleaned just like every other room in the house. So, on that point, we made a compromise.

After we finished "cleaning" our respective areas, we would meet at the base of the grand staircase and, from there, four of us would go down to clear the cellar together while someone again stood sentinel at the door.

Once we entered Moldavia, Lucas and Patrick carried the corner chair out of the parlor and propped it up against the front door to ensure it stayed open. Meanwhile, Wes drifted farther into the foyer, ogling the walls and ceiling as Lucas had done when he'd first entered the house, moving with slow, careful steps toward the downed chandelier.

While Wes crouched to one side of the mangled fixture, I turned my attention to Lucas, who unzipped the duffel Charlotte had left on the corner chair. Then, one at a time, he began to extract small whitish-gray twine-wrapped bundles.

Before I could ask what the bundles were, Wes interrupted.

"Problem," he said, his voice uncharacteristically sober. "The chain on this chandelier."

"What about it?" Lucas asked, as he handed me one of the bundles, which turned out to be small wads of dried and tightly wound leaves.

With a *clink*, Wes held up the end of the chain still attached to the fixture. "So, this chain didn't just give . . . It was cut."

"Uhhh," said Patrick, who squinted at the chain. "Maybe *we* should cut."

Charlotte shot him a glare.

"Aaaafter we're done here," he amended.

"Cut?" Lucas repeated. "It's metal. How could it have been cut?"

"Um," Wes said, examining the severed link. "With something really . . . really . . . hot?"

Wes peered up at Lucas, who had been watching me. Quickly, Lucas looked away, striding to where Wes stood to hand him a bundle, not even sparing the chain a second glance.

"You and Stephanie should start in the attic," Lucas told him. "Cover the second-floor bedrooms next, and then work your way back down."

"Right," Wes said, dropping the chain and simultaneously shooting Patrick a questioning side-glance. Patrick's gaze widened in return.

So. They were starting to pick up on the fact that Lucas hadn't told them everything. He'd asked me to trust him, but at what point was that just me participating in recklessness? When did I speak up to tell these people who, with the exception of maybe Charlotte, had become my friends that the word "spirit" did not even begin to cover the problem here?

"What does this stuff do exactly?" I asked, holding up the dried leaves, attempting to ease the tension.

Lucas straightened his glasses and handed a bundle to Charlotte, keeping one for himself. Next, he withdrew a grill lighter.

"The burning of sage helps to drive out negative entities," Lucas explained.

"This is a lot of sage, though," said Wes, who lit his bundle with a silver lighter from his pocket. He blew at the flames, causing tendrils of smoke to rise from its end. "For one house."

"Not for *this* house." Lucas gave Wes a side-glare.

"Normally, cleansings aren't where we begin," explained Patrick while setting up a video camera and tripod. Charlotte, in the meantime, began tracing long air-designs with the smoke in doorways and around windows in the foyer. "But . . . since we're not here to investigate, we're starting with the sage."

"It's a ritual a lot of paranormal investigators rely on when confronting or trying to clear malevolent energies," Lucas added. "But spirits can react negatively to sage smoke, so everyone . . . just be on your guard."

"That's geek-speak for 'we're all scared shitless,' " Wes said as he approached me. He reignited his lighter before holding it out to me. Taking my cue, I applied one end of my own bundle to the flame, letting it catch before blowing it out as the others had done. Vines of smoke then began to drift up from the slow-burning leaves, carrying a warm and earthy aroma—that same part of Lucas's scent that, until now, I'd never been able to pinpoint.

"You'll hold my hand if I get scared, won't you, Armand?" Wes asked.

My cheeks flamed. So did Lucas's, though less from embarrassment than anger. "Are you seriously going to be like this, man?" he asked. "Here?"

"Being insufferable is a defense mechanism," said Wes. "And like I've been saying since the very beginning of SPOoKy, what we *really* need in situations like this are (a) a real actual ordained priest and (b) holy water."

At this, Patrick raised a finger. "Just want to throw out an impartial observation here, but I thought that involving a priest is what supposedly started this whole mess in the first place."

"A triviality," replied Wes.

"Your *brain* is a triviality," countered Patrick.

"My brain, I'll have you know, is the second least trivial thing about me."

The sage would no doubt leave a smell in the house, which I'd have to conjure up an excuse for when Dad returned. But that was the least of my problems, especially since I'd already successfully concocted excuses for what happened last night.

Back at the hospital, when Dad had finally come to, he'd immediately started haranguing himself over the chandelier, apologizing for not checking the fixture the moment we'd moved in. Of course he would think the fitting had rotted. What would he say when he saw the chain? When he'd asked what had made me panic, I'd explained that I'd suffered from some kind of waking night terror. Which had, in a way, been true. He'd immediately asked about getting me tested for carbon monoxide poisoning, and I'd put him off, promising I'd check the alarms in the home first and call someone if the levels were bad.

Thing was, the levels in the house *were* bad. And I had called someone. Just not about carbon monoxide. And now, while both Charlie and Dad were away and safe, I had the help of four people who believed I was dealing with the otherworldly.

What no one in SPOoKy—including Lucas—seemed to be grasping, though, was that there was something in the house that *wasn't* bad.

Those eyes. The way they'd gazed at me before being dragged back inside the house. His mask might have hidden his features from me, but not those two faraway lights. There had been someone inside those eyes. Behind that mask. There was a *person* within that empty body I knew to be real because I had held it.

"Hey." Wes bumped my arm, offering me his elbow like we were about to walk down the homecoming court together. "Let's go smoke a ghost, shall we?"

"I thought you said it was a demon."

"And I thought you said you were single," he said through a wolfish grin.

That's when Patrick gave Wes a disapproving once-over. "Man. Quit being the creepiest thing in this building and get your weird ass up those stairs. I'm not chaperoning you. I've got enough to worry about being down here alone on the set of the *Insidious Children of the Conjuring Corn.*"

Wes gave me another of his mysterious, conspiratorial winks. Then he dropped his proffered arm and stalked to the base of the steps. Patrick in the meantime moved to take his station by the door, next to a camera, its lens aimed at the parlor doors and the back hall where Lucas had told the group most of last night's "activity" had taken place. Had Lucas been listening, though, when I'd told him none of it had happened on this side?

"Ruh-roh, Raggy," Wes said as a low *boom* of thunder sounded in the distance. "We'd better step on it, before the lights go out and suddenly we're all starring in *that* movie."

"Something tells me we might already be there," said Patrick.

Wes started up the stairs, and I moved to follow but paused to glance after Lucas, who'd gone into the parlor with Charlotte. I only caught a glimpse, but that had been enough to show me they were arguing. I didn't want to think it had something to do with me but then, what else could it be?

"Saint Michael the Archangel, defend us in battle," Wes chanted. "Be our protection against the wickedness and snares of the devil . . ."

I halted on the steps while Wes muttered the next portion of the incantation—or whatever it was he was intoning—under his breath.

"What's that?" I demanded. "What are you doing?"

Ignoring me, he continued, his volume building again. "And do thou, by the power of God, thrust into hell Satan and all evil spirits who wander through the world seeking the ruin of souls. Amen."

I gaped at Wes, images of hellfire leaping in my head, and of *Erik* being dragged backward again, this time into an inferno instead of the darkness of Moldavia.

Reaching the topmost step, Wes, sensing I hadn't followed him there, turned back.

"It's a Catholic prayer," he explained. "To help rid a space of evil forces."

"But," I said, still unnerved, "what if there's an entity here that *isn't* evil?"

Wes's expression underwent an odd change. He frown-scowled. Then, squinting one eye, he tilted his head at me.

"Sorry," he said, "but . . . that question seems to imply you have your doubts about the thing we're about to engage with. Even after said monster dropped a chandelier on your father."

He gestured over the banister, toward the wreckage.

"If there's a dark entity here—and there is," I said, "isn't it possible that there could be a good one trapped here, too?"

"Hoooold on just one freeze-dried minute," Wes said. "You said your *sister* had spoken to one of the entities. But what about you?"

Lucas. *Why* had he left out the details surrounding my interactions with Erik? Why, when Erik was the reason we were here?

"I . . . might have," I admitted. Because if Wes was going to put himself on the line, he deserved to know.

"What'd she just say?" called Patrick from the doorway.

"You . . . *might* have?" asked Wes, speaking loud enough for Patrick to hear. And the way Wes had asked this told me how big of a misstep I'd made.

"Does Lucas know about that?" asked Patrick, causing me to glance his way until Wes took several steps back down the staircase, stopping when we were eye level.

"Stephanie."

Wow. Was this the first time he'd called me by my first name? His voice had lost its wry and flirtatious edge, too.

"Whatever is in this house," Wes said, "it's not your friend. It's not in need. It's not trapped." He began ticking off fingers. "It's not a little girl, boy, pet, doll, goldfish, old man, old woman, mermaid, unicorn, or any other cute or benign *thing*. You understand that . . . don't you?"

His kohl-rimmed eyes bored into mine.

Rain started pouring outside, its hush like a too-late warning. I spared a quick glance once more to Patrick, whose anxious expression mirrored my own. And that doubled my worry that Lucas had made a horrible mistake in keeping the specifics from the rest of the team. Or had it been my mistake not to insist that I be the one to tell them what happened?

"He—" I started, but Wes cut me off.

"*It*," he corrected. "What did *it* tell you?"

"No," I said, because Erik wasn't an "it." I paused, stalling for time and wishing all the while this guy would freaking *blink*. Instead, his eyes grew wide. Afraid like Patrick's. Like because I hadn't told them about my interactions with both Zedok and Erik, we might now be in more danger than we knew.

Again, I looked to Patrick, whose eyes bounced between me and Wes, as if he only needed the slightest signal to shift his sneakers into marathon mode.

That's when the deafening *bang* of a downstairs door made us all jump.

A scream followed.

Charlotte's.

FORTY-SIX
Zedok

I had still been in the kitchen when they arrived—Stephanie and the small band of investigators I had warned her to never allow on the premises. Of course, her young man was among them.

I had stood there listening. To every word exchanged between the five of them.

That was, until it became clear that *she* would be heading upstairs.

Stephanie. She had come back. As I'd known she would. But why this entourage?

Of course. Erik. She had come back to rescue Erik.

The rose in my chest contracted, strained by the notion that this all could have been avoided if only I had told her the truth.

The rose, though. It bought me time.

Promptly, I crossed out of Stephanie's kitchen to stand upon the top step leading into my cellar. My plan was to lure Stephanie from the company of her cohorts in order to speak to her directly—something I could, if we were lucky, manage without losing my new heart. I had halted just short of closing the door to my side, however, when my attention was arrested by a fervent argument that, along with the useless sage smoke, drifted down the hallway toward me. The argument would not have commanded my attention except that it had contained, of all things, my name.

"You should have told us about Erik," came a young woman's unfamiliar voice.

"I did." This from the boy.

So, Stephanie *had* shared information with him regarding our interactions. But what? And how much . . . ?

"No, Lucas," argued the girl. "You actually didn't. You basically told everyone that we were dealing with a demon."

"Because that's what it has to be," he said. "Erik can't be real."

"Except you *just* told me that's not what Stephanie believes."

"Because she's in the first stage of oppression!"

"You don't know that."

"She admitted to caring about him."

"So. What. You're jealous? Is that what this is really about?"

"Don't be stupid."

"You're the one who is being stupid, Lucas. What if there really is a spirit stuck here?"

"That's just it, Charlotte. We're not talking about a spirit. She said he was tangible—a person. But you and I both know that's not possible. The legend isn't real. It can't be. So the only other explanation is that it's playing her. There *is* no Erik. Nothing else makes sense."

Sneering, I tightened a fist.

"Okay, fine," said the girl, Charlotte. "Say there is a dark entity here. That doesn't necessarily make it demonic."

"It melted metal," replied the boy. "It almost killed her dad. Besides, this thing's been coming to her in dreams. It told her not to have investigators to the house. She said Erik was why she *wanted* to come back here. Name one thing about any of that that doesn't scream demonic activity."

So, Stephanie had told him quite a bit. Had she truly said she cared for me, though? Whether she had or not, was not her return to Moldavia proof enough that she did care?

"I *knew* I should have asked her why she wasn't saying anything," said Charlotte. "It wasn't because she didn't want to. It was because *you* told her not to."

"Because we would have all sat there wasting time, debating about what this thing really was when the answer was obvious."

"You know," said the girl, "you're starting to sound just like Wes."

"I do *not* sound like Wes."

"You do. And while we're on the subject, what is going *on* between you two?"

"Nothing," snapped the boy.

"Clearly it's not nothing. Lately, he's been trying to get a reaction out of you any chance he gets. Why?"

"He likes Stephanie, okay?"

"He said that?" Charlotte asked.

"Yes. Actually. He did."

She laughed. "And you *believed* him?"

"Hey," said the boy suddenly, his voice at once clearer than before. "The basement door. Look. It's open."

The scuff of a shoe on the tile warned me of his approach. If he looked beyond the door, though, there could be little doubt now that he would see me.

"Lucas, stop. Stephanie said not to—"

Quickly, I yanked the door shut. The resulting *bang* resounded through the house, inciting a scream from the girl.

FORTY-SEVEN

Stephanie

"You stay there!" I shouted at Patrick as I darted past him, bolting into the back hall with Wes on my heels.

Patrick's instinct had been to rush toward the source of the scream. But we'd all be screaming soon if he didn't keep his watch over the doorway.

Rounding the corner into the kitchen, I skidded to a stop on the tiles, confronted with the sight of Lucas battling to open the basement door. Charlotte stood nearby, her back pressed to the kitchen counter, hands covering her mouth.

I tore past her and, without thinking, grabbed one of Lucas's hands, prying it free of the locked handle and inserting myself between him and the door. Flustered, Lucas backed off.

"The door," he explained. "It . . . it shut on its own. Just before it did, I . . . I thought I saw—"

"No one goes into the basement alone," I said. "You promised."

His shocked expression told me that, in that moment, he hadn't been thinking about what he'd promised. He hadn't been thinking at all.

"It's locked now," he said, gesturing to the door. "So none of us are going down there."

Maybe, for right now, that was for the best.

"Guuuuys?" came Patrick's voice from the hall.

"Everybody's okay," Wes called back. "Though I can't really say it was a false alarm."

"No," called Patrick. "All of you. Get in here."

Lucas was the first to move, though not without grabbing my hand along the way. With forceful steps, he led me back down the hall and into the foyer. Charlotte and Wes followed close behind.

"Whose room is that right there?" Patrick asked when we arrived, pointing at a second-floor door.

"Mine," I said.

"Yeah, well. Your door just opened all by itself."

"Did you get it on camera?" asked Lucas.

"Negative," replied Patrick. "Camera was aimed toward the back hall. Couldn't pivot it in time."

"Grab a digital, Wes," Lucas said. "You and I can go check it out. You three"—he gestured to me, Charlotte, and Patrick—"stay together."

"Like hell," Charlotte snapped, snatching a camcorder from the duffel bag before starting after him. "I'm coming with you."

"It's Stephanie's room," said Wes. "Shouldn't *she* go with Lucas?"

Charlotte and Lucas looked at Wes, dumbfounded.

"Charlotte and I can finish this floor," Wes continued. "We stick with the plan to get the house cleaned. Obviously, we're having an effect."

Wes and Lucas shared a glare. But then Lucas broke from the group and, still holding my hand, took me with him. As we climbed the stairs, I got the distinct impression that Wes had orchestrated things for his own purposes, the way he had at the dance. Lucas, on the hunt, remained none the wiser. But I was certain that, as soon as Lucas and I were out of earshot, Wes would tell the others what I had let slip to him.

Lucas dropped my hand, but only once we were both beyond the threshold of my door. Was he taking me more seriously now after what he'd seen? And about that . . .

"What was it?" I asked him as he made a beeline for my closet. "What did you see?"

"This door," he said, opening the closet. "Do you remember if it was like this last night? Closed, I mean."

"Actually . . . I opened it last night," I said. "Looking for Charlie. I'm pretty sure I left it that way . . ."

He swung toward me. "You might not have?"

"It matters?"

"Probably not," he admitted. "At any rate, I think something just came through here. C'mon."

Lucas took up my hand again and tugged me out of my room and down the rear hallway, like he knew the lay of the land as well as I did. But then, my house *was* all over a documentary.

"Lucas, where are we going?"

"Up," he said. "To the attic. Like Wes said, we stick to the plan."

Trailing sage smoke in our wake, Lucas and I climbed up, around one tight bend and then the next, our feet creating a hollow racket on the stairs that everyone had to be hearing. Everyone and everything.

I'd never seen Lucas this hell-bent. Until now, I'd have wagered that aggravation wasn't an emotion he possessed.

We cleared the final steps, emerging into the dusty and antique-filled attic. Above us, rain pounded the roof, the storm issuing a low groan of thunder.

Then Lucas did something that shocked me. He slung me gently out into the center clearing of the room, releasing me in the same motion. I stumbled backward a step into the weak patches of light straining to stream through the rear windows. He scowled at me, ready, it seemed, to start yelling.

He didn't, though. Instead, his steps hit the floorboards hard and fast as, with determination, he closed the distance between us, dropping his sage bundle along the way so that his hands could reach for me.

His palms, warm, took my face.

And then . . . then he kissed me.

FORTY-EIGHT
Zedok

F rom my side, I had entered Stephanie's by way of her closet. I'd made a show of pushing her bedroom door open before retreating once more to my Moldavia, taking care to shut the closet door behind me. From there, I went to my old room and exited by way of the closet into Charlie's. Sequestered there, I eavesdropped on the stir I had purposefully initiated long enough to ascertain that Stephanie would be returning to her room with the boy.

My aim was to continue to cause confusion that would lead to separation.

From there, I would isolate Stephanie at first opportunity and seize my final chance to explain everything.

Through the slit of Charlie's partially open door, I marked Stephanie's movements as she, conjoined at the hand with that infernal boy, was forced to follow his every step. Just when I had been sure he would bring her my way, their approach presenting me with the not-altogether-unappealing prospect of my having to incapacitate him, he turned sharply with Stephanie, veering for the rear portion of the second floor.

His conduct toward her, all but forceful, drove me to the window of Charlie's bedroom. Concern for Stephanie now tearing at me, I climbed out onto the external iron staircase that had been installed two decades prior.

Scowling behind Valor's mask, I scaled the fire escape through the pelting rain to its apex.

To the attic window that, shielded from the torrent by its gable, showed me . . . everything.

FORTY-NINE

Stephanie

Lucas. He was kissing me. As in no-holds-barred, no reserva-tions, no hesitation *kissing*.

And it was . . . *amazing*.

The rush of his scent, a mixture of sandalwood, peppermint, and sage smoke, sent my mind reeling and my body into autopilot.

I kissed him back, my hands lifting to press his chest, fingers curling into the fabric of his shirt. Eyes falling shut, I relished the sensation of his seeking lips. Soft and strong as his touch, they sought mine out in slow but fervent strokes.

Then those big hands fell to my hips, where, pulling me into him, they radiated the heat of desire.

It was a heat I felt all too keenly myself—from my toes to the electrified tips of my fingers.

Dismissing the small voice in the back of my mind that kept pos-ing too many questions—and more distantly asking about someone else—I looped my arms around Lucas's neck.

In response, Lucas's steel arms enclosed me, wrapping me in a devouring embrace that drew us flush. He deepened the kiss then, obliterating the reserves of my thoughts with a sinful sweep of his tongue.

My blood racing in my veins, roaring in my ears, I sought from that point to keep up with the kiss that began to run off with us both.

That's when Lucas stepped into me, walking us backward all the way to the wall, where he pressed me into the plaster—and then himself into me.

With no brain cells left to tell them not to, my hands somehow found their way beneath his shirt, fingers trailing over all the muscles I had always known they would find.

His hand cupped my face again, his thumb brushing my cheek, delivering in this heated moment the sweetest of caresses before, abruptly, he broke the kiss.

I blinked up at him, dazed, my chest rising and falling quickly from the run up the steps. And from the kiss, unexpected as it had been.

Lucas stared down at me, his brow pinched, like he was trying to figure out if he really had just kissed me that way. Urgent. Impulsive. Incredible.

In a moment, he would start talking. Why, though, when all I wanted was for him to kiss me like that again? In that insistent, demanding, and sexy-as-hell way that proved beyond a shadow of a doubt that, despite appearances, he wasn't *all* good boy.

"Do you like Wes?" he blurted, breathless himself.

I froze. And squinted at him, nonplussed. *"What?"*

FIFTY
Zedok

S he stood with her back to me, her arms lifting to wind around the young man's shoulders—not out of fear, as had been the case when they had wound around mine, but out of longing. For *him*. This wretch who took with ease what I had known all along could never be mine.

In spite of that knowing, this moment brought with it, for me . . . pain.

Along with the final unfolding of all I had sought to avoid.

No. Not so soon. Not yet. Not now.

The agony—the same from two nights ago—it came despite my plea, returning full force to ransack me from the inside out, exploding into being from the very core of my person.

I groped at my chest, wadding into my fist the waistcoat and shirt that concealed my ravaged form. But, as before, that did nothing to assuage the reckoning that occurred inside me—the likes of which I had never known. Not even when Rastin had applied his powers to my desolate soul.

That kiss.

The vilest of poisons could not have slain a man any better than that kiss killed me. And, like the twisting pain, their embrace wore on and on.

Weakened by the mounting intensity of both, I had no choice but to lean into the window that trapped within its frame this hated picture. One that, though I could not bear to watch, I found impossible to look away from.

How well their bodies conformed to each other. How lovely and alive they looked entangled. And how poor a judge *I* had been. To think that the worst could have ever been prevented. To think that, in her presence, a heart—any heart—would not break.

Another swell of pain rocked me. With it, though, I managed to tear myself from the window, from the scene that would forever replay in my hollow head.

His lips on hers. Her answering embrace. Their desires united and undenied.

My footing compromised by the slickness of metal, I staggered forward to grab the railing. When my hand came away from my chest, though, it brought with it rivulets of red. A glance down at my personage showed a stain of crimson spreading its way out from my sternum, saturating my already soaked white dress shirt.

But . . . how could this be?

I descended, my feet clanging over the stairs that brought me to the landing below. With difficulty, I reentered Charlie's room, where both rainwater and blood dripped from me to the floor. I could not stay here on this side. Not in this state that would quickly have me discovered. And yet, with the rose obliterated, I could not dare to return to my Moldavia, either.

Undecided, I staggered to the hallway door as thunder rumbled overhead. But I did not have to grasp or turn the knob. For the door, with a low and ominous creak, opened all on its own.

Beyond, against the backdrop of the lit chandelier that, on my side, still hung perfect from its chain, stood a figure resplendent in crimson. The plush hallway runner under him softened the booted steps that brought him nearer to the threshold. The one that, for the second time that day, stood as the only barrier between us.

"Even now," I said, my voice little more than a labored rasp, "I cannot let you win."

"You speak as though you have not already lost," he replied, the calmness in that horrible voice slicing deeper the pain that resonated all the louder within me.

Stephanie. My Stephanie.

"*Ours,*" hissed the figure of Wrath.

"No." My hand returned to clench the inexplicable wound in my chest, stoppering the blood, the presence of which should not have been possible.

"I shall not cross," I wheezed, taking a step back, away from the door and from him. "And . . . even you cannot take . . . what does not lie within your reach."

"I can only agree," he said before ever so slightly tilting his head at me. "But when, dear Erik, have any of us, least of all me, ever truly existed outside of you?"

With these words, Wrath parted the cloak that had heretofore swathed his figure, revealing a pit in the center of his own chest. But the hole was not hollow so much as it was a transparent nothingness through which the wall behind him could be viewed.

And that nothingness. It grew.

"W-wh—" I murmured, unable to comprehend what it was I was witnessing. One of my masks dissolving from the center out?

That's when the horror of the correlation occurred to me.

With terror I glanced down at myself, at the blood that, even as it covered me, transformed me, vanquishing Valor's garments in favor of heavier vestments of the deepest and most devouring of crimsons.

"You . . . cannot," I said as I moved into the doorframe and then through it, toward the figure whose form peeled back on itself from the center, dissolving even as the same crimson garbs began to envelop me. "Please. *No.*"

Wrath spread his arms, several of his ringed fingers gone already.

"Take heart, Valor," he said mockingly, his mask disintegrating now, too. "If you held any power to stop this, do you think I would just stand here?"

Panic gripped me. I grasped for my mask, prepared to rip it free.

But . . . then, with gloved and ring-lined fingers pressed to the mask's altered outline, I halted.

Because was I not now free? As free as I might ever be? Unfettered and at liberty to now take what I desired? And to destroy, in good time, what I loathed.

Was there anything I wanted more than Stephanie?

Contrarily, was there anything I hated more than the boy?

FIFTY-ONE

Stephanie

"Wes," repeated Lucas as he took a step back from me. "After the dance . . . he told me he was going to make a move if I didn't. *Do you like him?*"

I folded my arms, trying to get a grip on his thinking. Two seconds ago, I'd been showing him just how *much* I liked him, and now here he was asking about *Wes?*

"You asked me on a date," I took the liberty of reminding him.

"Y-yeah, I know."

"And I said yes."

"Yeah, but you guys were dancing together last night. And I didn't know if maybe you—"

"I don't like Wes," I said. "Do you think I'd have let you kiss me that way if I did?"

A flicker of hope flashed in those stained-glass blues.

"Hello," I said. "I like *you*. A lot."

A beat passed. Then we each took a simultaneous step toward one another. Lucas reached for me a second time, eyes hungry. I drifted into him, allowing his arm to slip around my waist, his hand to press into my lower back, bringing us together once more.

We both halted, though, our progress toward a second and possibly even steamier kiss arrested by a distant first-floor shout. That of someone calling out for Lucas.

The two of us snapped apart. Grabbing our fallen sage bundles, we hurried for the door. On the way out, I caught sight of the desk from which Erik's music had floated that first day I'd come up here. The desk now lay on its side—toppled. I frowned as Lucas and I wound down one set of steps after the other, halting only when we reached the middle of the grand staircase.

Patrick stood below, peering up at us. His words were enough to distract me from my questions surrounding the desk, which couldn't have thrown itself over.

"It just opened," he said.

Lucas and I didn't have to ask what he meant by "it." Instead, we both hurried down to the foyer, then streamed past him into the kitchen, where Charlotte and Wes stood facing the open basement door.

"Did you see it open?" asked Lucas.

"Heard it," replied Wes.

"Patrick!" Lucas yelled to the front of the house.

Patrick's steps pounded down the hall, slowing as soon as he reached the kitchen, a sage bundle in his own hand now.

"Watch this door, will you? I think . . . I think whatever we're doing . . . it's working. We've got this thing cornered now. But we don't want it locking us in."

"Yeah," said Patrick, glancing back the way he'd come, probably thinking about the now unguarded front door. "How long have I been saying we need two of me?"

"If you hear us scream," said Wes.

"Run," finished Patrick.

"You'll feed my fish?" asked Wes.

"If I get that far," mumbled Patrick as he stared into the darkened doorway. With that, all of us grew silent in the face of our new task, one that Lucas had assured me would be our last. Was it possible the sage could eliminate the evil that resided here? I wanted to believe it could.

Lucas hit the light, illuminating the basement's bare-bones wooden stairs. Emboldened, he then passed beyond the threshold of the cellar door. The three of us followed behind.

Once in the basement, all of us went from corner to corner, spreading the smoke, Wes muttering prayers under his breath. Then, with the deed done, we gathered in the center of the room, our backs pressed together, as if suspecting something would jump out at us, or that one of us would become possessed like Rastin.

"Is it over?" called Patrick to us, his voice tense and uncertain.

"Hopefully," said Lucas. "But it looks like we won't know for sure until later."

I let out a long low breath, eyeing the shafts of sunlight that sneaked down the stairs from the kitchen.

Erik.

No matter what he was—was it possible he was free now?

Was it possible *I* was?

THAT NIGHT, DAD came home in a cast.

After picking him up, I'd gone to get Charlie, and we all returned to the house.

Though I'd waited for questions to come pouring out of Dad, none had. Not until we'd settled back into the house that I hoped would stay as quiet as SPOoKy had left it.

First, as I expected, Dad had asked about the smell. He'd assumed I'd cooked something, and since he couldn't go upstairs to find the smell up there, too, I let him think that I had.

Then, all too predictably, came the questions about Lucas. Had I been with him all day? Were we a "thing" now?

"Maybe," I'd told him as I'd brought out a stack of blankets for him to sleep with on the couch. Tomorrow, I'd have to see about getting a bed set up on the ground floor, at least until the cast came off. Something that presented still more complications. Namely, halting my father's progress on this house, which ensured we wouldn't be moving until, earliest, spring or summer. Dad was going to be miserable until the doctor cleared him to work. But the trade-off amounted to more time with Lucas.

Dad, probably still groggy from pain meds, hadn't pressed for more details about Lucas or last night. And once I had him situated on the couch, I took Charlie upstairs to my bedroom, still not trusting to leave her in her own.

I texted Lucas as soon as I had Charlie tucked in with me, and put my phone on silent as she finally began to nod off.

After giving Lucas the all's-well update, he texted back.

> Are you still coming to school
> tomorrow?

I smiled and typed a response.

> Not sure yet. I want to see
> everyone and thank them again.
> It depends on Dad. Knowing him,
> though, he'll probably insist.

> Did he ask about us?

> He asked if we were a thing.

Only two seconds passed before his next text.

> And?

> And I put him off. But I think he
> knows we are.

This time, a delay of several seconds before Lucas's answer.

> Maybe I'll still get to kiss you one
> last time before I die.

I rolled my eyes, unable to suppress a grin.

Maybe.

♪ ♩ ♪

I *FELT* THE dream first.

The sensation of smooth gliding layered over an almost imperceptible swaying.

The soft lapping water . . .

All of that told me where I was even before I opened my eyes.

When I *did* open them, it was to see the deep velvet-blue nighttime sky colored by patches of cerulean and spattered with bright stars, all of it glittering like swirled diamond dust.

Lying on my back in the boat, its wooden edges in my periphery, I couldn't help the soft "ohh" that escaped my lips.

Had I ever seen anything so *beautiful* in my entire life?

The slow passing of the sky and the sound of disturbed water had me sitting up fast in the boat, so that I suddenly found myself face-to-face with the answer to that exact question.

He stood at the stern, sculling us forward over the water with the long staff he held between both hands.

"Erik—"

He made no reply. Just watched me with a steady and serious stare, grave and breathtaking as any dark angel.

The glassy waters of the lake mirrored the sky, giving the disturbing illusion that the world had no up or down. Trees lined the darkened shore that surrounded us on all sides. But no sounds or movement emanated from the forest, and no wind whisked over the waters. We were somewhere, but also, as had been the case with the other dreams, nowhere at all.

And like always, it was just the two of us.

"Erik," I said, my voice too loud in the near silence. "What's happened? Where are we?"

"There exists on the grounds a lake," he said. "Not too far into the woods. Didn't you know?"

I scowled at his response, as the growing sense that something wasn't right began to expand within me. Dad had mentioned the lake, but that the realtor had told him it now belonged to an adjacent lot.

"Why did you bring me here?" I asked him.

"I wish to thank you, Stephanie," he said coolly. "For setting me free."

"S-so," I stammered, "it worked. The curse. It's broken?"

"I told you. The curse can never be broken."

I frowned, tilting my head at him, confused. Why was he acting this way?

"Did I do something wrong?" I asked. "Did . . . did we somehow make it worse?"

To that, he said nothing, just lifted and lowered his staff, driving us toward the shore that never seemed to get any closer. The ripples raced one another to infinity over the star-specked waters. As they vanished, I redirected my attention, noting for the first time what I was wearing.

A gown.

Satin drop-shoulder sleeves adorned my arms, linking with a burgundy bodice that hugged my torso. Layered skirts and petticoats covered my legs—garments of another time.

Erik had always been responsible for how the world appeared in these dreams, but this marked the first instance that I myself had incurred any change. And this dress. I'd seen it before. On the masked figure. The one who had attempted to draw me into the basement. The one who had looked so much like . . .

"Did you do this?" Returning my gaze to his, I gestured to the gown. "You should probably know that dresses aren't really my thing."

"The list of transgressions I am to beg pardon for grows, then," he said without sounding sorry at all. "But it does become you."

Fear shot through me at this response, driving my heart to speed up.

I shifted. "Erik. What is going on?"

He raised the pole, slid it back into the water, and pushed off.

"Eri—"

"*Erik is dead*," he snapped.

I blinked, taken aback by this sudden show of temper. He'd been short with me before. But never unkind.

My sense of alarm growing, I swung toward one side of the boat and peered down into the waters, hoping to catch sight of the bottom that, as evident by Erik's use of the gondolier pole, couldn't be too far off.

The eyes of my own frightened reflection met with mine.

"Do take care," he cautioned. "Should we capsize, you'll wake, and my spell will be ruined."

Spell?

"What's happened to you?" My fear grew twofold. "You're—"

"The boy," he said, cutting me off. "You must forget him now."

My mouth fell open. This wasn't the first time he'd mentioned Lucas. I shut my mouth, my jaw flexing with the unwelcome thought that Erik might have witnessed the kiss in the attic. And that prospect summoned within me a snarl of complicated emotions. Because Erik himself had almost kissed me once. And in that moment, I had wanted him to. That kiss had never happened, though. And Lucas *had* kissed me. Besides that, Erik was . . . he was . . . God, what *was* he?

Whatever he was, he was not alive, which must have been why he'd stopped the kiss. Because he knew as well as I did that the two of us were separated by more than just time.

At least we had been . . . until last night.

"I . . . didn't mean to hurt you," I said in a whisper.

"I can assure you that is quite impossible for you to do," he said without meeting my gaze.

"You saw us, didn't you?"

His eyes narrowed on me. "I see *everything* that happens inside of my house."

My heart clenched suddenly tight, heat rising to my cheeks along with an odd sense of guilt over my kiss with Lucas.

I couldn't sit here, though, and let myself be surprised that Erik cared for me. After all, I came back into this nightmare house because I had grown to care for him.

"L-last night," I said. "Erik—"

"I told you not to call me that."

"No, you didn't." I gripped the sides of the boat. "You said that Erik was dead. But you're not dead, are you?"

"It no longer matters what I am."

"Last night," I pressed, "I was really there with you on the other side of the house. It *wasn't* a dream or a hallucination. And that's why you wouldn't take off the mask. You didn't want me to see that you don't look like this. That the stories about what happened to you are true. That's what you were trying to tell me in the conservatory."

"The music," he said, pretending like he hadn't heard me. "Now that you are here, that is all that shall matter."

My frown deepened. Because the way he'd said the word "here" had felt somehow . . . loaded.

"But . . . this is a—"

The words dried in my mouth, stolen by my own sense of suddenly screaming alarm.

Erik had brought me here for a reason, to a setting that confined me to a boat. And the conversation he'd led me through, full of holes and non-answers, had been meant only to distract me.

He must have seen the realization dawn in my eyes. Because he stopped rowing, a small smile touching his perfect lips. It was a smile, however, that did not reach his eyes. Eyes that no longer carried the warmth or sadness I had seen in them before, but now suddenly displayed far-off, inhuman, light-like glints.

The boat rotated, and my gaze fell from his tall, straight form to his image reflected in the water's surface.

Panic surged into my heart, sharp, piercing, and cold as an ice pick.

Though I wanted to scream at the sight of his reflection's crimson garb and death's head mask, I acted instead, remembering what he'd said about this dream being a spell—his spell.

I pushed out of the boat and dove for the waters.

Though my body made a splash as I hit, I did not end up in the lake. I instead toppled—awake—from someone's arms, landing atop a floor of beautiful carpeting.

At once, the sound of lapping water revealed itself to be the soft ticking of a clock, and I found myself faced with a fireplace outfitted with tiles showing feathery paintings of birds on porcelain. The carved deer's head watched me from its mounting over the hearth, its antlers casting long, wicked shadows up the wall.

No . . .

The stag was too small to have owned the whole of those curved, spiked shadows. Their true source came from something that loomed behind me.

I dug my fingers into the carpet, and my breathing came quick now. Because there was no question of who I would see when I dared to turn and look.

What.

PART

II

FIFTY-TWO
Lucas

"You have to be *certain* if we are seriously going to do this," said Patrick. "Absolutely, positively, irrevocably *certain*."

I glowered at him from across the restaurant table, irritated at him and the rest of the SPOoKy crew all over again.

"Yeah, because you know me," I snapped, folding my arms as I leaned back in the booth. "I really like to make stuff up. Especially when there are people's *lives* on the line."

"No," said Charlotte. "You don't make stuff up. You just leave stuff out."

"Preach," said Patrick while giving his sweet tea a stir.

I sent Charlotte a glare, one that she gave right back until I had to look away. Because, as much as I hated to admit it, she was right.

"You had it all figured out, didn't you?" she went on. "Didn't think to run any of the alternate-side-of-the-house stuff by us before deciding yourself what it all meant."

"This from the person who didn't believe Stephanie from the start," I muttered.

"Yeah, well, looks like you were the one who didn't believe her this time," Charlotte countered, her words burning. Because, again, she wasn't wrong. I *hadn't* believed Stephanie. Not until nearly a week ago when, after the sage cleansing, she'd vanished in the middle of the night from her house.

"Look," I said. "I've already apologized. Yeah, I thought I had the answer. I thought I knew what we were facing. I did what I did because . . . because I figured you all would have come to the same conclusion anyhow. For me, in that moment, the bottom line was that Stephanie needed help and we were all she had."

"Because we didn't even try to contact anyone else!" said Charlotte, who, along with Wes and Patrick, still didn't know about my reaching out to Rastin. Now, though, didn't seem like the best time to bring that up.

"In all fairness, Charlotte," said Wes, surprising me by possibly coming to my defense, "I can't say I don't follow Lucas's logic." He paused to aim his kohl-rimmed eyes at me. "*Not* that I'm excusing the way you handled things. But, at the end of the day, who's to say we would have approached the issue any differently if we *had* gotten the story straight from Stephanie. I, for one, would have still gone in."

"We *all* would have," snapped Charlotte. "That's my point. But what's yours, Wes?"

"My point," replied Wes, "is that, regardless of what Lucas did or didn't tell us, we'd still probably all be sitting here right now talking about Stephanie, who would still be missing."

"That's the thing, though," said Patrick. "This discussion right here?" He stabbed the table with a finger. "It isn't about whether or not we would have gone in. It's about whether or not we should go *back* in."

"And why the hell wouldn't we?" I challenged.

"Lucas," said Patrick. "They found Stephanie's blood on the floor in Charlie's room."

"Yeah," I said, my temper rising by another notch. Because we'd already had this conversation. "I *know* the cops found her blood, but—"

"Apparently, her dad also has a record." Wes again. "*And* he resisted arrest."

Okay. Now I wanted to throw something. Instead, I took a pause and a breath before speaking again. Because I had to be reasonable if I wanted any of them to see reason. "*You* might resist arrest, too, if someone you loved went missing and, instead of being able to look for them, you were getting locked up."

"We're not saying we think her dad hurt her," said Charlotte.

"Really? It seems to me like you are." I frowned at my hands on the table, at my untouched food, at the enormity of the mistake I'd made in ever letting Stephanie walk back into that house. Also, in putting my own judgment ahead of hers after she'd been brave enough to confide in me.

Now here I was kicking myself like I'd done every hour since the morning she'd failed to show up to school. Not to mention officially groveling for help from my own paranormal investigative team. And if I couldn't talk *them* into joining me on an admittedly insane-sounding interdimensional rescue mission? What then?

"Mr. Armand's looking pretty bad right now," Patrick said. "And if we get involved, we're bound to also. That's all I'm saying."

I sighed. Because I couldn't argue with that logic.

So far, I'd been able to talk myself out of going into Moldavia and facing whatever dark figure I'd glimpsed behind that door alone. With the house under investigation, I couldn't have approached the grounds anyway. Today, though, marked the first day since Stephanie's now six-day disappearance that Moldavia wasn't crawling with cops. We knew this because, after Stephanie's father had been arrested, we'd set up one of Patrick's trail cameras on a tree beside the entrance. That was the main reason behind why I'd called us all here. Because tonight, the house would officially be empty.

Well. One side of it would be.

It was true I hadn't believed Stephanie about there being another house inside of hers. But now that she was missing, it stood to reason that perhaps there really was another side to Moldavia.

"Let's just say you actually have it right this time," Patrick added. "Say there *is* an alternate side of the house in which something or some *things* physically dwell, like Stephanie said. Before we go barging back into a situation like that—one that has obviously been out of our league from the start—shouldn't we at least consider other options?"

"That's what *I'm* saying," said Charlotte.

"Like what?" I challenged.

"Like we could approach the church," said Wes predictably.

"Or bring in one of the local clairvoyants we know," offered Patrick. "Someone who can give us something solid to go on."

I pulled my glasses off to rub at eyes that had gotten virtually no sleep since Stephanie's vanishing. "If I can't get any of *you* to believe me that she's been taken by this . . . thing, then how am I supposed to get anyone else to?"

I certainly hadn't dared to tell the police my suspicions when they'd questioned me. The last thing I wanted was for them to think me unstable. I'd admitted to the truth, that I'd been in Stephanie's house that morning, though I'd left out the precise reasons why. When they'd asked me if I was her boyfriend, knowing they would have read my last text exchange with Stephanie, I gave the only answer I could.

Yeah, I was.

"You tell me, then," said Patrick. "What are we supposed to do when we get in there? Start knocking on doors hoping Steph's behind one of them? I don't think I need to remind anyone how the sage—which is *still* all we've got—didn't work."

"Regretfully," added Wes, "the Saint Michael prayer didn't seem to have the desired effect either."

Silence returned to the table, making me think they were all waiting for me to lay out my master plan. Which, of course, I didn't have.

I put my glasses back on, certain for the first time that I'd have done better to go to Moldavia by myself instead of requesting this meeting. Truth was, I could still go. Sure, the whole estate was now a crime scene, and I'd be breaking about twenty laws just by stepping foot inside. But if I could somehow reach Stephanie, she could be back as soon as tonight. If, in the process of trying to rescue her, I didn't get us both killed. Or myself arrested and put officially under suspicion.

Except *Wes* was the one equipped with the prayers and talismans and the jokes that, though more annoying than not, sometimes helped to keep us all sane. And Patrick was the levelheaded one who always asked the right questions and kept us all from doing stupid crap. Like running into *any* situation solo—regardless of what it was.

And Charlotte. Charlotte had always been our best debunker and sounding board. The second half to my mastermind. Not just for SPOoKy, either. She was my best friend. Which was why we hadn't worked as a couple.

Sometimes I thought the only reason we'd tried to be together was because everyone already assumed we were. But, romantically, Charlotte and I had mixed as well as a bulldog and a chicken.

We'd come out of it all right. We still had our awkward moments, and maybe a few lingering hard feelings. Some confused feelings, too.

When it had come to Stephanie, though, there'd been nothing to be confused about.

I'd had it for her from day one and wanted to bet that I always would.

Word had gotten around at school about someone moving into Moldavia. Stephanie was the only new student at Langdon. So, two and two had amounted to one breathtaking girl.

From that slow-motion moment when she'd first passed me in the hall, Moldavia became, for me, a house inhabited not by a monster but by a walking dream. Yet, all along, there had been a monster inside, too. And perhaps, despite my previous misgivings, a ghost as well.

Erik Draper. Perhaps he wasn't my enemy after all.

Could it be that *he* was the key to reaching Stephanie?

And so, was that my plan? To go in and appeal to the figure Stephanie had been convinced was a walking dead man? Was it possible he had any power to combat this monster who had terrorized and killed?

And that threat of death. It made me get why my paranormal team was so reluctant to go after Stephanie. At the same time, though, Stephanie had *become* one of us. She'd become ingrained into the group—part of its heart. She was certainly part of mine.

So I had to believe there was still some way to reach her.

I had to because I was in love with her.

And for that reason alone, I *would* go back to Moldavia. With or without backup.

"Kind of quiet back here tonight," said Sam, our usual waiter, as he sidled up to our table. "I'd ask if somebody died, but that's typically why y'all are here."

None of us looked up or even cracked a smile.

"Wow," laughed Sam. "Okay. Anybody want a slice of Death by Chocolate to go with their Doom and Gloom?"

"I'll take some more ketchup," Patrick said, even though he'd killed off most of his fries already.

"Well," said Sam as he pivoted. "At last one of y'all's acting normal."

I scanned the table after Sam left but sighed when, again, no one would meet my gaze.

"So that's it," I said. "That settles it. I'm on my own."

"Now, wait just a second." Wes raised a pale palm to me. Like I was one of the entities he liked to rebuke. "Might I take this moment to remind you that, despite your surly sea captain attitude toward us, none of us has said no. We're just trying to be sure there is, in fact, a plan. One that we're *all* in on this time."

"Because, you know," said Patrick, cutting me off before I could say a word, "we do all have things like permanent records, reputations, and major arteries that will suffer the consequences."

"And if we roll up into this house," added Wes, "break in, and start trying to find Stephanie in the walls? At *best* we stand to get arrested."

"Yeah. And at worst we stand to get killed," added Patrick, pulling out his phone after it buzzed with an alert. "Which, by the way, is why you need to give us a solid heads-up before you omit any more vital information or Leeroy Jenkins into any more crazy shit. I do not have time to be dead."

"You mistake our apprehension for doubt," said Wes, raising a finger. "And how can we help it when, if what you're saying is true, and Stephanie was taken by—"

"Zedok *has* her," I said, not caring anymore if I sounded crazy.

Wes cringed at my use of the entity's name, but I didn't care about that, either. *Whatever* I needed to do or say to get through to them, I *would*.

"Yeah," said Wes. "That guy. It's just that . . . if what you're telling us is true, then that means that the whole 'Phantom Fury' episode wasn't a hoax. And if what happened to Rastin was real, that also means this thing really did kill Joe Boq. And—"

"Car," said Patrick suddenly, prompting the three of us to glance his way. He held his cell phone closer to his face, eyes scanning its screen. "Black Beamer. Just now, on the trail cam. I saw it pull onto the lot."

"Another cop," Wes said, which was what I'd been thinking, too.

"No," Patrick said quickly. "I don't think so."

"Who, then?" asked Charlotte.

"I . . ." Patrick said. "The windows were tinted, but the driver's side was rolled down halfway. Dude had sunglasses on, and I can't be sure, but I . . . I *think* . . ." He stopped himself, shaking his head before stuffing his phone into his pocket and nudging Charlotte.

"Move," he commanded. "Everyone move. We have to go there. *Now.*"

Patrick had seen something. Someone. Though he wasn't telling us who. I personally didn't need an explanation if it meant we were going back to Moldavia. Wordlessly, we all dug cash out of our pockets, leaving it on the table for Sam just as he arrived with Patrick's Heinz 57.

"Y'all are off in a hurry," he said.

"Sorry, Sam," said Patrick. "We gotta bounce."

"It's cool," Sam said, wiggling the bottle at us as we filed past him. "We can ketchup later."

FIFTY-THREE

Zedok

Despite his delay, he came, as I'd known he would.

The medium. *Rastin.*

And while I could not say his arrival was unexpected, his choice to approach me in corporeal form *was.* Because, by now, Rastin must have learned of Stephanie's disappearance and the ensuing investigation. Could he have deluded himself into believing I might still be complicit to carry out the plan the two of us had made?

Bypassing the yellow tape, he entered through the front door I had left unlocked for him. And now the medium stood in the center of the foyer, where he turned slowly in place, his glasses catching a glint from the weakening sunlight as he searched the gloom-filled archways and murky hall.

Stationed within a corner of shadows, I observed him from the balcony overlooking the foyer, the grand staircase, and the chandelier that still lay shattered in its hole.

If he were only to glance up, he would see me. But he was Rastin, a man as oblivious as he was intuitive. So, he did not.

Like me, Rastin never learned from his mistakes.

And his hopeless optimism—it looked as though it *would* be the death of him after all.

"Erik," said the medium, aware of how, even at a whisper, he would be heard.

I did not answer. Of course, I would. But . . . not yet.

In truth, I had hoped *not* to have to dispatch him. But then, I *had* warned him. And by returning here, was not Rastin making it clear that his plan was to stop at nothing to undo me?

"Erik, there's no use hiding," said Rastin. "Show yourself. Whatever form you've taken, I wish to speak. That is all I want. For today."

I smirked under my mask at that final amendment—before entering Charlie's vacated bedroom, where I passed through her closet door into my Moldavia.

Exiting Erik's opulent and emerald-adorned chamber, I strode over the balcony landing once more. Pausing at the first step, I spared a glance to Myriam's shuttered door, behind which Stephanie had remained for the majority of the time she had been in my world, emerging only when her appetite got the better of her. I had so far stayed away, waiting for the moment when she would approach *me*. Though my patience was wearing thin, and so I had resolved to end our stalemate tonight.

With his timing, though—impeccable as usual—Shirazi now presented another delay.

I descended the grand staircase, crossing through the very space Rastin occupied on the other side. I then drew back the parlor's closed pocket doors in silence, once again exiting the splendor of my

Moldavia for the ruin of the current-day one. Turning, I glanced to where Rastin stood with his back to me at the base of the steps, his gaze fixated on the landing I had vacated mere moments ago.

Ah, Rastin. Always rushing at me headlong. And always one step behind . . .

I waited for him to notice me. For all his meddling, he deserved, if nothing else, to see me coming.

FIFTY-FOUR

Stephanie

I still wasn't ready to believe there was no way out.

Not even when, no matter what door I tried, I never got through to my side.

Worse, I never woke up. In spite of everything, I kept hoping this was just another dream.

Just like I kept waiting for the sun to rise.

Dawn never came, though, and I never opened my eyes to turn off my alarm or to find Charlie's small nose two inches from mine.

The night he, Zedok—*Erik*—had brought me here, I'd run away into the snowy woods. My goal had been to put as much distance between us as possible, wanting to escape what I couldn't accept. That my abductor and the beautiful boy I'd tried to free were one and the same.

Without a coat or shoes, I'd barreled through the frozen forest only to have my path loop back to the house again and again, no matter which route I took.

Finally, unable to stand the cold, I'd barricaded myself inside the freezing conservatory, surrounded by the vines of all the roses that, like Erik, had once lived here but were now dead.

Curling up under the mountains of furs I'd found on the settee inside, I couldn't be sure if they, along with the mug of hot tea on the nearby table, had been meant for me. Like the house had foreseen my taking refuge in the conservatory. Like *he* had.

Lucas. God. He'd been *right* to suspect Erik. Because, on that boat, everything about Erik had changed so drastically that I now suspected this shift in him was what he'd been trying to warn me about all along. And I hadn't listened. Hadn't read between the lines. But how could I have ever anticipated *this*?

"Music," Erik had claimed as his reason for bringing me here. But there'd been something more lurking behind his words. Something deeper, darker—and far more frightening.

The memory of our almost-kiss surfaced in my mind for the hundredth time. Only now, when Erik drew nearer to me, the perfection of his face deteriorated, skin shriveling and cracking, sucking inward to hug the skull of a long-dead mummy.

I banished the image before I could picture those papery dead lips pressing mine. Sickened, wishing I was far away from here—safe somewhere in Lucas's arms—I wrapped my own around myself and walked to the window. Every day its frame showed the same scene of white grounds and darkness. I put my back to it, having already learned that it was useless to wait for the snow to stop. Though on the other side of the house this room was mine, on this side, the powder pink walls and pillow-piled bed told me that I now occupied Myriam Draper's room. If she was here along with Erik, though, she had yet to show up.

So far, I had not encountered any masked figure but the crimson-clad one that had brought me here. But there *were* more of them lurking about. Sometimes I'd hear whispering and once, a strange laugh. Doors would slam, too. Also, the masquerades had surrounded me that night I'd found myself on his side of the house, and Erik had fought them all off. Only now he was wearing the mask of the most frightening of them.

That night, it had also been Erik who'd possessed the lights-for-eyes that Charlie had told me were Zedok's. I should have made the connection then. Because they were the same eyes of the figure who'd brought me here.

Over the past few days, I'd had plenty of time to contemplate the other clues that had surfaced in my mind. The red-masked figure referring to himself and Erik as "us," and poor Charlie's encounter with the figure that hadn't resembled the Zedok she had known. Had I paid more attention, had I looked even just a little harder, maybe I would have come to the answer sooner.

That Erik was both figures and somehow, I was beginning to suspect, all figures . . .

How that was possible, there was no way to know. Not without asking. But facing him in his current state was not something I was prepared to do. Which was why I'd stayed in this room as much as possible, behind a locked door that I didn't really believe would stay locked if he didn't want it to.

His power scared me. His appearance scared me. What scared me even more, though, was the prospect that, in speaking to my captor, I would not find a trace of the boy I had come to know. Or maybe I was afraid that I would.

Daylight might have given me some bravery, but dawn never came, and it was the thought that I might never again see the sun that nearly broke me. Mostly because it also promised that I'd likely never again see my small and thoroughly shattered family. Or Lucas.

And reaching them again, getting back on my side of the house, was, at the very least, a goal. And as long as I had a goal, then I could still keep myself mentally okay.

Okay enough . . .

Until today, optimism had been easier to hold on to because I hadn't seen him again. Zedok.

After catching sight of him through a window earlier, a crimson smear in the snow, I now couldn't be sure of how much longer he'd leave me alone.

After just a moment of my staring, he'd turned to look back at me, making it clear he'd known the whole time I'd been watching him.

Maybe his appearance today had even been a signal. A warning that my adjustment period was about to end.

And now had arrived the part of the day I'd come to dread. This hour when my stomach complained loudly and painfully enough that its voice drowned out the questions, the doubts, the fears, *and* the rage. This hour when my choices ran out.

So far, each night I'd spent here had ended with my hunger driving me from the frilly, pink-adorned girl's room. Drawn by the intoxicating smells that began to fill the mansion at this hour, I'd crept downstairs and into the empty dining room to find the table crammed with platters packed with freshly cut fruit, meat, cheeses, and bread. On a separate table lay a spread of coffee, tea, and delicate cakes.

Even though I always found a feast awaiting me—more than I

could ever eat on my own—no other figure ever joined me.

Whenever I returned to my room, though, I always found that anything I'd moved had, in my absence, been returned to its original state. Any food I'd brought up with me also vanished when my back was turned. These changes happened too quickly to be caused by him or one of the masks, though. It was almost as if the house was somehow resetting itself. Rebooting like a computer.

Preparing to leave my room again, even knowing he might be waiting for me this time, I stood in front of my door, steeling myself, and reached for the doorknob.

But the muffled yell—that of a man—caused my fingers to retract.

Only silence followed, which was what prompted me to take hold of the knob again.

Slowly, I opened the door and slid out of Myriam's room, stepping as lightly as I could as I ventured all the way to the banister.

"Stephanie!"

I jolted at the low thump that followed the sound of my name, my head snapping in the direction from which the muffled racket had come.

That voice. Though it struck me as somehow familiar, it wasn't one that I could place. But the far-off way it had come through the walls told me that it hadn't emanated from this side of the house.

I gripped the banister, prepared to shout back. But I stopped myself.

Think. What if this was a trap?

"Stephanie Armand!"

The sound of my full name incinerated my reservations.

"I'm here!" I shouted. "Help me! I'm here!"

My heart jumped into a breakneck gallop. With quaking hands, I pulled myself along the banister, all the way to the stairs, where I waited for the man to shout again, to tell me what to do.

"Stepha—*grrh!*"

"Oh God," I whispered at the sound of my name being cut off by—

"No!" I screamed as I barreled down the stairs. "Run! Whoever you are, run! Get away!"

The voice—the man's. It had come from the same place I stood now in the foyer.

Someone was in the house. Someone who not only knew who I was but understood that I was trapped here.

But the stranger had been ambushed, and now there was only horrible silence.

Of course, it must have been *him*. On the other side. Attacking the man who had come to save me and who I was powerless to rescue in return.

Rushing through the parlor doors that had once served as a gateway between realms, I found myself again in Erik's parlor, where the black clock on the mantel ticked endlessly away.

The man groaned, and a low thud sounded in the foyer, prompting me to whirl.

"Erik!" I screeched. "Stop it!"

Someone was about to die for me. If he hadn't already.

My eyes darted over the pristine furniture, the lavish décor, and, finally, the spotless stained glass of the front door that Erik had once also used to transport me.

Desperate, I lunged toward the door, and grabbing the handle I swung it wide. But instead of a cool autumn breeze, an artic one blasted my heated face.

Twisted dead trees lined the horizon, their skeletal limbs powdered white.

Helpless. I was helpless to do anything to stop what was happening.

My breath fogged and my eyes stung from the cold. Yet, through their blur, I saw a sliver of what the trees, in their fullness, had always hidden from me on my side.

There, in the distance, gleamed *the lake*. The one Erik had used to convey me here.

That had been in a dream, yes, but didn't everything here mirror the other side? Hadn't I heard the piano notes and the ticking clock and now the man's voice through the walls?

The waters of the lake were, perhaps, a barrier, too. Could the lake do for me what the doors had so far not been able to?

I didn't have anything else.

I clambered down the stairs, rushing into the screen of falling snow. Then I began to run as hard and fast as I could in the direction of the forest.

Toward the lake.

FIFTY-FIVE
Zedok

I'd grabbed the dagger Wrath kept sheathed in one boot.

After turning to spot me, Rastin had lifted a hand, but I advanced on him anyway, giving him no time to utter even a single syllable before I struck, slicing the palm he'd hoped to stay me with.

A crimson arc slashed the floor, but his shout struck me more as one of surprise than pain. He swung away, his left hand gripping the wrist of the injured right. His back to me, I swiveled the blade in my grip, prepared to drive it through his ribs. Except I did not strike.

Because I *could* not.

The pain. Debilitating and arresting, the sudden rupturing in my empty chest caused me to stagger. I somehow managed to keep hold of my weapon while my free hand rushed to stifle the wound that had torn itself open again.

Rastin shouted Stephanie's name as he whirled—charging at me. His outstretched hand, streaming blood, met with my equally bloody sternum—an action that rendered me paralyzed.

He drove me backward, and I went—halting only when I collided with the wall.

It was then that Rastin unleashed the full power of his mind, sending into me his first retaliation.

Emotions, thick as blood themselves, flooded me. Rastin's.

His anger and the bitter sting of betrayal burned behind his pain. Not physical pain, but something much more potent. *Regret*.

Still, I laughed at him and took yet another swipe with my knife.

Wisely, Rastin jumped back, taking his psychic attack with him. *Un*wisely, he called again for Stephanie. This time, he even received an answer.

"I'm here!" she shouted from my side of the home. "Help me! I'm here!"

Rastin, on instinct, swung toward her voice—toward the grand staircase.

"You cannot reach her," I reminded him in a snarl. "It is hopeless, and you know it."

At once, Rastin turned to me, fists clenched, eyes alight with a strange fire I had never seen there before. "*She* is not who I have come in hopes of reaching!"

In an instant, my dark mirth morphed, transmuting wholly into fury.

This . . . *pity*. Rastin's. It was what made me loathe him.

I lunged for him but, displaying unexpected dexterity, he dodged me. Turning on him a second time, my cloak snapping as it whirled behind, I feinted toward him. Unflinching, he sent me an exasperated glare, as if to say he knew better than to fall prey to any trick of mine.

And with that look, rage dug its claws into my nonexistent innards—and twisted.

No more games. No more patronizing from *either* of our sides. No more deluding myself.

With my open hand, I reached toward Rastin, and with my mind, I dove into his chest.

Rastin had called for Stephanie again, but stopped cold, convulsing with my invasion. She shouted in response, urging him to flee, but it was too late for that now. Holding him in my sway, I shut my eyes and narrowed my focus on that beating muscle just behind his sternum.

Fear thrummed in him and his heart hammered as I closed my mental hand around it. Overcome, Rastin collapsed with a groan to his knees, grasping at his chest.

"Erik!" came Stephanie's shrill but muffled shout. "Stop it!"

Her command. It won my hesitation. And that mere flicker of resolve allowed him to slam me with his most vicious attack yet.

This time, instead of anger or regret, Rastin pierced me through with a feeling so unexpected, I had difficulty even identifying it.

Until suddenly, I knew it.

Relief. It coursed from his spirit—from his soul—and came pouring into me, striking with more force than any blow could have.

He was *glad* to be here? Compassion, above all, coated the snarl of everything else. *Including* his fear. His anger.

I let him go. Because I could not bear to be faced with this irrefutable proof that he *did* care. About me.

"Why?" I asked him as I drew back, clutching the knife tighter, as if willing myself to use it again. "Why do you seek to save me when you know it is useless? *Why do you care what becomes of me?*"

Rastin ignored me, shouting once more for Stephanie, though

his tone had changed. Now he seemed to be calling after her rather than for her.

"Erik," he then huffed between labored breaths, peering toward the door. "The . . . girl—"

"I'll not give her up," I said. "Not now, not ever."

"The lake," he wheezed. "Erik . . . she's . . . *the lake . . .*"

At once, his meaning occurred to me. Stephanie had gone silent after crying out. And Rastin was now insinuating he could sense Stephanie's whereabouts on the grounds. But . . . this must be a distraction. A ploy. For what reason would Stephanie have to go to the lake? The lake that, on my side, was sheeted by ice.

Without another word, I departed, leaving Rastin there, gasping and bleeding on the floor as I hurried to the front door that returned me to my realm.

I left the porch, my gaze fixed upon the white-hazed horizon that held no sign of either movement or silhouette. My boots crushed the fallen snow that continued to barrel in currents from the sky, hurrying to fill the tiny grave-like prints left by a smaller set of feet.

The prints led away from the porch and from me, trailing across the grounds in a straight line that terminated at the trees.

The lake. Rastin's voice, full of warning, rang through my skull.

But . . . *why* would she go there?

There was only one reason I could think of.

And it was a reason that made me run.

FIFTY-SIX
Lucas

I hadn't even finished shifting the Dart into park next to the empty black Beamer when we heard the shout. Someone inside the house calling out for—

"*Stephanie.*" I pried off my seatbelt, leaving my keys in the ignition and my friends in the car.

"Lucas, wait!" Charlotte called from the front passenger's seat. But I charged straight toward the house and the open front door, not bothering to look back.

"C'mon, man, I thought we had this talk," growled Patrick, his steps along with Charlotte's and Wes's now pounding the pavement in time with mine.

As my feet thudded up the porch steps, a blast of frozen air slammed straight into me. I ignored its warning, ducking under the yellow crime scene tape before bursting through the door and into the darkened foyer.

Arcs and splatters of crimson slashed the floor. *Two* sets of footprints tracked the blood this way and that, and there—in the center—knelt a man.

He gripped his chest with one blood-soaked hand. Reaching toward me, he beckoned with the other.

"Ho-ly man on the TV," Wes said from behind me as I rushed to the man's side, not recognizing him until his outstretched arm took hold of mine. His eyes. I had seen them countless times before. I'd even spoken to him once. At that convention. And there was the email I'd sent. Did this mean he'd gotten it?

"You have got to be kidding me right now," exclaimed Charlotte, her voice emanating from the door.

"I *knew* I'd seen him on the cam!" shouted Patrick. "I figured it *couldn't* be, but—"

"Please," said Rastin, heaving for breath as I helped him to his feet. "Autographs later."

I swiveled to find Patrick hovering close by. Wes still lingered in the door, his face a mask of pure shock. Charlotte stood beside him, dumbstruck.

"Joking aside," said Rastin, looping an arm around my shoulder. "We need to get out of here."

"But—" began Patrick, gesturing to where Rastin gripped his shirt.

"Now!" Rastin rasped, and then he nearly collapsed.

I caught him and hauled him upright, bearing as much of his weight as I could.

My brain told me to get him out of there, stat.

My heart, though. It knew I wasn't finished here yet. "Stephanie—"

"She lives," Rastin said. "But *we* will not if we stay."

"Wes, get his keys," I said as I helped Rastin toward the door. "Charlotte, you and Patrick take the Dart. Follow us out."

No one argued. Wes dug through Rastin's blazer pocket, the one the medium indicated with a nod.

"*Go,*" Rastin urged. "All of you. Before he returns."

Patrick, hurrying to Rastin's other side, helped me usher him out. Charlotte, in the meantime, ran ahead to the Dart.

"You swear she's alive?" I asked as we ambled to the Beamer.

"He will not let her die," said Rastin, even as he faltered again, his knees giving.

"What the hell is that supposed to mean?" I propped him— maybe a bit roughly—against the side of his car while Patrick broke off to catch up with Charlotte. Rastin winced. It was then that I got a better look at his chest—the source of his pain.

His shirt, though spattered with blood, showed no slashes or cuts.

That only left room for an internal issue.

His heart.

Wes, rounding the Beamer, climbed in on the driver's side.

"C'mon," I said, deciding that, for the moment, it would have to be enough to know that Stephanie *was* alive. And so long as Rastin was here, well, I couldn't let him die. "We have to get you to the hospital."

"No hospital," said Rastin as he slid into the back seat.

His head lolled to one side before he passed out.

"Just go," I said to Wes as I climbed in next to the medium. Wes shifted the car into gear before I could even pull the door shut.

We peeled out, tires kicking up gravel as we raced back the way we'd come, Charlotte and Patrick in the Dart barreling after us.

"Dibs on the car if he croaks," said Wes as he gunned the gas.

"It's a rental," murmured Rastin.

"Hey!" yelled Wes, his gray eyes flashing in the rearview. "Are you faking back there?"

"Sometimes . . ." Rastin murmured as he faded out again, "I wish I *were* a fake."

FIFTY-SEVEN

Stephanie

Half running, half sliding, I rushed down the steep, tree-covered embankment of white that sloped to the lake's edge.

Though my ears burned from the cold and my fingers went numb, the threat of hypothermia didn't concern me as much as the thought of what he would do when he discovered I was gone. Because as far as I knew, he had just killed whoever had come to help me.

Embedded in a wide clearing, the lake, frozen and black, stretched as wide and long as it had in the dream. Only the faint hiss of the falling snow and the sound of my own panicked breathing disrupted the muted silence of the night.

Every few stumbling steps, I kept checking over my shoulder, searching for any sign of red amid the trees. Then, skidding to a halt at the bank, the stitch in my side loosening by a fraction, I scanned the surface of the lake for a weak point.

Flawless, the ice reflected only the darkness of the forest, as well as the overhanging tangle of white-laced limbs. My own face, haggard and frightened, nearly unrecognizable in the onyx ice, begged for the answer of what to do next.

"Lucas," I whispered aloud to the ice, and his name left my lips in in the form of a cloud. One that I imagined could, like a prayer, somehow find its way to him.

Nearby, I spotted a jagged stone poking through the snow and seized it.

When I made it to my world again, would I find Lucas there, too? Had he also been trying to reach me? Could he have possibly even come here with the man?

Tap . . . Tap . . . Tap . . .

The sound of my steps on the ice pierced the bubble of my swelling hope. It reminded me of the ticking clock on Erik's mantel. A sound that must have plagued him for years. Decades.

Over a century.

I couldn't do that. I couldn't stay in a place like this for my whole life and beyond. I'd go insane. Like I was right now. Ready, apparently, to die if it meant I got a chance to live.

Reaching the center of the lake, where the ice thinned enough to creak and whine underfoot, I stopped and peered down again at my reflection and took a simultaneous breath.

Then I slammed a heel hard into the frozen barrier.

A crackle split the silence, but I didn't go through. Instead, white spiderweb splinters burst out in jagged lines beneath me.

The impact hadn't been enough.

Determined, I knelt onto the crack and raised the rock over my head before bringing it down as hard as I could, hard enough to cause the edges of the rock to slice into my flesh.

Multiplying, the white veins shot farther outward, spiking thinner offshoots.

A growl that started in the back of my throat transformed into a yell of frustration. Again, I slammed the barrier separating me from the water—from home—and this time, along with a sharp crunch, there came a soft and eerie *ping*. I blinked, startled by the unexpected sound. The way it echoed through the silent wood caused me to pause. And strangely, to want to hear it again.

As if answering my unspoken request, the sound repeated—an ethereal and almost musical peal—like the far-off snapping of a metal cord. Confused, I lowered my hands, now bleeding.

Stilling, I waited for the moment when the pinging from the ice would stop.

If *I* wasn't moving, though, then there shouldn't—

I lifted my eyes with sudden understanding.

Slowly, I turned my head.

He stood on the ice at a distance of thirty feet, those two pinprick lights fixed on me, shining from within the depths of the silver mask that gleamed cerulean in the gloom.

He had thrown back his cloak. The garment spilled from his shoulders to frame his crimson uniform, which, against the backdrop of white, blazed brighter even than the blood that smeared his chest.

The pinging of the ice had stopped the moment my eyes met his, confirming my suspicion that it hadn't been *my* movements that had caused the lake to sing that way . . . but his.

Now there was only the sound of my frightened breathing—my heart banging a death-metal rhythm in my ears.

How had he reached me so quickly? Could he appear where he wanted on a whim?

He showed no sign of exertion. No clouds of breath appeared in the vicinity of that mask.

Holding him with my stare, trying not to blink, I abandoned my rock, pressed my hands against the ice . . . and pushed to my feet. Slowly, the weakened ice groaning beneath me, I pivoted toward him.

"Don't," he said.

But just as I faced him, the ice at last gave.

Then he, along with the world, rushed up and out of sight, like a curtain being torn away to reveal a polar void.

The water, more frigid than I could ever have imagined, pierced me everywhere—a thousand stabbing knives.

I gritted my teeth as I sank, and, fighting the cold, I willed my limbs to move me farther *down*. Only, instead of ending in a place where the bottom of this lake broke through to the surface of mine, the blackness carried on, proving that this was not the same shallow body of water from the dream.

The glimmer of hope I'd felt when I'd beaten on the ice began to fade. And then that small light dimmed, readying itself to do what all lights eventually did. All lights except for perhaps two . . .

I stopped swimming and tilted my head up toward the unbroken sheet of ice that was my sky. The hole I'd fallen through. It had vanished.

Panic gripped me, and I pedaled for the surface, raising both hands above my head.

But it wasn't until the moment my fingers grazed the frozen

barrier that I remembered the way things reset themselves in this world.

The ice. I should have realized it would follow the same rules.

I wanted to scream. Instead, without meaning to, I inhaled.

Water flooded my lungs. And the darkness that I had hoped would deliver me home came to take me where it would.

FIFTY-EIGHT
Lucas

"Curious," said Wes. "Is that the blazer you wore in the Halloween episode of *Ethereal Encounters*?"

He was talking to Rastin, who now sat at the far end of our usual gaming couch in my basement, an ice pack pressed to his head, the bloodstained blazer in question draped over the arm of the couch.

"You know," Wes prattled on, "the one where Jordan and Graham got chased by that shadow figure and you helped that old guy cross over? Can I try it on?"

"Absolutely not," Rastin snapped even as Wes rose from my computer chair to go for the blazer. Plucking the garment up, he looped his too-long arms through the coat and settled it onto his shoulders. Grinning, he put his hands on his hips and nodded. "Oh, yes. Wessed to impress."

Shortly after we'd made our escape from Moldavia, Rastin told us that, in spite of appearances, he would be okay and that taking him to the hospital would only delay our reaching Stephanie. So, I'd told Wes to drive him back to my house.

And now . . . here we all were. Sitting in my basement with the world-famous Rastin Shirazi, who was now dressed in one of my '50s-style button-downs.

Luckily, Mom was at an event and Dad was upstairs absorbed in football and grousing at the TV.

After Wes had parked the Beamer on the street, I'd hurried ahead into the house. I'd said my usual "What's up?" to Dad before rushing down the stairs to let Wes and Rastin in through the basement door. Patrick and Charlotte followed shortly after.

"Dude," said Patrick. "Does your dad know he's here?"

"*No*," I said. "And can we keep it down, please? I'd like it to stay that way."

"I thought I was going crazy when I saw him on the trail cam," Patrick said. "And now he's in your flipping basement. I can't even handle this right now."

Rastin pinched the bridge of his nose and peeked at Patrick with one eye.

"One might also point out how his presence here erases all lingering doubts about his being the real deal," said Wes.

"Hey," said Patrick, pointing at Wes. "Didn't we have a bet about that?"

"That's what I was leading up to. You owe me a Frappuccino."

"Are you sure you don't owe me one?"

"Would I have brought it up if I did?"

"You are all really very annoying," grumbled Rastin as he squeezed his eyes shut again.

"Oh, I'm sorry," said Wes. "Pardon us. We'll try to save your life a little less annoyingly next time."

"What are you even *doing* here?" asked Charlotte.

"At last," muttered Rastin, "someone speaks to me as though I am present."

I glowered at him. "Excuse me if I didn't know how to be more direct than *emailing* you."

Everyone turned to look at me now.

And wow. Yeah. I guess I kind of did just say that out loud.

Rastin alone dropped his gaze. He sighed, shoulders sagging.

"I take it your being here means you got my message," I said.

"I got your message," Rastin's reply caused the anger within me to wind that much tighter.

"You sent Rastin a message?" Patrick asked.

"And again," said Charlotte, "you didn't think to tell us?"

"*Now* who do we need the spray bottle for?" asked Wes.

"Stephanie came to me," I said. "She started explaining stuff that . . . that I'd never heard of happening before. So, I thought, what the heck? If he wasn't a fake like everyone thinks he is, he'd reply. He never did, so I never told you guys."

Though Rastin winced at the word "fake," he didn't say anything. So, while I had everyone's attention, I decided to ask the million-dollar question. "Why didn't you write me back? You knew what was in that house. You knew it could hurt people, and you didn't respond."

"You are amateurs," he said. "*Children.* You don't know what you're doing."

"We're teenagers," I snapped. "Besides, I didn't tell you how old I was in the email."

"Uh, Lucas," said Patrick from his spot in the yellow beanbag. "He's psychic."

"There was nothing metaphysical about it," Rastin interjected. "You linked your website."

Oh. Yeah. I did.

"Besides," Rastin went on, "even if you *weren't* kids, I wouldn't have involved you. Emailing you back would have involved you."

"Except my email told you I was *already* involved," I argued.

"You don't understand."

"I understand that you saw Stephanie," I said, trying to push my anger aside enough to forge forward and get somewhere with this guy who, I was trying to remind myself, I'd always admired, even during the days when the others had doubted him.

"I *heard* her," corrected Rastin. "I called for her, and she answered. But . . ."

"That's when it attacked you," Wes guessed.

"Him," Rastin was quick to correct. "Erik."

"*Erik?*" Charlotte blurted.

"Yes," said Rastin. "Erik."

"So, what are you saying?" Patrick asked. "That there *are* two entities in the house."

"No," he said. "And here is what you do not understand. Though it would seem there are many entities in the home, there is truly only one."

Everyone in my basement went silent. All eyes rested on Rastin, who still had his head hung. Finally, he raised his stare to meet mine.

"Erik is there," Rastin began. "His soul is indeed trapped in Moldavia. But . . . there is no ghost."

"So, we *are* facing a monster," interrupted Wes.

"*No*," answered Rastin. "And don't call him that."

Wes blinked, struck speechless for perhaps the first time since I'd known him.

We all stared at Rastin then, waiting for him to give us a single clue as to what we were really up against. And why, if it was evil enough to abduct Stephanie, kill people, and attack him, he would be so adamant about what we chose to call it.

"Erik. He is . . . a *boy*," Rastin explained. "Like you." He gestured to me.

"So, the stories," Patrick said, "about the curse. They *are* true."

"There *is* a curse," Rastin admitted. "And Erik *is* its victim."

"But not its only victim," I said.

A beat passed before Rastin replied. His answer came with a tired, sad expression. As well as a note of resignation. "No."

"Stephanie," I continued.

"She is Erik's prisoner," conceded Rastin, his frown deepening. "That much is evident."

"But?" I folded my arms, certain I wasn't going to like the next turn this conversation took. But if the signposts pointed to Stephanie, then it was time to hit the gas.

"*But*," began Rastin, "Erik, too, is a prisoner."

"Uh," interjected Wes, and for once, I was glad he did—because it saved me from having to. "A prisoner who nearly crushed your heart. For the second time, I gather?"

"You *must* believe me." Rastin shut his eyes again, like his headache had only grown in the time he'd been here. "But Erik is currently not himself—and has not been for a very long time."

"Zedok and Erik," I said. "Tell us once and for all. What is their relationship to one another?"

Rastin laughed, and the mirthless, *hopeless* sound of it caused the hairs on my arms to stand on end.

"They are the same," he confirmed. "And yet . . . they are not."

Wes smacked his lips. "Well. Now that that's cleared up . . ."

"It *is* difficult to explain," sighed Rastin. "Nearly as difficult as it must be to understand."

"But maybe it won't be so hard to explain it to *us*," I said, hoping he would hurry up and realize that, just as he was the only one who knew for sure what we did about Stephanie—that she was a prisoner in an alternate dimension—*we* were the only ones in a position to hear him out on anything regarding the creature keeping her there.

We needed Rastin's help. But it was growing more and more apparent that he was going to need ours, too.

And *that* was really where this conversation was headed. Now that he'd recovered, why else would he still be here? Regardless of what he was hoping to accomplish, our overall goal was bound to be a unified one.

Get Stephanie out.

"If someone will make me hot tea," said Rastin, "chai, preferably, I will tell you all I know about the curse, and about Erik. I cannot ask you to pity him as I do. Perhaps none of us—myself especially—can afford to pity him any longer. But . . . if one is to understand their enemy, then one must be willing to put oneself in their enemy's shoes. Or, in this instance, perhaps it is better to say . . . we must put ourselves in his masks."

Silence pulsed.

Then Charlotte sighed and, turning toward the stairs, said what she knew none of us would since we didn't know how.

"I'll go make the tea."

FIFTY-NINE
Zedok

She awoke with a start, eyes springing wide to focus on the blazing hearth.

Darkness swathed the parlor, the fire and the silver glow of the winter moon through the window serving as the room's only sources of light.

She lay draped upon the chaise that I'd had Guilt and Guile lift and draw closer to the fire. Sitting up, she searched for me, yet her eyes did not wander to where I'd sat for the past several hours, keeping watch over her. Instead, she turned toward the sound that, though softer than the fire's crackling and the mantel clock's ticking, had awakened her.

The whispers. Those of Envy and Spite.

Having had their usual perch stolen from them, the gossiping duo loitered nearby, their forms silhouetted by the moonlit bay window.

"Shh," hissed Envy. "She's awakened."

"Oh, *this* ought to be interesting," answered Spite.

I took that as my cue to stand. Better I reveal my presence to Stephanie now than have it betrayed by one of that pair.

"They are nothing to fear," I said.

Stephanie's head snapped in the direction of my voice, so much altered from the one she had come to know.

I moved forward, melting out of the darkness and just into the outer rim of the firelight.

In response, Stephanie pulled the quilt Desire had laid over her tighter to herself with the hands I had bandaged.

"What happened?" she asked, her hushed tone implying she was asking herself rather than me. Still, I chose to answer.

"You fell into the lake, and I extracted you."

"The ice," she said, her memory rejoining her. "It closed over."

"Yes."

"How did you . . . ?"

"I am stronger than I appear."

"But . . . I was drowning." She pressed a hand to her chest, fingers tightening around the white fabric of the cotton nightgown she now wore.

"You expelled the water while unconscious."

The truth was that I had forced her lungs to eject the water, utilizing the same abilities to preserve her life that I had employed to nearly end Rastin's. But she had been through enough, and that information would only serve to alarm her further.

"The man," she said with a gasp, as if she had somehow read my thoughts. "The one who came for me. Did you kill him?"

"That man lives," I said through a sneer.

"You let him go?"

Could I say that? I could. Though it would be more accurate to say he escaped.

"I have said I did not kill him. Believe that or don't."

She glowered at me, hating me as she did. As perhaps she now always would.

"You can't be him," she said, shaking her head. "You can't."

I frowned beneath Wrath's mask, the pain in my sternum twisting. By "him," of course, she meant Erik.

"To that, I have but one answer," I replied. "Within this Moldavia, I am the only 'he' and, in fact, besides yourself now, the only *one* there is."

"The other masked figures—" she whispered.

Her expression shifted in the firelight, betraying how she had already solved the riddle of the masks. But perhaps it would be best for us both to leave her no room to doubt.

"They are all, and have always been, me," I finished for her.

"But then . . . you *lied* to me."

The vehemence with which she spat these words suggested that this was, for her, the most egregious of my crimes—more unforgivable even than the act of abducting her.

"The others, perhaps," I allowed. "But not I."

"You tried to kill my father."

Here, she had me. While I regretted Madness's actions, I could hardly argue I had not meant to cause Mr. Armand harm.

"Again, it was the doing of another mask," I said, though without hope she would believe me. "I . . . am relieved your father will recover."

"He won't, though," she argued. "And neither will Charlie. Not if I don't come home."

To that, I reverted to silence, for I could not disagree. No more than I could permit myself to entertain her reasoning. Now that she was here with me, mine at last, I preferred to forget there existed anyone else.

"If they really are all you," she said at last, after the silence swelled to an unbearable volume, "then I want to talk to the other one. The blue-masked figure."

"Valor, you mean. Sadly, he is no more. You understand I could not have him usurping my plans any longer."

She hitched a breath, and from seemingly nowhere, a pair of tears fell, though I surmised from the sternness of her expression that she hated that I had borne witness to them.

"I don't believe you," she said.

"Again, you doubt my word. Soon, though, you will learn as I have that Wrath has little cause to lie."

"He is Valor and you're Wrath?" she asked, banishing the tears with one bandaged hand.

"He *was* Valor," I said. "And yes. I *am* Wrath."

"And all of you are Zedok. Erik?"

"Erik is dead," I said calmly.

"But you *were* Erik. Once."

"I told you—"

"The man who was here," she said, abruptly reverting subjects. "Who was he?"

"He *is*," I replied with care, "an old . . . associate."

"Yeah," she snapped. "You two sounded *real* friendly—*hey*." Glancing down at herself, she noted for the first time the white nightgown. "Where are my clothes?"

"You were soaked," I answered simply, having prepared myself for this topic. "It is a wonder you did not suffer hypothermia."

"So you *undressed* me?" Fear once again crept into her now shaking voice, overshadowing any outrage.

"Certainly not," I said. "I daresay you would know if I had." I gestured to my sternum, hoping the blood there spoke for itself. She would not find a trace of it on her person. I nodded in the direction of the bay window. "The two masks there saw to your garments. I did, however, bandage your hands. Your wounds needed tending."

"But..." She trailed off, her eyes leaving me briefly to spare another glance for Envy and Spite. "The masks. You . . . you said they *are* you."

"I have but one pair of eyes," I assured her with discomfort. Were we really going to dwell on this? Could she not take my word for it? And why was she looking at me *that* way?

"I cannot see what they see," I continued. "Be assured your propriety has in no way been compromised."

She blinked at me. I, in turn, looked away. As if I had a face that wasn't already hidden.

"I understand your concern," I said, speaking yet again when she let that horrible silence drag on. "Circumstances being what they are, I can, of course, only expect you to assume the worst of me. But, despite what you must think . . . What I mean to say is that I meant all that I said before. In the parlor, and the conservatory. Regarding my . . . I wished only to preserve your life. I'll thank you now not to twist my actions and accuse me of indecency when I merely—"

"Oh my God," she said, the words escaping her lips in an awestruck whisper that silenced me immediately.

I shut my mouth, ceasing the tirade that now struck me as rambling. Reluctantly, I shifted my gaze to her once more.

"You're *embarrassed*," she said.

I stiffened and kept silent, all too aware that any denial on my part would only prove her right. Yet it did mortify me to think she would assume I had behaved ungentlemanly toward her. Or was I mistaking her concern for repulsion over the fact that I had touched her at all?

"I must know if you intend to continue to try to kill yourself," I snapped. "Or has that particular itch been sufficiently scratched?"

Her scowl returned in an instant, deepening toward rage. "I wasn't trying to kill myself!"

"You wished merely to go for a subzero dip?"

"I was trying to get away!" she yelled, tossing off the quilt and launching to her feet. "From you!"

Behind her, Envy and Spite burst into titters. One of them even snorted.

"And *you two*," she said, wheeling on them. "Don't either of you have anything better to do than hiss like a pair of snakes in a basket?"

To my surprise, Envy and Spite went silent, neither seeming to have anything to say. An absolute first.

"They won't answer," I said. "I've ordered them not to speak to you."

"They have to do what you say?" she asked, veering on me once more. "The others. Why do they listen to *you* but not Valor?"

Because none of them wanted what Valor wanted.

"Do sit," I said. "You very nearly succeeded in drowning yourself, and you're bound to catch cold if you do not now rest."

Her eyes burned into me. "I told you. I was only trying to get out of here."

"By way of the lake." My words dripped incredulity.

"That was how you brought me here, wasn't it?"

Ah. Now it made sense. Relative sense.

"That was a dream," I explained.

"I *know* it was a dream."

"You could have died."

"I. *Know.*"

Quiet claimed the air between us. And indeed, what could I say to that?

"You are that desperate to leave, then?" I asked, shocked that I had uttered this aloud.

She did not answer. And that *was* my answer.

I pivoted from her, retreating into the cover of darkness again. "You are saying you will try the lake again? Even if I tell you it is useless."

"Erik—"

"Do *not* call me by that name."

"Where are you going?"

Where *was* I going? Here I was about to walk away from her like a wounded dog. And there *she* was asking after me.

"You wish me to stay?" I growled, irritated with her. With myself.

"No," she said, providing me with both the answer I had expected and an excuse for the escape I sorely longed for. I slid farther into the shadows.

"Wait—yes!" Taking a step after me, she thrust her hands

blindly into the dark, as though she hoped to catch me. "Yes—*stay*."

I stopped where I stood, a dog once again, obeying the command of its mistress.

"Just now," she began anew, "you said that you meant the things you said before. In the conservatory. That means that you *are* still Erik."

To this I said nothing. What good would it do to either affirm or deny? She may have guessed the truth, but she still did not understand.

"In the beginning," she continued, "you were trying to get me out of the house. Weren't you? Even before I ever spoke to you. That's why you appeared to Charlie."

Again, I answered, though this time in my mind, *not I*.

"Because . . . a part of you knew *this* would happen." Her voice became softer even than before. "Or something like it. When you were Valor, you were trying to prevent it. You even tried to tell me the truth that night, when you almost . . . when *we* almost . . . But then something went wrong. That's why you're bleeding. Isn't it?"

You are right, Stephanie. Something did happen. But how do I tell you that that something . . . was you? And the boy. He is what went wrong.

As far as the blood goes and from whence it came . . . who could say?

"Answer me," she hissed. "*Please*."

I vacillated on whether or not I should confirm her guesses as true, for it was all irrelevant now. But then, had she not once acquiesced to me when *I* had pleaded? Unlike that instance, though, when she had played for me, I could not give her what she longed to hear. I could, however, still grant her what she asked.

"You see me accurately for who I was," I allowed. "Know, though, that I am that no longer."

"So then what are you now?" she challenged after a pause. "Erik, why did you bring me here? What does kidnapping me accomplish? What does *any* of this accomplish?"

I scowled, disarmed yet again. And her question needled at me, boring through that place inside me that both did and did not know how to articulate an answer for this particular inquiry.

"Did you expect me to be happy here?" she pressed. "Do you expect me to ever be? Or are you doing this to punish me because of Lucas?"

"He is unworthy of you," I snarled.

"You don't get to decide that!"

"If I was in your world," I said, "if I was *of* your world, and your time, you would not have chosen him."

"There was no choice, Erik."

And what was this? Her way of saying she had never even considered me? Now who was the liar.

"I would have made you forget him," I promised her. "I would have given you everything. I would have snatched you out of his grasp. I would have made you mine. I would have—"

"But you're not any of those things," she said, her words once more slicing through mine—rending me in two as well. For again, she was right. "By the way, you can't *make* someone want to be with you. And I know you know that."

I did. Powerfully so.

"That's why I'm here, though, isn't it?" she asked, her tone dry, brittle, and black as charcoal. "Because you do know it. You just don't care anymore."

Even in *this* mask, I could not hide from her.

"What is it going to take," she asked, "for you to realize the truth? Erik, when are you going to let me go?"

Let her go? Could it be she still didn't realize what she was to me?

"You wish me to release you."

"I'm telling you that you have to," she said.

Apparently, she had yet to learn that there was very little Wrath could be compelled to do. But if she wanted to make demands of me, I would of course oblige.

"Very well," I said after a pause. "I shall release you on one condition and one only. Say that you *are* mine. Swear that you will stay in Moldavia. Better still, say that you will marry me."

She went silent and still. The crackling of the fire filled the room, as did the ticking of the clock.

"*What?*" she said at last.

"My words were plain," I replied. "They should not bear repeating."

She shook her head, the fingertips of both bandaged hands rushing to cover her mouth.

"Erik," she whispered, "you're dead." As if this was something I could have forgotten.

"And yet I stand before you," I said, anger searing the edges of my patience. "I speak. I walk."

I feel.

"You know that's—"

"The request is a simple one," I cut her off. "The answer should be, too."

She drew a breath. And, like a well-aimed arrow, her expected answer split the quiet—and pierced me through.

"Never."

The clock ticked, and Spite whispered some triumphant utterance to Envy.

The truth was that I had known she would deny me. Truer than that, I had been counting on it. If the growing pain in my chest was any indication, however, there had apparently existed some part of me that had hoped in vain for some other reply. Any other.

"The masks by the window," I said. "They have been instructed to watch over you. And prevent any similar scenario like the one today."

"You can't keep me here forever," she said, strength returning to her voice. "Deep down, you know that, too."

"The hour is late, and your exhaustion is plain," I replied as I turned to go. "I should leave you to your repose. Perhaps, though, when next I see you, you will feel recovered enough to revisit the ballad you already know."

"Erik."

"It should please you to learn I have finished the score."

"It *doesn't* please me. Erik, *none* of this pleases me."

"I have also composed lyrics. They should prove easy enough to memorize."

"I'm not going to sing for you!" she shouted. "Not ever!"

Silence boomed through the space between us, a raw scream of nothingness.

"'Not ever,'" I repeated after a long pause. "'Never.' So be it, Stephanie Armand. But then let your answers stand for us *both*."

With that, I brushed past her, leaving her to the care of her solitude—and the watch of her new guard dogs.

SIXTY
Lucas

O ver tea, grape sodas, ginger muffins, and, in Patrick's case, nearly half a bag of fun-sized chocolate bars, Rastin had told us what he'd claimed to be, quote, "everything."

The medium had then asked us not to speak and requested that we instead "meditate" and reconvene with him the following night to discuss next steps. To me, though, the plan seemed clear enough. But for once, Charlotte had been the one to make the final call: we would do what Rastin asked and wait to talk.

Rastin had left shortly after, assuring us he was fine to drive himself back to his hotel. Before he went, he gave me his cell number.

Now, as I lay in bed staring up at the slowly rotating arms of my ceiling fan, I imagined how the Lucas Cheney of one year ago might have reacted if he'd known that, come November, he'd have Rastin Shirazi's personal cell phone number saved in his contacts.

Probably, Past Lucas would not be quite as agog about the number as he would be to learn of the events leading up to the connection.

Hours ago, SPOoKy had agreed to meet the next evening. Then, per Rastin's instructions, later that night in the lobby of his hotel to devise a plan with the medium, who we were going to need—no way around that, either.

Mom had arrived home shortly after everyone had left, and I'd tried to act normal over Chinese takeout and all the "Where've you been all day?" interrogations.

Oh, you know, I'd answered in my mind, *just went to Stephanie's cursed mansion to rescue a famous guy from an invisible bloodthirsty mummy—the usual.*

After dinner, Mom and Dad had streamed a movie while I'd retreated to my room.

Now it was almost one in the morning, and both darkness and silence had set up camp in the Cheney household.

Unable to resist any longer, I grabbed my cell phone from my nightstand, keyed in the passcode, and opened my pictures. Thumbing through, I arrived at a photo Patrick had snapped of me and Stephanie the night of the dance.

We leaned against my car, both of us smiling, my arm looped around her shoulders. There was something in Stephanie's eyes, though, that I hadn't noticed that night. A distance. A worry that dimmed the enthusiasm of her smile. How much else had I failed to pick up on? Until now, I hadn't thought much.

Somewhere along the way, even in spite of everything, I'd gotten distracted.

Hard not to do around her.

And at the dance, it had felt so good just to hold her. Then there'd been that kiss. The one full of heat and desire and everything I had, up to that point, kept myself from saying out loud to her.

God. I missed her.

What was she doing right now? Was she okay? Was she think-ing of me, too?

Guilt, heavy as a cinder block, returned to my chest. If she *was* thinking of me, then she had to be wondering what was taking me so long. Or had she assumed I'd given up on her?

Dropping my phone to the bed, I glared harder at the ceiling fan, my gaze shifting past the blades to the shadows they cast on the smooth white ceiling above. And as my focus switched from phone to fan—from Stephanie to those shadows—a shift took place inside of me.

From love to hate.

For Erik.

Rastin had told us he believed the creature had taken Stephanie because he'd fallen in love with her.

And that hadn't even been the most difficult part to swallow. Then again, maybe it had been. For me.

Insane at is it seemed, I could see it happening. It had happened to me, after all. But exactly how . . . Well, there was the mystery.

Stephanie had told me about her recurring dreams of Erik but never mentioned what those dreams contained. Only that Erik had spent the majority of them trying to warn her about Zedok.

Turned out I'd been wrong in my assumption that Erik had been just a front for something much darker. But then, in a way, I'd also been right.

If only I'd delved a little deeper, plied Stephanie until she told me what, specifically, had gone on in those dreams. Then I might have suspected even more of the truth.

I hadn't, though, and now Stephanie was with him. In his world. Trapped.

Regardless of what Rastin or anyone else said or believed—that wasn't love.

Human or not, cursed or not, Erik was evil. And that meant he had to be stopped—for good.

Already, I'd made up my mind that I would be the one to do it. Based on everything Rastin had divulged about how to destroy the monster, there seemed no other way.

According to the medium, the lore about the Mothmen and the mummy unwrapping had been true. And while Erik had incurred the wrath of the mummy by disturbing and inadvertently reawakening him, he had also succeeded in extracting the power he'd sought. Power that had afforded him certain abilities, like the conjuring of apports—which was basically making something appear from nothing. He also possessed other dangerous psychic powers aside from the ability to infiltrate and manipulate the dreams of those who entered onto the property.

Fortunately, though, his powers both began and ended at the original property lines.

That tidbit of info had prompted Patrick to ask about Joe Boq, and Rastin had surprised us all once again by revealing that Erik had not been responsible for that particular death. Instead, Rastin believed a separate entity from a different investigation was to blame. That news brought little comfort. Because even though that meant we were all safe for the moment, it didn't change the fact that all bets would be off once we stepped foot back in his world.

Rastin claimed that Erik's lust for power had derived from his longing to mold and bend his life—and therefore his fate—into the shape he wanted.

The day Erik was born was the day his parents had set him on the track to becoming a physician. And before he'd died, he'd been faced with the decision of marrying one of two wealthy debutants—neither of whom he was in love with, or even liked.

From early childhood and on, though, he'd exhibited an almost otherworldly talent for music and a matching thirst for the mastery of it.

Each of us in SPOoKy had always heard of Erik Draper's abilities with music. During his time, rumors had spread that he'd been visited by angels or that he'd signed a pact with the devil. Those were the only stories the Victorians could come up with to explain how he'd ended up with the voice and face of a god.

But in the end, Erik's aspirations hadn't mattered to his parents.

In their eyes, music and love were frivolities that their only son could ill afford to indulge in. Not at the cost of more worthy pursuits.

"So . . . this whole mummy thing was a fit of teenage rebellion?" Wes had asked Rastin.

"Erik was on a path from which he could not deviate," Rastin replied. "The way he saw it, the path was one that would cost his very soul."

"So, he wanted to be a musician," Patrick observed.

"A composer," Rastin replied.

"Aaannd . . . running away wouldn't have solved that?" Charlotte asked.

"Who is to say?" said Rastin. "Why leave your family, your

inheritance, and your legacy if you believe you have found the answer to fixing everything?"

Just as the legend stated, though, things hadn't gone according to plan for Erik.

The Egyptian priest had indeed risen from the dead and, after killing Erik and his family, had taken Erik's body into the alternate Moldavia, where he'd torn out his heart. It was this action that doomed Erik to walk as a corpse forever.

Though that particular piece hadn't been new to us, everything Rastin shared from that point forward was.

Since the heart was indeed the seat of the soul, as the Ancient Egyptians believed, Erik's became splintered. What was worse, each shard of his spirit became its own entity represented by a figure imbued with its own mind and characterized by its own mask. Twenty-four seven, he was literally surrounded—and tormented—by these pieces of his decimated soul. Yet Erik himself could only wear one mask at a time, which meant that he could also only *be* one facet of himself at a time. Something that made him all the more dangerous since Erik's powers also allowed him to traverse, at will, the barriers between each version of Moldavia, all while remaining invisible to anyone who did not believe in him. Which was why only Charlie had seen him at first. Then, when Stephanie's mind began to open to the idea, she had seen him under that sheet. As a result, I had contacted Rastin. Which, in turn, had prompted Rastin to visit Moldavia by "remote means" to confront Erik directly.

"Astral projection," Rastin replied when Wes had asked what he had meant by "remote."

"Huh," Patrick said. "So that's really a thing."

"A thing that allows me to enter *his* Moldavia," Rastin said. "As he is the only one who possesses the ability to open doors between the two sides."

From there, Rastin went on to tell us about his long-standing agreement with Erik that he would leave him be so long as Erik kept people out of the house. Rastin had also described his habit of dropping in on Erik intermittently to be sure he was holding up his end of the bargain.

"Normally during my past check-ins with Erik," he said, "I've found him in some unreasonable state. If we conversed, it was never for long. Always, I would leave before I could be trapped again."

"Trapped?" asked Charlotte.

"The documentary," Rastin replied, his eyes going far off. "I trust you've all seen it."

"*Oh yeah*," Patrick said, stuffing another candy bar into his mouth. "Ar yu ckhidding?"

"We replay the moth-barfing part every time," Wes added. "Your tonsils are *huge*, by the way."

When I asked what really happened during that episode, Rastin told us how, after mistaking Erik for a malevolent entity—a mistake I couldn't blame him for since I'd been guilty of making the same one—he'd immediately tried to exorcise him. An action that had resulted in disaster, as evidenced by the documentary.

"I didn't know what I was dealing with," said Rastin.

"You mean you didn't know he was actually human," guessed

Charlotte as she shot me a pointed look that I ignored, in spite of deserving it.

"Exactly," said Rastin.

And, according to Rastin, it was Erik's humanness that changed the whole game.

"Erik believes it is the curse that binds him to this world," said Rastin. "But, over time, I have become increasingly convinced it is his shattered state."

In the past, Erik had apparently used various objects as stand-in hearts since, for a time, the substitutes focused his soul, allowing him to play music. But the hearts never lasted. Eventually, they gave out, resulting in chaos for Erik.

"Wait, though," said Charlotte. "The fake hearts restore his spirit? Before, you said you thought Erik's soul was stuck here because of its splintered state. So that's the answer right there. That's what needs to happen."

It was then that Rastin revealed how Charlotte had guessed his plans exactly, and that he'd proposed this very solution to Erik multiple times, offering to perform the ritual again except, this time, with his soul focused.

Erik had always refused. At least until Rastin's last remote visit, the very drop-in that had been prompted by *my* email.

"Not only did he agree," Rastin said, "but it was his idea."

I didn't like this detail. Because it meshed with what Stephanie had told me about the masked Erik she had encountered on the "other side" of her house that night after the dance. And because I didn't like that it proved she'd been right about Erik wanting to protect her—that he truly did care about Stephanie. Not when hating him outright gave me strength. And a target.

"So it comes down to that, doesn't it?" I asked. "He needs a heart."

"That is just one of the things that would need to happen for us to have any chance at success," said Rastin.

"You'll have to perform the exorcism again," guessed Patrick.

"A cleansing this time," corrected Rastin.

"Soooo," said Wes, "call it a hunch, but I don't see ole Nosferatu sitting very still for any of this."

"We'd have to get him to come to us, too," said Charlotte.

At that, Rastin became very still and silent.

"What?" I asked him. "There's something else. Isn't there?"

"He does not know this," said the medium, speaking quietly. "In fact, no one does. But I believe that I harbor within me . . . a fraction of Erik's own spirit. A mask. One that I unwittingly absorbed that night I attempted the exorcism."

Silence reverberated after that revelation—the biggest we'd been given so far. Because, yeah. Dust from bombs *that* big took a while to settle.

"Hope," Rastin said when none of us spoke. "That is the 'mask' I carry. Ironically, I now think that his hope has become ours. For my possession of it has already once bridged our two worlds."

"That moth," I said. "The one from the documentary."

Rastin nodded. And then he said something that changed everything.

"That link between us might . . . just enable me to open a door to his side."

At that point, everyone in the room had erupted into dissent—everyone except me.

"I'll go with you," I volunteered, and even though my voice was quiet, it had been loud enough, apparently, for everyone to hear. Simultaneously, Patrick, Wes, and Charlotte went silent. All eyes, including Rastin's, turned to me.

"A cleansing occurs when I open a portal for spirits to pass on," said Rastin. "Yet the opening of a portal to the afterlife always requires all of my faculties as a medium and most of my strength. Even when dealing with normal spirits. This means that, once we are on Erik's side—if the shard of his soul I carry does indeed enable us to cross to him—I will be absorbed in that task utterly when the time comes. In fact, the reason for my delay in meeting Erik was that I could not convince a friend of mine to perform the darkest part of the task, which neither Erik nor myself would be capable of."

"You need someone to destroy the heart," I said.

"Precisely," Rastin affirmed with a nod, which resulted in a second barrage of balking remarks from my friends.

It was at that point that Rastin had stood, collecting his things. He had a plan, he said. One that we could begin to enact as soon as tomorrow. But one that he advised us against deciding to take part in tonight.

The conversation had ended shortly after, with Rastin telling us about tomorrow's rendezvous.

All night, the whole meeting had played on a loop in my head. Certain I couldn't be the only one not sleeping, I contemplated calling Charlotte. Mostly to see if she'd decided to go with me and

Rastin or not. Could I blame her, though—or any of them—if they said no this time?

And Erik. What would I do when I saw him? And I *would* see him, because I had already. That slice of moving darkness visible through the cracked basement door.

My gut twisted with the thought of meeting him eye-to-eye. Face-to-mask.

Sitting up, I pushed off from the bed and rushed to my closet, pulling down the camera I'd taken to Stephanie's house that day I'd first entered Moldavia. Flipping through photos, I slowed when I got to the ones I'd snapped after opening Charlie's door to that empty hallway. The hallway I'd perceived as empty.

I'd already viewed these pictures once and found nothing.

Hands shaking, I clicked forward.

Nothing. Nothing. Nothing.

And then.

Midway up the flash-darkened backdrop of the hall, near Stephanie's room, a blurry, disembodied, and transparent face. Set right at a man's height.

Except, as I studied the photo harder, scrutinizing the blue-white negative-like image, I realized I *hadn't* captured a face.

I'd captured a mask.

SIXTY-ONE

Stephanie

*S*ay that you will you marry me.

The force—the whole notion—of his words caused an atom bomb to detonate in my gut.

I didn't get it.

I didn't get *him*.

Nor this pair of bug-faced, serpent-tongued gossips. The ones who called each other Spite and Envy.

No wonder they were so insufferable.

Ever since the previous evening's disastrous conversation with Erik, the two masked figures had followed me everywhere. If I shut the door in their faces, I would turn to find them *inside* the room with me, seated on the settee like they'd been there the whole time. Not only that, but they'd glance up at me from behind their fans as if *I* was somehow interrupting *them*.

I'd already tried telling them to shut it when their constant bickering, along with the nagging presence of Erik's sheet music on Myriam's dresser, had made sleep impossible.

Eventually, they did pipe down. Despite my utter exhaustion, though, I'd still gotten zero rest that night. This time, however, it hadn't been because I was afraid.

If my dip in the lake had accomplished one good thing, it had been the significant diminishing of my overall fear of this place. And, perhaps, him.

Zedok had fished me out of that lake, after all. Saved my life. Made me an offer of marriage.

Not exactly the behavior of someone planning to murder me in the night.

Now, seated in Myriam's canopied bed, I ignored the sheet music that remained permanently on her vanity, the white papers waiting, obstinate and unrelenting, convinced that I wouldn't be able to resist them indefinitely.

Firm in my resolve that I would not indulge Erik's demands—any of them—I'd refrained from so much as looking at the papers. Which only led me to study the flawlessly wrapped bandages encasing my sliced and burning, frostbitten hands. And, for the first time, I found myself believing that Erik and Zedok *were* the same.

Last night, hadn't he exhibited some of that tenderness he'd shown in that dream in the conservatory? There'd been cruelty and coldness, too, though.

The monster and the angel. They were one and the same. Yet possibly, even with me here, still at war.

Eventually, unable to withstand my own curiosity, I gathered up Erik's music and retreated with it to the bed, telling myself I only wanted to sort through it in case the lyrics might hold some key to understanding him.

By his own testament, the words that looped along beneath the notes had been written by Wrath's hand. Yet there wasn't so much as an ounce of anger in any of them. Beauty and sorrow infused in the melody instead.

My heart twisted at the words that demanded careful reading. Simple and elegant, they painted his feelings in stark black and white, and like a spell, they drew me in.

He'd written a love song.

First my abduction and then his proposal. And now this?

What else could it mean, except that Erik had somehow, some way, fallen in love with me? And if that were the case, did that mean *he* had, too? Zedok?

"It *is* rather confusing, isn't it?" said Envy.

The retort caused my head to jerk in the direction of my wardens. Because I hadn't spoken my inquiry aloud. Was it possible she had heard my thoughts? The way Envy now stared at me, as though she was waiting for an answer, suggested she had.

"Yes, dear Envy," said Spite, her voice tight and full of warning. She gave Envy a *thwap* with her fan. "Your asking random questions *is* rather confusing."

They bowed their heads together and raised their fans again, as if they had lips I could read, and returned to their viper hissing.

Setting the music aside, I rolled over in the bed, giving them my back, but then the spot next to me, empty of my little sister's sleeping form, became just another torture. It was then that I gave up on sleep. Abandoning Myriam's room and Erik's music, I went to roam the house, going from room to room, telling myself I wasn't looking for anything in particular. That wasn't entirely true, though.

After scouring the house and finding no trace of him—well, other than his masks, which refused to interact with me—I started checking the windows and the grounds. That was just an act of avoidance, though. Because I already knew where he had to be hiding.

When I began to make my way toward the kitchen, however, my masked companions took pains to obstruct my way. Pushing past them, I found myself standing just outside the closed basement door.

The very last door I'd yet to try.

He was down there. He had to be.

Stalled outside the basement, I focused on the door handle and willed myself both to concentrate on the list of things I needed to address with him and to just *do it already*.

Don't knock. Don't deliberate. Just *go*.

"Do tell her the basement is forbidden," hissed Envy, elbowing Spite.

"We're not to speak to her, you ninny," said Spite. "Really, is it that hard to remember?"

"*She's* the one who can't seem to remember anything!"

Geez. Did *he* ever have to put up with this? The snapping back and forth and the passive-aggressive potshots? If they behaved this way around him, it was a wonder he wasn't more unhinged than he already was.

"Look!" said Envy. "She's opened the door. What are we to do now? We certainly can't follow her there."

"Well, he didn't tell us to stop her from going into the basement," reasoned Spite, whose tone now gave me the impression she'd be all too happy to see me come up against whatever consequences Envy feared.

"Yes, but he does not wish to see her."

To this, Spite gave a snorting laugh. "Only as much as he does."

Suddenly, with the door half open to the darkened stairway, I stopped dead, though not because of the conflicting words of the masks. Rather, it was due to the *sound* that issued from the bowels of the house.

Soft and mournful, the heartrending cry of a violin strained to split the silence.

The same note came a second time, followed by an awful teeth-ringing screech from the instrument.

Another fluid note beckoned me a step closer. The notes that followed, though, came like screams of pain, loud enough to cover the sound of my feet on the stairs until he came into view.

With his back to me, he didn't see me coming.

He stood at the far end of the shadowy room, his angular form thrown into relief by a single candelabrum that stood atop a simple wooden table—which counted as the only simple object in the room. A horde of priceless artifacts lined the walls and crammed the corners. A small chest of polished silverware sat next to a crate of fine china, and propped against the far wall, the eyes of Erik's long-dead family members watched me from their portraits.

So. *Here* was the fortune Erik was rumored to have taken.

The violin screamed again, warning me to stop, to go back, and that I shouldn't be here. And it was true. I *shouldn't*. I should be at home. In front of the TV with Charlie in my lap. Or with Lucas in his car.

He had brought me here, though. And so he could deal with having me here.

Slowly, as the steps in front of me became fewer, the sour notes began to lessen in frequency and the beautiful ones began to link together. As they did, my trepidation morphed into grim fascination. In the darkness, he moved like a flame—a wavering pillar of red in the gloom. And like one of his moths, I kept coming . . . enthralled by the sight. By the *music*.

It swirled around me. Through me. Making something inside me sing with it, like my soul had no hope but to resonate right along with the melody.

I paused only when I reached the final step.

As the song slowed, I marveled at the fluidity of the arm that controlled the bow, and of the figure's slight frame as it swayed with subtle motion.

And the way he cradled the violin . . . There was that tenderness again.

The last step creaked as I left it, and with an abrupt and horrible shriek of strings, he whirled on me, slashing the bow downward like a sword, causing it to whistle.

His twin light eyes focused on me and I froze, half expecting to drop dead right then and there.

My face began to burn. And the longer the silence continued with that pointed stare aimed straight at me, the higher the heat in my cheeks grew.

That's when I reminded myself it had been my *intention* to interrupt him.

"I'm . . ." I began, but trailed off, nixing the impulse to apologize.

Tensing, I braced myself for his reaction.

He spoke then, and his voice—almost a deeper, more distorted version of the violin's—held no trace of outrage.

"My playing disturbed you," he said, and it took me a moment to process his words.

Truth was, a lot of things here "disturbed" me.

But his playing, unearthly as it had been, might have been the one and only thing that had not.

"You'll forgive me if . . . I lost myself," he said. "I've not been able to play for so long. As you know, I should not be able to now."

I wavered in place, so much less certain about what to say now than when I'd made the decision to come down here.

"The curse is supposed to keep you from playing," I said, keeping my voice even while, beneath me, my feet itched to take me back up the stairs.

"Playing . . ." he said. "In the past, it has always required a heart."

I waited through another horrible patch of silence for him to explain further. When he didn't, I went ahead and pressed.

"So, that's true, too. You lost your heart."

"I have lost them all," he said. "I am as hollow as this instrument."

A beat passed in which I tried to make sense of that statement.

"Like so much else, it is a mystery," he said. "But mark my words. In another hour, the ability will be lost to me again."

Turning toward the table, he laid the violin in its case and then secured the bow in its slot.

Without the instrument, he no longer resembled a wavering flame—but a cold taper.

His chest gleamed in the firelight with the blood that never went away or dried.

"Tell me," I said, making a feeble gesture toward the portraits, the faces identical to the ones in the photo I'd found in the attic. "What were they like?"

This wasn't how I'd planned to begin tonight's conversation, but it struck me as a good way to segue into what I'd come to ask of him. Anything that might walk him back to his true self, to Erik.

"My family?" he asked, swiveling toward the paintings. "They were . . . cold. And warm. Flawed . . . yet simultaneously perfect."

"So you take after them," I said, the words leaping free of my lips before I gave them permission to, a nervous and ironic laugh underscoring the observation.

He turned to regard me, that skeletal mask free of any trace of humor. Pressing my lips together, I banished my almost-smile and forged forward.

"It must be painful to have their likenesses, their ghosts, so close."

"They are everywhere," he said with barely any voice at all, his gaze returning to the portraits. "Forever as present as they are absent."

"We . . . don't put up pictures of Mom," I said. "I have them, of course. But . . . they're hard to look at. Even after all this time. I can't imagine what it must be like walking through a house filled with so many memories. But, then again, after today . . . I guess I can."

"It's always as if they are merely in the next room," he said. "Or as though I have only just missed them."

"Like they've been gone for years," I said. "But at the same time, only just—"

"A day," he finished.

Quiet pulsed, and my bravery grew. Again, I scanned my mind for some way to gently steer him in the direction I needed us to go. Before I could utter another word, though, he spoke.

"Charlie does not know about your mother."

Charlie. My whole chest seized at his uttering of her name. Tears stung my eyes.

"She's too young to understand," I said. "We're afraid she . . . We don't want her to know the truth. It's too much."

"There will be pain either way," he said.

Will be? With a thrill of hope, I ventured on.

"One day, when we're both older, when she knows, I'm going to take her back to Syracuse. To see her. Mom, I mean. Even if Dad doesn't want to go."

"Oh?" he asked, and it wasn't lost on me that he didn't jump to forbid this.

"I sometimes wish we'd never left," I went on. "Because even though she's gone, even though it's hard to look at pictures, it's also hard being so far away. I can't go see her. And sometimes—a lot of times, actually—it feels like I would be able to bear missing her a little more if I could just be close to her. I'm not sure if that makes sense—"

"It makes perfect sense," he said, his voice a little less Zedok and more . . .

"Now Dad and Charlie are gone, too," I said. "But also, just like you said . . . everywhere. Except I've been here days. You, though. You've been here for—"

He swiveled his head my way, those startling eyes stopping me yet again, warning me I might have gone too far, stepped too near to his edge . . .

Now, I told myself. *Say it now.*

"Erik. I want to—"

"No," he said. "You mustn't tell me why you've come. Allow me instead to guess."

I wrapped my arms around my middle, chilled by his words.

"You've had time to reconsider my suit," he went on, the softness in his voice gone, replaced by frigid irony that bordered on sarcasm. "And you've sought me out to offer your acceptance. What say you, then? Will you wear my ring?"

Ice water replaced my blood.

I'd been so close. Close enough that I couldn't say if I'd said one word too many . . . or one too few.

"If you're trying to scare me," I said, "it won't work."

It *was* working. But he couldn't sense that . . . could he?

"Well," he said through a clipped laugh. "At least I've graduated to *trying*."

"I came to talk to you," I said. "Before, in the dreams, you would always talk to me."

"I am no dream."

"If you would just—"

"You tire of your companions," he remarked, addressing the violin. He had one hand on the lid of the case—like it was a coffin he was reluctant to shut. "I wager nothing less could have driven you to seek me out."

With these words, something inside of me snapped.

"Don't *do* that!" I shouted at him, and before I even knew what I was doing, I found myself stalking toward him, hands curling into fists at my sides. "Stop assuming you know everything about me. I'm not one of your masks."

His shoulders went rigid, the reaction letting me know I'd struck a chord.

"You're saying they are *not* the reason you're here?"

"No," I snapped. "They're actually not."

The truth was, I had come to negotiate.

"I'm here to offer a trade," I began, fear creeping over me again, because I needed this to work. "A promise for a promise."

"I have already stated my terms."

I'd prepared myself for those words. Still, they came like a knife to the stomach. Because even though I kept sifting through the darkness that had consumed him, desperate to find a glimmer of the light I'd glimpsed in him before, I never found more than a trace of it. Forging on, I pushed the pain aside.

"So long as you're like this," I said, "I know better than to ask you to let me go."

Again, he glanced at me with something that might have been surprise, and for a moment, I felt an internal check of victory at having stolen his certainty.

"You wish for something more than I would freely give you?"

"Yes," I said. "And . . . if you give it to me, I promise to stay here. Meaning . . . I won't try to leave again. And if someone comes to my rescue, I won't go with them, either."

He tilted his head at me, letting me know I'd taken him off guard. "I have stolen your freedom," he said. "And so I *am* curious. What could you hold as more precious than that?"

The way he'd said "freedom." It seemed to suggest he assumed I didn't realize the worth of what I'd placed on the table.

Maybe I didn't. I did, however, recognize fully the power *he* held. And not just over me.

"You have to promise not to hurt anyone else," I said.

He laughed, becoming a monster fully once again.

A bitter taste rose in the back of my throat, and I resisted the urge to recoil from him.

What was I doing? Giving away the very last of my power to this nightmare he had become?

No. That wasn't it. I was buying it back. Piece by piece.

Peace by peace.

Because I could bear it here more easily if I knew my friends were safe. And if this worked, the demand for my release would come next. By then, if I played my cards right, he would hopefully be under the influence of another mask. But . . . one thing at a time.

"These are *my* terms," I said. "I won't try to escape again. And I won't ask you to let me go. But, in return, you have to swear you won't hurt anyone."

"In exchange for such a promise . . . you would agree to willingly remain here?" he asked. "With me? Indefinitely?"

"I have to stay anyway, don't I?" I asked.

If that man who had tried to get to me yesterday came back, or if

Lucas or anyone else from SPOoKy came for me, what would he do to them? If I could protect them, if he would strike this bargain with me, then . . . did I have any other choice?

"You expect him to come for you," he said, his voice becoming dangerously quiet. "The boy. *That* is why you ask."

With this outright mention of Lucas specifically, my heartbeat thundered harder than ever.

"You can't do anything to him," I said, the words flying out. "You can't touch him at all. Or anyone else. They're my friends. *That's* why you have to promise."

"And if I agree, then you will tell him of your decision to remain here with me and that you do so of your own free will?"

"Yes," I forced myself to say, only pausing afterward to contemplate what his question implied. Because . . . if he needed my reassurance that I would remain, that suggested the opportunity to escape *did* exist, or at least that my rescue *was* possible.

"You understand what will happen if you break this oath."

The same thing that would have happened if I'd never made it.

"Yes."

"*Done,*" he said as he shut the violin case.

Picking up the candelabrum, he then extended it to me.

Stunned by his abrupt and unquestioning acceptance, I took it from him, my hand brushing his gloved one.

The deal had been struck without haggling or negotiation. And now this must be his way of telling me that I was . . . dismissed.

Numbed and addled by the swiftness of the exchange, I almost turned away. I caught myself, though, forcing my hand to set the candelabrum back down. Though I had gotten what I'd come for, I hadn't gotten everything I wanted. I'd come so close to stoking an ember of his old self into flame. Perhaps it wasn't too late—or too soon—to try again. And, if I wanted to be honest with myself, I *had* come armed with more than just words.

"There is one more thing," I said tentatively. "I want you to take off the mask. I want to talk to you without it. I want to see your face."

"This *is* my face," he hissed as he slowly turned his head my way, revealing the skeletal profile of the shining silver mask.

"No, it's not," I said, even as my heart sped up with renewed fear. "I've seen your true face. You yourself showed it to me."

"The dreams were a lie," he snapped.

"I'm not talking about the dreams."

All at once, silence supervened.

I took a shaking breath, steeling myself for what I needed to do—something I'd already promised him I wouldn't. But, well before that, in that dream full of roses and regret, I had also made him another promise.

> "*Walls between us,*
> *Time and death, too.*
> *Heartless, our worlds divide us.*
> *Still, I hear you.*"

Turning from me, he tensed all over.

In spite of my reservations, I continued with the lyrics that, just as he'd predicted, I'd memorized easily. Without even really trying to. And the melody? Well, I'd known that already.

> *"Silence deafens.*
> *Shadows grow long.*
> *Yet, in the soundless nothing,*
> *Your name is a song."*

He pivoted to me then, a gloved hand gripping his crimson jacket, the bloodstain glistening black in the glow of the candlelight. I took a step toward him, though, and as I did, the blood seemed to recede. His form straightened, and his eyes beamed with a sharper light.

> *"Sing to me, angel.*
> *Sing, and I shall come.*
> *We'll be but a breath apart*
> *Before the night is done."*

I took another step. And then another. But then I paused, my breath stolen by his voice as, beautiful even in its distortion, it cleaved the darkness.

> *"Sing to me, my love,*
> *Sing to me and see*
> *All the dark hath kept hidden*
> *From you and from me."*

Compelled myself, I went to him, my voice rejoining his, ringing in perfect harmony. Working also, somehow, to drive the blood back into him the closer I came until, as I stopped to stand just before him, it vanished.

> *"Walls between us,*
> *Time and death, too.*
> *Heartless, our worlds combine us.*
> *Still, I—"*

It had been the reflection of the firelight in his mask that had reminded me the barrier existed. My hand, rising of its own accord, took hold of the silver.

The mask came away easily.

Then everything went wrong.

He swung away, lifting his cloak with one arm while the other knocked aside the candelabrum, throwing the basement into pitch-blackness. Then a gloved fist gripped the wrist of the hand that held his mask. I tightened my grasp on the cold metal, determined not to return it to him.

He drew me to him, and helpless to resist, I went, an echo of muted, far-off pain cinching my chest as we came together. Still, I wasn't afraid. Not even as darkness closed in on my consciousness, causing my legs to give out underneath me. Not even as, in almost the same instant, he swept me off my feet and into his arms.

Fighting his influence, the same he'd used to lull me into a state that had allowed him to bring me here, I kept his mask in a death grip and groped for his collar with my free hand. My fingers wound in the stiff fabric, and as they did, I murmured his name. His real name.

These actions served as my only defense against his severing of this moment I had fought so hard to win. In the end, they did not amount to enough, and my mind went where he pushed it—into the darkness of another dream, one in which he himself was nowhere to be found.

SIXTY-TWO
Lucas

"You know this hotel is haunted, right?" Wes asked, slipping into Rastin's room as soon as the medium opened the door.

"Please," Rastin replied, his tone wry. "Won't you come in?"

I wandered in next, followed by Charlotte and Patrick.

Rastin gave us a weary and tight-lipped stare, as if hoping we'd all catch the drift that this wasn't what he'd had in mind when he'd asked us to meet him at the Brown Hotel.

"I see you all made a collective decision *not* to wait for me in the lobby as we had discussed," grumbled Rastin. "How did you get my room number?"

"Patrick hacked the hotel's computer system," Wes answered, lowering himself into an armchair with a heavy sigh.

"Cool middle name, by the way," Patrick said. "P.S. You don't *look* thirty-eight."

Rastin, visibly peeved, perched on the window ledge.

"Here," said Charlotte, handing him a coffee cup. "We brought you some chai."

"How considerate," muttered Rastin.

"So, what's the plan, Stan?" asked Wes.

"The plan *was* for each of you to listen to me."

"Yeah, we did a lot of that yesterday," I said. "I thought today was for taking action."

"Oh?" Rastin went to the only other chair in the room and took a seat, crossing his legs. "Then you have come to my room with a strategy in mind. Let us hear it."

"See," said Patrick, "we were sort of thinking that since *you're* the one harboring a fraction of the enemy's soul, *you* might have the strategy."

"Obviously, you are not interested in my plan," Rastin remarked before turning his attention to Charlotte. "This is very good tea. Where did you find it?"

Charlotte shrugged and held up her own paper cup. "Heine Brothers'. It's a local chain. Their coffee will turn your brain into a grow lamp."

"Mm," said Rastin appreciatively. "I'll have to try it."

"*Obviously*," I said, cutting in, "the plan is to go back to the house. This time, we go in prepared to fight and to get at least one of us onto the other side. To find Stephanie . . . and bring her back."

"Ooh, ooh," said Wes, snapping his fingers. "I've seen this movie. We come out of the ceiling at the end all gross and covered in ectoplasm. But we're gonna need ropes and a small lady with a high-pitched voice."

"That is a very swift way for one or all of us to get killed," said Rastin.

Scowling, I put my hands on my hips. "So, we're not going back in?"

"Oh, we will go in," said Rastin. "Two of us must, at least. And one tonight. But I would prefer to do so more covertly than your own plan suggests."

"You want to try going back in remotely?" I guessed. "And what exactly is that going to accomplish?"

"If we're lucky," said Rastin, "a conversation with Stephanie."

"I'm all for catching up," said Patrick, who leaned one shoulder against a chifforobe. "But what good is that supposed to do her or us?"

"Stephanie can do what none of us can," said Rastin. "At least not without forfeiting our lives."

"Which is?" asked Charlotte.

"The heart," I said, interrupting. "You want her to be the one to implant the heart."

"We *need* her to implant it," corrected Rastin, "or else convince him to do it himself."

"No way," I said.

Rastin spread his hands. "I am ready to hear your alternate plan."

"I have one," said Wes. "I call it 'How about We Just Open Up a Door with Your Slice of Stolen Soul, Smuggle 'Er Out, and Run'?"

"Emphasis on 'run,'" added Patrick.

"Not bad," Rastin said. "If we are successful, Stephanie will be free to return to her house later, when her father is acquitted of murder."

To that, we all went quiet. Rastin had done his homework.

"Fine," I said. "Say we do things your way. Say we tell Stephanie what she needs to do and she's somehow able to do it. Then what?"

"*Then* we go get her," he said. "So long as he has no heart to focus his soul, we have no chance of casting that soul into the hereafter. It should be clear to you by now that Stephanie can only be free when Erik is."

"I don't like it," I said.

"I am already skeptical about our ability to come close enough to destroy his heart," replied Rastin. "If you're suggesting one among us also implant the heart beforehand, then I know we will fail. As Wes so acutely observed yesterday, Erik, given his current state, is unlikely to submit himself to such an operation."

"Acutely," Wes said. "Did you all hear that? Yesterday I was annoying, but today? Today I'm *acute*."

"So what makes you think Stephanie could do it?" I asked.

"Short of letting her go," said Rastin, "I think he would do anything to please her. Even that. At the very least, it is worth a shot."

The silence in the room thickened with that, the tension radiating from each of us.

"You are her friends," Rastin went on to say. "Your willingness to rush to her aid suggests that you share a strong bond. It should not be unimaginable that Stephanie would be willing to meet us halfway."

I took a sharp, quick step toward Rastin, but Patrick moved to block my path.

"Whoa," Patrick said. "Simmer down there."

"You said he wouldn't let her die," I spat. "But what happens if he figures out what she's trying to do?"

"I told you he is in love with her," said Rastin. "He will not harm her."

"He *is* harming her," I snapped.

"Lucas," said Charlotte, her voice soft but chiding. "Rastin is trying to help."

She was right. I knew she was. I just wanted his urgency to match ours—mine.

I retracted my step and, turning away, ran a hand through my hair.

Again, Charlotte spoke, though this time she addressed Rastin. "So, if you think the next step is talking to Stephanie, why haven't you tried?"

"Because," Rastin said, "she doesn't know who I am. She will not be as apt to listen to me as she would, say, to him."

I spun toward Rastin, who had his coffee cup raised in my direction.

"Me?" I asked. "But . . . I can't astral project."

"Which is why we"—Rastin gestured to himself and the others—"will be sending you into her dream. Why do you suppose I requested we meet so late?"

To increase the likelihood that she would be asleep. Of course.

"You can do that?" Charlotte whispered while I stood frozen, at once swayed to Rastin's side just by the mere prospect of seeing Stephanie tonight.

"I am glad you all decided to come," Rastin said. "After yesterday's attack, I'll need the extra psychic energy. Are you ready to try?"

I glanced first to Charlotte, then to Wes and Patrick, searching for one face that was, in fact, ready. None of them looked keen on this.

"Yeah," I said anyway. "We are."

SIXTY-THREE

Stephanie

Charlie was born in June, so it had been warm then. Now, though, a pall of snow covered everything, softening my steps as they carried me over a slim stone pathway that wound between gravestones and monuments.

White flecks poured from the sky. The moon, a brilliant silver disc, peered down at me, illuminating the way I shouldn't have known. Because this place was huge, and I hadn't been back here since the burial. I'd only been eleven at the time, staring out the window of the limousine, watching the trees and stones file past.

After walking for just a little while, I turned the corner of a shed-sized mausoleum. And there, surrounded by other stones like it, stood the same unassuming granite marker my broken family had abandoned six years ago.

In that moment, it was as if winter itself snuck into my veins to freeze my heart solid. My throat clenched tight, and I swallowed. But the emotion wouldn't go down. Instead, it welled up inside of me, spilling out in the form of stinging tears.

I gripped the corner of the mausoleum, half hiding behind it as if the marker were an actual person and not just the reminder of one.

The tears fell as I pushed off from the sepulcher, staggering forward a step. My knees met with the frozen earth when I came to the foot of her grave.

Mom wouldn't have wanted me kneeling at her headstone crying. She would have wanted me smiling and happy—all the things I'd found it so much easier to be when she was around. Now, even though the two of us were close again, she remained unreachable. Cold and alone. Just where we'd left her before Dad had uprooted us to one city after another.

Poor Charlie. Moving around was all she'd ever known.

Charlie. I missed her so much, too—and Dad. Where were they now? I must have come back here, to New York, without either of them.

And what was I *doing* here anyway? How had I even entered the cemetery?

Shifting into a sitting position, I propped my jeans-clad knees up and wrapped my arms around them.

"Mom, I'm lost," I murmured. "And I know that must be why I'm here now. Except . . . I can't remember where I went wrong. Or if I'm too late to fix it."

No answer came from anywhere, none but the hiss of the snow—a sound I'd heard before and recently. One that now caused my skin to prickle and my pulse to race.

Turning my head, I laid my cheek against my knees, my focus shifting from my mother's simple marker to another, more elaborate one. An old stone figure's hooded form stood sentinel over another grave, poised atop a plinth with its head dipped low, its hood draped forward to shield the face I couldn't be certain the statue even had.

And that was somehow familiar, too.

Sniffing, I pushed once more to my feet, stepping in the direction of the other grave, certain that if I cleared the snow covering its plaque, I would know the name inscribed there, too.

Before I could touch the stone, though, I froze, arrested by the whispered sound of my name.

I hesitated, afraid of who I would find there when I turned. With a scrape of my heel on the stone pathway, I spun—and started.

"*Lucas?*"

The sight of him standing there in the snow without a coat or scarf, the moon glinting off the lenses of his black-framed glasses, caused everything to come rushing back to me. All at once, I understood exactly how I'd gotten here. And where *here* really was.

"I'm dreaming," I said to him. "This . . . is a dream." I laughed a little to myself. Then the tears started again, streaming too hot down my cold face. Because while it would have been an act of kindness for Erik to send me here after what I'd shared with him, it struck me as unbearably cruel of him to bring Lucas into this. No doubt this was a trick. Erik's way of mocking me over our bargain. Or was he seeking revenge because I'd stolen his mask?

"It's a dream, but it's real," Lucas said, his tone hushed, like he was trying to convince himself as well as me. "Or . . . I am."

He pointed at himself, his fingers trailing over his heart, the words making me hitch a breath. Because this had happened before but in reverse, with Erik. I hadn't believed him then, and that had been a mistake. One I was still paying for. One I couldn't afford to make again.

"Lucas," I whispered as I started toward him. Because I knew how these dreams went. They could lie and they could pretend, all while seeming *so* real. Worst of all, they could end at a moment's notice. I couldn't let this one end without at least touching him first.

Lucas opened his arms to me, seemingly as stunned as I was that he was here. I ran to him, and as I flung my arms around his middle, wrapping him tight, I told myself that for at least as long as I got to hold him, it didn't matter if this was real or not.

"I want it to really be you," I said through a choked sob, half of gladness, half of despair, reveling in his warmth and that familiar scent. "Tell me you're not a lie."

"It is me," he assured me, squeezing back. "But . . . I don't know how much time I have here with you. If you wake up, or if the circle gets broken—"

"Circle?" I pulled back enough to peer up at him, pressing my hands into his chest like that could keep us both here, and connected, no matter what.

"There's no time to—" He stopped himself, a scowl erasing his anxiousness as he took my hands in his. He turned them palm-up, examining the bandages Erik had wrapped them with. Had the bandages been there when the dream began? Or had they appeared only after I remembered everything?

"The blood," Lucas said. "*This* is why there was blood in Charlie's room."

"Charlie?" Terror flashed through me. "What's wrong with Charlie—is she hurt?"

Suddenly desperate to know with more certainty if he was or wasn't a dream, I gripped his hands, ignoring the pain it brought to my own. Like Lucas's presence, the pain was welcome, though, because it vouched for the realness of this moment with him. But then maybe I shouldn't want him to be real as badly as I did if he'd come to tell me something terrible had happened to Charlie.

"No. She's okay. She's . . ." He stopped himself and then began again. "Stephanie, the police are looking for you. They found blood in the house after you went missing. After he took you."

I shook my head, not comprehending. "It's . . . not mine."

"It was," he insisted, presenting my own hands to me as proof. "He did this to you. He must have. Or . . . did he make you forget?"

My hands curled into fists, the palms burning. Even if I tried to explain to Lucas what happened, he wouldn't understand.

"He didn't do this," I said. "It . . . was . . . sort of an accident. Lucas, where's Charlie? Where's my dad?"

A flash of anguish twisted his features, telling me that whatever the answer was, it wasn't a good one. His lips started to form words, but nothing came. I wanted to give him a shake or a shove, something to knock the truth out of him. But then, at last, he spoke.

"They're okay . . . Charlie's with friends. Your dad . . . he's fine but . . . Stephanie, there's something more important. It's why I came. I need you to just listen to me without saying anything. It . . . it's about *him*."

My fingers leapt to press Lucas's lips. He hadn't said either of the names. But what if he did? Speaking the name would surely call him here. Unless he was already present. Watching. Listening . . .

I scanned the vacant cemetery, fighting to see through the screen of snow that, in thickening, turned the light of the moon bleary.

Life-sized angels populated the grounds, some leaning grief-stricken into crosses, others shedding tears over their stones, their wings outspread or tucked close to form the silhouettes of hearts.

I shoved Lucas backward, and he went at my insistence, both of us stopping at a craggy oak. The two of us then hid behind it, huddling close to each other. In reality, there was nothing that could shield us from Erik's sight—not if he was determined to see, to hear. And Erik must have been the one to bring me to this dream.

If that was the case, Lucas had chosen an inopportune moment—perhaps the most inopportune—to come to me this way.

"We're coming for you," Lucas said. "But if our plan's going to work, there's something we need you to do."

His words and our surroundings still warring for my attention, I shook my head. Because while I wanted more than anything for Lucas to come and take me out of Erik's dark world, the idea was also something I couldn't bear the thought of. I'd made my deal with Erik. If Lucas showed up now, I wouldn't be able to leave with him. Not if I wanted us both to make it out alive. Not if I wanted him to.

"Whatever you're planning," I said, speaking fast to keep him from trying to interrupt me, "don't. It's too dangerous. He's already attacked someone. He—"

"Rastin," said Lucas, uttering perhaps the one word that could have muted me in that moment. "Stephanie, that man who came looking for you, that was Rastin."

"Rastin?" I blinked rapidly, my heart beginning to race. Because the pieces kept coming together to suggest Lucas *couldn't* be a figment.

Lucas nodded. "He got my message. That's how I'm even able to be here right now."

I gaped at him, his words sparking in me a potent hope. Again,

I gripped Lucas by the arms, my nails digging in this time. Because that voice that I'd heard shouting my name from the other side of the house—it had been familiar for a reason. Because I had heard it before. Through one of the earbuds Lucas and I had shared that day in the library.

"He's hurt," I said, fear squeezing my words. "God. Is he okay?"

"He's okay. Stephanie—"

"How did he—?"

"None of that's important!" Gripping my arms in return, Lucas shook me once. The action won my silence, but only long enough for a soft flutter to catch and steal my attention.

"Shh!" I commanded him, turning my head sharply. "Did you hear that?"

The noise had been like the flap of a bird's wing. Or the hem of a heavy cloak . . .

"Whatever it was, it's not real," Lucas said, attempting to turn me back to him. "Nothing here is but me and you. This is a dre— Stephanie, where are you going?"

Though Lucas tugged my arm, I managed to pull away. I drifted out from behind our tree, my steps returning me to the clearing near my mother's grave. Again, I scanned our surroundings, searching for the source of the noise.

Then a horrible sensation, like the ground and all of reality had dropped out from under me, caused my stomach to plummet.

The plinth that had previously supported the solemn and hooded stone figure now stood empty, vacated by its guard.

"Lucas," I said, my breath leaving me in the form of a small white ghost. "Lucas, you have to go."

"I *can't* go! Not without—" His steps crunched in the snow, growing nearer until, along with his words, they halted abruptly.

Dread overwhelmed me while my mind painted pictures of what I would find when I turned. I spun anyway, my heart stalling at the sight of the black-hooded form brought to life. He loomed behind Lucas, one gloved and ring-lined hand clasping the hilt of a dagger, the wavy blade of which he held to Lucas's throat.

"She has instructed you to depart, sir," came that distorted voice from within the hood. "You may take your leave or, if you prefer, I will see you out."

Lucas's bright blue gaze dulled with hate. He remained frozen, though, seeming to understand completely just how real all parts of this dream were—how real the consequences were about to become if he didn't do as I'd told him.

More seconds elapsed, however, and Lucas remained in place.

"You can kill me," said Lucas at last, his words shocking me almost as much as Erik's sudden appearance. "You can kill anyone who comes near her. You must think I'm still here because I don't understand that, but I do."

"Lucas, *don't*," I warned, able to sense where he would go next and knowing there would be no coming back from it.

"You can keep her forever and never let her go," Lucas continued, ignoring me. "But what you don't seem to understand is that none of that is ever going to make her love you."

The hand clenching the knife tightened, prepared to strike. But in that same instant, Lucas moved, uncoiling himself from the arm that, when it should have killed him, simply . . . let him go.

This was my chance. I sprang forward and, inserting myself

between the two, as if that could do anything, I flung my arms wide, giving them each one of my bandaged palms.

"Leave, Lucas!" I screamed at top volume, recognizing fully that the only reason Lucas was still alive was because Erik had so far decided to keep his promise. With Lucas instigating this way, though, goading Erik, how much longer could I hope for that resolve to remain?

Instead of listening to me, Lucas squared off from his enemy and let loose more words—his only weapons.

"You're *dead*!" Lucas yelled. "You don't belong here."

"Lucas, *please*!"

"Even if you were alive and not some *thing* of nightmares, she would *never* choose you!"

"Erik, *no*!" I screamed as, with that, the hooded figure darted forward, lunging past me toward Lucas, who only narrowly avoided the swipe of the blade that sang as it sliced lengthwise through the snow and air. Lucas delivered a return swing with his fist. The cloaked figure dodged it, the motion fast enough to cause his hood to fall back—and reveal the flawless face I had not seen since that night in the boat. *Erik's.*

The sight of it, even twisted with hatred, caused something within me to shift and upend. Because unlike the horrible silver death's head mask, this face was one that I had come to know. And the pain beneath the beauty in those features, beneath the fury—it echoed my own.

"Erik, he's leaving," I said. "He'll go. Lucas?"

With a growl, Lucas rushed Erik again.

"Stop it!" I shrieked at both of them when, in response, Erik slashed Lucas's sleeve open, sending a spatter of crimson over the snow. That strike had been yet another warning—no doubt Erik's final. Lucas had to know this. Why, then, was he swinging at Erik yet again? Did he think being in a dream protected him? Did he think he could win?

Erik's face. What about it had tipped Lucas out of defiance and into rage?

"You belong in *hell*," said Lucas through gritted teeth even as Erik shoved him against one side of the stone sepulcher. "And even if it kills me, I swear I *will* be the one to send you there."

The words stunned me, cracking my heart in two. Not just because they were filled with hate but because they proved that, in this moment, what Lucas cared most about . . . was revenge.

Dropping the knife, Erik seized Lucas by the throat with both hands.

Lucas cringed, clawing at the gloved fingers that squeezed harder, threatening to crush his windpipe.

"Erik!" I ran to him, latching on to his arms as if I had the strength to pry them off. But now he wasn't listening, either.

Lucas's knees buckled. But Erik held him fast against the stones, fury contorting his expression past the point of recognition.

"You swore!" I shouted at him.

Erik froze. He held his crushing grip a moment longer. Then, with a roar of rage, he released Lucas and, still glaring his hate at him, backed away several steps. Gasping for breath, and before his knees could meet the frozen ground, Lucas vanished, no doubt waking up wherever he had gone to sleep.

That left Erik and me alone.

"Do you believe him?" he asked me, his voice no longer Wrath's but his own.

Obviously, he was asking about something Lucas had said. Maybe all of it.

Slowly, with two staggering steps, Erik turned to face me. Blood poured from his chest, streaking a form no longer clad in his crimson officer's uniform but rather in a silver brocaded waistcoat, one lined with buttons. An indication he had changed masks?

He wavered on his feet, about to go down.

"He's right," said Erik. "Of course he's right. But . . . it wouldn't matter . . . not if you didn't believe him."

I bolted to him, catching him by the arms before he could fall. Unable to keep him upright, though, I went down with him until both of us were kneeling in the snow and the blood.

There, Erik gripped his chest, pain seizing him.

Though I took hold of his wrist, attempting to pull his hand from the wound, he flung me off, the motion causing the world to invert and the dream to end.

SIXTY-FOUR
Lucas

I drew a ragged breath, and my lungs flooded with air—almost too much.

Someone, a girl, screamed my name. Her voice drew me backward through the darkness. And then other voices joined hers. Including one that I recognized as my own.

"Stephanie!" I shouted into the light that burst into being above me, revealing shadowy, amorphous shapes that, in the next instant, became familiar heads and faces.

"Lucas, *oh my God*," gasped a teary Charlotte before she launched herself at me.

"*Sheez*," said Patrick. "Eff that. We're *never* doing that again."

"Give him space," commanded another voice, this one coming from my left. Rastin's.

Someone peeled Charlotte off of me, and still gasping for breath, I pressed my hands into the carpet and struggled to sit up, drunk with confusion and disequilibrium. I clasped my throat, the skin of which still held the memory of being squeezed almost to the point of collapse. Then a warm, wet sensation on my bicep drew my attention to my white sleeve, now stained crimson with blood. Only when

I saw the wound—the slash I'd been dealt in the dream—did the pain rip its way through my arm.

"Stay back," commanded Rastin, his face appearing to hover over mine, contorted with worry—and anger. "What happened?"

"I didn't get to tell her," I said. "I didn't get—you have to send me back."

"No!" wailed Charlotte.

"He found you," said Rastin, releasing a breath. "Tell me you didn't try to fight him."

"Send me back now," I hissed to Rastin, locking eyes with him, my anger at last trumping my fear.

"You are not going back there," Rastin said.

"I'll kill him." I pushed against the medium, trying to stand.

"Don't be stupid," snapped Rastin, shoving me down again.

"Get away from him!" Charlotte screeched.

"Charlotte, I will not harm him."

"You already have!" she yelled. "Something was choking him. He stopped breathing. Look at him, he's covered in blood!"

"He is all right," Rastin assured her. "He will be all right. Please, calm yourself."

"Calm myself?" sobbed Charlotte.

Above me, the turning ceiling fan sped into a swirling drain—a whirling funnel that threatened to swallow me.

Nauseated, I shut my eyes and fought the urge to puke. Shunting Rastin's staying arm aside, I sat up.

"Charlotte," I managed. "It's not Rastin's fault."

"You almost died!" she yelled—loud enough for our sleeping hotel neighbors to hear.

"I didn't die," I said. Because I didn't have an argument. Only a purpose I couldn't walk away from. Especially now that I'd faced and confronted the monster head-on. Officially, Erik had become some-*one* and not just something. The legend about him was true, too. He had the face of a god. Still, the face I'd seen wasn't his real one. Not anymore.

"Someone fetch me some towels and warm water," said Rastin. "Use the ice bucket."

"Lucas, this has gone too far," said Charlotte. "You can't go in that house again."

"Charlotte," I said as the rotation of the room began to slow. "I have to."

"No, you don't," she snapped. "Stephanie doesn't want you to die for her."

I scowled, not caring for Charlotte's new stance.

"This is *insanity*, Lucas," said Charlotte. "Look at us. We're not equipped for this." She thrust an arm toward Rastin. "*He's* not equipped for this!"

"Stephanie doesn't have anyone else," I said, keeping my voice as reasonable as I could make it while my brain was still trying to sort through all that had happened.

"She has me," Charlotte said, gesturing to herself.

"What?" snapped Wes.

"*I* will go in with Rastin and talk to her," said Charlotte, caus-ing a stunned silence to chill the room. I gawped at Charlotte, who didn't leap to take her words back. "I'll go in," she said. "However I need to. But not you, Lucas. You're done."

I shook my head, baffled. "There's no way I'm let—"

"You don't get to *let* me do or not do anything," she said. "Erik hates you. He'll kill you the moment you step foot in his world. But he's not going to hurt me."

"Are you insane?" I asked her. "Of course he'd try to hurt you!"

"There are no certainties when it comes to Erik," said Rastin, cutting in quickly, his eyes straying to me with a reluctance I didn't like. "But . . . knowing what I do about him, I believe Charlotte's theory is sound. He may just allow Charlotte to speak to her."

"No," I told him, before repeating the word to her. "No. There's no way."

"I don't like it either," said Patrick, "but I think we should hear Charlotte out on this one."

"No," said Wes. "I'm with Lucas. That's a bad idea."

"*This* is a bad idea!" hissed Charlotte as she gestured to my arm.

"You hate Stephanie," I reminded her.

"Who said I hated her?"

"Why this change?" I pressed. "Why, all of a sudden, do you want to be the one to risk going after her?"

"Because I . . . because I didn't ask her why she wasn't saying anything. That day we went into the house. I knew something was the matter. I *felt* there was something she wanted to say. I should have asked her. I *wanted* to. But . . . I didn't."

Silence swept in between us all. Everyone stared hard at Charlotte. Me hardest of all. Because she was talking about that day in the coffee shop. When I'd briefed everyone on what had happened at Moldavia after the chandelier incident.

"That was my fault," I told her. "I was the one who told her not to—"

"It doesn't matter what you told her," said Charlotte. "I could tell something was wrong just by looking at her, and I could have pulled her aside and asked her and I didn't. Instead, I let a stupid grudge get in the way. She would have told me about Erik if I'd asked her. Probably everything."

"What do you mean by 'everything'?" I challenged.

"There's something else going on here," said Charlotte. "You don't want to see it, but there's some part of this we're missing. And it has everything to do with Stephanie."

"If there was, she would have told me."

"No, she wouldn't have," said Charlotte, shaking her head. "You're not going to understand, Lucas, so stop trying."

"Why—"

"Because!" She threw her arms open. "You love her. It's obvious to everyone how you feel about her. But it's also clear that you're letting that blind you."

"To *what*?"

"Lucas, she went back in for him," Charlotte said, like I was missing something that stood out as painfully obvious to her. "She told you that straight. But you didn't tell us. And that's because you preferred to believe that it was some kind of demon you could smudge out of existence instead of someone who she truly cared for."

"She doesn't," I said, my words coming out strangled.

Charlotte shook her head at me. "You're still not ready to hear it. This is crazy, Lucas. *You* are crazy. And I'm not going to stand around and wait for you to get killed because you think you're the only one with a stake in this."

With that, Charlotte turned and stormed out the door.

I struggled to stand, to go after her, but Rastin again stayed me. This time, I let him. Because the room was starting to spin again.

"Patrick," said Wes. "Where are you going?"

Glancing up, I saw a scowling Patrick stop en route to the door.

Though I wanted to believe he was going to retrieve Charlotte, or at least talk her down, the reluctant way he pivoted toward us told me otherwise.

"Look," said Patrick. "I'd be lying if I told you Charlotte hadn't just said out loud everything I was thinking."

"So, what? You're leaving, too?" asked Wes. "Now?"

"All Charlotte's trying to do is get you to ask yourselves a question," said Patrick as he scanned the three of us with an accusing finger. "And that's whether or not Stephanie's got some part in this we're not seeing. And you." He shifted his finger to me. "Whether you want to see it or not, you're getting more and more reckless. This isn't just about Stephanie anymore. Not for you. Or else you would start listening to someone other than yourself."

Inside my chest, my already thundering heart plummeted into my gut.

Before I could demand that Patrick retract what he'd just said, the door to Rastin's hotel room swung shut a second time. And while there was a small check of comfort in knowing that Charlotte would not be alone in her abandonment of the group—of me—there was a deeper pain surrounding the fear that Patrick might just have a point.

As much as I wanted to, I couldn't deny that Charlotte had one. We *were* in over our heads. That alone made me want to look back and question everything that had brought us to this moment.

I didn't want to think Charlotte could be right about Stephanie and Erik either, but hadn't I just seen for myself that there *was* something between them? Why, until this moment, had I not questioned what that something could be? Rastin had already told us Erik had fallen in love with Stephanie. Was that something that could occur without her encouragement? The dreams Stephanie hadn't told me about until that day we went into Moldavia—what had happened in those dreams?

Erik. With a face like that, I could imagine any number of things happening between them.

What hadn't Stephanie told me? And why had she insisted that I not come for her? She'd been afraid for me. But there'd been a silent exchange that had happened between her and Erik, too. She'd alluded to an oath. Whatever it had been, she had either made it for me. Or . . . she had made it for him.

"She's right . . . isn't she?" I asked Rastin in a quiet voice as Wes returned with the requested towels, one of which the medium pressed to my still-bleeding arm.

"She . . . raises an interesting concern," conceded Rastin. "One I admit I had not considered. One that . . . might offer an explanation for an odd occurrence."

"Which odd occurrence?" asked Wes bleakly.

"When Erik attacked me yesterday," Rastin said, "I detected his presence within the house as usual. I knew he was still without a heart, because I could not pinpoint his whereabouts. But . . . I also felt Stephanie's presence on his side. Her whereabouts I *could* detect. Until now, I felt sure that my awareness of her had more to do with the fact that her soul is out of place in his world. Now, though . . ."

"Now, though, *what*?" I asked through a growl, daring him to say what he ought to know not to.

"I'm not sure," said Rastin, glancing toward the door through which Charlotte had left. "But . . . if Charlotte makes a point, so do you. Stephanie and Erik. They have no one else."

Stephanie *and* Erik. With those words, I shifted my deadened stare to Wes. I found his gaze already there, waiting for mine.

I sent him a question with my eyes only, one I needed an answer to tonight.

Wes pressed his lips together.

Hands going to his hips, he dropped his head.

And just when I thought I had my answer to whether he, too, would abandon me to side with Charlotte, Wes—my biggest critic, the biggest pain in my ass—looked up . . . and made his stance clear.

"For those of us still on Team Lucas, we get T-shirts, right?"

SIXTY-FIVE

Stephanie

I awoke with a start, sitting up in Myriam's bed, to which Erik must have returned me after the incident with his mask, *Wrath's* mask. Which miraculously still lay under my hand.

He hadn't taken it back.

My fear didn't subside, though. Instead, it grew, magnified by the sight of Myriam's room tinted in tones of red.

A fiery glow emanated from the window, casting everything in an eerie luminescence.

Leaving the silver skull mask amid the covers, I pushed myself to sit on the edge of the bed. All around, black shadows clogged the corners of my room as though hiding from the glow.

Confused, I stood, bare feet hitting the frozen floorboards that I'd half expected to find burning—like everything else seemed to be. But the cold did little to ground me.

I grabbed the long white dressing gown that draped the vanity's chair and drew it on, tying its satin ribbon at the waist. Next, I rounded the bed, heading toward the garnet window, folding my arms against the freezing air as I went.

A blizzard raged outside, reams of tattered clouds shooting across the sky.

Beyond the bluster, the normally silver moon blazed blood red, its glow casting the snow-covered grounds a gory pink.

But . . . something wasn't right with the way the snow currents fell. That's when I realized the snow wasn't falling. It was *rising*—the innumerable flecks of white flying upward into the sky that, sometime during the last few hours, had transformed itself into a bloody maw.

I left the window and hurried to the nightstand, fumbling for the oil lantern that always doused itself when I relit it. Lighting it again, I grabbed it and made for the door. My hand halted just shy of the knob, though—stalled by the soft sound of sobbing in the hall.

A woman.

The sound . . . It had to be coming from a mask. But, as far as *female* masks went, I'd only encountered the three.

Reminding myself that the masks weren't separate people but separate shards of one person, I took the knob again and, turning it, opened my door.

I stuck my head out first, surveying the empty hallway and red-tinted darkness swathing the landing as I tuned one ear to the soft sound of wailing. My bare feet sank into the plush carpet runner then as I made my way down the hall, stopping only when I rounded the top newel post.

She sat in the center of the steps, head in her hands, shoulders shaking, her emerald skirts fanned out around her, making her look like a toppled creampuff.

Gathering the skirt of my nightgown in my free hand, I steeled myself for whatever sort of interaction I was about to have with this mask . . . and began to descend.

Either oblivious or indifferent to my approach, Envy didn't budge or lift her head. She didn't stop crying, either. Not even when I came to stand beside her, the circle of light I'd brought with me no doubt alerting her to my presence.

"What's happening?" I asked her in the whisper that the surrounding silence demanded.

I lifted the oil lamp so that I could survey the bottom of the stairway and the foyer. Though I searched for Spite—Envy's until-now constant companion—I found no trace of her anywhere.

Just when I was starting to think this place had a normal . . .

Swallowing with sudden and growing unease, I returned my attention to the weeping masked figure at my feet.

"*Answer* me."

Immediately, she stopped crying and peered up at me, her grasshopper eyes actually glistening in the glow of my lantern.

"You love him . . . don't you?" asked the mask.

I froze with the question.

"Of course, why *wouldn't* you?" she snipped, turning her head away. "Clearly, he would die for you."

My knees weakening, I sank to perch on the step above hers.

"You mean Luc—"

Her hands rushed to cover her ears. "Don't say his name."

Frowning, I peered behind us, to the vacant foyer and the parlor's pocket doors, but I saw no sign of Erik.

"Tell me what's happening," I demanded of the mask who had gone back to crying.

"It's our heart," said someone else.

I swiveled my head up toward where the second female voice had come from. And though I expected to see Spite, a different mask occupied the top step. None other than the one who had appeared to me in the open basement door that night. The one who had extended her gloved hand to me—a hand I had almost allowed to take mine.

She now stood hovering over us, garbed in an opulent white-lace wedding gown.

A gauzy, floor-length veil shielded her mask, the features of which too closely matched my own.

"I thought he didn't have a heart," I said, terrified by the change in this specter's appearance.

"We don't," she replied. "There is nothing this time to break. And yet . . . it does."

"Who are you?" I demanded of the mask. Then, thinking better of it, I rephrased. "*What* are you?"

"I'm a dream," said the mask as she took a descending step in my direction, her long train whispering after her. "I'm a falsehood. I am a beautiful lie that I can't seem to help telling myself."

"Don't talk to Desire," rasped Envy, grasping my wrist. "She's not supposed to speak to you. You're not supposed to know about her."

Desire?

My scowl deepening, my panic building, I glanced between the two of them—ultimately settling my attention on my ghostly twin. The bride whose name strangely did not scare me half so much as the chaos within which she'd made her appearance.

"Erik," I said to the veiled mask, ignoring Envy's warning. "Where is he?"

"That untasted kiss," said the white-masked figure. "The one we almost stole. The one he claimed in our stead. That is what killed us then. But . . . seeing you with him again. That is what kills us now."

Pushing off from the stairs, I stood, my legs carrying me down the steps, away from the two masks and my abandoned lantern— toward the darkness of the foyer.

"Erik!" I cried, remembering how I'd left him in the dream. Dying. Just as the mask had said.

"*Erik!*" I shrieked again, hating this helplessness that I could never get away from here, no matter *what* I did.

But then I spun to see his crimson-clad form standing in front of the mantel clock and the fireplace, his back to me. Uncaring that he wouldn't have his mask, I rushed over to him. Rounding him, though, I stopped, arrested by what waited for me within the hood of his cloak.

Nothingness. Wrath's hood was empty.

Still, the hooded figure turned his head toward me, and as I stood in terror beneath his invisible gaze, the fear inside of me suddenly morphed into something more like alarm.

Wrath lifted a gloved hand. His fingers drifted toward me. Then his knuckles grazed my cheek with the softest of caresses.

"Wh-where is he?" I demanded in a whisper.

Somehow understanding, the cloaked figure shifted away from

me to point to the dark smears of blood that marred the parquet floor, trailing past the piano, which glistened with wet handprints, as if he'd faltered against it.

Immediately, I spun from the phantom cloak to follow the blood trail into the hall, toward the back door, which stood open to the cold and the crimson storm.

Only scarcely visible through an upsurge of pinkish white, a long scarlet smear stained the snow, leading all the way to the conservatory.

Not caring that I had neither cloak nor coat, I rushed out, bare feet crunching in the snow as I began to run, chasing the scarlet path to the glass house.

SIXTY-SIX
Zedok

Never before had the world that encapsulated me so chaotically rebelled.

Never had this body, which could hardly be referred to as such, so violently revolted against me.

The hemorrhaging had started just as it had after the kiss that had rent my last heart.

This time, however, the blood flowed from me in more copious amounts. Not only that, but it came with an unrivaled chaos that had arisen the moment I had ended the dream. Just after I had somehow managed *not* to kill her young man. I'd still had enough of Wrath coursing through me that I might have had she not reminded me of our bargain. The very same she had perhaps been in the midst of planning to break. I had not overheard enough of the conversation to tell. Only enough to ascertain that Mr. Cheney had joined forces with the medium.

And the boy. Though he'd been foolish to challenge me, his words had hit their mark, dealing more damage than he could know.

I had emerged from the dream to find my world and my masks in disarray. And now here I was. Running from *her* as well as them.

But I had known better than to hope for respite from either. Or that she would not catch up to me nearly as swiftly as my masks.

The metal-frame door of the conservatory shrieked on its hinges. Her sharp intake of breath alerted me to her presence.

"Come no farther," I commanded.

Miraculously, she stayed put. Most likely not because I had told her to, though.

The roses. Doubtless *they* had been what had stalled her.

Myriam's roses. They had returned from the grave. Going one step further than I had, they had returned to *life* as well.

With blooms too numerous to count, they ambled over the frosted windows of the conservatory. Perhaps, though, these were not the ghosts of Myriam's roses resurrected. For Myriam's had varied in hue, ranging in color from the palest parchment to the deepest violet. These roses had instead taken the likeness of the dozen Stephanie had brought into Moldavia—the externally white and internally crimson variety from which I had plucked my last failed heart.

Never again had I thought I would see them in bloom this way. At least, not outside of a dream. Defying the rules of the natural world as well as this unnatural one, they had simply appeared. Suddenly present where there had previously been nothing. Not unlike what I had come to feel for Stephanie. What I continued to feel despite having no heart with which to feel it.

"*Go*," I told her. "Return to your room and lock the door."

Though I disliked frightening her, I understood her fear would do a better job of keeping her safe than I could in my current state. Because I could not recall when and how I had come to be garbed in the long black frock coat and half-scarred iron mask of Tumult. Nor how, after the changing of masks, my hands had managed to keep Wrath's rings. I remembered taking Stephanie to her room. Leaving Wrath's mask in her unyielding grasp, I had walked backward out of her quarters, barefaced, watching her as I went.

No sooner had I arrived in her doorframe, though, than did ten more hands seize me. I had abandoned myself to them, fleeing their melee mentally in order to take refuge within the latest dream I had spun for her, uncaring which mask assumed control next since none could be as bad as the one she had helped me to shed. Of course, I had forgotten all about Madness.

His top hat now lay nearby on the floor, dropped by the figure who had followed me here, waiting for the moment when the confliction that made me Tumult swayed too far one way . . . or the other.

Stephanie took a step toward me. In response, I made a retreating one, but I faltered, nearly slipping in the congealing pool of my own blood. She extended her hand to me.

"Damn you, *go*." I turned away, pressing a palm to my chest to stifle the blood as I moved toward the nearest glass wall. Once there, the pain slammed me again. And this time, it nearly sent me to my knees.

I fell toward the glass, bracing myself against the wall with my free hand.

Turning, I saw that she had ventured as far as the center of the room—just below *him*. The masked figure that floated above us, swirling in its own mire.

Madness.

His amorphous body of eddying clouds and silent violet lightning seemed to be having a difficult time ordering itself. Hatless, his three-faced mask sailed this way and that, eyeing me as a circling vulture does its dying prey.

"He'll have me soon enough," I warned her. "You mustn't be here when he does."

"What is he?" she asked.

"*Dangerous*," I hissed. "The chandelier. It was *his* doing."

I did not think Madness, or any part of me, could harm her physically. But it was his nature to be destructive. He could damage her mind with his words. Worse, he could show her our face. At the very least, he would be incapable of keeping any pretty promises when her young man showed. Wrath might not have won the hate from her that he'd deserved, but Madness would. And if she stayed in this room with me for much longer when I knew she loved another, he would win me.

"Your masks," she said, "what's happening to them?"

I both did and did not know the answer to her query.

Pandemonium had occurred here before, though never quite like this, and only after the shattering of a heart. But this time . . . *This time* . . .

Wincing under the new mask, my body seizing with another wave of pain, I tilted my head back and shut my eyes.

> *Your question. Is now a good time to*
> *remind you she never answered it?*

These words whisked through my mind, uttered by the highest

pitched of Madness's three voices. The lowest of his voices answered before I could.

> *You said yourself the boy was right.*
> *On all counts.*

That's why you should have killed him!

"Quiet," I said. "Both of you. All of you."

"Who are you—"

"I thought I told you to go!" I roared at her.

Bare feet padded against the floor, but not in retreat.

Tenacious, obstinate—too bold for a woman—she came to where I stood, propped against the roses, still clutching at the pouring wound. I did not mark her progress toward me through my own still-closed eyes, though. Rather, I viewed her approach from above. From the vantage point and through the empty eyeholes of Madness.

No. Not now. Not him.

She came to within a foot of where I stood, and lifting her hand, she reached, unafraid, toward my bloody figure.

Forcing my physical eyes open, I found myself back in my body. Back behind Tumult's mask, which I covered with one bloodied hand, uncertain if I could truly keep her from seeing what she was determined to behold.

Instead of reaching for my mask, her small, pale hand did what it had tried to in the dream and took mine—the one covering the wound.

"What are you doing?" I asked, helpless to stop her as she began to tug my fingers away, prying them up with her own, which fast turned scarlet.

No sooner had she taken my hand from the wound, though, than did she abandon it to the air. And it hung there, as stunned as I when the digits of both her hands curled into the fabric of Tumult's waistcoat.

"It cannot be helped," I rasped as she began to undo the long row of buttons.

Stop her, urged all three of the voices Madness possessed. The voices that would soon possess me.

But, shocked into stillness by this—her newest and most astonishing act of bravery yet—I found I could not obey.

SIXTY-SEVEN

Stephanie

Terror, I realized in the moment I reached for his collar, was something that could—in certain situations—be set aside.

Later, I could open that parcel. *Later,* sometime after this moment ended, I could afford to scream and break down.

That later *would* come. Even now I could see it winking at me from its dark corner in the future. But for now, so long as I just kept going, my unborn terror would stand aside long enough to let me do what I needed to. Even if I didn't know yet what that was.

Button after button, I undid his waistcoat, my hands shifting down after each unfastening, my bloodstained fingers moving on autopilot, repeating the same unhooking motion over and over. Next, I went to work on the buttons of his soaked dress shirt.

I kept my eyes on the task, not daring even the smallest of glances up at the new mask he wore, a glowering, mouthless metal face, pristine and polished on one half, but scarred and corroded on the other.

The obvious tumultuous nature of this mask combined with his silent stillness made me nervous. What was he thinking? Why had he stopped trying to stop me? And what would he do when the reality of what *I* was doing caught up to him? What would happen to *us* when my terror leapt from its corner to seize and devour me anyway?

Madness. That was what.

And that meant I had to keep it together. Already, though, my hands had begun to shake.

Because the chest that waited behind the drenched fabric belonged to a corpse. Someone who had been dead for a long time. Someone who shouldn't be *standing* or walking, let alone bleeding.

Of course, I'd known what I would find. Conceptually.

After catching that glimpse of his cheekbone, I hadn't had difficulty picturing what he must look like under his regalia. And that image hadn't been any worse than what now lay before me. But it had been in that hazy, uncertain space inside my head where horrors could lurk but not live.

God. His ribs. I could have counted them. Together, they formed a cage shrink-wrapped by dark yellow and, in places, blackened skin.

Still, my now dripping fingers worked at the buttons that seemed never to end until, abruptly, they did—leaving me to stare at a stomach that made my own churn.

His entire torso resembled the shriveled core of a rotten apple, shrunken and withered and *wasted*.

Taut, leathery flesh stretched unbroken over his abdomen. If there was nothing inside of him, though, if everything had been removed, then where was all this blood *coming* from?

I swallowed, the memory of what Lucas had told me in the dream resurfacing in my mind. He'd said they'd found blood in Charlie's room. Blood that had not been hers or my father's. It was obvious now whose blood it had really been. But then, if the blood they had found was Erik's . . . why had it matched mine?

My gaze trailed down the left side of his sunken, concave stomach, to where there ran a black slit. An *incision*.

Past it, one of the roses that had bloomed on the previously dead vines caught my attention, its petals snow white on the outside, blood red on the inside. Just like the ones I'd brought to the house that day.

In the basement, when I'd asked about his heart, he'd said that he'd lost "all of them," before referring to himself as "hollow."

Nausea crept over me as my fingers went to the bloom. I seized the flower—and pulled it free.

Cradling the rose in my right hand, I made a loose fist around it to protect it. Then, without letting myself think, I passed my fist into the papery opening—where his organs must have been extracted.

He made no move to stop me. And because he wasn't breathing, because he *couldn't*, I couldn't either.

The total hollowness he'd alluded to awaited my hand, and weirdly enough, that helped me not to stop dead in the midst of what I still wasn't sure I was doing.

He remained motionless as my wrist and then half my arm vanished inside him. As my bid to deliver a heart to him brought us closer, I caught, under the coppery tang of blood, the scent of lavender and honey. The same scents I'd smelled that night he'd brought me here in a dream.

I smelled salt, too. And frankincense.

Embalming scents.

I hitched a gasp, my fingers releasing the rose that, amazingly, remained suspended.

I waited several seconds. For what would happen. For something *to* happen.

Mindful to keep my eyes from meeting his, I watched the blood recede as it had last night, moving toward the invisible wound in his chest before vanishing. The devastated, ruined state of his body, though. *It* did not change.

Had I expected it to?

But *something* more about him had to change. Didn't it? Would it bring *him* back to me?

The sound of my own shallow breathing sounded loud in my ears as, carefully, I began to withdraw my arm, which came away clean—no traces of blood.

Before I could get very far, his hand caught the back of my elbow.

With renewed strength, he stood from where he'd been leaning against the wall. He stepped into me, recovering the slim distance I'd made. And keeping me close, he loomed tall over me once more.

My own heart quickened inside my ribs.

"Take it back," he said.

Even as he spoke, my fingers curled into a refusing fist.

"It is sure to shatter," he said. "And when it does, I cannot be expected to keep my bargain. I scarcely kept it this night."

"You won't break your promise," I whispered. "I know you won't."

I withdrew my arm, and he let me.

Once we were parted, he swung away, as though wanting to hide the horror that had already been revealed. But several panes of darkened glass not covered by roses reflected the sight back to us.

I willed myself not to look away as he lifted those luminous twin light eyes to mine.

"Do you want to know how I know?" I asked him.

To this, he made no reply but, gripping his jacket with both hands, he clutched it closed.

His eyes then went to the ceiling, and only when they left me did I give myself permission to follow their stare.

But the masked figure he'd been so fearful of taking over had vanished. As had the blood. And the red glow from the moon. And the flying snow.

Instead, *raindrops* now began to patter the glass, making it shine.

"Because no," I whispered. "I don't believe him."

SIXTY-EIGHT
Lucas

The next day, for the first time in high school history, I arrived at lunch to find our table empty. Though I wasn't surprised, I slammed my tray down all the same, not caring when half my fries spilled from their paper boat. I forbade myself from looking up and taking in any of the stares I'd attracted. I didn't want to scan the crowd and find wherever my so-called friends had relocated to, either.

For a moment, I just stood there, fighting the urge to pick my tray up again, dump everything at the station, and go to the library. Except the library was where Stephanie and I had first met. And there, her absence would ring even louder than it did at this table.

Just in case Charlotte, Trick, or both were watching, I gave up and fell into my usual chair. I forced myself to eat a fry. A moment later, a shadow eclipsed my burger.

"This is ground control to Major Tom," came Wes's voice. "Got your helmet on?"

"Don't tell me," I replied, already suspecting what was coming. Ever since I'd arrived at school that morning to find our usual meeting spot in front of the first-floor radiator as deserted as this lunch table, I'd been waiting for the other shoe to drop. Or, should I say, the last remaining buckle-lined black boot.

"She cornered me this morning," Wes said, sliding into the seat across from mine. "Which is why I wasn't there."

Elbow propped on the table, I put my still-aching head in my hand.

"So why are you here now?" I asked, even though I could guess.

"I told her to let me talk to you before she did anything rash," he replied. "Convince you to change your mind about letting her go in with Rastin. At least before we all go through with her plan to tell the counselor about you."

"What about me?" I asked.

"That you're not coping, and that you're a danger to yourself, and we're worried for your safety. And your mental health. From there, while you're put under lockdown, she plans to go in without you."

"You're being serious."

"It's pretty hardcore," Wes admitted. "Even for her."

"So that's it?" Lowering my hand, I leveled him with a glare. "You think I should be cool with letting Charlotte go in there with just Rastin? You and I *both* know who Rastin is more worried about."

"Charlotte's convinced you're going to get yourself killed," he said. "And now I'm convinced that, if she gets her way, she's going to get *herself* killed. She wants to go tomorrow, after school. That's the real reason I'm here. Because it comes down to this: there's no way I'm letting her go back into that house with just Rastin. You don't want her to go, and I don't want her to go. And that is why you have to let me punch you."

My head snapped up from my plate. "What?"

"That's good," he said. "That's your really pissed-off look. You don't wear it often, because it clashes with your Captain America thing. Keep it, though. Work with it. Feel the burn. But seriously. I've gotta deck you. There's really no way around it." He sighed. "I mean, I would let you hit *me* first, but I've got to be the one to start the fight or she'll never buy any of this."

"Are you even listening to yourself?" I asked him.

"Maybe if I'm lucky, she'll still give me a chance when this is all over," he said. "More importantly, though, she'll be safe. Plus, she'll never suspect that I'm planning on going with you to Moldavia tomorrow morning while she's here at school. Think about it. It's genius. Our parents will be at work, and we'll both be suspended. By the way, you have to hit me back in order for the zero-tolerance rule to apply. Left side, please."

I blinked at him, trying to sort through what, exactly, had just come pouring out of his deranged mouth.

A moment more passed. Then I tilted my head at him.

"Wait a second. Are you saying that . . . ? What do you mean by give you a chance?"

"I'm in love with Charlotte," he said, his voice monotone. "But I'm not going to ask your permission to date her even though you two used to be a thing because that's just weird."

I sat back, flabbergasted. "*That's* weird?"

"Just for the record," he said, waving a hand between us. "I'm cool with the dancing. It makes me insanely jealous, but I'm developing some coping mechanisms. Like dancing with your girlfriend while you dance with mine."

"Charlotte's not your girlfriend."

His eyes widened, blazing ice through my soul. "I'm working on it."

"Wait a second." I placed my hands on the table. "You mean to tell me this whole time you were *never* really into Steph—?"

"What would you have done?" Wes asked, cutting me off. "What would you have honestly done if I *hadn't* told you I was planning to move in on Armand?"

I frowned at him, absorbing all of this. Was Wes playing a double agent right now or, in true Wes fashion, some kind of jacked-up *triple* agent? In other words, was this a setup that was supposed to throw me for a loop and get me to see reason? *Charlotte's* reason?

That made no sense.

But Wes liking *Charlotte*? That made even less sense.

Except . . . it also made perfect sense.

Because if Wes had *really* liked Stephanie, if he'd really wanted to make a move, why inform me? He and I were friends, but Wes would have thrown anyone under the bus if it meant getting what he really wanted. But, apparently, who he'd really been after was Charlotte. He *had* been sitting next to her a lot lately. And hadn't I caught sight of them dancing together at the competition?

"I'll tell you what you would have done," continued Wes when I didn't answer. "You'd have sat on your ass and done your take-your-time 1940s good-boy thing. And not been aware of anyone else but Stephanie. So just like right now except Stephanie might not be your official girlfriend."

"It was all an act," I said, shaking my head at him.

"An act to get *you* to act," he said, his face expressionless, his eyes dead serious. "Because I knew the quicker *you* moved on, the quicker Charlotte would be able to."

I stifled a laugh. At him and the whole cold, calculated, and overthought game.

"How long?" I asked him. "How long have you had it for her?"

"Let's just say I might have plotted your murder a few times while the two of you were dating. But, in my defense, so did Patrick, because that whole episode was weird and made you both insufferable."

I burrowed my eyes into his, searching for his level of sincerity. Because, when it came to Wes, he always left you guessing.

"You're saying the reason you haven't moved in on Charlotte is because you think she still has feelings for me?"

"I don't *have* to say it," he snapped, genuine irritation—genuine hurt—backing his words. "She said it herself last night."

"*When?*"

"Hello. When she said she'd go in for Stephanie. She feels bad for Steph, but more than that, she's trying to protect *you*."

I opened my mouth to tell Wes he'd read too far into that. But another question pressed past that one.

"Does . . . does Trick know how you feel?"

"Just you," Wes said, swallowing, his jaw flexing. "It's a delicate thing, you know? Just because we survived the dating of two members before doesn't mean we will again. But Stephanie . . . once she entered the picture . . . Well, she changed everything."

He was right about that. Stephanie had changed the whole dynamic of SPOoKy. Regarding the stuff with Charlotte, though, Wes didn't have everything about her pegged. Having grown up with Charlotte, I knew her better than he did. She might have been protective of me, and maybe a little jealous of Stephanie for a while. But it was my belief that Charlotte's animosity toward Stephanie had always been more about how Stephanie was changing our relationship—mine and Charlotte's. And now that I knew about Wes's feelings for Charlotte, I could see where she was coming from. I couldn't exactly say I was super keen on the two of them dating. But what would Wes say if I told him the truth about me and Charlotte? That *she* had been the one to break up with *me*. Would he change his mind about this whole jealousy theory?

Maybe I would tell him. When all this was over, and we were all together at prom or something. For the moment, he and I had another issue. Namely, this half-baked plan of his.

"So, let me get this straight," I said. "You think Charlotte will abort raising the alarm about me just because we get into a fight? Why don't we just tell her that you convinced me to let her go without us, and then you and I skip school in the morning?"

"Because, Lucas, you're a damn Hufflepuff."

"What?"

"You're a horrible liar."

He had me there.

"Still," I argued. "Won't a fight just *help* her case if she does go to the counselor?"

"Think about it," he said. "This is strategy, so I know that's hard for you, but I need you to try."

I scowled at him, my hand twitching toward becoming the fist I might just end up throwing after all.

"Her goal is to sweep you off the board," he said. "Only problem is, if you don't go along with the program, she's got to nix her own rook while she's at it. But if you sacrifice your knight to her bishop, meaning me, then we can storm the castle while the queen is in chemistry."

"You're an idiot."

"She needs Rastin," Wes said. "However, she's also willing to go in without him and try reasoning with Masks R Us directly if that's what it takes to keep you safe. Which means that, if you *don't* get put into a mandatory time-out, her next step will be to tell the authorities about Rastin's involvement just so he won't be able to help you. That's her plan B. But. If you're already preoccupied with being in trouble, then she'll stick with her plan A and go straight to Rastin after school tomorrow. Thing is, you and I will have already been in and out."

I huffed a laugh at him. "And starting this fight. That's supposed to help your case with her . . . how?"

"I don't *have* a case with her," he snapped, shaking his head at me. Like he thought I was as stupid as I was oblivious. "And I don't expect to get one, either, until Steph is back. So I'll worry about that later. Now, are you game . . . or not?"

"You'll seriously go with me and Rastin?" I asked him after a pause. "Tomorrow?"

"No Trick, no Little Lottie. No muss, no fuss. Rastin opens the door. We special ops in. You *Ocean's Eleven* her out, and we worry about figuring out a way to stake the vampire later."

It sounded good to me. It sounded like maybe, if we could get Rastin on board, it could even work. At the very least, it was something—a plan.

"I'm in," I said.

With that, Wes stood from the table. Taking the cue and deciding to trust him even if his plan was insane, I stood, too.

"Quick," said Wes. "I'm a method actor. Give something to work with."

"What?"

"Piss me off, Lucas."

"Uh . . . Charlotte's bra size is thirty-two C. Her favorite one has pineapples on it?"

"And that works."

What that, he pulled back his fist and, no-holds-barred, took his shot.

Pain erupted in my jaw, ricocheting in and through my head so that the unanimous shouts of surprise that arose from the cafeteria hit my ears as a dull roar. The thought that he hadn't needed to hit me so hard, or that he could have possibly just pretended, entered my mind first. And stoked the rage I'd felt the night before back into full flame. I swung at him. At his right side instead of the requested left. He took the punch, not even trying to block. And it felt good—so good—to land the blow that I hadn't been able to last night. Even if the target had changed.

Wes hit me again, and somewhere I heard Charlotte screech my name. Not Wes's. Mine.

Wes closed in on me again, his face twisted with an anger too real for me to buy that this was all fake.

He shoved me hard, and I toppled backward, into a table that went sliding, its occupants scattering with shouts, screams, and spilling sodas.

I pushed off from the table—and dive-tackled Wes. He slammed to the floor under me while chants of "Fight!" chorused from the crowd gathering around us.

"People really do that?" Wes grunted, his hand shoving my face back.

"Apparently," I growled, elbowing him in the nose.

"Kind of sad, really," he snarled, flipping me scary-easily onto my back before delivering a second punch—one that caused my lip to split. "Like getting your ass kicked twice in as many days."

I latched on to his shirt, and gritting my teeth, I rolled us. Getting him under me, I slammed him down amid rising cries and screams—causing his head to bang the linoleum.

"Ouch," grunted Wes through a cringe. "That tickles."

Inserting a knee between us, he kicked me off, and I went pedaling backward before sprawling flat.

We both hopped to our feet, blood running from his nose and my lip. But then Patrick appeared over Wes's shoulder, both hands catching Wes's coiled arm. Wes didn't pull or lower the punch though. Not until, with a blur of blonde, Charlotte came flying between us.

Immediately, Wes lowered his fists, no longer bothering to try to fend off Patrick, whose pull he began to follow instead.

"What's wrong with you?" she screeched at Wes, almost making me feel bad for the guy. And maybe I would have. If our fight had turned out to be as fake as he'd said it was going to be.

Charlotte had enough time to turn around and gape at me before Mr. Corey, the lunchroom monitor, grabbed me, yanking me back from Wes.

Charlotte's expression, tortured as it was, made me hope Wes would turn out to be right about one thing at least.

That our fight, fake or not, really would buy Charlotte's silence. For at least one more day.

SIXTY-NINE

Stephanie

I didn't see him the rest of the night or, so far, this morning either. He'd not been back since the rain had started.

After last night, after the fading of the strange phenomenon and the dissipation of the snow, I hadn't encountered a single one of his masks. Just like him . . . they'd all vanished.

While I couldn't say where the masks had gone, I sensed that he—*Erik*—had gone to the other Moldavia. And that he'd done so because he wanted to be away from me.

After I had implanted that heart inside of him, an odd change had taken place inside of *me*, too. I didn't just think he'd gone to the other Moldavia—I knew it. Because now, I carried within me an internal signature of him, a strange buzzing awareness of his presence and, more loosely, his whereabouts.

Something had happened between us—*to* us—in the conservatory.

But the rose couldn't have brought about the change. Not on its own.

Something else had occurred. Something I couldn't make sense of. But then, the clarity that I was missing would only come to me when he did.

So, I spent the day walking through the whole of Moldavia, waiting for him. To come to grips with the fact that I'd seen exactly what he was.

Disgust and terror should have caught up to me by now—sent me into the tailspin I'd been so worried would overtake me. But the moment that heart had found its home, all my fear of losing control, of losing my mind, had fallen away. Something inside of *me* had clicked.

Last night, he'd left me standing there in the conservatory. I'd let him go, too, stepping aside as he'd brushed passed me. Because, well, he had let *me* go. Released me when I'd needed him to. And the way he'd caught my elbow, keeping us connected that way . . .

While I *did* believe he'd wanted me to remove the rose, I also now believed he'd held me those few extra moments for the same reason he'd allowed me to touch him in the first place.

How long had it been since he'd experienced any tenderness?

That question repeated itself the most during the quiet hours that passed between the sunless dawn and the early afternoon, all part of the same unending night.

Then, just when I thought I'd have to stoop to calling out to him in order to get him to come back and speak to me, another shift took place in my chest. One that told me he'd come back and that he was near again.

Jumping up from the velvet-upholstered balloon chair on the second floor, I hurried down the hall and to the top of the grand staircase. Stopping there, my heart hammered at the sight of him standing below in the foyer.

He still wore the split iron mask whose name I'd yet to ask, even though I didn't really need to. Wasn't it obvious which part of him this mask represented? The divide itself. That narrowing rift between his worst self and his best.

"You're back," I said.

"Yes," he replied.

"You were gone for an entire day."

He only nodded, causing anger to wind through my confusion.

"It was so quiet here. Your masks . . . they're all gone now. Not that I missed them, but for a while I felt like I might go crazy."

"Yes," he said again through a soft laugh that kept me from breaking and unloading on him, berating him for abandoning me to this empty tomb of a house. Because that "yes" held too much understanding. I'd been alone for one day. Him, though . . .

"Why?" I asked.

This time when he spoke, he angled toward me. "All morning it has rained. The snow that has fallen on this side of Moldavia for over a century has begun to melt. Previously, the moths could be found around any corner on the property. Yet they have vanished. There are now *live* roses growing in the conservatory. My masks are, as you have already observed, nowhere to be found." He gestured to his chest. "My plague of blood is gone. What is more, I feel your presence in this house. I can tell where you are. No heart has ever done so much. Because of that, I am certain it all bodes something catastrophic."

I folded my arms, doing my best to keep my expression impassive. To wear my own mask. So, apparently, he *didn't* have an answer for what was happening to his world. Only that it was something *he* was experiencing, too.

"What makes you so sure it can only end badly?" I asked. "The heart. It . . . stopped whatever was happening last night."

"I warned you yesterday," he said. "It won't hold. For me, no false heart ever has. And this intermingling of our spirits. As beautiful—as blissful—as it is, can it not be assumed that the inevitable consequences can only match in severity?"

I frowned at him, both baffled at his words and able to see his reasoning.

Why did that hurt so much?

"I am here before you now against my better judgment," he went on without further prompting. "While I wish I could say that I have come to prepare you for whatever will transpire next, I can lie to you no more. And so I will tell you that I have returned simply because the misery of missing you has, at last, outweighed the pain that comes with being in your presence."

I couldn't have hidden my shock if I'd wanted to. Because those words, simultaneously as ardent as they were devastating, couldn't have come from Zedok. Only *Erik* could have said such a thing to me.

"Would the pain be any more to bear," I heard myself whisper, "if you let me go?"

"Stephanie—"

"I would come back," I hurried to say. And maybe, possibly, I even meant it.

"It's not—"

"I miss my family." I started down the stairs toward him. "I miss Charlie and my father. They're gone because I am. And I know they're not going to come back until I do. They need me. Erik, please."

"You don't understand." Turning, he headed into the parlor. I went after him, stopping in the doorway while he went to the fireplace. With one gloved hand, he picked up the ticking mantel clock.

"This was once my father's," he said. "Every hour of every day, it reminds me of him. Stephanie, it eats at me. Erodes the fractals of my soul the way sand devours a forgotten relic."

Stepping back from the mantel, he hurled the clock into the hearth with sudden violence, the shattering of glass and the cracking of wood making me jump.

Next, he crossed to a short table stacked with books, which he kicked over. Then, turning, he stormed toward me.

I held both my breath and my ground, fearful I'd be the next target on his tirade. But he merely took me by the hand, something he'd *never* done since bringing me here.

"Listen," he said as he pulled me out with him into the hall again, his bony fingers dropping mine the instant we'd passed fully into the foyer. "Do you hear it?" He pivoted to face me, standing closer than he had ever dared to come on his own outside of a dream.

I listened, searching the darkness that contained his eyes . . . but I didn't hear anything.

But then the mantel clock resumed its quiet ticking.

He pressed a hand to my spine. Then, gently, he guided me back into the parlor. Once more, he parted from me, pointing to where the unmarred onyx clock sat on the mantel. The books and table had righted themselves once more, too.

But . . . I didn't get it. He wasn't showing me anything new.

"The house resets itself," I said. "Nothing changes."

"And why is that?" he asked.

"Because of the curse."

"Because that is the house's *nature*," he corrected.

I frowned at him—at the way the change had overtaken him. No longer was I in the presence of a monster. There was no creature here. Just . . . Erik.

Could a rose truly be responsible for this significant of a shift?

In implanting it, what had I done? What had I *really* done?

"Are . . . are you saying that you won't release me because it's not in your nature?"

"I am saying that I *cannot* release you," he said as he strode away from me, back in the direction of the fireplace. "The curse. It renders me *incapable*."

"But . . ." I began, telling myself to tread carefully here—and ignore my knee-jerk need to argue. "You *want* to?"

"More than anything I have never wanted."

"Don't make jokes."

He hung his head, bracing a gloved hand on the mantel. "I haven't breathed in nearly a century," he went on to say, "and yet you have become as air to me. How could I joke about such a thing?"

I was glad he'd turned his back to me, because the flush had returned to burn my cheeks.

"For over a hundred years my world has remained shrouded in

shadow and snow," he said. "Then you appeared. I have never wanted to keep you against your will. Valor's efforts, I hope, proved that to you. But, more deeply than that . . . I admit I have never wanted you to depart. That is truly why you are here now."

He glanced over his shoulder at where I stood stiffly on the oriental carpet, my eyes wide, ears burning along with my face. What could I say to that? Wrath might never have lied, but he'd certainly never been this honest, either.

"You'll remember I attempted to rescue and steal you all in one night," he said through an ironic and humorless laugh. "But you don't know the most disturbing part . . ."

What could be more disturbing than the contradictory statement he'd just uttered?

"Wrath. The whole reasons he made plans to abduct you was because he knew of Valor's plan to—" He stopped himself there. "Well, to get you to leave."

I frowned at him, sure he'd almost said something else.

"It's true this heart makes me whole enough to set you free," he said, plowing on. "Yet the threat of your departure stands only to rupture it anew. And so we are gridlocked. For so long as the curse binds me to this world, I will stop at nothing to keep you. You must already understand my volatility. Or you would not have made that bargain with me."

"I . . . I just don't want anyone else to get hurt," I murmured, a statement that now and had perhaps always included him, too.

"After much thought," he said, "it is my wish to cancel our agreement."

A silent bomb went off somewhere in my midsection.

"You want . . ." I whispered, shaking my head. "You want to break the deal?"

"I wish to propose a new one," he said, glancing at me from over one shoulder, but only briefly. "Timid" was the only way to describe him in that moment. Not a word I ever imagined using in reference to him.

I grew cold all over, the blood rushing out of my veins.

"You want me to marry you," I muttered, my stomach clenching.

"I want you to *agree* to," he corrected. "If you agreed . . . I think I could release you in exchange."

My insides withered with the weight of the fear his suggestion sent coursing through me. "But that makes no sense."

"It buys you your freedom," he whispered. "Your release."

I stood there, dumbfounded. Trying to process the logic behind his plan.

He turned to face me—suddenly grim and awesome once more. "You would only be required to *agree* to my proposal. We would be engaged but nothing else. You could think of it as . . . as a game."

I scowled, my horror growing. Because it *sounded* like a trick.

"You're forgetting that you almost did kill him," I whispered, hating having to bring up Lucas. Because *any* attention on Lucas was too much. "And that was after you'd promised you wouldn't. What would keep you from hurting him if I accepted this new agreement?"

"So long as you have promised me your hand, swearing off all rivals . . . I will be unable to treat him as such. To behave in any other way would deny my trust in you."

"But . . . once I go home. What happens then? I still won't be free. And I *can't* marry you. I'm sorry, Erik, but—"

He turned toward me, his gaze meeting mine full-on.

"*Stephanie*," he whispered, like I'd missed his whole point. Like it had been the simplest of math equations I'd failed to solve for and not the bombshell he proceeded to drop in my lap with his next utterance. "That is why you must betray me."

SEVENTY
Zedok

H er eyes. Within them, I saw the spark of hope ignite.

In the next instant, though, she set her jaw as though she feared I had noticed.

Had she forgotten I could feel her now as she could feel me? Her fear over the prospect of being joined together with one such as I. Had it not decimated me? Nearly as much as her hope now buoyed me.

"This heart you have given me *will* rupture," I told her, touching my chest. "There can be no avoiding it. And so, once our deal is done, you must leave Moldavia."

Her eyes shone unblinking in the lamplight. Was it too self-indulgent to think a portion of her unshed tears might have been for me?

"Even if I agreed," she said. "How can it work when you *know* I don't really mean it?"

"I have thought of that as well," I said with a nod. Clasping my hands behind my back, I turned to pace over the carpet. "And *that* is why you must leave the grounds as soon as you can. Only this time, you must never return. The heart. It should last at least until you are gone for good and I am sure I shall never see you again. So long as *it* remains . . . any plans of betrayal on your part . . . Well. They will not matter."

"Why wouldn't they matter?"

"Because," I snapped, wheeling on her. "That is what true love is!"

It was out before I'd known I'd said it.

She gaped at me, awed and horrified. And still *so* beautiful.

"Oh, I don't expect you to believe it," I said. "What cause have I given you to? How can such a thing as *love* survive in a place like this? In a thing like me? It does, though. Perhaps it is what caused the roses to return and the snow to vanish. I *know* it is the thing that allows me to stand before you and consciously offer you the key to my undoing."

"And what happens if . . . if I say no?" she asked, trembling.

"Then . . . there *will* be blood."

SEVENTY-ONE

Stephanie

I watched him in disbelief. And yet I believed him all the same.

He turned from me and went to the piano, where he paused to remove a ring from one gloved finger.

The silence in the room swelled. Between clock ticks, the metal ring clicked loudly against the piano's smooth and polished black surface.

"You don't have to say a word," he said. "You don't have to say yes. I know it frightens you. Just . . . take the ring. Take it, and that will be enough."

More ticks and tocks. More silence. Then he moved to walk past me, out of the room.

"Wait," I said, stopping him by placing a hand to his chest, my lids fluttering in shock at my own words. "Don't go . . . yet. I . . . I'm not ready to be alone again."

He'd said he'd missed me. Had I just admitted to having missed him, too?

"You prefer my company to solitude." His gaze went from my hand to the clock. It wasn't a question. I could tell by the way he'd said it—like he was just repeating the punch line to a joke he'd found funny. "Things really have gone too far . . . haven't they?"

I tilted my head at him. These lucid questions. They kept coming. Evidence of his growing awareness? His mannerisms and his demeanor, too, had shifted toward those of the boy who had appeared in my dreams. So much so that I halfway wanted to ask if this *was* a dream.

But. Would he be wearing a mask if it was?

"Before, in the basement," I said, withdrawing my hand from his form once I was sure I'd stayed him. "You told me you hadn't been able to play. But now you can. Does that count for the piano, too?"

For a moment, he didn't move, only glanced between me and the enormous instrument.

Just when I thought he would refuse, revert to his colder self, and whisk out of the room, he took a seat on the piano bench, placing his hands to the keys. As he did, my eyes went from his gloved fingers . . . to the place where he'd set the silver skull ring.

Its ruby gaze stared into me—rooting me to the spot.

Then he began to play, the first and all-too-familiar notes of "Für Elise" wandering out of his fingers and into the space between us.

I shut my eyes, fighting off the pain that came with the beauty.

Perfection poured from the piano, the mellow, meandering notes collecting themselves gradually and with tentative steps into a surer shape. Then the melody shifted into certainty, trilling and tripping along, light as the rain that pattered on the window. Then the song fell again, settling into its original pace.

Opening my eyes, I found myself moving toward the music, floating nearer to him. I came closer. And though I expected my nearness to disrupt him, it didn't.

He went on and so did I. And when I arrived at his side, I did the impossible. I lowered myself onto the bench beside him so that we were sitting just as we had in the dream, when all the walls had still existed between us and not just a single remaining mask.

Directly in front of me, his skull ring glinted—its crimson eyes unblinking, as dead as they were serious.

Suddenly, the song changed, darkening the way the sky does when storm clouds move in, his left hand repeating a low A while his right shifted between the accompanying chords.

With my shoulder barely brushing his, I found myself leaning into him. Together, we weathered the dark until his right hand climbed toward me, taking us out of the danger before falling away in a quick descent to rediscover the main theme that had started everything.

And then he killed me with the final fading, those dying notes that caused my heart to ache, though I couldn't be sure if the pain was all mine. And when at last he *did* stop, the silence swam in to swallow us both, as cold and shocking to the system as the frozen lake had been.

Seconds elapsed. All of them counted and chronicled— *stolen*—by the clock.

Catching the faintest hint of lavender, I shifted toward him on the bench.

He turned his head to me, but not all the way, almost as if he'd known what I was about to do—even before I did.

I did it anyway, my hand rising between us, moving on a slow collision course for his mask.

He let my fingers come as close as his cheek. And then, he caught me by the wrist.

Without moving, I waited. He said nothing. Just held me in a grip that, though not tight, remained wholly inescapable.

Finally, I spoke.

"You once asked me if I trusted you," I said, my eyes trained on the hand that held mine. "Now, after everything, you're asking me to do that again."

He made no comment. Just held my wrist, like he was trying to decide what to do.

"Won't you do the same for me?"

He kept his hold on me. I didn't pull away, though.

Another moment of intense nothing elapsed between us in which even the clock seemed to hold its breath. Suddenly, he released me.

I paused. And then my hand moved again, my palm closing the distance, impossibly settling on the cold—nearly freezing—surface of the iron mask.

With the smallest of tugs, the barrier came free.

I fought to keep my hand from quaking even as I held the metal mask, so much heavier than Wrath's, in place. Inside my chest, my heart boomed a warning that my blood carried through to every cell of my body.

Ignoring it, I took my hand away and with it . . . the mask.

SEVENTY-TWO
Zedok

Eyes shut—no courage in me with which to face her—I braced myself for the scream that would split my mind and bring Madness down upon us both. For the tenuous heart inside my breast would surely disintegrate at her horror—shrivel and become as dead as me.

Her words had made the truth clear, though. She would not budge if I did not give in. And if I had learned a single thing about Stephanie Armand, it was this: that my determination to stay hidden would not win against her determination to see.

But . . . as air, as breath—*hers*—touched my coarse flesh, the scream I so feared never came.

Still, the rose in my chest clenched itself tight as an angry fist.

Any moment, it would rend, regardless of her reaction.

Just when I could bear no more, warm fingertips brushed my right cheek.

I scowled, still unable—still unwilling—to open my eyes.

Not even when I felt the impossible sensation.

Of her . . .

Leaning closer.

SEVENTY-THREE

Stephanie

When it came to the question of what lay beneath his mask, I didn't *really* need an answer.

Hadn't I seen more than enough last night?

Amazingly, my hand stopped shaking the moment I began to lower the mask—the moment I began to see.

The mask had always given the impression that his twin light eyes had existed in pits of solid nothing. That had just been an illusion created by shadow, though. He had eyes. Real eyes. Sunken and deep-set. Would they match the eyes of the boy from my dreams? I wouldn't know until he opened them.

I waited for that moment to come, and in the meantime, I allowed my own gaze to wander . . . and absorb.

Parched, yellow-charcoal skin, eroded enough in one place to expose sinew and cheekbone, did what it could to cover a human skull. His other cheek, the one I'd glimpsed before when he, as Valor, had fought Wrath, jutted sharp as a blade, threatening to break through the barrier of leather flesh.

Feather light, I brushed my fingertips over the curve of the bone—just so that he would know I wasn't afraid. The scowl knitting his brow deepened with confusion, the motion causing a pang of sorrow to resonate through me.

Because it told me that, whatever he'd been expecting from me, *this* hadn't been it.

Though I waited for him to open his eyes again, face the moment—and me—he didn't. And I smiled slightly, sadly, with the thought that the trust he had for me could only come this far.

Granting him another moment's refuge, I continued my close study of his features.

His face, once so beautiful, now looked like anyone else's might after decades in a tomb. Though the longer I searched, the more I began to find evidence of a likeness to the boy from my dreams. High cheekbones. Strong chin. Gentle jaw.

Training my focus on the thin straight line of his once full and perfect lips, I kept my hand to his cheek. I brushed my thumb along his jutting cheekbone.

His eyes opened, their gray gaze meeting mine. And there he was. My Erik.

I leaned in close. Close enough to press my own lips softly to those papery ones.

He smelled of salt and lavender. And too many years to count.

He didn't move an inch.

I lingered, reluctant to pull away. Because this wasn't a fairy tale. Because I wasn't going to draw back to find him alive and beautiful again. Not that I had kissed him because I thought for one moment I might.

He wanted the fairy tale, though. With everything in him.

Why else would he have brought me here?

No. I'd kissed him—was kissing him still—because I couldn't stand the thought of leaving him here with the false assumption that I did not care what inevitably became of him.

Or that things couldn't have been different if . . . if they'd only been different.

In parting from him, I turned away, leaving his mask on the keyboard.

As I rose, I scooped his silver ring from the piano, and hurrying from the room, I slid the ruby-eyed skull onto my ring finger.

I went to the stairs, tears slipping down my cheeks as I began to climb.

Because I knew he would keep his word.

And because I knew that meant that I would have to keep mine as well.

SEVENTY-FOUR
Lucas

To ensure Rastin would come to Moldavia, I'd texted him early in the morning that we were there already and that we'd give him exactly one hour before we went in without him. After that, Wes and I had waited in my Dart, which I'd parked just outside the house.

"Have you heard from her at all?" I asked at last while we both watched the sun rise through the windshield. "Charlotte?"

"Called me a lot of names over text," Wes said. "But." He shrugged. "I kind of liked the attention. You?"

"Just one text," I said. "She wanted to know what caused our fight."

"And?"

"All I said was that it wasn't Stephanie."

Wes got quiet. Then after almost a full minute, "She didn't say anything after that?"

"She didn't."

More quiet. And then, out of nowhere, Wes said, "You know my mom cried when she found out we got into a fight. She likes you. Says you're a good influence."

"Really? Because my mom kind of hates you."

Wes jutted his bottom lip out and nodded. "I feel that."

Gazes meeting squarely for the first time since yesterday, we both grinned in spite of ourselves. Because my mom was always making Wes food when he came over. And sending him and Patrick home with leftovers and cookies.

"Think Charlotte will ever forgive you?" I asked him.

"For kicking your ass? She might. When she finds out the truth."

"You mean that we faked the fight?"

"No, moron. When she finds out we were fighting over her. Or . . . that I was. She's a Leo, so she'll think it's super hot."

I rolled my eyes, then looked up at the cracking of tires over gravel. One glance into my rearview showed me Rastin's Beamer ambling down the long drive. He'd come more quickly than I had thought. Quickly enough to suggest that he might have even already been on his way. Had he planned to go into the house on his own? It was certainly looking that way.

"That was fast," I said.

"Faster than Jimmy John's," muttered Wes.

"Don't give him time to argue," I said.

"None," Wes replied as, simultaneously, we climbed out of the Dart.

Then I frowned as a far more familiar green Corolla pulled onto the lot.

"Oh God," said Wes beside me. "We're dead."

"Yeah," I murmured, neither of us even giving Rastin a second glace as he got out of the Beamer. Oddly, he didn't pay us any mind either as he hurried straight up to the house, stopping just shy of the front porch. "By the way, great plan, Wes."

"Hold me" was all he said as the car skidded to halt near the Beamer, its blonde driver having caught sight of us both.

Immediately, she tore off her seat belt and kicked open her door.

"What in the *hell*?" Charlotte screeched at us as she emerged from her Corolla. Seated on the passenger's side, Patrick shook his head at us through the windshield, and though I couldn't hear anything he was saying, my lip-reading abilities told he'd *almost* gotten through all the really bad words.

Her face going scarlet with rage, Charlotte stormed up to us both. Patrick emerged from the car, holding up a hand and continuing to shake his head as though he truly had run out of words to say to us. Or maybe he was praying that Charlotte would not eviscerate us. Hard to tell . . .

"You two idiots *planned* this?" she railed.

"She's so beautiful when she hates me," muttered Wes at my side.

"What do you mean *we* planned this?" I asked her. "What the heck are *you* doing here?"

"We both realized yesterday that you weren't going to stop," answered Patrick as he slammed his own door shut. "No matter what we did. So, in a bid to save your crazy twitterpated ass, she and I cut school and went to get Rastin."

"He wants to kill *you*, Lucas," she said. "And you're so wrapped up in your feelings for Stephanie that you keep wanting to let him!"

"What else was I supposed to do?" I shouted back at her. "Wes said you were planning to go in there *by yourself*!"

"Shut up, Lucas," warned Wes. "I swear to God your whole face needs to shut up right now."

It was too late. Charlotte veered on him next, actually delivering a shove to his shoulder.

"*You!*" she snarled at him. "It's going to be *your* fault if he gets hurt again, do you hear me? I *trusted* you."

"I just . . . didn't want you getting hurt either," said Wes.

"So instead of telling me that, you told Lucas? And then staged a fight?"

"Yeah?" he said, suddenly timid in her presence, which presented a funny picture given their drastic difference in height.

"Well, that *is* how you operate, isn't it?" she challenged. "You're so insecure you don't tell anyone anything that's real—least of all how you feel about something. Or, God forbid, some*one*. Instead, you hide behind your jokes and try to scheme and finagle your way around to getting whatever it is you think you want so that *you* don't get hurt."

"That's . . . not true," he mumbled back, though without his usual conviction, and seemingly at a loss for any of his customary quick-witted rejoinders.

"Yes, it is!" she hissed. "And, while we're on the subject, can I just say that I am so *sick* of waiting for you to actually work up the nerve to ask me out? You're a tool, Wes."

With that, she brushed past the both of us, heading up toward the house where Rastin still stood facing the front door.

"Charlotte," Wes called, taking a step after her. "Uh. W-will you go out with me?"

She rounded on him. "Try not to *die* and I'll think about it!"

Suddenly, without warning, Rastin turned to face us. "There's something wrong," he said.

"What?" I started toward the porch, terrified he was about to tell us all we were too late.

"His hope," Rastin said, touching his sternum. "That part of him I've harbored for so long. I felt it go from me the moment we entered the lot. But now . . . now that it's gone, I can't sense him at all. His spirit. It's . . . gone."

"What about Stephanie?" I demanded.

"There's nothing," Rastin replied. "Either this is a trick . . . or he is not there."

"The curse," said Wes. "Are . . . are you saying it's broken?"

"It's impossible," Rastin whispered, though more to himself than to us.

Then, without warning, he hurried into the house.

SEVENTY-FIVE

Stephanie

Mirrored walls surrounded me on all sides of the enormous room.

Golden chandeliers hung in twin rows from a vaulted ceiling filled with French-style portraits of angels. The angels' robes billowed against azure skies, their wings stretching the width of the golden frames that separated the depictions. Ambling down, those decorative gold barriers joined with the pillars that lined the grandest ballroom I'd ever seen.

Gilt statues of robed and masked figures stood sentinel atop the pillars. One held a lyre, another a violin.

No sooner did I notice their instruments than orchestra music—a ghostly waltz—began to pipe in from nowhere.

Turning, the voluminous skirts of my dark blue ball gown rustling with the movement, my slippers tapping against the shining marble floor, I searched for the music's source.

Instead, I found him.

He stood mere feet away, wearing no mask. Erik never needed one.

His own steps made no sound as he approached.

Keeping one arm folded behind his back, he came to a stop in front of me and offered his other.

A dance?

Uncertain, I placed my right hand in his left.

He drew me to him, settling his free hand on my upper back. I placed mine on his shoulder. Then he began to lead me in a waltz, and it didn't matter that I didn't know the steps. Because this was a dream, and he did.

We revolved through the empty ballroom, the golden walls and mirrors blurring into smears of color and refracted light. Our reflections chased after us, splitting us both into a hundred versions of ourselves.

Though I waited for him to say something—anything—he never breathed a word. He just bored his crystal gray eyes into mine, their intensity and beauty robbing me of words.

The music echoed around us, warbling and distant, as if it was coming from some faraway dimension, or from a memory.

He danced us closer to the far end of the room, to the place where a black partitioning curtain hung over the opening to another room, the interior of which remained shrouded in obscuring darkness.

We turned toward the curtain and then beyond it, leaving the ballroom and the music and the angels for a strange candlelit realm of nothing. He let go of me and I stepped back from him, suddenly apprehensive, too afraid to ask him where he'd brought us—and why.

Maybe my fear stemmed from having already known.

Because my heart. It told me things about him. And said things about me. Things he must have somehow heard, because then he stepped up to me. His strong hand returned to my back, trailing down to press into the base of my spine. He pulled me into him, his other hand cupping my cheek. He bent to me, his lips, warm and alive, meeting softly with mine.

The scent of lavender assailed me, and I inhaled him, melting into the kiss that, even in this dream state, felt more real than any I'd ever experienced.

Though he'd closed his eyes, I held mine at half-mast, enough to see his brow furrow with an almost painful bliss. That bliss, that pain—it resonated through me, too. The love he'd professed for me echoed through him, resounding with enough force to make my knees go weak.

I leaned against him, my hands braced on his chest, my body responding all on its own, awakening to desires no longer latent. Both his . . . and mine.

My fingers curled around the lapels of his jacket. Answering his kiss with my own, I drew him to me, as if being as close as possible still wasn't close enough.

With these small actions, I stoked within him a hidden fire, inciting the kiss that up until that moment had been both chaste and cherishing to become something more consuming.

Fervent, even urgent, his lips sought mine with a sudden hunger that told me just how long—how *much*—he'd yearned for this. For me.

In response, my heart beat with a wild rhythm—one that begged me to forget all that I'd branded impossible and put my trust in him.

His thumb brushed my cheek. In answer, my hands unfastened his cloak. Next, they trailed down the fabric of his waistcoat.

Encountering buttons, my fingers performed, again, the task of their unlatching, shaking even more uncontrollably than they had the night before last, though now for entirely different reasons.

This time, I wasn't afraid of what I would find. I was afraid of what had found me.

These feelings. This yearning.

He let me undo the waistcoat, and he didn't stop his pursuit of my lips, either. Not even when I untucked his shirt. He just kept kissing me while my fingers crept under the barrier of the fine fabric. As I pressed my palms to a sculpted and smooth abdomen—the flesh there as real and alive as the rest of him—his own hand went to his throat, where he loosened and then pulled free the cravat, letting it drop.

Stripping away the waistcoat next, he let that fall, too.

Breathing hard, my heart a thunderstorm, I stepped back and watched him not breathe at all.

His stare burned through me a moment longer. Then he closed the distance between us again, backing me toward and then *onto* the black-curtained bed I had sensed was there all along.

I scooted myself backward, drawing him with me onto the mattress. The moment my head hit the heavy blankets, his lips found mine again. Only now, with growing abandon, he deepened the kiss, his dark hair falling around us to block out the candlelight from the countless tapers that surrounded us.

My world, my whole awareness of everything, then zeroed in to exist only at our points of contact. While my palms took his face, he trailed a hand down the front of my bodice, causing the night-blue dress to become my dressing gown. And only my dressing gown.

He slid in closer, our bodies lining up, the heat of him radiating through the thin barriers of fabric that yet remained. I matched his lips brush for brush, a soft sigh escaping me as I relished the feel of his skin, of his realness—his closeness.

His right hand gripped me behind the knee, and he hiked my leg to the side of one hip.

Taking hold of the collar of his open shirt, I tensed at the sudden escalation. Of *everything*.

Velvet soft, his tongue swept mine, and his kiss, passionate and incinerating, now beckoned to the most buried parts of me.

My whole body, my whole soul, sang with this intensifying duet, anticipation warring against the apprehension that unraveled as his hand, in a caress, traveled from my knee to my thigh. From there, his fingers followed the curve of my hip, then slid up over my rib cage, barely bushing the outer curve of my breast before scaling my arm to capture my left hand.

From there, he inserted his thumb into the fist that held the iron grip on his shirt, and, loosening it, he laced his fingers with mine. Then he squeezed, causing the metal of the skull ring to bite into my skin.

What was he telling me? Where would he take us from here?

But then . . . where else was there to go?

"*Stephanie.*"

Eyelids fluttering shut, my mind left me the moment he said my name, so that there weren't any clear thoughts to be had. Just fragments evoked from the next kiss he captured me with.

Erik. Heat. Love. *Now.*

He pressed into me, his free hand roving where it would. My

own clamped his shoulder while my heart thumped against the one I had given him.

Our bliss spiraled. Carrying forward for one moment longer.

Until, suddenly, Erik stopped.

He parted the kiss. His hand unraveled from mine, and without warning, he drew back.

His eyes found mine in the gloom, the sudden twin flashes of light within them replacing my momentary delirium with fright.

He let go of me then, retreating through the darkness.

"Erik!"

I sat up fast, shouting—*reaching* after him.

Into a cold and empty room filled with the stark and blinding white light of day.

SEVENTY-SIX
Zedok

I had not planned to do what I had done. Neither, when I'd been in the midst of its euphoric unfolding, had I intended to stop where I had.

But when had my plans ever panned out in the way I conceived them?

After Stephanie had fallen asleep, I had stolen into Myriam's room and had transported her, as I had promised, back to her own room, exiting my side of Moldavia for hers through Myriam's closet. After laying her into her own bed, I had returned to my Moldavia, shutting the door after myself, aware in spite of our betrothal that I would not find her there again.

From there, I had resisted as much as I could stealing into her mind, creating around us another dream. In the end, though, that had proved a battle I could not have hoped to win.

Something yet called to me. Some part of her. It came through the mysterious link that had been forged between us. Harkening to it, I'd halted at the doorway of the parlor, noting my chair inside. The one from which I had projected my mind those times I had entered her dreams.

I'd touched the scarred cheek of Tumult's mask, beneath which my leathered skin recalled the grazing of those delicate fingertips. My lips. Did they not also still hold the sensation of the soft caress of her own?

These lips. She had kissed them.

Mine.

She had kissed me. Touched her angel's lips to my dead ones.

The heart Stephanie had given me. If it had held through that kiss, would it not also hold until her final departure?

Heedless of the answer, I gave in to the need to see her one last time. In entering this final dream, I had only meant to show her the truth of the feelings I had contended with all this time, no matter what form or mask I took. And she had not run from me when I'd invited her to dance. My daring grew, encouraged by our invisible connection, her seeking eyes rendering me powerless to resist the desire that I had theretofore managed to keep at bay, if not deny.

She had gone with me into the dark, too. Even knowing what I sought.

How could she not when, due to our connection, there was no way for me to hide from her? But then, had there ever been?

There, in the nothing, I did what I had wanted to so fiercely that night I had first begun to love her, bending to take her lips with mine.

And oh, how her own had answered.

Her hands had dared to wander over my garments—and then so boldly beyond them.

Continuing as it morphed into something else entirely, our dance proceeded from there into forbidden territory. Dauntless, we accompanied one another there. Our entwinement—had it not been made all the more irresistible, all the more unstoppable, all the more ecstatic, by the precarious mingling of our two souls?

As it all escalated into rampant fire, which of us could have hoped to stop the other?

It was my contention that neither of us would have. Certainly not I.

Except . . . there were people in the house.

SEVENTY-SEVEN
Lucas

"**E**rik!" shouted Rastin as Wes, Charlotte, Patrick, and I entered through the front door behind him.

"Well," muttered Wes, who turned in a slow circle, "so much for the element of surprise."

"He's gone," said Rastin, who pressed a hand to his forehead. "His spirit. I can't feel it."

"Lucas?"

"Oh my God," said Patrick at the sound of my name, uttered by the softest of voices that had all five of us pivoting toward the grand staircase. Stephanie stood at the landing, her eyes hollowed with disbelief, her dark hair tousled, her expression at once bereft and lost.

"*Stephanie*," I said, taking one halting step toward her, afraid that this could be a trap.

"Lucas," she said again, blinking in the brightening sunlight. "What are you doing here?"

I started at her response, my steps taking me to the base of the stairs. "I . . . I told you I would come for you. But . . . how did you get back?"

Her hands went to cover her mouth. Pain etched itself on her too-pale features. And then tears appeared on her cheek. Tears of relief and . . . torment.

A huge silver ring gleamed on her left hand—a skull with glistening ruby eyes.

I knew whose ring that had to be. But . . . what was it doing there on her left ring finger?

While Rastin and my friends watched on, I began to climb the stairs toward her. As I did, Stephanie's tears began to fall more readily.

"Lucas," she said. "I'm sorry. I'm . . . so sorry."

"Why?" I asked, scarcely able to believe it could really be her. I took another step toward her but paused, utterly shocked when she took a sharp step back from me. I scowled, confused.

"No, I've . . . I'm," she stammered, but her words wouldn't come.

"Stephanie," came Rastin's voice next. He approached the base of the stairs, peering up at her. "What has become of Erik?"

"He . . ." Trailing off, she glanced down at herself, shaking her head again, like there was something about her being here she couldn't understand. Almost like she thought it couldn't be true. Or even . . . like she didn't want it to be.

I glanced back at both Rastin and the members of SPOoKy, searching their faces for an answer. Wes's eyes darted between me and Stephanie and back again. Charlotte frowned, uncertainty knitting her whole frame. Patrick shook his head, his gaze roving the foyer, the parlor, and the hall, like he expected an ambush.

"Erik," Rastin prompted again, his voice breathy, almost desperate. "Where is he?"

"He . . ." Stephanie began. "He brought me back while I was sleeping. I didn't know it. I didn't expect . . . He left. He told *me* to leave. He's on the other side. I . . . I can feel him there."

"What do you mean, you can feel him?" Patrick asked, giving voice to the question we all had to be thinking.

"It's the heart," she said, her delicate fingers trailing over her chest. "I gave him a heart. Somehow . . . that connected us."

"Wait," I said, my scowl deepening. "You gave him a heart?"

"What kind of heart?" asked Rastin.

"A rose," Stephanie answered, her voice shaking, fingers twisting and twining themselves with one another. "He says it will break, though. And that . . . something awful will happen. That's why . . . it's why he brought me back."

My eyes met with Rastin's and with that look, we exchanged all we needed to say.

Rastin turned, exiting the foyer by way of the back hall.

"Guys," I said to Wes, Charlotte, and Patrick, "take Stephanie and get out of here. Now."

"Lucas," Charlotte began, but I shot her a glare that silenced her.

"We won't get another chance," I told her, keeping my voice low, so that Stephanie wouldn't hear my words. Though I wasn't sure why.

With that, I made to follow Rastin.

"Lucas?" Stephanie called after me. "Wait. Where are you going?"

I ignored her and, skirting the fallen chandelier where it still lay, I trailed after Rastin as he entered the kitchen—moving in the direction of the door I knew he would open next.

I paused in the center of the kitchen as Rastin opened the cellar door to reveal a darkened stairway. He shut it quickly, then opened it again.

"It's as I feared," he muttered, shutting the door a second time. "With my connection to Erik now severed, there is no link binding us together any longer. The heart Stephanie gave him. Somehow, it must have focused his *entire* soul. Including the missing shard. There is now no way for me to reach his side."

"The only thing that matters at this point is that he has a heart," I said. "There's got to be a way we can draw him out."

"Erik!" Stephanie screeched, causing me to whirl in the direction of the hallway. "Erik, no, *you can't!*"

At hearing these words, Rastin and I made a break for the kitchen entrance, both of us jumping to the conclusion that he'd crossed back to this side, to Stephanie. We halted, though, at the unlatching of the basement door, which then creaked open.

Neither of us turned. Not even when a voice emanated from within the cellar.

"I am here, gentlemen."

A spear of ice pierced me through the gut. Together, we spun, Rastin and I, to find a figure in the doorway. A masked one.

Shock rooted me to the spot.

I had come here knowing I would face him. Still, nothing could have prepared me for the sight of him.

Tall and rail-thin, cloaked and garbed in ebony, he emerged from the nighttime blackness of the cellar into the daylit kitchen, twin lights glinting at us from within the eyeholes of his split metal mask.

Unable to help it, I stumbled back a step, into Rastin, who quickly pushed himself ahead of me, an arm extended. As if he could have done anything to protect either of us.

"Erik," said Rastin. "What trick is this?"

"No tricks this time, Shirazi," the creature said.

"Erik, no!" Stephanie screeched again, her voice coming from farther away now. Because the others. They must have taken her out of the house.

Stephanie, though . . . Why was she yelling at him like that? Like she was afraid. Less of him and more . . . *for* him.

Her fear. It didn't seem to stem from where it had before, in the graveyard—that he would kill me. But that didn't make any sense.

"Why is she calling to you?" I asked him. Because I had a right to know if I was reading this all wrong. If Stephanie was shouting for him because he was in the process of killing me already. But then, in that case, wouldn't Stephanie have been shouting *my* name?

"She senses your plan," the monster said, surprising me by answering. "She senses it because *I* sense it."

Confused by these words, and by Stephanie's panic, I risked a glance in the direction of her distant shouting. If Stephanie knew what we were going to do, though, why would she want to stop us?

As though in answer, an echo of Charlotte's words from the hotel room swam through my mind, banishing the remnants of my doubt that she had known what she was talking about—that she'd been able to perceive something vital that I hadn't.

And Stephanie—she'd said he, Erik, had let her go. She'd also said he'd told her to leave.

Now here Rastin and I were, more defenseless in this phantom's presence than either of us had thought we would be. Still, he'd yet to make an attack. Or even a threat.

His having a heart. According to Rastin, didn't that mean his soul was, for now, intact?

What, though, did it mean that he and Stephanie could now sense one another's whereabouts and, in a way, each other's thoughts?

"Mr. Cheney."

Numb, I snapped my attention to him, the figure whose mask hid the face of a dead man. A creature who had called me by my name. And had so far refrained from cutting my throat.

"Rastin," it—*he*—said next. "Both of you. This way, if you please. So she cannot interfere."

With that, he stepped suddenly between Rastin and me, his shoulder, real and tangible, faintly brushing my own as he went. I turned my gaze to follow the sharp path he cut past us, my expression of astonishment briefly mirrored in the polished side of his iron mask.

Then he vanished around the corner, heading in the direction of the rear door.

Rastin moved ahead of me to follow after him. It took me an instant longer to jar myself into action.

Though Rastin went straight through the open back door, passing into a world of rain and melting snow—a world that had inexplicably turned to night—I hesitated.

"The girl," Rastin called after Erik, following his cloaked form down the path and into the dark. "How did this connection come to be forged between you?"

Drawn to the lip of the doorway, the one leading straight into his domain, I hesitated before drifting through, ending up outside on a perfectly restored porch.

Ahead, *he* waited on the muddy pathway leading to the conservatory.

Rastin was halfway to him when all three of us turned back to the open door at the sound of his name.

"Erik!" Stephanie called, her shouting growing near. Along with the thump of running steps.

"Mr. Cheney," said Erik. "I find myself incapable of shutting the door. Her will to reach me keeps it open. And so, the task falls to you."

What? Me again?

"Mr. Cheney," he said, this time with more force. "The door."

I turned my head toward the hall as Stephanie appeared, her face white with terror, her mouth open. Calling someone's name. But . . . not mine.

"She will never be free if you let her cross to me again," he hissed. "Never."

And that was the only thing he could have said to make me do as he had commanded.

Catching the door, I pushed it shut just as Stephanie reached it, our eyes meeting for one brief and horrible moment. I'd never seen that look in her eyes, either. Or in anyone's. A beseeching stare. One of horror and utter devastation.

From the other side, she screamed to me. "Lucas, please don't!"

I glanced back at him, the monster, Erik, who now clutched a hand over his heart.

"Very well" was all he said as he turned from me and Rastin, continuing down the path to the conservatory. "Follow me. Quickly."

SEVENTY-EIGHT

Stephanie

I crashed against the door as it slammed shut, blocking out the sight of Lucas, and of Rastin and Erik.

"Lucas!" I gripped the handle, but when I opened the door again, it was the sun and the day that greeted me. Things I should have been glad to see again.

I wasn't glad, though.

Terror for Erik's plan, the one I felt in my heart, seized me.

"Where did they go?" asked a voice behind me.

I whirled to find Charlotte there.

The boys. They'd held me back, pulling me to Charlotte's car. That was until Charlotte had ordered them to let me go.

"They're going to kill him," I told her.

"Lucas?" Patrick asked as he and Wes entered the hall behind her.

"No," Charlotte answered for me. "Not Lucas."

Had she seen him shut the door on me like that? She must have.

"Zedok," said Wes.

"Erik," I corrected in a breath.

"They're going through with the plan," said Charlotte as she passed through the door and onto the porch, like she thought doing so could still take her to Lucas. "And Erik's going to let them."

I gripped my heart, a horrible ache ricocheting through me with her words. The pain was the same he must have felt all those times. An ache more of the soul than of the body.

"I can't lose him," I whispered, robbed of the ability to breathe, my steps taking me out into the world I hadn't quite been ready to return to after all. "Not when I just got him back."

"It's true, then," said Charlotte out of nowhere.

I looked up to her, searching her for the answer I didn't have but, apparently, she might have found in all of this.

"You love him."

I gaped at her, awestruck, because she'd put into words what I'd been unable to. Not even to the person to whom it would mean the most. To whom it would mean everything.

"I'm sorry," I told her. And she would know why. She'd warned me not to break Lucas's heart. He didn't know it, but I already had. Because it *was* true. Without meaning to, without even realizing it, I had fallen in love with Erik.

And now I wouldn't ever get to tell him.

"Charlotte, I'm sorry," I repeated.

"No," she said, coming to take my hands in hers. "*I'm* sorry."

I was taken aback by this response, even in the midst of my panic. Still, I gripped her hands tight with my own, because in my tilting world they felt like something to hold on to.

For a moment, her expression mirrored my anguish. Then she shook her head, as if despair and helplessness were things that could be thrown off.

"You said you were linked," she said, wringing my hands in hers while she wracked her brain for any scrap of hope she might offer. "Before we got here, Rastin said he and Erik were linked, and that their connection might allow him to open a door to Erik's side. What if . . . what if that means you can open the doors between your worlds now, too?"

My mouth fell open at this suggestion. One that struck me as possible.

Was it, though? I'd opened the door after Lucas had shut it to no avail. At the same time I hadn't thought I was capable of traversing sides. And maybe there was a trick to it, some method Erik used whenever he wanted to cross from one side to the other.

"I don't know how," I said.

"You never saw him do it?" Patrick prompted.

"No, he never—"

"Come on," said Charlotte, grabbing my hand. "They were headed for the greenhouse."

We burst away from the porch at a run, the boys following after as we rushed down from the ruined porch, taking the path to where I sensed him now.

The conservatory, the door to which, on my side, stood ajar.

SEVENTY-NINE
Zedok

Roses all but coated the inside of the glass house, the vines tangling to the point that they would soon devour the door. No doubt they would all die when I did.

I'd left the door ajar behind me and, coming to a stop at the far window, the one against which I'd pressed myself the night Stephanie had given me my new heart, I waited.

Rastin entered first, the boy close behind him.

"My soul," I told them both. "I believe it has somehow become entangled with hers. Enough so that she now mistakes the love I feel for her as her own emotion."

"You're saying she thinks she's in love with you?" the boy asked, and I was glad to note his bravery had grown since my initial appearance. He would need it in these next few moments.

"Crudely put," I said. "But that is my guess, yes."

"Your guess?" Cheney challenged. "What if you're wrong?"

"You allowed Stephanie to reenter this house at great risk," I replied. "You cannot disagree that action has helped to bring us here. If you love her even half as well as I do, then I know I can count on you *not* to gamble with her freedom a second time."

"Her soul," said Rastin, at last speaking up. Could I count on him to be the voice of reason? His next words told me no. "If it's entwined with yours, as you now claim, then it's too dangerous to do as we had planned before."

"It is too dangerous *not* to do as we had planned," I argued, unlatching my cloak and tossing it off. It unfurled in midair, dissipating to nothing. That's when I unsheathed Tumult's wavy-bladed kris dagger, the same weapon with which I'd attacked the boy in the dream. Flipping it in my grip, I now offered it to him, pommel-first.

He blinked at me from behind his glasses, no longer the man I'd faced in the graveyard but the uncertain boy who had first entered Moldavia, an unbeliever of all the truths he had told Stephanie regarding what I was.

"I can't," he said, holding up both palms and shaking his head in refusal of the blade. "Not if Stephanie doesn't want—"

"Stephanie wants what I want," I snarled at him. "And that is for her and me to be together for all time. She wants this because her heart has been poisoned to want it. My soul overshadows hers. And I have now come to be certain that, if my soul is allowed to shatter, hers will follow suit. Need I remind you, though, that *she* is alive?"

"You're saying she'll die?"

"That will be the least horrific fate to befall her," I said.

"And the worst?"

"My greatest fear?" he said, shaking his head. "That she could become as I am."

"If we destroy your heart," said Rastin, "those two ends are stopped how?"

"Because the rupturing of my heart and its destruction by an outside force are two different things," I explained.

"You're saying if we destroy it while Rastin has the portal open, the bond will automatically be severed?" Cheney asked.

"It must be," Rastin answered for me, his tone turning as bleak as his expression. "His soul, cut free of its anchor, will extract itself from her."

"Think of a frozen flower," I told the boy. "Crush it, and it shatters. Remove the ice, though, and—"

"It still won't live," he said, his word actually serving to silence me.

And so. It seemed I would have to change tactics.

"You made a promise to me," I said to him. "One that, for her sake, you must now find the courage to keep."

He shook his head at me. "She—"

"When Rastin opens the portal, my spirit, so long as it is bound by the curse, will revolt. My incapacitation means that *you* must do it. Now take the dagger."

A long stretch of seconds passed. And then, surprising me once again, Mr. Cheney at last accepted Tumult's blade.

EIGHTY

Stephanie

I broke from Charlotte, running ahead with a cry after I caught sight of movement through the broken windows of the conservatory—a fluttering of red rose petals.

Without stopping, I crashed into the rickety metal-framed door and pushed my way through only to find myself in a room of shattered nothing.

Shards of dingy glass littered the mud-caked stone floor along with dried brush and broken bits of wicker. I whirled under the domed ceiling, searching its exposed frame for some sign of night.

The sun glared down on me instead, its unwelcome heat drawing from me a sob.

A shout echoed it. One I heard partly with my ears and party—more clearly—within my mind.

Erik's.

I sprang away from the center of the room, back to the open door through which Charlotte, Patrick, and Wes, standing at a distance, watched me unravel with helpless despair.

Grasping the doorframe, I hung my head and fought the urge to collapse. Instead, I passed through it again, imagining where I wanted to be—where I wanted this doorway to take me. To a place I made myself believe it *could* take me. To the other Moldavia. His. Ours.

When I looked up again, though, I found my friends still there.

I would have broken down then, if Patrick hadn't stepped forward to point at me. Or rather, at the doorway behind me.

"Stephanie," he said.

Turning, I saw that the scene within the doorway had changed.

Green tattered vines clung to the walls. Rose petals flew.

And there was Rastin. And Lucas.

And . . .

EIGTHY-ONE
Lucas

A breeze arose from nowhere to shake and stir the heads of the innumerable blooms, amplifying their already heady scent to a nearly noxious status.

The monster—who'd disconcertingly yet to behave like one—said I'd made a promise to him.

He must have been talking about something I'd said to him in the graveyard. Trying to remember what words I'd used, I wrapped a hand more tightly around the dagger he'd proffered to me. And as the cold metal of the handle bit into my flesh, I recalled exactly what I'd said.

I'd promised I'd be the one to send him to hell.

A glance toward Rastin showed him putting his hands out, palms up, like a sage preparing to raise the dead instead of a medium preparing to do the opposite. He closed his eyes. At the same instant, the monster—Zedok—doubled over, contracting into himself.

This was happening. All without my say-so. I'd taken the dagger. I'd taken it, but . . .

Another rush of air gusted through the waxy leaves of the roses, strong enough to tear whole heads free. Petals filled the air like confetti, funneling into a whirlwind.

At the center of the vortex stood Rastin, who murmured to himself, lips moving, voice silenced by the flutter of leaves and the whip of wind. Lowering one hand, the medium opened his eyes, a glower of determination setting his features as he extended the other hand toward Erik.

The windstorm, raging against him, sent the monster staggering backward several paces. A low roar of defiance emanated from him, growing loud enough to rise above Rastin's whispered prayers and the blustering. The monster reclaimed surer footing, even as a white halo of light began to radiate around him.

Conflicted, still remembering that look on Stephanie's face as I'd shut the door on her, I gripped the dagger at my side, its handle already slick with sweat. The light surrounding the monster expanded then, revealing itself not to be an aura . . . but a portal, one that would remove him from this world forever.

A glance to Rastin showed the medium's focus locked on his target. Beads of sweat trickled down his temples. He'd widened his stance and now held out both hands. What would happen, though, if his strength failed him?

Still undecided, I spun back in the direction of the monster.

His black jacket began to disintegrate, the fabric thinning, then molting away to reveal tattered and time-yellowed skin and bony limbs.

The glowing white rift tore itself even wider behind the creature.

Then the mask itself dissolved, crumbling to pieces.

The monster screamed. Impossibly, he took a staggering step toward me, straining all the while against the portal that, like a vacuum, began to suck the loosened rose petals, leaves, and flower heads into it.

And then. Then the creature did something awful.

Lifting an emaciated, skeletal hand to its chest, it pried fingers between its own ribs—and ripped downward, tearing bone and papery flesh away to reveal the rose.

Again, I twisted the dagger in my grip, trying to make myself believe that I *would* do what Rastin needed me to. What Stephanie and her family and this monster did, too.

But now that the moment had come, the point of no return, something about it felt . . . wrong.

I peered again to Rastin, who gritted his teeth, his arms trembling against the creature, who took another step in my direction.

Then, with a roar of his own, Rastin shoved both hands forward, and the monster went flying back, straight at the portal. And, as if the portal was not an opening but a wall, the creature slammed against it with a demented cry of pain, his face distorted in rage and agony.

He began to claw at his own chest, at the heart that caused him so much pain. The heart that was now the only thing keeping him here, locked in his ruined body and caught in this warped existence. The only thing besides me, that was.

He couldn't remove it, though. Even so, his hand fastened

around it, he squeezed and screamed, dead muscles straining.

Do it. I should.

I'd said I would.

And I would have. If I hadn't glimpsed within the centers of those two pits what Rastin had seen and perhaps now Stephanie, too. Not a monster. Not a creature. But a soul. A person.

God. He loved her.

He really loved her.

The truth of that came crashing around me, landing hard enough to break my own heart.

Why hadn't it dawned on me before this moment—when it was already too late—that he wouldn't have asked me to do this if that had not been completely and utterly true?

The light Rastin had summoned had now begun to shrink. The portal was closing. My chance—*his* chance—was fading.

Erik's heart would collapse when the portal did. I had no doubt of it. Then his soul would shatter. Now that it was linked with Stephanie's, what would that mean for her?

I shook my head and locked eyes again with Erik.

Tightening my hand around the dagger, I started forward. Then I ran right at him.

He uncurled his skeleton's hand from around the rose, his arm falling away as I raised the blade.

And plunged it home. Into the target that had been too easy to impale: the rose.

As I used both hands to twist the knife, destroying the flower completely, several things happened at once.

The light inside those two pits for eyes went out. The portal holding him up closed with the sound of a snapping live wire. And, as the now lifeless corpse fell, dagger and all, to the petal-strewn floor, someone screamed.

EIGHTY-TWO

Stephanie

I gripped my chest as my eyes took in the scene before me. As if I had been the one stabbed.

Tears rushed down my cheeks, seeming to bring the silence with them.

Both Rastin and Lucas stared at me, but I didn't see them. I couldn't.

I only saw him. Lying crumpled at Lucas's feet. Dead, but now also gone.

My breath abandoned me as my feet hurried to the form that, somehow, during the last moments, had been rendered a *thing*, lifeless and inanimate.

Someone said my name. Lucas.

I couldn't hear him, though. I could only *see*. This thing he had done.

I fell to my knees beside my ghost. My hands then went to his chest but stopped short of the broken cage, which, in addition to the dagger, still held the remnants of the heart I'd given him.

"Oh." The noise escaped my lips.

And instead of touching him, I drew my hand up to stifle the sob that burst forth.

Pain came with the sight of his face. His *skull*. His closed eyes.

He has lights for eyes.

Charlie's words from that night swam from the black mire my mind had become while I watched and waited for those eyes to open and the lights to return.

"No," I murmured when they didn't. "No," I whispered again as I took his face in my hands.

Bending over him, I pressed my lips to his forehead. "I mean yes."

I shut my eyes, tears tumbling onto the face that I had realized too late I loved more than any other. "Yes, damn you."

But now he wasn't able to hear my answer. The one I should have given him before but had not been brave enough.

"Yes," I whispered again.

He stayed still. Silent. And dead.

And, inside my chest, my own heart at last ripped itself in two.

EIGHTY-THREE
Lucas

No sooner had I done it than I realized it had been the wrong plan.

He'd been wrong. *I* had been wrong.

Seeing Stephanie draped over the now empty shell, I also understood the most important fact of all. Something I had overlooked perhaps because I simply had not wanted to believe it.

Stephanie loved him *back*.

Erik must have been telling the truth about wanting to keep Stephanie safe. But her current state told me he'd been wrong to think she had mistaken his love for her own. Would he have asked me to do what he had if he'd known?

"Stephanie, I'm sorry," I told her as I neared her, still not certain if she would hear me. At first, she didn't look at me. "He . . . told me to." I touched her arm, but she jerked away, confirming what I'd feared. That she could now only hate me as deeply as she had cared for him.

The next instant, though, she pulled away from the body. She stood and, flinging her arms around me, she sobbed into my chest.

"He told me to," I whispered again, my own voice cracking as I embraced her in return. "I didn't realize."

The truth was, I hadn't *wanted* to realize.

But how did I apologize for that?

I looked over to where Rastin sat exhausted on the floor. But instead of watching me or Stephanie, his own stare roved over the walls of the conservatory, the mostly decapitated roses, the vines of which still clung to the glass.

He shook his head once, like something about that—the roses specifically—didn't add up.

The others now filed in through the door of the conservatory that Stephanie had left open. The one that her link with Erik must have allowed her to open. Patrick frowned at Charlotte, who took the scene in with as much sorrow and shock. Wes's eyes flicked to me and Stephanie.

Rastin started to rise, and Patrick hurried to help him to his feet.

As Rastin stood, he nodded once to Stephanie, then lifted a finger to his lips.

"Shhh," I soothed Stephanie, rubbing her back and drawing her slowly away from the body, which Rastin approached with caution, his movements stiff and difficult, one hand over his own heart.

He knelt beside Erik. But, as if Stephanie had sensed something was amiss, she pushed from me, turning on the medium.

"What are you doing?" she demanded. Gently, I held her back. "Don't touch him," she snapped as Rastin lifted free the dagger that I'd thrust through the mummy's heart.

She pulled from me again, and this time I let her go. She

approached him—Erik—and retook her own kneeling spot next to Rastin.

"The vines," Rastin told her. He gestured toward the glass walls with the blade, his voice marveling. "They live."

"What is it?" I asked him. "Rastin, what's happening?"

The medium turned toward me, expression lost. "His world. It should not still stand. The roses . . . this dimension . . . they should have ended with him."

"Erik," Stephanie whispered to the corpse. "Wake up."

And though she did not see the limp skeleton's hand twitch . . . I did.

EIGHTY-FOUR

Erik

Poppies crowded the field.

I stood knee-deep in the redheaded stems, surrounded on all sides by their beauty.

And the blooms stretched on forever, terminating in a horizon just above which peeked a hazy twilight sun.

Silver clouds hung still in a cobalt sky. Tilting my head back, I gazed up at them, but then shut my eyes to the sensation of the wind on my naked face.

Was this the breath of God that now stirred my hair?

Should I thank him when the two of us finally met face-to-uncovered-face? For the gift of seeing Stephanie one final time?

I had seen her push through the door just before the boy had plunged his knife through the rose. Though I despaired to know that the sight of my demise had brought her pain, I relished the final vision all the same.

That glimpse alone had all but erased the urge to unleash upon God the fury that had seeded itself in my nonexistent heart for nearly all of my earthly existence.

She, after all, was free.

I inhaled, long and slow, my lungs filling with the perfume of the poppies—so different from that of the roses. When I exhaled, I imagined myself releasing all that Rastin had always hoped I would.

The masks. My separated soul. My mistakes.

It was then, just before I opened my eyes, that I felt a small hand slide into mine.

I glanced down again, to the short figure now at my side.

She wore her Sunday hat, its yellow ribbon dancing in the gentle breeze.

"Myriam?" Her name left my lips as a whispered wish—a prayer that both asked for and knew it to be truly her.

My little sister, whom I had thought of and longed to see every day of my death, offered a small, close-lipped smile. She squeezed my fingers in hers, and then she spoke.

"The curse," she said. "It's not broken, brother. You cannot come home yet."

A short laugh escaped me. Because, while the sight of her brought such happy tears to my eyes, her response struck me as absurd. I had existed so long under the impression that I would never see her again, let alone any other "home" outside of Moldavia. Rarely, as well, had I allowed myself to entertain the idea that there existed a future in which I *could* go on to something better—no matter what prattle Rastin spewed. My crimes. Had they not been too heinous?

"Yet?" I asked her.

"You can't come home without your heart," she said.

My face fell. Did those in heaven truly not know my fate?

"Myriam." I lowered myself onto one knee before her, gripping her by the shoulders. "I haven't a heart."

"Yes, you have," she replied, the smile returning to her lips, though sadder now than before. "Stephanie gave you one."

I tilted my head at her, a hundred questions piercing my brain like so many arrows.

So. Myriam knew of Stephanie. My family. Could they see me from wherever their spirits now existed? Had they watched over me all along? From the beyond I had unwittingly sent them to?

Perhaps Myriam had not seen everything. Like the moments that had elapsed before I had arrived here—wherever here was. A dream that, this time, was not of my making.

"The rose—it was destroyed," I told her. And I might have dreaded what this would mean for me. But I had already spent so long in purgatory that the prospect of more time in a realm of in-between held little horror for me.

"But you see," said Myriam through a giggle. She took both of my hands in hers. "The rose—*that* rose. Brother, it never counted."

"What are you saying?" I asked her. "Please. Speak plainly."

"You've been lost so long," she whispered, touching my cheek. "In a dark forest where all the trees were you."

I touched her cheek in return just as the wind rushed up between us, carrying off her hat. As if I had never missed a moment between the last day I had seen her and this one, I rose immediately to go after it. But I was struck still and dumb by the sight that awaited me.

Two figures now stood in the distance.

Mother. Father.

Arm in arm, positioned exactly as they had been in their wedding photo, my parents watched me with their own matching set of sad smiles, their expressions far from condemning.

My mother waved. Taking hold of my sister's hand, I started toward them.

My family. They had come. Despite what I was. What I had done.

I swallowed against the bitter taste of Myriam's previous words. Her claim that I could not return home.

So then . . . what was to happen now?

"*Erik.*"

My sister came to a stop—forcing me to do the same. I wheeled around to look at her, panicked for the first time.

"You *cannot* come with us," Myriam stated.

Hell. This was when she would tell me where I *would* go. The boy had been right. But could the devil do any worse than I had done to myself? It was true I had blighted my own existence. Yet I wanted it also to be true that Stephanie had winged me at last to release.

"Why?" I asked, fear and anger ripping through me anew. "Why can't I?"

"Because." Myriam stepped up to me, placing her warm hand over my sternum. "Your heart. Your true heart. *It beats on.*"

She shoved me. Lightly. But the small effort on her part was all it took to send my spirit floating back from hers. Up. Over and above the poppies.

Toward the sun that had not been a twilight sun at all, but one of dawn.

My mother and father. Both waved to me now.

As they did, Myriam ran to where they waited, Mother holding her hat.

Then the light that had brought me here took me into its embrace a second time.

A beautiful voice beckoned to me from within it, urging me to wake up.

But then that voice began to hum, and the risk of losing its beauty made me hesitant to heed its command.

Immediately, I recognized the ballad as my own—our own.

And the voice. I would know it anywhere.

I opened my eyes to find hers closed. Tears coursed from beneath her fringed lids, trailing down to fall upon my naked face. Though her pain destroyed me, I could not bear the thought of missing even one tear.

And so, I commanded my hand to move. My fingers merely twitched at first, and then . . . my arm found the capacity to lift.

She gasped at my touch, those brilliant blues bursting open with shock . . . and hope.

Stephanie. My heart.

The meaning behind Myriam's words at last became clear.

Stephanie had become my heart. By bequeathing me hers.

Had not the bleeding stopped the night she had given me the rose? The night she, the rose, and I, the briar, had become as one?

The night her actions had done what I thought only her words could.

The night she had said "yes" without either of us truly knowing.

EIGHTY-FIVE
Lucas

"Woh-kie dokie," said Sam as he arrived at our usual table. "Let's ssssee here, burger special and ketchup with a side of fries."

"Lycopene is my friend," said Patrick, who now sat next to me, seeing as our seating arrangements had unofficially undergone an official change.

"Street tacos and nachos for the lovebirds. Safe to say that's on one check, Darthemort?"

"Did you hear what he called you?" Wes asked Charlotte as he accepted the plate they'd ordered to share. Just like the booth seat, where they now were cuddled up to one another. It was a little absurd. What with Wes drenched in his usual ensemble of solid black and Charlotte in tones of honey and cream, her blonde hair secured in a high ponytail and accented with glittery heart-shaped barrettes.

"Because, between the two of us," said Charlotte in her trade-mark monotone, "I make a way more passable dark lord."

"Should I defend your honor?" asked Wes.

"Don't you have to have your own first?"

Wes grinned. Like that retort was all he'd wanted. "One check's good," he told Sam, who fought off his own grin as he plucked up the final item on his tray: a huge soda-shop-style milkshake in a tall old-fashioned fountain glass.

Though I expected him to cart the shake off to one of the surrounding tables, he instead set the dessert in front of me.

"What's this?" I asked.

"It's a vintage-style milkshake," replied Sam.

"But I didn't—"

"You said you didn't want anything," Sam said, cutting me off. "Usually, when a customer says that—especially one of my normally hungry regulars—it's because they've recently missed out on something they *did* want."

I blinked at him, my stomach twisting, my heart giving an extra painful thump.

"Now," Sam continued, "ice cream can't fix that. But it's on the house and it tastes good, and sometimes a small, sweet reminder that good things are still in the pipeline helps to ease the sting of whatever didn't work out."

With that, he left me to stare laser beams into the milkshake he'd made special for me.

No one said anything. But I was sure all my friends were staring at me.

I really had meant it when I'd told Sam I didn't want anything. I'd even made an effort not to sound as dejected, defeated, or lost as I felt. But he'd still seen right through me.

Next to me, Patrick lifted his burger and took an enormous bite. Across from me, Charlotte and Wes dug into their tacos.

I sighed, then took an obliging sip. Though the coldness brought a sting to my eyes, it wasn't the bitter sort I'd been fighting the last two weeks since Stephanie's return. And something about the icy, familiar vanilla taste brought a comfort I hadn't been sure I'd be able to feel again. And Sam had been right. The milkshake did taste good.

As if my acceptance of the treat lifted some kind of gag order on the group, Wes cleared his throat.

"So, food's here. Shall we officially commence?"

Usually at our meetings, the rule was that we could shoot the breeze on non-SPOoKy stuff until the food came. After that, we shifted to official business. I was usually the one who called us to order, but I didn't mind Wes taking the reins this time. Really, it came as a relief.

"We've gotten a few emails while we've been, uh, busy," said Charlotte, thumbing through her phone. "One from this couple who just moved into a house in J-Town. Then we got an inquiry from this antique shop called Time and Again. Turns out they heard about us from that investigation we did at that little bookshop on Bardstown Road last fall."

"List of complaints?" prompted Patrick before chomping another bite of his burger.

While Charlotte started rattling off purported phenomena that might have been impressive to us at one time, I zoned out, my focus trained on my milkshake, mind spiraling back through time. To the glass house when I'd plunged Erik's knife into his chest.

I'd meant to end his misery with the action. I'd meant to end Stephanie's. And mine.

I'd meant to do the *right* thing.

And at the time, violent as the action had been, it seemed like it was. But how and when had right and wrong gotten swapped? At what point had Erik become Erik again and Stephanie no longer mine . . . but his?

Stephanie hadn't been in school for the past two weeks, which wasn't surprising. I hadn't heard from her much, either. Her father was home with her now, cleared of all charges and almost half-way through recuperating from his injuries. Charlie was back, too, returned from her stay with friends. Stephanie's family had been pieced back together, another member seemingly added, unbe-knownst to all but Stephanie herself.

I wasn't sure yet how Stephanie had explained away her absence to her father or the authorities. Probably, she'd tell us when she was back. When she returned. To us. Her friends.

Friend.

It wasn't what I wanted to be to her. But being someone's friend meant you'd be there for them when it was hard. Or impossible.

Erik and Stephanie. They struck me as so impossible.

How could they be together? Even if they did love each other? How were they going to share a life when, technically speaking, only one of them was alive? What was going to happen with stuff like prom and graduation? What about college? What about see-ing the world? Those weren't things they were going to get to do together, were they? Maybe, though, since they shared a heart now, they would.

But I guessed the answers to those questions really weren't for me to know. I wasn't part of their one-plus-one-equals-one equation.

And I guessed that now, as Stephanie's friend, it was my job to be okay with that.

Really, what was the alternative?

"Lucas?" asked Charlotte.

"Yep." I glanced up and took another sip of the milkshake.

"That's all the info about the emails," she said. "But we were wondering if you've heard anything from Rastin."

I nodded, certain they knew I hadn't paid a lick of attention to Charlotte's email debriefing. But they were being patient with me, and friends made a habit of doing that for each other, didn't they?

"He called me," I said. "Asked for a check-in, and I hope you don't mind I gave him the rundown on each of us. He also asked who would be turning eighteen by summer and who would need official parental permission."

"Why would he ask that?" prompted Patrick, the table going silent.

I inhaled deeply. "He might have mentioned something about featuring us on this new show he's signed on for, *Phantom Stalkers*," I said in one breath.

Charlotte's eyes bugged. Patrick's head swiveled my way.

"Uhhhh," said Wes, pausing with his glass half lifted to his mouth. "Come again?"

I smirked. I hadn't been holding out on them. Just waiting for the right moment. The one in which I could deliver good news with something akin to cheerfulness.

"He said he'd fly us out."

"Shut. The. Freak. Up," said Charlotte as she gripped Wes's arm.

"Ow," said Wes. "I mean wow."

"I know you aren't messing with me right now," said Patrick.

"He has a case in mind for us," I went on, forcing more eagerness into my delivery of the news than I felt. Maybe, though, by the time the opportunity arrived this summer, when we'd all graduated, I would be excited. "He wants us to help him investigate the Waynesfield Wraith."

The table erupted into noise. Then faces split into wide grins. And with good reason. Because the Waynesfield Manor was known for being one of the most haunted locations in the United States. That everyone seemed to be on board meant that Moldavia had strengthened us way more than it had weakened us. Also, if we played our cards right, we might actually—if we were lucky—launch an official career for ourselves.

I smiled at my friends, which wasn't so painful now that the split in my lip had finally healed. From there, I just listened to the conversation that careened into unbridled elation, everyone gushing and throwing out speculations over what the summer was going to bring. And here it was, one of those sweet in-the-pipeline deals Sam had mentioned. With whipped cream and a cherry on top.

When it was apparent their excitement wasn't going to be something I could wait out, I tapped a spoon against the side of my glass, calling for order.

At once everyone sobered, eyes shifting to me. The seriousness of my expression caused Charlotte's brow to knit.

"What is it?" she asked.

"The last official order of the day," I said.

"Which is?" Patrick prompted.

"Stephanie," I said.

To that, no one said anything. Pain flickered across my features, but I wasn't interested in hiding it. I'd seen the damage masks could do.

"She's not an official member of the group," I said. "But she texted me that she'll back to school on Monday, and that got me thinking."

"About?" Charlotte asked.

"Holding a vote."

"On Stephanie joining us officially?" asked Patrick.

"That's the protocol we decided on," I said with a shrug. "So. Those in favor say 'aye.' Those opposed? Well, you know."

My friends all shared uncertain glances with each other, until Wes suddenly spoke.

"Aye," he said.

"Aye," said Patrick.

"Duh," remarked Charlotte when I flicked my eyes to her.

Her response made me smirk.

"Aye," I heard myself say.

Then everyone's smiles became more lopsided. Like they wanted to be happy about this but weren't sure if I was ready for that. My heartache wasn't theirs. But that they were willing to share it with me still slapped a bit more balm onto all the hurt.

"A toast?" said Patrick, lifting his soda. "To SPOoKy?"

"And its newest member," added Charlotte, raising her lemonade. "*Finally*, another girl."

"To Stephanie," said Patrick.

"And to looking soooo damn good." Wes. Of course.

I picked up my milkshake glass. "Hear, hear," I told my friends.

Because that seemed better than telling myself, "There, there."

And then the four of us clanked our beverages together—a sound like old things breaking away. And like new ones coming together.

EPILOGUE

Stephanie

December Twenty-First

I finished placing the last ornament, settling it into the fragrant branches of the live Christmas tree Dad had yanked into the house and erected in front of the parlor's bay window.

Together, the three of us had piled on lights and filled the boughs with memories.

Still, the tree had never seemed complete. At least, not until now.

In between Dad's yellow hardhat and Charlie's purple octopus, and directly next to my music note, there now hung the rose ornament I'd smuggled home that afternoon.

I took a step back, eyeing my handiwork, at last satisfied that each of us had a place on the tree.

Tick, tock, tick . . .

We didn't have a clock in the parlor on our side of the house, but the ticking floated to me through the walls the same way his music did, though I never had to strain to hear the piano or the violin. Or that voice . . . calling to me.

I glanced in the direction of the mantel and smiled at the fireplace's in-progress state.

Now that his leg was better, Dad had restarted work on the house. The doctor had advised him to begin with smaller projects and tackle the bigger ones in the spring. Currently, he was out of the house. On a hunt for supplies with, of all people, Ms. Geary, the school librarian. The *single* school librarian.

This wasn't their first excursion, either, and somehow during their last one, she and Dad had found ceramic tiles with birds on them. Though they weren't the same as the originals, Dad had matched them closely enough to make my heart flutter with happiness.

Eventually, Dad did ask about Lucas, like I'd known he would. In answer, I'd told him truthfully that the two of us had decided to just be friends. He'd pressed for more information, of course, so that's when I turned around and started asking a few of my own questions about Ms. Geary. After that, he stopped prodding so much. I returned the favor, and in that way, we reached an unspoken truce about not prying.

Now the bird tiles he and Ms. Geary had scored sat in a small pile next to the fireplace A few of them had already been set. Dad had also located the figurehead of the deer for the center, which he'd promised to let me install when the time came.

I still found it interesting that even after I'd convinced Dad to let us stay here—to keep this house—he continued to take the greatest care with its restoration. Aside from slowing down and accepting a construction job in town that would start in the spring, nothing had changed regarding his plans for Moldavia.

And maybe that had something to do with the fact that Erik still sent him dreams.

I still had dreams, too. Except I knew they weren't dreams.

Wanting to check on Charlie, who had returned to sleeping in her own room after I'd delivered the news that Zedok was no more, I spun toward the open pocket doors—and jumped to see him standing there.

Erik's gaze gave nothing away as it beamed at me from behind the familiar mask—that of Valor—that he still wore, though more for his sake than mine. His face, unchanged from the one I had revealed that day when he'd played for me, wasn't one I would have cringed or shied from. Still, the barrier helped *him* to navigate a reality—or rather, a love—where all others had been obliterated.

Pressing a hand to my thundering heart, I released the breath I'd almost swallowed.

Despite our connection, he still held the power to sneak up on me.

"Have you chosen a school yet?" Erik asked, nodding to my laptop, which lay open on the coffee table next to an accompanying stack of college catalogs.

I shook my head. Because I hadn't. Stanford had been my original first choice, but after some discussion, Erik had convinced me to also apply to Carnegie Mellon and Juilliard—schools with legendary singing programs.

"Legendary programs for a legendary voice," he'd said, making me yearn to see myself the way he did through those two bright lights.

He made me feel like I could do it all. What was more, our daily practice sessions made me *believe* I could.

College, though, meant distance. From my family, my friends, Moldavia, and from him.

For now, that hurt too much to think about. Not in the debilitating way my heart had burned during those moments when I'd been certain I'd lost his forever, but enough to make me go to him and welcome myself into the arms that enfolded me only after I wound him in my own.

He always embraced me with reverence, like every hug was our first. Or maybe his fear was that it would be our last. But the bond tying us together was stronger than that. Strong enough to override a curse, and restore a soul. *Two* souls.

I guess, though, he still needed some convincing that we weren't destined to unravel.

Perhaps, ironically, he just needed time to figure it all out. And maybe I did, too.

Our whole situation *did* seem so . . . incredible. And I wasn't sure how it was all going to work. But, simultaneously, I *was* certain about one thing.

And that was that it would.

Pressing my cheek to his silent chest, I closed my eyes and breathed him in, relishing the feel of something I'd been missing for far too long—that indefinable feeling of *home*.

That had been another thing I'd lost when I lost Mom, who Charlie now knew about. The questions had come pouring from her almost as soon as she'd been returned to us, delivered to our arms by those of a mother—one whose mere existence had made her want to know where her own had gone.

The buried pictures and mementos came out shortly after and, with them, all the pain Dad and I had tried to run from, out-maneuver, and deny.

Charlie had struggled with the news, but she was doing better now that Dad had returned to counseling and was getting some help on how to handle her grief and confusion as well as his own.

And the pain of loss. I still carried it, too. As I always would.

I opened my eyes again, though, arrested by the realization that, in that moment, the faraway and deep-seated ache I harbored within wasn't entirely my own. Pulling back, I focused on the sapphire pin embedded in the black satin of Erik's cravat.

"I wasn't sure you'd want to play tonight," I said. "Or if you'd want company."

He tucked a gloved finger beneath my chin, tilting my face to his mask. "How could I stay away when my solace, my heart, is here?"

I smiled in spite of both of our aching and, taking his hand in mine, turned to draw him to our preferred place of retreat—of respite.

"So that means you're still up for teaching me this crazy middle part, right?"

I seated myself at my super-early and super-enormous Christmas present—the piano Dad had, at my behest, restored.

Eager to begin, my hands went to the keys. Starting with that low booming A that pounded like a heartbeat, I then layered in the chords that spoke of approaching doom. In other words, my favorite part.

Faltering in the same place I had yesterday, and the day before, I began again.

"That would be good," Erik said, taking his place next to me. "If it wasn't so dreadful."

"*Hey,*" I said. "It wasn't that bad."

"I've heard worse," he allowed, reaching across me to correct the position of my fingers on the keys. "Just yesterday, I think it was."

Settling his hand over mine, his fingers aligned with my own, eclipsing the silver and ruby-eyed skull ring I still wore.

"I'm going to let that one go," I said.

"Ah, you're kinder than your playing," he said, making me laugh this time. He pressed his pinky down on mine, and the repeated heartbeat note filled the room, beautiful and resonant.

Normally, whenever Dad was home or Charlie was about, I'd cross to his side for practice sessions, or just to talk. Sometimes, though, when Dad was out and Charlie was sleeping, we'd meet in my parlor. Always, we had the piano, our music, and each other.

"This seems like the easy part," Erik said, "but it's not. The single repeating notes, they must stay constant through the chord progressions. Or the whole thing falls apart."

My right hand flowed through the chords while he guided my left through the repetitious single A. When it came time for my left hand to switch, he released me and let me go on.

The moody middle of "Für Elise" stormed on from there, the lighter notes intertwining with the dark ones to become two halves of one whole.

"Beautiful," Erik remarked when, arriving at the place where our last lesson had ended, I had to halt. "Now again. From the beginning."

Replacing my hands on the proper keys, my fingers moved with a new and hard-won fluidity as they tiptoed over the somber notes my mom had ushered me through in my younger years. Next, I waded into the lighter ones that Erik's instruction had helped me to grasp.

He let me play on, his right hand interceding at the point when all the high notes came flying out one after the other in the sequence we'd yet to take on together.

Then the dark part arrived again, and this time, he let me take it all on my own.

I made it through without a lapse, grinning to myself when I did, and then his hand again swept in to play the climbing and falling section.

After that, the both of us played, each of us carrying a half all the way to the point where the end of the song came to mirror its beginning.

And then, when we were done, as we always did, we began anew.

Acknowledgments

Over the course of several years, this book has transformed many times and each version, each draft, revealed more and more to me regarding the story I *truly* wanted to tell. This is that story. As a result of this journey, which has brought incredible rewards—not the least being that I get to share this book with the world—I have many people to thank.

An enormous and heartfelt thank-you goes first to my incredible agent, Janna Bonikowski, who worked tirelessly to help me refine this book and also to find the perfect home for it. Janna, I want to thank you for believing—in me as well as this story. Your guidance, dedication, passion, and tenacity paved the way for this project to become a reality. I am immensely grateful for all you have done and, as well, to have you in my corner.

Additionally, it has been my great honor to collaborate and conspire with my incredibly talented editor, Dana Leydig. Dana, your leadership, thoughtful input, ideas, and love for this story have helped to shape it into all I have ever hoped it would be. Your direction, dedication, intuition, and expertise enabled me to polish (and, at times, reign in) an ambitious retelling. Thank you for encouraging me to dig deeper and also to chip away and let go of the things that didn't belong. You heard the music of this story so clearly, and it now sings because of you.

On that note (yes, all my puns are intended), I would like to thank my incredible team at Viking for their talent, time, and attention. Books always bear their author's name on the cover, but each page within bears the invisible yet invaluable influence of those working behind the scenes. I am deeply appreciative to you all for working so hard to usher this dream of mine into the realm of tangible reality. Thank you to my copyeditors, my authenticity readers, my design team, and to all who have lent their minds and magic to push *Phantom Heart* toward success and to deliver it to the hands of readers. For your input, thoughts, time, and artistry, I am profoundly grateful.

When I began writing this book, Stephanie's voice came quick, easy, and fast. Zedok, on the other hand, lurked onto the page in a far more mercurial and amorphous way. My dear friend Katie McGarry was the first to agree with me regarding his potential. What was more, she did so with an enthusiasm that fed my own. I am indebted to you, Katie, for encouraging me to follow my phantom through his dark world, to seek after his voice, and investigate his past. In particular, thank you for your help in shaping THAT chapter. You know the one. The one that changed more times than Zedok has masks. And thank you also for believing in my monster. You were right about him. As always, you were right.

Sometimes when I pass by a bookshelf, I catch myself imagining what trials each author went through to see their books become a reality. And I know there were trials. Both successes and setbacks inevitably pepper the path of anyone who strives toward any worthy goal. Immediately after one deeply discouraging moment on my journey with this book, I got a knock on my car window. When I looked up, I found my good friend Gina Possanza peering in at me. She had pages in her hand—pages of this book, which she had read and loved. Gina, after banishing my despair, you told me to keep going. Thank you. I am so very glad I did.

I am fortunate in so many ways and one of my truest blessings in life has come in the form of my exceptional critique group. Together, its members comprise a powerhouse of knowledge, expertise, creativity, ingenuity, passion, and heart. A tremendous thank-you goes to Kurt Hampe, Bill Wolfe, Colette Ballard, Bethany Griffin, and again to Katie McGarry. While reading through the various drafts of this book, I would always smile at all the moments each of you helped me to include and refine. Thank you all for cheering me on through this project, for encouraging me, for believing in me, and for continuing to sharpen me into a better writer.

While writing this book, I have also received support and encouragement from many incredible friends. Thank you, April Cannon, for reading every single version of this book and for offering such wonderful input. I appreciate your friendship, your advice, and your willingness to read, reread, and read yet again, more than you will ever know. Thank you as well to my good buddy and sounding board, Nick Passafiume, who also read multiple drafts and who lent an ear to long rants about plotting. I'm so glad we get to sit at the Slytherin table together.

Thanks also go to Marcus Wynn for checking in on me, for believing in me, and for being a constant and enduring source of the best kind of inspiration. Just about every word you say is gold, my friend. Oh, and judo chop.

During the last rounds of this book, I struggled to come up with a particular line of dialogue, which required a touch of brilliance. Good thing I happened to meet up with the ingenious Lindsey

Carter Palgy, who solved the issue right quick due to being a comedic mastermind. Thanks, Lindsey. It was the *perfect* one-liner.

Thank you also to Megan McIntosh, who kept telling me to chase this story, inspiring me all the way by chasing her own stories. Your tenacity rubbed off on me!

A huge thank-you goes as well to my friend Andrew Buchanan, a gifted musician. The first time we met, you were dressed as one of my characters. From that moment forward, you have continued to shower my creative endeavors with galvanizing exuberance and enthusiasm. Thank you for singing about it, dancing about it, and for literally cheering me on. Also, for lending your musical knowledge and for sharing your expertise regarding the piano.

I wrote the earliest drafts of this novel while living in the preservation district of Old Louisville, where the grand historical Victorian homes helped to inspire and mold my vision of Moldavia. But I've also been lucky to have another source of inspiration in the form of lush and beautifully written books by my friend, fellow author, and Old Louisville historian David Dominé. David, thank you for your wonderful research and for always encouraging my writing.

Jeannine Buhse. You might not remember that day years ago when we were outside your old apartment talking about my crazy dream of becoming an author, but I do. I carry that moment in my heart like a good luck charm. Thanks for believing I could do it, for following me on all my field-research escapades, for being my friend through it all, and for encouraging me through yet another book. Also, for making me the best bracelet ever.

Writing this project required research into many subjects, which included parapsychology and ghost hunting. I have so enjoyed listening to *The Paranormal Podcast* by Jim Harold; *Jim Harold's Campfire*; and *Beyond the Darkness* and *Darkness Radio*, hosted by Dave Schrader and Tim Dennis. Jim, your shows are so engrossing and I appreciate your meticulous approach to conducting interviews as well as your enthusiasm for so many different subjects surrounding the unknown. Thank you also for writing back to me regarding my question on closets. I now take care to always close mine at night.

Dave and Tim? Your knowledge, candor, and gift for humor inspired me to create a fictional ghost-hunting team infused with the same attributes. When listening to your show, I am always either scared, laughing, or some delicious combination of the two. Thanks for creating such wonderful, entertaining, inspiring, and thought-provoking content.

Extra-special thanks go to my teenage nephew, Ethan Creagh, who listened to several plotting sessions and offered ingenious solutions and input. I know I embarrassed you that day in the grocery store when I kept ranting about open portals, alternate sides of houses, ghost-hunting Lindy Hoppers, and masked figures running amok. I didn't know I was talking that loudly, but now that I think about it, I suppose there *were* a few stares . . . Anyway, thanks for putting up with that excursion, for still being seen with me in public, for taking the time to pop your head in when I was writing to see how it was all going, and for schooling me on swing-eighths.

I would also like to extend my deepest gratitude to my family, who have offered their support and encouragement through all of my writing endeavors. In particular, I would like to thank my mom, who has always believed in me and my projects and who also fostered and encouraged my childhood obsession with the arts and with

The Phantom of the Opera. Thanks for buying me the book, the theater tickets, the music, the fancy programs, and all the art supplies I used to obsessively draw characters from this classic tale that, to this day, remains my all-time favorite. Mom, you truly are the best.

To my readers: thank you for reading this book. I am immensely grateful to all who have taken the time to fall into this world and visit with these characters I have created. Your support and enthusiasm bring me limitless joy.

Finally, I wish to thank God, who has gifted me, along with so much else, a talent for storytelling and wordsmithing. To honor this gift, I use it. Some days that is difficult. Others, the act of writing is joyous, easy, and enthralling. Years of experience in both craft and faith have taught me that God is there through it all and that sometimes it's those really tough days that serve as the stepping stones that lead to experiencing the best days. And today, a day in which this project, so dear to my heart, nears completion?

Well, it counts as one of the *very* best.